NEWS FROM
THE GALACTIC FRONT!

Reported by . . .

Christopher Stasheff
"PIRATES"

The truce is broken by Khalian space raiders—who will die before they surrender!

Anne McCaffrey
"MANDALAY"

With one war over and another beginning, a little R&R is impossible—or is it?

David Drake
"SMASH AND GRAB"

Teleportation means the ultimate sneak attack—but there are still a few bugs in the system!

Janet Morris
"BIRTHDAY PRESENT"

It's hard to fight a war when you can't trust your technology—or your tech officer!

. . . and many others!

*Ace Books edited by David Drake
and Bill Fawcett*

THE FLEET
THE FLEET: COUNTERATTACK
THE FLEET: BREAKTHROUGH
THE FLEET: SWORN ALLIES
THE FLEET: TOTAL WAR

TOTAL WAR

THE
FLEET
BOOK 5

——— *Edited by* ———
David Drake *and* **Bill Fawcett**

ACE BOOKS, NEW YORK

This book is an Ace original edition,
and has never been previously published.

THE FLEET
BOOK 5: TOTAL WAR

An Ace Book / published by arrangement with
Bill Fawcett & Associates

PRINTING HISTORY
Ace edition / September 1990

ISBN: 0-441-24093-3

To Bob Asprin
It's all your fault

CONTENTS
Book 5   Total War

PIRATES

by Christopher Stasheff

THE MERCHANTMAN JABBED at the marauder with a spear of light—but the smaller ship leaped aside, almost seeming to disappear and reappear. The huge Terran vessel jabbed again, this time with its rear cannon, but the tiny marauder danced away, mocking them.

"By all that's holy!" the navigator swore. "Only a quarter our size, and we can't hit them! What's the matter, Captain? Don't your boys know how to aim?"

"I was top gunner at Target, Lieutenant," the first officer snapped back. "But these aren't exactly state-of-the-art lasers—and I only have two of them. *Damn* that mosquito!" He jammed the heel of his hand on the firing patch.

On the screen, light blossomed where the smaller ship had been a half second before.

"This is a liner and freighter, Lieutenant," the captain said heavily. "We only carry minimal armament—not like that Navy ship you pushed until you signed on with us."

"If I'd known . . ." the navigator muttered—but he broke off, because the Khalian destroyer was suddenly much larger in the screen, and swelling.

"He's inside my guns!" the first officer yelled. "I can't lock onto him, he's too close! How the *hell* . . . ?"

A grinding crash jolted the whole ship. The captain was

1

the first to recover enough to pull his webbing loose, crying, "Pass out small arms to every able-bodied passenger, and fight for your lives! That ship just grappled us! They're going to be cutting through and boarding, any second!"

The crew scrambled to their feet, broke open the gun locker, and headed out into the passenger compartment, arms full of weapons.

They were barely into the cabin before a section of wall blew in. Passengers screamed as sinuous Weasel shapes materialized out of the cloud of smoke, ruby beams stabbing out at the crew.

The navigator howled and went down with a hole through his chest, exactly circular and neatly cauterized. The navigator and captain dodged aside, dropping the extra weapons and snapping shots at the invaders. One speared a Khalian through the shoulder; the creature screamed but caught the gun with its other hand and fired. The captain leaped back toward the bridge, and the Khalian's beam scorched the wall. But the first was firing, enough to make a Weasel duck before he shot back. The beam reflected off the officer's insignia and cut a furrow through a passenger's arm, setting her sleeve ablaze. She screamed, and her husband shouted, batting out the flame. Then a slug thrower cracked, and a hole appeared in the wall right near the captain's head. He returned the fire, and a Weasel shrieked—but so did the passengers as they felt the wind of atmosphere swooping toward the hole in the ship's side and the vacuum beyond. Then the slug thrower cracked again, and the first dropped, blood spreading out from his shoulder.

But a large, bulky shape rose up behind the pirates, a civilian in a business ensemble, drawing out an old-fashioned blackjack and clubbing at a Khalian. He connected, and the Khalian tumbled just as it squeezed off a beam at the captain, a beam that scribbled across the hull and went out just before it reached another screaming passenger. The captain's own beam speared the largest Khalian, sending up smoke from leather armor, but the Khalian howled and shot back, and the captain tumbled, his gun falling loose.

The big civilian swung at the armored Khalian.

Another Weasel swung his arm up, deflecting the black-jack with a yell, and the big Khalian swung around in time to see the sap swinging toward him again. He screamed and ducked down, hurtling forward, and knocked into the big human, jolting him back into the aisle and shredding his jacket with sharp claws. The human started to lift the black-jack again, but five needle-sharp talons poised over his face, and the Khalian shrilled, "The course of wisdom is to relinquish your weapon."

The Terran dropped the blackjack, as much from astonishment as from fear, and the Khalian erupted into the squealing hiccups that served as the laughter of his race. "Yes, you are startled to see that I speak such excellent Terran, are you not? But then, warrior-in-disguise, I was a translator in our Khalian Intelligence during the war. And you? Surely the only one of these monkeys who dared fight must have been a warrior once. What is your name, what was your rank?"

"Sales," the Terran ground out. "Lohengrin Sales, Lieutenant Commander."

"Ah, yes! The quaint custom of your kind—to give name and rank only! But was there not something more? A number? Yes, you Terrans are numbers as much as names, are you not?" And the Weasel gave his shrill, piping giggle again.

"And you?" the Terran grunted. "*Your* name?"

The talons danced dangerously. "Be wary, Sales. I honor you for having fought, but not so highly as to give you the power of my name. You are vanquished, after all."

"No," Sales spat. "We conquered Khalia."

The claws darted down, but halted a fraction of an inch from Sales's eyes. He kept his face carefully immobile—and was shocked to see that the Khalian was doing the same. The Weasel had exercised self-control!

"You did not conquer," the Weasel hissed. "Some few of my more tenderhearted countrymen were infuriated to discover that we had been deceived by our supposed allies of your kind, the Syndicate, and in their anger allied with you." The talons danced again. *"Is that not so?"*

Sales ignored the glittering points. "If you know that, why have you attacked us? We are not of the Syndicate! We are your allies!"

"No, not mine," the Khalian hissed. "Alliance with an enemy? Never! I, at least, would not accept such dishonor! See what comes of it—monkeys like these around us, thinking that Khalians did surrender! No, never will I be party to so disastrous an alliance! I will die fighting you, if I can, as I should have before the truce! And all of my crew wish to do so, too. But we will take as many of you as we can, first! We will slay you all, any of your race! We will punish all humans—the Fleet, and its Terran sheep—for killing Khalians."

"It is wrong," Sales gritted. "Deaths in war should not be avenged during peacetime."

"Peace has not come for me! The war has never ended! Rightly or wrongly, the only safety for Khalians is punishing those who kill Khalians! And we will slay those of the Syndicate, for exploiting us—suborning and then betraying us. We will bring you all down to death, or dishonor."

"Your own people have commanded all Khalians to lay down their arms! If you do not do so, you will be an outlaw!"

"An outlaw," the Weasel agreed, "never to see my ancestral hold again, never to feel the earth of Khalia beneath my feet, never to scent its sweet breezes!" The talons danced, and one drew a line of pain down Sales's cheek. "You are unwise to remind me of this!"

Sales ignored the pain, and the alarm that fed it. "The ways of wisdom do not always accord with the ways of honor."

"Honor, yes. Honor demands signs of victory." The Khalian's gaze darted down to Sales's chest, and his snout split with a grimace that was a Khalian smile. His other hand moved at Sales's throat, and the Terran tensed, but the Khalian laughed. "Softly, Sales, softly! What is a strip of cloth, after all, against a life?"

Everything, Sales knew—to a Khalian. Any sort of trophy taken from one of them was dishonor. But he was a human, so he lay frozen as the Khalian whipped the brightly colored band from around his neck. "Is it not pretty?" the Weasel cried, then whistled the same phrase in his own language— and his crew laughed with him.

They sounded like a psychotic calliope, Sales thought. He knew what the big Khalian had said to his men, because he knew Khalian as well as the Weasel knew Terran.

The leader draped the tie around his own neck and bent it into a clumsy knot. "There! See, I too am a Terran businessman! This is my trophy! Do each of you also take one!"

With whistles of agreement, the Khalians turned to tear at the civilians' neckties. With cries of dismay, the men untied their decorations quickly.

"Thus shall you know me, if ever we meet again," the big Khalian told Sales.

The Terran smiled, without mirth. "Shall I? Or shall we all burn, when you are done looting this ship?"

"Oh, we shall take the whole ship for our loot! But you have a launch, have you not? A 'lifeboat,' that is your term for it. Yes, we shall set you adrift in that, those of you who are not foolish enough to fight, and not skilled enough to die fighting."

Sales reddened.

The Khalian showed his teeth in a grin. "Be glad, Sales. Your clumsiness has saved your life. No, I will let all of you go, alive, to carry word back to your fellow Terrans of me and my crew—that they may know not to dare ply the space about Khalia again, lest we fall upon them!"

"Indeed," said Sales, with the closest he could come to scorn. "And how shall we tell them of you, when we do not know your name—you who are so good of heart as to let us live?"

His sarcasm was lost on the Khalian. "Good of heart? Why, that will be a most excellent name! Yes, tell them I am Goodheart, and that they shall know me by these brightly colored strips of cloth my crew and I shall wear! Tell them of Goodheart, that they may tremble in fear!"

"Goodheart," Sales agreed, with a sour smile. "Goodheart, the pirate."

"Goodheart!" the Khalian shrilled to his crew in his own language. "Do you hear? He has given me my name, the name which shall make Terrans tremble! From this time forth, I am Captain Goodheart!"

The crew's approval was a chorus of whistles that fairly drilled through the Terrans' brains.

The launch was jammed full, and the Khalians were none too gentle about pushing the passengers aboard. The women screamed in fright, and some of the men, too. Then Captain Goodheart snapped, "Stand clear!" and two of his Weasels stepped in, brandishing rifles. The crowd screamed and pressed back away from them, jamming up against one another.

Then, while the two crewmen held them back with their rifles, two others brought in an improvised stretcher with the captain's unconscious form on it. They went out, then returned with the first officer, again unconscious. Lastly, they brought in the draped body of the dead navigator. They stepped out, and the passengers were silent, awed. Then the two guards backed away, and Sales stepped in.

He turned to face the big Khalian in the hatchway. "I thank you for your courtesy to my fallen countrymen."

"I honor them," the pirate answered. "They fought, willingly if not well." Then his lips writhed back in a grin. "Remember me, Sales—and remember my kindness."

He hit the pressure patch, and the hatch swung closed.

"Oh, don't worry," Sales murmured. "I'll remember you, all right."

"You damn fool!" a passenger cried. "You damn near got us all killed back there!"

The crowd, given a scapegoat, suddenly turned into a mob, all shouting blame and accusation at Sales.

He whirled about and, in his best quarterdeck voice, bellowed, *"Grab hold!"*

Cries of incredulity answered him, but some of the civilians had been in the Fleet, and grabbed for the nearest seat-back or rack, yelling to others to do the same. Sales himself just barely managed to grab hold of a tie-ring before a giant kicked their ship like a football, and it shot out into space.

People screamed, and the ones who had ignored Sales slammed down against one another, then ran stumbling backward to be plastered against the aft bulkhead. Sales felt sorry for the ones on the bottom of the pile, but he knew someone had to direct this launch, or they'd be off course before they even began.

Assuming, of course, that the Weasels weren't planning to use them for target practice.

He didn't think they were, Sales thought, as he struggled fore through the press of bodies. The Weasels wouldn't have wasted a good ship that way. Goodheart had already shown that he cared a lot about public opinion; he wasn't about to shoot down helpless refugees.

He elbowed the last passenger aside, ignoring his angry shout, and pulled himself into the cockpit. Just then, the acceleration eased off, and he almost fell against the forward port, but caught himself in time, pushed himself back into the pilot's chair, and pulled the shock webbing across his body almost by reflex. Then he reached out and turned on the board. Lights winked across its surface, and the big screen next to the port glowed into life. Sales slapped at patches, activating the sensors, but not the beacon.

The merchantman was already moving. Goodheart wasn't wasting time—he was getting out, before Sales could call for help.

Passengers jammed the hatch behind him, and a man called out, "Just what the hell do you think you're doing!"

"Calling for help," Sales answered. But he kept his eyes glued to the screen as he turned on the log recorder, watching and noting coordinates until the merchantman suddenly blurred and winked out, into hyperspace. Then, finally, Sales reached out and turned on the beacon.

He turned around and said to the men jamming the opening, "Tell everyone to find seats, if they can, and see if there's a doctor or a nurse to keep an eye on the captain and the first."

One of the men turned away to carry the message, but another glared in outrage. "Who the hell put *you* in charge?"

"Yeah!" said the other man. "Who do you think you are, anyway?"

"Lohengrin Sales," he answered. "Lieutenant Commander, Fleet Intelligence."

"Sit down, Commander," the admiral said, not looking up from his desk screen. Sales relaxed a little and took the straight chair in front of the desk. The walls were almost invisible in the murk left by the single pool of light on the admiral's desk. The glow of the screen was brighter, though, and lit the man's face from below, giving him a supernatural look. *Good*, Sales thought. *It takes something supernatural to fight demons.*

The admiral looked up. "You acquitted yourself admirably, Commander. It's just lucky for those civilians that you happened to be on a mission to Terran HQ."

"Thank you, sir."

"But why did you have nothing but a blackjack, may I ask?"

"Spaceport security, sir. Civilians aren't allowed to carry weapons aboard, and blackjacks don't show up on screens— if they don't have any metal parts."

The admiral nodded. "We've sent your courier pack on to Terra with another messenger. It was lucky those pirates didn't think to search you—diplomatic documents with Khalian seals would never have gotten past them."

"They would have used them for kindling, sir. Now that that mission's out of my hands, may I request reassignment?"

The admiral smiled. "To what, Commander?"

"To pirate extermination, sir," Sales answered.

The admiral nodded. "Good idea. I was just about to assign you to track down Captain Goodheart, as it happens. And, by the way, you're promoted—to full commander."

* * *

There was discussion among the crew about the captain's taking of a Terran name, of course.

"I could understand his giving the humans a name to call him by," said Pralit, one of the CPOs, "but abandoning his family name, his clan name? How can this be good?"

"There is a way," Xlitspee, a crewman, assured, if somewhat desperately. "There must be—for our captain is the bravest of we orphans of Khalia."

"What did you say?" Houpiel snapped.

"That the captain is the bravest," Xlitspee answered, frowning.

"No—you said we are 'orphans of Khalia'!"

They were silent, letting the implications of the term sink in.

"If that is so," said Pralit, "perhaps his taking of a new name is fitting."

"Even if it is only a human name, translated to the Khalian tongue?"

"Of course." Pralit managed a grin. "*We* understand the meaning of it, in all its sarcasm."

"Not that there is not something of truth in it," Houpiel temporized, "though more of irony."

"Far more of irony," Xlitspee said, suiting his tone to the word.

They looked up as Saulpeen, the first officer, came in. "What says he?" asked the second. The officers had so far been silent.

"That we, too, should take new names," Saulpeen answered. "More, he wishes you each to take a name that is an aspect of his."

The wardroom filled with shrill cries of consternation.

"Be still!" the second cried. "You have seen sense in his change of name; hear his sense in changing ours!"

"Why," said Saulpeen, "the sense is that your names will show your allegiance to him—as will be needed, if your clan names are forgot."

"Forgot!"

"Forgot," Saulpeen said, his tone hardening, "for the captain means to gather in your fellow exiles—all they who

are Khalia's new orphans—and he does not wish that age-
old clan feuds should arise to divide we outcasts, who need
each other most.''

The wardroom was quiet as the crew looked at one another, then looked away. They were all men of one clan,
and the thought of alliance with enemies was detestable—
but Khalian enemies were better than human.

''And,'' said the second, finishing the train of thought,
''if there are no clan names, there can be no clan feuds. It
is very wise, Saulpeen.''

''Very,'' the first agreed, ''but from this time forth, I am
Saulpeen no longer. I shall henceforth be Throb.''

They were silent, letting the impact sink in.

Then the second nodded and said, ''I shall be Tender.''

And, slowly at first, then in a rush, they began to choose
names.

It wasn't just a matter of manning a ship and going out
to track down the pirate, of course. Sales had to earn that
ship, by figuring out where Captain Goodheart would appear next. He set up a computer scan, having every shipping
report routed through his office, and set a program to search
for key words, such as ''raid,'' ''lifeboat,'' and ''necktie.''

Reports began to come in, of a Khalian pirate who outgunned and outmaneuvered a merchantman, then matched
orbits, clung to the ship's side with magnetic grapples, and
blew a hole through the ship's skin. Then Weasels boarded—
and the biggest one always wore a loud, garish necktie. He
was unfailingly polite while his crew killed off the pilot and
navigator, then stuffed the passengers into a lifeboat.

Soon, Captain Goodheart was notorious for his lightning
strikes, his ruthlessness, and his neckties.

The ship shuddered, the section of hull fell inward, and
the half-dozen men and women of the crew started firing.
But Weasel faces ducked out, snapping off shots, and the
crew fell. A large Khalian bounded in, and the women
shrieked. The men struggled to their feet, pale and determined to die well. . . .

The Khalians swarmed all over them, and they were down and out cold in an instant.

"My husband!" a woman screamed, but the large Khalian said, in surprisingly good Terran and with amazing politeness, "I doubt not your husband is well, madame, though unconscious—unless he is a much better fighter than I expect. My crew does not kill civilians."

"Your crew?" the woman gasped. "But—who *are* you?"

"You may call me Captain Goodheart—for, see, I leave you your lives. But only your lives." The big Khalian held out a hand. "Your jewelry is forfeit. Give it to me, please."

With trembling hands, the woman unfastened her necklace and placed it into his hairy paw, then added her bracelet. Behind, the Khalians rose, taking the men's wallets and watches with them. All but one still breathed; most were unwounded.

Two women screamed at the sight of the others, and fell weeping over their bodies.

"The safe," Goodheart said to First Mate Throb, and the first turned away, with a whistle of assent.

The last of the women was surrendering her jewelry to the Khalians. Then half the crewmen fell to untying the men's neckties.

"But . . ." the first woman swallowed, plucked up her nerve, and asked again, "why are they taking our husbands' neckties?"

"Their neckties?" Captain Goodheart touched the garish strip of cloth around his own neck. "As mementoes, madame. Surely you would not begrudge us souvenirs?"

"And even our neckties!" the civilian shouted, purple with rage. "What kind of Navy do you think you're running, if these Khalians can just pop up wherever they want and play pirate with us?"

"Neckties?" The naval officer seemed suddenly more intent on the civilian's report of the piracy. "Just yours? Or everybody's?"

"All our neckties, dammit!" the civilian shouted. "What am I paying my taxes for, anyway?"

But Commander Sales only nodded as he stood and said, "Thank you for your information, Mr. Bagger. You've been a great help." He started to turn away, then stopped at a thought and turned back. "By the way—what were you coming to Khalia for, anyway?"

"Why, to buy some of that bargain real estate the Khalia are selling, of course! And set up a department store! There are fortunes to be made there, man!"

As Commander Sales turned away, he was almost ashamed to admit that he could understand at least part of what drove Captain Goodheart.

Sales set up a holotank with Khalia's sun represented by a glowing ruby at the center, then plotted the pirate's ambushes in yellow dots, connecting them with traceries of faint yellow lines. Slowly, the pattern grew. Goodheart seemed to be everywhere and nowhere, in a sphere about three AUs out from Khalia. That was the point at which ships had to drop out of hyperspace into normal space, because they were getting too close to the gravity well of Khalia's sun—and sometimes Goodheart was there to meet them, and sometimes he wasn't. It didn't seem to matter which side of Khalia's sun they dropped out on—Goodheart ambushed ships from every direction.

Sales couldn't patrol every inch of a sphere that size, of course—but he could outfit a cruiser and wait in ambush near the breakout point from Target, that being the most frequent traffic from and to Khalia. A cruiser that was nonmetallic, and black, and far enough away so that it wouldn't be visible to the naked eye—but close enough so it could rendezvous with any inbound ship within fifteen minutes.

All he needed was permission.

"Sorry, Sales. We can't risk you in combat now. You're the only one who knows that Weasel, his mania, his patterns of raiding."

"I've left complete notes, sir," Sales said. "The locations of his raids, the times, the pattern—everything's there, in the computer."

The admiral just sat, frowning at him. Sales could almost hear him weighing the greater chances of eliminating the pirate, against the chance of losing the only man who had any feel for how Goodheart thought. Sales held his breath.

The admiral decided, and nodded. "All right, Sales. You can have him."

Sales's heart was still soaring as he stretched his shock webbing across himself and leaned back, waiting for take-off. To be in command of a ship again was wonderful enough—but to be in command of a ship that was chasing Captain Goodheart was sublime.

The ship waited near the breakout point, its black hull virtually invisible in the eternal night of space. It waited for a week and, during that time, watched a ship a day break out into normal space and shoot onward toward Khalia. It waited for two weeks, and the crew began to grumble. They were getting tired of backgammon and calisthenics. They wanted action—or shore leave.

Finally, after three weeks, the alarm beeped, and the sensor op called, "Khalian on scope."

"Commander Sales to the bridge," the captain snapped into the intercom. "All crew, combat stations!"

The klaxon hooted, and the ship filled with the thunder of pounding feet.

Sales burst into the control room and stilled, staring at the image on the telescope screen. Infrared-sensed and computer-enhanced, the silhouette of a Khalian cruiser seemed to float in space.

"We've got him!" Sales hissed. "Full acceleration, Captain!"

"Full acceleration," the captain told his engineer. The alarm wailed, and reflex sent Sales into his acceleration couch. He was stretching the webbing as the boost hit and two gravities' worth of acceleration slammed him back into the cushions.

A point of light shimmered on the screen, a new star.

"Widen coverage!" the captain snapped, but the sensor op was already increasing the field.

A new ship appeared on the screen, hurtling toward the Khalian—but it was ten times the size, and the silhouette was Terran.

"There's what he's after!" Sales snapped. "A freighter!"

"Torpedo," the captain directed. There was no feeling of recoil, but after a second, a gunner called, "Away."

"He'll move before it gets there," Sales warned, but the captain was already nodding. "We'll launch as soon as we can tell vector and velocity."

Then, suddenly, the Khalian jumped—but away from the freighter. It flipped over, bow facing toward Sales. Fire burst, and the torpedo exploded well away from the ship.

"He knows we're here," Sales grated. "Any more legs on this ship?"

"Range!" The gunner didn't even finish the word before the captain was bawling, "Fire!"

It was fast, then—the head gunner keyed the computer for full fire, and the helms op keyed his for evasive action. The ship slammed them from side to side and back and forth, jumping about in its progress toward the Khalian—but the fire computer read each change in vector as soon as the helm computer generated it, and compensated in its aim. The ship's full armament blazed, picking off the Khalian's torpedoes and evading its lasers, while it probed and stabbed with its own cannon and missiles.

The Khalian, of course, had done the same, and its image jittered about the screen, its cannon blazing at the Terran, evading and returning fire.

Computer against computer, the pirate strove against the Fleet vessel—while, beyond them and all but unknowing, the freighter sped silently past and on toward Khalia.

But Sales had an advantage that the Khalian didn't—a dozen PT ships, spawned at the sound of the klaxon and arcing high above the plane of the ecliptic. Now they fell, stabbing fire, guided by computers independent of the fire-control brain.

The Khalian rolled and jumped, trying to evade this new menace. Then an explosion lit it amidships. The screens darkened to compensate for the extra light, so Sales could only see a dim picture of the Khalian turning tail.

"Got him!" the captain shouted, clenching his fist. "Go get him, Helm!"

"Chasing, sir," the helm op gloated, and the warning hooted just before the ship jumped into two g's acceleration again.

On the screen, the pirate shrank as it sped away.

"He might be sucking us in," Sales reminded.

"We're watching," the captain answered.

The pirate began to grow in the screen again.

"We'll catch him," the captain gloated. "We'll blast him out of the night!"

Suddenly the pirate began to glitter.

"He's jumping!" the sensor op yelled.

"He can't!" Sales shouted. "He's wounded! He could blow himself into oblivion!"

"If he stays, we'll do it to him for sure," the captain grated.

The glitter covered the ship completely, faded to a twinkle, and was gone. The screen was empty.

"Got away!" Sales slammed his fist against the arm of his couch. "He got away from us!"

"Maybe not!" The captain's voice was leaden. "He was too close to another mass—us—and too close to a standard breakout point, where the curvature of space is kinked. Could be he's blown himself to hell."

"Not this weasel." Sales glared at the screen. "Could be, but it's not. He may be hurt, but he's alive."

He lay back in his couch, forcing himself to relax. "You fought damn well, Captain, and you gave him one hell of a chase. I couldn't have asked for better."

"Thank you, sir—but I could." The captain's face was grim. "We lost him—so it wasn't good enough. The crew did a fine job—but there must be something we could have done better."

"I can't think what." Sales suddenly felt very tired.

"You will, though, sir. You will."

* * *

"We must know who commanded that ship, Throb! It was no chance encounter; he was waiting for us!" Goodheart paced the chamber, vibrant with anger.

"He must, indeed," Throb agreed.

"We must have knowledge! Information! We must set spies to tell us of the slightest sign that some Terran seeks us out!"

Throb frowned. "But how can we know what the humans think, Captain? We cannot have agents among them."

"Can we not?" Goodheart wheeled about, eyes glowing. "Have we no Khalians who dwell among humankind? Are there none on Target, none on Khalia, who would favor us?"

Throb stared, struck by the notion. "There must be many!"

"Make planetfall secretly!" Goodheart commanded. "Set each of our men to talk to old friends! Let them sound out those who are loyal to Khalia, not to the clan chiefs! Those few who are, give them transmitters and codes! Let them pass each word they hear that might have meaning back to us!"

"At once, my captain!" Throb sped away, leaving Goodheart to plan alone.

He paced the chamber, reviewing possibilities. Language—he must teach all his crew the human languages, those of the Fleet and the Syndicate, and set them to scanning the humans' broadcasts. He must begin to collect news printouts from every vessel he boarded—he had chanced upon a copy of a shipping schedule on the last Syndicate ship he had taken. He needed knowledge.

Old friends talked to old friends, and they talked to new friends. No one could say who had asked whom, but half the Khalians on the home planet soon knew to which old friend they should mention anything interesting. Petty, perhaps irrelevant . . .

Or perhaps not.

"Commander Lohengrin Sales?" Goodheart stared at the picture on the screen, recorded from a newsfeed and trans-

mitted to his ship, secretly. He frowned at the human face.
"Why does that name itch at the corner of my brain?"

All the crew were silent, watching their captain out of
the corners of their eyes.

But Goodheart scarcely saw them; he was concentrating
on memory, reviewing all that had happened since he had
decided to turn pirate. . . .

"Sales!" he cried. "The civilian who fought us, when
we first captured a Terran ship! Have they set *him* to chasing
me, then?"

"We shamed him, Captain," murmured Throb. "He lusts
for revenge."

"Even as I do—now!" Goodheart bared his teeth in a
grin. "Would he chase me, then? Well, let us seek more
information about him, and more—for I will chase him!"

For some reason, the prospect filled Throb with forebod-
ing.

And perhaps he was right—for, alone in his cabin, Goodheart paced the deck, claws emerging and retracting,
simmering with anger and frustration—because he realized
that, more than anything else, he needed human agents.

How could he recruit even one trustworthy human, when
all were so loyal to their race—or so treacherous that they
were willing to sell anything for their own wealth, even
honor? He didn't know—but he would find a way. "I must
have a human!" he breathed. "I must!"

The other kids never liked Georgie Desrick when he was
growing up. Long in the torso and short in the legs, he was
never much of an athlete—and whether his clumsiness
was inborn, or only the result of the other kids never wanting him on their teams, it was nonetheless extreme. Add to
that a face with a receding chin, buck teeth, and huge, bulging eyes (from the distortion of the thick contact lenses he
had to wear), and you had a person who didn't exactly gather
friends. Nonetheless, he was very religious, so he managed
to put aside all thoughts of revenge and filled his time with
books.

Storybooks, "How To" books, encyclopedias, dictionaries—he soaked up everything he could read. By fifth grade, he was already reading high school physics and chemistry; by seventh grade, he was soaking up cybernetics and electronics. Those clumsy hands managed to acquire a modicum of skill with a soldering iron and a chemistry set, and his mind developed compartments for listening to the teacher separately from working on his latest math problem. School lessons would have bored him stiff, if he'd actually had to pay attention to them—after all, they were several years behind his reading—so he became adept at tracking the classroom lectures, able to snap to full consciousness at the mention of his name, and answer the question that had just been asked, while the back of his mind went on planning his next electronic invention.

He got straight A's, of course. Which made him even less popular.

By the time he graduated from high school, he had several patents to his name and a very good income from royalties—so a high-pressure Navy recruiter talked him into going into the Fleet, promising that he could attend the best colleges on old Earth at government expense for as long as he wanted—provided that, when he graduated, he would work on some problems the government wanted investigated.

And, the recruiter pledged, he'd have companionship.

The companionship turned out to mean that he was quartered with other officer candidates, that they all had to sleep in the same room and eat at the same table. It didn't mean they had to talk with him.

So they didn't—they talked past him, over him, and by him, and when they did look at him, their faces held anything but friendship. They were fine-looking, sociable, athletic young men, all of them, and they resented him fiercely.

Georgie threw himself into his studies more fervently than ever.

His roommates took it as snobbish aloofness and disliked him even more.

Georgie graduated in three years—with a doctorate in physics. He stayed another year, to pick up master's degrees in chemistry and metallurgy. He was starting work on his third dissertation when the Navy told him it was time to collect.

But they had to take him to the planet where the problem lay, so he was signed on as supercargo aboard an FTL training cruiser.

Within a week, the crew resented him for not having to get his hands dirty.

A new midshipman, trying to build a personal power base, chose Georgie as the obvious scapegoat and unified the rest of the middies by building up a huge grudge against the oddball who just stayed in his cabin and read.

Rough hands woke him in the middle of the night, jabbing a gag in his mouth and shackling his hands and feet. Young men, snarling obscenities, rushed him through the darkness and locked him inside a space-going coffin labeled a lifeboat. A mule kicked him in the seat, and he blacked out.

They were caught, of course—but their midshipman leader managed to put it down to a sophomoric prank that had gone too far. The officers let the rest of the crew off with severe discipline, but the leader was cashiered. He turned his back on the Navy and started trying to figure out how to manipulate those around him into making him rich.

Georgie woke in the dark, with no light but the faint instruments on the control panel. He yanked the gag from his mouth, found the water bottle in the emergency rations—not easy, with handcuffs—took a couple of gulps, and remembered that he was marooned. He forced himself to cap the bottle and studied the control panel.

His heart sank.

When the middies had kicked him out of the ship, the lifeboat had dropped back into normal space. It was thirty light-years from the nearest sun.

He started the beacon, but with almost no hope. He started a strict rationing program, so his air regenerator gave out before his food and water did, two weeks after he'd been drifting alone in the darkness.

The loneliness, he was used to. His religious faith sustained him, until the end.

But, as the excess carbon dioxide muffled his thoughts and he began the slide down into unconsciousness, the despair he couldn't quite contain opened the channel through which all the resentment, bitterness, and years of repressed anger tore loose into a river of hatred—hatred against all things human, who had been too snobbish to befriend him, had sneered at him all his life, and who could not, when last came to last, even leave him alone. The religious part of him cried in dismay, but finally had to admit that burning, tearing hatred that boiled up in a lust for revenge against all of humanity.

A shrilling pierced Georgie's ears. He winced and forced his eyes open. He was astounded to realize he was still alive.

He was even more astounded to realize he was staring up into the face of a Khalian.

The snout split in a grin—Georgie was flabbergasted; he hadn't known the creatures could smile—and a furry paw came up to pat his cheek. Then, even more incredibly, the Khalian spoke—in Terran. "Do not be afraid. We have rescued you from your lifeboat—and only just in time, too. Minutes longer, and you would have been dead. You are safe now, and among friends."

Georgie could only stare.

Then sleep claimed him again.

When he woke a second time, the Khalian in attendance looked up, saw him, and shrilled something into a grille on the wall. Georgie was just trying to struggle up to a sitting position when the Khalian he'd seen before came in and pushed him gently back. "Please, not yet. Give your body time to recover."

Georgie sank back, realizing that the Khalian was much bigger than most of his kind, and wondering why he was wearing a bright, gaudy necktie. "But—why would you save me? I'm . . . not even your kind. . . ."

Captain Goodheart grinned, all the more widely because

that was the same question Throb had posed. "We cannot but admire the valor with which you strove to survive in that lifeboat, when all must have seemed hopeless. We Khalians understand valor. How long were you adrift? A week? Two?"

"Two," Georgie agreed.

"And how did you come to be there? Shipwreck? Accident?"

"Exile." Georgie's jaw firmed. "My own kind threw me out."

"Ahhhh." Captain Goodheart lifted his head. "Then we are alike, you and we."

Georgie frowned and asked, "How can that be?"

Goodheart began to explain.

"But, Captain! How can a human choose a Khalian name?"

"In the same fashion that you and I have, Throb. And for much the same reason—he renounces his kind. He says that we are his kind, now."

It made sense, from Georgie's viewpoint. He was dead to the human race, and by their own doing. Sure, only a few spiteful young men had actually thrown him out—but the Navy itself hadn't shown much concern, surely not enough to come looking for him. As to the rest of the race, why, they scarcely knew he existed, even though most of them were already benefiting from the improved hyperspace communications link he had invented.

And the Khalians didn't care what he looked like.

In fact, they seemed very friendly, treating him like one of their own. Which he was; he would willingly have done anything Captain Goodheart asked now, up to and including suicide. After all, he owed his life to the captain; surely it was his to call in, whenever he chose. Besides, there seemed to be neither Khalian nor human here—only pirates, together. True, he heard one or two now and then joking about "the captain's pet human," but Throb and the other officers were quick to punish the offender.

Georgie had never had a friend stick up for him before.

The total lack of interest in athletics, though, they could not abide. They were, after all, medieval warriors, no matter what their technological skills. But Goodheart tutored Georgie himself, slowly and with immense patience and good cheer, gradually teaching him how to defend himself, then turning him over to Throb, who coached him with equal patience into learning to attack—until, after a year's time, Georgie actually knew how to fight and was amazed to find he was physically fit. He had even learned to endure pain without flinching.

And if, between sessions, Throb stormed and ranted to the captain about what a worthless being Georgie was— why, Georgie had no need to know it. And the captain didn't mind. He knew Georgie's true worth—at least, to himself and his raiders. And if, in his most secret heart of hearts, he thought of Georgie as a traitor, he was quick to counter it with the charitable thought that this genius of a human was really only a poor, gullible fool.

Sales had almost had him. That slimy pirate had almost been in his grasp! He felt it as failure, of course—but he had saved the merchantman, damaged the raider, and at least proved he knew how to find Goodheart. So the admiral gave Sales a dozen ships, and Sales stationed them at the points Goodheart was most likely to raid.

Of course, the pirate never showed up—near any of Sales's ships. He appeared in plenty of other places, gutted merchantmen and passenger liners by the score—but never where Sales expected him to be. He detected the cruisers in ambush, somehow, or maybe he had agents in the Fleet— now that they had Khalian allies, it was impossible to tell. Not that barring Weasels from the Fleet would have done any good—there had been traitors enough during the war, and Syndicate humans still didn't look any different from Fleet humans.

Would a Syndicate agent work for Captain Goodheart?

Of course—since he was fouling up Terran-Khalian traffic. Any little bit that weakened the Fleet was in the Syndicate's interest.

Sales considered the possibility that Goodheart might *be* a Syndicate agent, and decided against it. The Weasel simply had too much hatred for humans.

Then ships dropping out of hyperspace began to be boarded, light-years away from Khalia. There was either a research genius among the pirates, or the Syndicate saw a great deal of potential in Goodheart's activities. They would have had to have spirited the gadget in to Goodheart by a secret agent, of course—but that wasn't impossible.

Nor was the possibility of accident, Sales reminded himself. If the pirate had captured a ship with such a weapon aboard, he wouldn't have hesitated to use it—or duplicate it. His value system might have been medieval, but his technicians were modern.

Sales increased the scale on his holotank exponentially; the three-AU sphere shrank to the size of a baseball. He began plotting Goodheart's new strikes in red dots, then connecting them with very thin lines.

Gradually, a lacy red sphere grew around Khalia, about twelve light-years out.

He had to have a base, Sales knew—and it had to be inside that lacy sphere. It couldn't be outside, or he'd have had double transit time to the ambush sites on the far side of Khalia from wherever he'd set up housekeeping—and the reports of attacks came too frequently for that.

He had to have a base—but where?

"There! It is perfect!"

Throb frowned at the image on the viewscreen. "It is bleak and pitted, Captain. What can be perfect about a huge asteroid?"

"What! Can you not see?" Goodheart spun about to Georgie. "Perhaps *you*, adopted one! Is not my asteroid perfect?"

"Perfect, yes, as an asteroid," Georgie whistled. His Khalian was horribly accented, but comprehensible. It gave his shipmates much material for broad jokes—but at least

he could understand the punch lines. "For a pirate's base,
it is large enough to house the warriors of the cruiser, and
a dozen ships more."

Throb and the other Khalians lifted their heads.

"Some of those pits may be tunnel mouths," Georgie
went on, "and the rest could become so. Caverns could
become ammunition dumps and hydroponic gardens. Then
it is a small matter to close those mouths with walls or
locks, and you have your base."

"You see?" Goodheart shrilled to his crew. "You see?
Even the outlander sees what you could not!"

Georgie blushed, feeling the resentment rise around him.
"By your leave, Captain . . ."

"Anything! To one who can see so clearly—anything.
What would you say, Hemoglobin?"

The crew relaxed a little, smiling, and Georgie was glad
he had chosen a foolish scientist's name—it let the Khalians
feel comfortably superior, in the ways they believed really
mattered. So like humans . . . "Good Captain, would it
not be better to have a planet? A base that cannot run out
of oxygen or water?"

The ship became very quiet. Georgie twitched under the
weight of their stares, but held his gaze even with the captain's.

"Why, it would be so," Goodheart said evenly, "but
how would you defend it?"

"With the ships that form your current lair, the old merchant hulks, each mounted with many cannon and set in
orbit."

"Well thought," Goodheart purred, "but where would
we find these cannon?"

"On the small ships of the Fleet that we have never bothered with."

An appreciative whistle passed through the crew.

Goodheart grinned. "Well thought, Globin! But to take
off or land from such a world requires great stores of fuel!
Where shall we find it?"

Georgie hid his irritation at the blindness of people. "Our
engines are fueled by hydrogen, great Captain, and water

is hydrogen bonded to oxygen. We can loose it easily with small amounts of electricity. Choose a water world—with seas, to provide your hydrogen, and rivers, to turn the turbines that will make your electricity.''

The surrounding whistle increased in shrillness, and even Goodheart seemed a little shaken as he laughed and said, ''He does not dream small dreams, our Globin! But where are we to find such a world?''

''In Virgo,'' Globin answered, ''not far from Spica.''

And he gave them the coordinates. He did not tell them that this was his own world, the one that he had gleaned from the records of many, many exploration missions, sifted in the library in the long, lonely hours of college weekends. His own world, the one around which he had built his fantasy, his dream of escape from all the sarcastic people who belittled and insulted him, from the athletes who punched him around for fun, from the beautiful and condescending girls. He gave it to them without reluctance or hesitation, for he had found his escape—but with friends.

It grew in the viewscreens, a jewel of a world, a semi-precious stone polished to an oblate spheroid, a turquoise banded with white—too small, and too mineral-poor, to have been of interest for colonization, and too far from Terra.

But close enough to Khalia, and to the route from Khalia to Target.

The ship landed, the machines sampled atmosphere and water for chemical oddities and microorganisms, and pronounced the planet safe—as the records had said it was.

''Go and frolic!'' Goodheart cried. ''But stay close to the ship—we know not what monsters may lurk nearby!''

The hatches opened, and the crew boiled out in a manic tide.

''Some few must stay and guard, must they not?'' Goodheart glanced from screen to screen. ''You and I, Globin.''

It warmed the human's heart immensely. ''Will you show me how to fight on land?''

''Haw!'' Goodheart swiped at the human. ''He who had no love for the things of the body! Yes, Globin, I will fight

you—without claws.'' His eye gleamed as he watched the
screens. ''See them rejoice! Thank you for my world, Globin.''

''You are welcome, Captain.'' Globin would have given
his hero anything.

Goodheart's eye was still on the screen. ''What would
you name it, Globin?''

''Name?'' Globin looked up, surprised. ''Why, New
Khalia, of course!''

Goodheart shook his head. ''The past is closed to us,
Globin, and must be forgotten. Give me a new name, for a
new world!''

''Why,'' said Globin, ''Barataria, of course!''

Globin was sweating. He had always been uncomfortable
among his own kind, but had never realized it so thoroughly
before. He missed his friends, his Khalian pirate com-
rades—but the captain wanted it done, so Globin would do
it.

He stepped into the little town on Target, reminding himself that he could fight now, if he had to—but no one looked
twice at him.

He could scarcely believe it. He bucked his spirits up and
walked on down the street into the depot, feeling as though
all eyes were on him, but seeing not a single glance, no
matter where he looked. Perhaps, after all, the little, funny-
looking man in the gray ensemble wasn't worth looking at.

He bought a ticket for the hover to the capital, where he
checked into a hotel room, then booked passage for Terra.

''He will betray you, Captain! He is among his own kind
once again! He will tell the Fleet where we lair!''

''He dares not.''

''But he may be taken! He may be given drugs!''

''Ah, Throb! Have you no confidence in our own forgers?
We duplicated exactly that passport we took from a human—except in changing the name and the holo.''

''Of course,'' Throb grumped, ''but I have no faith in

the 'merchant' Globin goes to meet. He may be an agent of the Fleet come to bait a trap!"

"If so, we will lose our dear Globin—but the humans will not be much the wiser, for Globin knows nothing of us but the inside of our ship and the coordinates of Barataria. That, I would begrudge—and I daresay I would truly regret Globin's passing. But at least, it would not be a Khalian whose death I mourned."

"We will steer our ship into a trap, when we come to take the weapons the merchant has promised you," Throb grumbled.

"Perhaps—so there will be only two pirates who go to load the consignment." Goodheart took out the pasteboard with the human's name on it—"Seth Adamson, Expediter." The gall of the human, to press a business card on him in the midst of a raid! *I can be of service to you, Captain. We can be of service to each other.* Again, Goodheart squeezed the corner and saw the surface of the card change, displaying weapon after weapon, up to cannon and tanks, while a mouse's voice touted their virtues. "Is there no treachery too great for these humans," Goodheart murmured, "so long as it enriches themselves?"

"Why should that be any less true of Globin, Captain?" Throb demanded.

"Because, good Throb, *we* are his enrichment." Goodheart flipped the card into the air and watched it spin slowly down.

As Globin went through the whole process, the meeting in the Terran restaurant, the discussion under the privacy screen, the haggling over price, and the listing of the order, a part of him sat aside and marveled. He would never have had the nerve to do such a thing if Captain Goodheart had not asked it. He would never have had the confidence if Captain Goodheart and his crew had not given it to him.

The freighter dropped into normal space, shed velocity, and drifted, lights blinking in the prearranged signal, waiting. Goodheart's crew scanned the vicinity, but saw no trace of ships.

"Wait," said Globin. "Let me try my new detector."

Goodheart whistled with respect. "How can you detect masses in hyperspace, Globin, when we are in normal space?"

"By the interaction of interference waves between the two continua, Captain. . . . No, so far as I can tell, there are no other ships except the freighter, and us."

Goodheart pressed a patch. "Then go, Plasma and Saline!"

The small courier shot out from the pirate ship. It docked at the great ship's port, and the crew settled down for the long wait while the two Khalians inspected the cargo with a life-detector.

Finally, a smaller ship shot away from the freighter. Sometime later, a twinkle in the distance announced its departure from normal space.

"Terran yacht in hyperspace," Globin announced.

Goodheart hit the com patch. "Saline! Are you in possession of the ship?"

"I am, Captain. The merchant pronounced himself satisfied with the bonus."

"Then guide the freighter toward the rendezvous asteroid and begin testing weapons."

"How long until we are sure the whole ship will not blow up on us, Captain?"

"A day and a night should be enough. Enjoy your target practice." Goodheart signed off and turned to Globin, catching him by the shoulders and shrilling with delight. "Mission accomplished, Globin! Well done!"

Whistles of acclaim pierced the air, and Globin stood with a silly smile on his face, very proud and very, very happy.

"You actually went through the records of every surplus dealer on all the human planets?"

"Computers are wonderful," Lo assured the admiral. "Of course, the records of the munitions factories' output are submitted to us regularly—but as far as we can tell, they haven't been doctored.''

''Very good, Commander Sales.'' The admiral studied the hard copy on his desk. ''Small losses in shipment, from a dozen factories . . .''

''And a large number of sales of personal arms, to anonymous buyers, from a hundred surplus stores.'' Lo nodded. ''It all adds up to a very large shipment of human-made weapons.''

''Very good, Commander! And where did those weapons go?''

Sales laid the other hard copy down on the desk.

The admiral nodded, his face grim. ''Arrest Adamson.''

''We tried, sir. He disappeared.''

The whole tavern was filled with females. Throb should have been delighted to be surrounded by so many, some even beauties—and after more than a year without seeing anything feminine! But he had seen them stream out of the factory, saw the drab protective clothing they wore, and the signs of servitude sickened him.

Ri'isthin was easily the most beautiful of them all, and it should have been an almost intoxicating pleasure to share a drink with her, even if the brew had not been alcoholic. Still, he couldn't hide his agitation.

''You are brave, to come into a place filled with bitter females,'' Ri'isthin said sarcastically. ''Yet I can see you are troubled by more than being so greatly outnumbered.''

Throb couldn't hold it in any longer. ''How can you labor for the conqueror! Like slaves!''

Ri'isthin winced, but shrugged with determined fatalism. ''We choose to live—and so many males died in the war, so many more males than females, that we have no husbands. How else are we to find food and shelter?''

Throb took a deep breath, then took the plunge. ''What is the depth of your courage?''

* * *

The first shuttle blasted the pad and settled down. The hatch opened, the gangway extruded—and the females filed down, looking around them at Barataria in wonder.

Goodheart's crew shrilled with delight and shot out toward them.

Every crewman grabbed a female and whirled her away—but there were 180 males left unpartnered.

Not for long.

The second shuttle touched down, and the third—then the first blasted off to go back for its second load.

Goodheart stood watching them, controlling the raging tide of his own hormones with difficulty. "You chose my world well, Globin—and Throb has brought us life for it."

"It is wonderful to see them happy," Globin murmured, eyes on the men.

Goodheart frowned at the new note in his henchman's voice, and looked down at him. "Ah, poor lonely Globin! Shall we find you a female, too?"

But Globin shook his head with granite resolve. "The only ones who would want me, Captain, I would not choose. Even if they wished marriage, it would not be me they'd want; they would only accept me because they could do no better. No, let me take joy in my shipmates' pleasure."

That was when Goodheart began to think of Globin as a being in his own right.

"Are you *certain* there is no ship near, in hyperspace, Globin?"

"I am sure, Captain. My detector shows nothing."

"But it must be bait for a trap!" Goodheart paced the deck, agitated. "What else could it be? A passenger liner, dropped into normal space with its distress beacon screaming—why would the humans make themselves such easy prey?"

"Then wave a flag to show us where they are?" Throb echoed.

Globin said, "It *could* be a genuine emergency . . ."

"If so, we shall pick them clean!" Goodheart turned with decision. "And if it is a trap, we shall pick their bones! But if the snare is set, I will trip it alone! Prepare my pinnace!"

"No, Captain!"

"You must not risk yourself!"

"We would be lost without you!"

"I volunteer!"

"I volunteer!"

"And I!"

"And I!"

"And I!"

The pinnace shot away moments later, staffed with three valiant crewmen. Throb and the other officers eyed the captain as though they were ready to pounce.

The pinnace docked. Three spacesuited figures drifted into the airlock.

"Leucocyte?" Goodheart called. "Are you there?"

"The lock is cycling, Captain." Leuco's helmet-camera showed them the interior hatch. The green patch lit, and Leuco's hand came out to haul the hatch open. "We are entering." The edges of the hatch swam out of sight . . .

The screen was filled with Khalian faces.

Goodheart stood stunned. So did Leuco.

Then, as from a distance, Goodheart heard Leuco say, "Why have warriors come cold to the void?"

"We wish to enlist with Captain Goodheart," one of the Khalians answered.

Then, suddenly, the air was filled with keening.

"Do not leave us to labor in the conqueror's shadow!"

"Do not condemn us to fight for our enemies!"

"No clan will battle the humans! Give me a leader!"

"Take me!"

"Take me!"

"Take me!"

"Do not turn us away!"

"Volunteers," Goodheart murmured, awed.

Globin nodded, eyes glowing. "I know how they feel." He looked up at Goodheart, beaming. "You have made a new beginning for us all, Captain."

"A whole shipful of Khalians?"

"Yes, sir." Sales's face, beyond the shadow of the desk

lamp, was filled with disgust. "Don't ask me why the shipping company was willing to lease them a liner."

"Or why Emigration let them all get on the same ship? They're free beings, Commander, not slaves—we can't stop them without very good reason." The admiral scowled heavily at the list on the screen. "If they want to go, we can't stop them!"

"Even if they're going to kill humans?!?"

The admiral shrugged impatiently. "Prove they're going to join Goodheart—ahead of time. But with this ship lost, I don't think anyone's going to be interested in a charter for a band of Khalians again. You can tell the spaceports to watch the small ships, though, Commander."

Lo did—and they managed to prevent several yachts with "joyriding" Khalians from leaving port. The joyriders turned out to have an amazing amount of weaponry with them—but the warriors had not surrendered their personal arms, and they claimed they needed to be able to defend themselves in case of attack by pirates.

That they needed the weapons for the pirates, Sales didn't doubt.

But he couldn't prevent Khalians from booking passage on liners with human passengers. And if the pirates attacked, and some humans lived, but the Khalians failed to come back, who could be surprised?

Sales wondered how many Khalians were working only to save up enough money for another round trip on a liner, hoping against hope to be pirated.

"He calls himself Globin." Sales held up the candid shot for the admiral to see. It showed Globin at a newscreen in a spaceport; he seemed to be staring right up into the camera set next to the screen.

"Ugly enough." The admiral frowned at the picture. "He makes weapons deals for Goodheart?"

"We're pretty sure he's the one who made the three weapons buys, yes. But this time, he ordered metal."

"Metal?" The admiral looked up, frowning.

"Yes, sir. A superfreighter of manganese, aluminum, nickel, iron, and a whole list of more exotic supplies."

"That's industrial bulk. Just how big is this Goodheart growing, anyway?"

"He's got to have a base, sir," Sales said, "a mighty big base."

"Big enough to set up his own weapons factories! Shut him down, Sales—shut him down!" He tossed the holo back. "And if this Goblin ever sets foot on a human planet again, arrest him! I want him tied, tried, and fried."

"Yes, sir, Admiral." Sales didn't correct his mistake—he used it. And fed it to the rumor mills, and the public opinionators.

Within the year, there wasn't a human on Target or Khalia who didn't believe the psychotic Goblin was the worst villain the race had ever spawned.

"Why don't you ever attack Syndicate ships?" an aggrieved businessman wailed.

"Why do you think I do not?" Goodheart returned. "They are very profitable game, I assure you. Your valuables, please."

Every few days, now, word came of another raid by a ship that grappled and cut through the side of a merchantman, and sometimes even a destroyer, disgorging a horde of shrilling Khalians whose captain wore a brightly colored necktie, each one more garish than the last. His crew cut down anybody who resisted, and weren't terribly picky about innocent bystanders. Their last loot was always the men's neckties.

But they always left at least a few alive and set them adrift in a lifeboat—almost as though the pirate was taunting Sales, making sure he knew that Goodheart was still striking with impunity.

Either that, or Goodheart was very much aware of the value of publicity.

But one route had more ambushes than any other—the hyperspace curve between Khalia and Target. There was no way of telling where the attack would occur, within the twelve-light-year approach to Khalia, so Sales couldn't post sentry ships to cover every AU of it. But he could call for volunteers, order civilian suits for them, and start taking round trips on a ship that went from Khalia to Target and back. A very special ship. It looked ordinary, of course, like any other passenger ship—but Sales had ordered some very unique modifications.

The section of hull fell inward, and the Khalians leaped in among the passengers, guns leveled and ready.

"So, ladies and gentlemen." Captain Goodheart shouldered his way in among his crewmen. "I am delighted to be your guest, no matter how brief my stay. Come, come! Have you no greater hospitality than that? Will you give no refreshment, no entertainment? Ah, but you must offer me something! Your wallets and jewelry, as a beginning." He grinned down at the big, beefy man near him. "Come, will you not rise to greet your . . ." Then his eyes widened as he recognized the face he had seen in each of several news articles, that he remembered seeing last above this same civilian ensemble. "Sales!"

"Now!" Sales roared, a gun appearing in his hand. "He knows!"

Laser bolts seared the air. Weasels shrieked—then humans screamed. The stench of burning fur and flesh rose—for each "civilian" had concealed a pistol beside him in the seat, and the Khalians among them were caught in a murderous crossfire.

But they were quick, those Weasels. Even as barrels leveled, they dodged aside. A few were caught by bolts aimed at others, but most skipped back, wounded and furious, to the hole in the side.

"Back!" Goodheart shrilled. "So you do not smite your own! Then fight, as your fathers did at Target!"

· The pirates pulled back in a knot around their hatch—but grenades hurled from among the Terrans. Weasels shot into the crowd, but their beams scorched upholstery, though here and there a man or woman cried out. One bomb came whirling back toward the humans, but two others blew. Pirates keened, and one cried, "They have disabled the lock!"

"The outer lock only!" Goodheart cried. "Back, back inside, so that we may close the inner hatch!"

The pirates disappeared like water down a drain—but Sales leaped forward, pulling a crowbar from under his jacket, jamming it in the hatch, whistling in execrable Khalian, "I hear you, Goodheart!"

"Then hear your death!" The big Khalian burst out, and the hatch slammed aside, knocking Sales back against the lock wall. He recovered—to see Goodheart towering before him, eyes glaring, claws out. Before the humans could shoot, he had grappled Sales to him.

The big human stomped on the Khalian's foot.

Goodheart shrilled in anger and ran his claws into Sales's arm. Then he pulled back with a howl, a slash of red across his abdomen, as Sales shrilled, "I have a claw, too!" Blood dripped from the slender dagger he'd pulled from his sleeve.

Goodheart sprang, claws reaching for Sales's throat. Sales stumbled and fell, but drove a fist into the pirate's belly, shoved stiffened fingers into the central nerve plexus above it, and brought a fist up to drive the big Khalian back. Goodheart stumbled away—and a fuming sphere hurtled from the opened lock. Goodheart dove back through it and the door clashed shut as the human ship filled with tear gas.

Coughing and gagging, Sales scrabbled at the fallen section of hull. One of his fighters realized what he was doing and leaped to join him. Eyes streaming, they raised the steel plate by feel alone . . .

Then the ship rocked, and Sales knew Goodheart's ship had kicked off from his. Too late, the tear gas streamed out into the vacuum of space—but the damage was done; his fighters rolled in the aisles, eyes streaming. He and his helper threw their weight against the plate, holding it back as vacuum tore at it, trying to ease it up level with the side of the ship . . .

Then the door to the bridge burst open, and a crewman in a spacesuit hopped in, picking his way among bodies, lugging a tool chest. He dropped it by the hole and yanked out a wad of metallic cloth, shaking out into a huge, ten-foot square. He draped it between the alloy circle and the hole in the hull, pressing the adhesive edges against the metal all around it, stamping it against the floor. "Let it go now, sir!"

Sales and the agent eased the metal circle against the bellying tarp. The spacesuited man yanked another out of the tool kit, unfolded it, and pressed it into place over the huge disk. Then he pulled out a small welder and began to bond the edges of the patch to the metal of the hull.

Air pressure began to return.

Sales turned, and felt fingers dabbing at his eyes. Blessed coolness flowed from them, and he blinked away the last of the tears, managing to see a mottled image of his soldiers, pulling themselves to their feet, as the navigator and captain went on among them, smearing an antidote balm on their eyes.

The ship shuddered.

Sales lurched down the aisle, careful to avoid bumping soldiers, into the control room, staring at the viewscreen.

The image of the Khalian ship was just beginning to glitter. An explosion rocked its tail; then it was gone.

"How many times did you hit him?" Sales grated.

"Only that last, sir," the gunner answered. "His fire-control picked off all my other torpedoes. I got a couple of laser burns in, but I don't know if they did more than scar his armor."

The man in the spacesuit loomed in the door. "Mission accomplished, sir."

Sales turned with a grin. "We kept him busy long enough, huh?"

"Yes, sir," the man confirmed. "I bonded the telltale to his ship's skin."

Sales nodded and turned away. "Into hyperspace, Captain."

"That confounded human!" Goodheart snarled. He winced as the medic lowered him down to the acceleration couch.

"Sir, you really should be in your own berth. . . ."

"This is my berth, Doctor! I must see how my ship fares, how she moves! What damage was there, Throb?"

"His cannon deeply scored us in two places, Captain, but did not pierce. We will need to replace those plates at home. And his final torpedo removed a control surface; we will need great care if we seek to maneuver in atmosphere. In all other respects, we are whole."

"That, at least, is good fortune." Goodheart lay back and let himself relax for a few moments. He had actually thought his end had come when he realized Sales had ripped him open—the pain had been almost unbearable, until his rage had hidden it. "That treacherous human," he growled again. "To mask a war party as a passenger liner! To camouflage weapons turrets as control blisters! It was skillfully done, so elegantly done! A worthy adversary, worthy!"

"If he had been any more worthy, we would have been dead," Throb returned, miffed. For his part, he was glad Globin wasn't aboard on this trip—the crew might have blamed it on him, for no other reason than that he was human.

"There is mass behind us," the sensor op reported.

Throb and Goodheart were both still.

Then the captain snapped, "How much mass?"

"Enough for a ship, Captain—a cruiser."

"It is Sales!" Goodheart snapped. "He has pursued me, he will hound me to my doom—or his!"

"But how?" Throb cried. "How can he track us through hyperspace?"

"It is enough to know that he does it! Senses, does he gain?"

"No, Captain. He holds his distance, at a million kilometers. He must not know our detectors have expanded range."

"Holds his distance?" Throb frowned. "Why would he follow, instead of seeking to overhaul?"

"Because he wishes to trail us to Barataria!" Goodheart's teeth showed in a grin. "Then he would flee and return with a fleet! No, we will lead him away, far away! Helm, set course away from Target, away from Khalia—away from any settled territory that we know!''

"But where shall we go, Captain?"

"Galactic Northeast, above the plain of the ecliptic by thirty degrees! There is nothing there, nothing! Let him follow us to nowhere! Then we shall lead him too near a star and let him be sucked in to fry! Northeast by thirty, Helm!''

"Even so, Captain." The helm set his course, trying to smother his own doubts.

They cruised on through the void of a space measured in alien dimensions, lit by streaks of light that were segments of the lives of stars, to an almost-uniform grayness. It was as though they flew through fog, with here and there the lights of a passing city.

Then, suddenly, the sensor op called out, "Ship approaching on a nearly parallel vector, sir!"

"Sales?" Goodheart spun about. "Is he no longer behind? Has he realized our gambit?"

"It is not his signature, sir." The sensor op pointed at the screen. "The wave form is typical of the reflected shape of a Syndicate merchantman."

"Ah-h-h-h." Goodheart turned to the screen, feeling the pain of his humiliation diminish. "If we have lost one prey, we have found another! Lay our course parallel to his, Helm! We will surprise him when he breaks out!"

Onward they fled, with Sales only an impulse behind, a minor irritation. All eyes fastened now on the merchantman; warriors checked their pistols, and the gunner checked his magazines.

"As ever, Captain?" Throb asked. "Wait till they break out into normal space, then overhaul and grapple them?"

"Even so," Goodheart answered. "Senses, what of Sales?"

"He is lost, sir," Senses reported. "I think he has fallen behind, beyond my range."

"Then he shall not disturb us while we feed. Throb, sound battle stations!"

* * *

They fled on in near silence for an hour, a day, thirty hours. The tension stretched thin, among crew who slept in their battle stations, staving off hunger with hard rations and sips of water.

Then, suddenly, the wave form that showed the merchantman began to shimmer.

"He shifts!' Senses called.

"Shift with him!" Goodheart snapped. "Helm, *now*!"

The ship bucked and seemed to twist—a transition come too suddenly, with no time to prepare. Goodheart thrust away dizziness and focused on the screen. The merchantman lay square in the screen, and the scale showed he was only fifty kilometers distant.

Goodheart keyed the intercom. "Apologies for so rude a breakout—but yonder lies our prey! Action, imminently!" He released the patch. "Senses, expand scale! Let us see our field of battle!"

The merchantman shrank in the screen as the view increased. . . .

And the limb of a disk crept in at the edge.

"Expand by ten!" Goodheart snapped, and the disk was suddenly complete, a planet glowing across the full spectrum of visible radiation.

"What globe is that?" Throb breathed into the sudden hush.

"His destination!" Goodheart crowed. "We have found a Syndicate world! Come, pluck this fowl that lies before us, and let a few escape to bear the tale! Let the merchant traitors tremble to know that we flay their hides so close to home! Seize me that ship!" Then caution nudged his mind. "Com op, send a message torp. Let them know what we have found!"

Irritated, the communications operator slapped switches and trilled a brief message into the transmitter.

Even as he did, the helm op laid course and accelerated, and the pirate ship darted toward the merchantman.

Then, suddenly, the screen was filled with a dozen streaks

of light, swarming in at the edges, two swelling into the forms of Syndicate destroyers.

"They keep close watch!" Goodheart shrieked. "Torpedoes away! Rake them with cannon!"

The pirate ship spat fire; its progeny swarmed away toward the destroyers.

But a blister opened in the side of the merchantman, and flame gouted from a huge cannon. The screen filled with fire, and Goodheart had just time enough to realize the irony of his prey turning on him, before the luminescence caught him up, and he passed into the excruciating light of death with the knowledge that the clan leaders had been right, after all, and the humans of the Fleet had not been his enemies.

"He's gone, sir!"

"Break out!" Sales snapped. He settled back into his acceleration couch, savoring the revenge of knowing that it was Goodheart's own invention that had doomed him—that Sales's own spies had brought back word of Goblin's hyperspace mass detector. Just knowing that the thing existed, and who had invented it, had been enough—his own engineers had checked the records of Desrick's work, had found the concepts he'd been working with, and had duplicated his invention. Then they had gone on to transform the detector into a tracer.

They broke out within the range of that same tracer; Goodheart's ship had been just on the fringe. They had followed, hopefully out of his range.

Could Barataria really be so far from all habitation?

Perhaps. What better protection, than being beyond consideration?

The moment of dizziness passed, and Sales scanned the big screen eagerly, looking for the pirate's silhouette. He saw the rippling red circle of the detector's signal first . . .

Then saw the great disk looming over all.

And the darts of light that emerged into the forms of Syndicate destroyers.

"They're trying to fry *my* pirate!" Sales roared. "Blast 'em, Fire Control! Punch them out of space!"

"Torpedoes away," the chief gunner returned.

"Captain, get in there and fry those lice!"

"Aye," the captain answered, lips stretched thin in a grin. "Full acceleration!"

Two G's kicked them in the pants and stayed there.

Just then, fire erupted out of the merchantman, a huge spreading blossom that wrapped about the Khalian pirate, enveloping it, converting it into a ball of spreading luminescence.

"Those scum!" Sales shouted. "Those thieves, assassins! They can't kill my pirate and get away with it! Captain, burn 'em! A merchant ship that shoots is no longer immune!"

"Aye, sir," the captain grunted over the weight of acceleration. The light ball filled the screen, then swam up to the upper left corner as the converted liner dove around it. The merchantman swelled in the screen, but the helm op swung around the expanding flower, too.

Two smaller blossoms erupted at the heads of the streaks of light that were destroyers.

"Two out," the gunner chanted. "Port cannon raking two more—belly cannon raking three . . ."

Light exploded all about them.

Pain, unbearable, filled Sales's whole being—then passed; and, in the moment of consciousness left to him as a part of that luminescence, Sales, too, realized that he had been chasing the wrong enemy.

INTERLUDE: Aftermath

The surrender of the Khalian Council did not end hostilities with all of the Khalia. In a culture where independence and military prowess were the sole measures of success, even the surrender had a limited effect. On Khalia, where those loyal to the remaining members of the Council were dominant, it meant a near-instant finish to the fighting. Within a few days all resistance had ended and Khalians by the thousands were turning in weapons and even those ships that had survived the space battle against Duane's forces.

To the amazement of the occupying Alliance Marines, there seemed no resentment on the part of most individual Khalians. They had been bested, and so instead offered the thousands of humans that occupied their planet a grudging respect. The phrase used by most Khalians to describe humans gradually changed from hairless, defenseless prey to worthy opponent. It was a lot easier on the ego to be defeated by a tough opponent than a defenseless ape.

Attempts to integrate Khalians into human units met with mixed success. Orders for Khalian pelts to be destroyed were diluted as they passed down the chain of command until most sergeants interpreted them as requesting their commands to put the furs in the lower compartment of their foot lockers. Attempts at integrating competitive sports met with other difficulties. Football could be quite hazardous when played against an opponent whose instinctive reaction when faced by a larger opponent was to extend two-inch claws. Still mutual respect for the other's prowess provided the beginnings of understanding.

Elsewhere in Khalian space the acceptance of the surrender diminished with distance. Some Khalian raiders surrendered. A few of these were slaughtered by vengeful local inhabitants before the Fleet could intervene. Years of fear and frustration created some truly grisly scenes. This complicated the situation, giving many of the remaining Khalia a mind-set similar to that of the isolated Japanese soldier after World War II. The last of these had surrendered almost forty years after that war had ended.

The absorption into the Alliance of the entirety of Khalian space provided another rallying point for those who refused to accept defeat. Some of the remaining captains strove to reestablish a new Khalian empire elsewhere. Others simply continued to pillage until destroyed. Most soon found some excuse to resist Fleet units whenever they had the advantage and when outgunned surrendered when informed ''for the first time'' by the Nedge translators now carried on most larger Fleet vessels of their Council's action.

Still, within months after the fall of Khalia, the bulk of Khalian resistance had collapsed. Those pockets and ships remaining were proving particularly vicious. Their holding out and the battles that followed complicated the incorporation of Khalian units needed to bolster the badly depleted Marine companies of the Fleet.

Access to large numbers of Khalians also brought a wealth of information to the research services. This was quickly, if belatedly, turned into useful ways of combating the remaining Khalian centers of resistance. Like so much research, some of what was developed proved useful and other new inventions proved more a hazard to those using them than the enemy. A few developments, as is often the case, taught the Fleet scientists more about themselves than the Khalia.

PLACEBO
by Doug Murray

TROOPER GLASSMAN PULLED his helmet on, locking the gasket against the collar of his battle suit. He took a quick look at the little green indicator that showed suit integrity. Satisfied, he settled in to wait for his turn to enter the boarding tube. That shouldn't be too long: the ship was making a series of tiny course corrections like a spider's mating dance.

Unconsciously, he rubbed his hand over his left bicep. He was starting to itch. Maybe that shot they'd given him was starting to take effect. He hoped so; those films had really impressed him. Imagine being able to move as fast as a Khalian; wouldn't that be something! If he were that fast, maybe he'd finally be able to . . .

The ship jerked slightly, the sign that she had locked onto the Khalian pirate. Glassman watched as the entrance of the boarding tube dilated open—they were definitely locked on now. Weapon ready, he strode into the tube behind his platoon leader. The tube seemed shorter than usual. He was almost halfway through . . .

"Freeze it there." Commander Rodman's voice carried easily in the large lounge of the *Sabatini*. He commanded the attention of the five senior officers seated at the long table facing the wall of monitor displays, all frozen on the same scene. "This is where the injection took effect—you can see him gain speed as he moves into the tube. The Scalosian drug has already started to move through his bloodstream. Now, watch what happens . . ."

Glassman edged up the passage toward the control deck; Trooper Verzyl paralleled him on the opposite side. Glassman had always been a little nervous before combat, but this was ridiculous. He'd begun sweating even before he got through the boarding tube, and it was worse now.

He took another pull from his drinking tube, his third in the last few minutes. There *must* be something wrong with the suit's environmental controls, he thought. Just like maintenance to screw 'em up just before a mission. Better have a few words with Tech Karty when this is over.

Glassman took yet another drink and saw a flash of movement in the dimness ahead of him. "Khalia!" he barked over his com system, bringing up his slug projector as he yelled. Couldn't use heavier weapons here, might puncture the hull—or the fusion bottle—the brass wanted prisoners, not a shipload of corpses.

Another movement caught his eye, a bit farther ahead, then Verzyl was yelling and the two of them were scant meters from being engulfed by a horde of Khalians, swarming out of the darkness with claws and knives and pistols. Glassman squeezed his trigger and prepared to die . . .

"The first encounter with a Khalian force took place in corridor number four, just five hundred meters from the entrance to the command bridge. A squad of Khalians, charged with the protection of the control crew, were able to creep within five meters of the Marine patrol without being detected." Rodman thumped the table in front of him for emphasis. "Five meters! Computer record searches have shown that in *all* past encounters, Khalians within a five-meter radius of our troops have inflicted fatalities eighty-five percent of the time!"

"Think of that statistic. Eighty-five percent! This time . . ."

Glassman was surprised at how slowly the Khalians seemed to be moving. Or maybe it wasn't them. Maybe it was the drug the Fleet technies had put into him just before jumpoff.

The Khalians moved as if they were swimming through a heavy liquid. Glassman grinned. He'd fought Weasels before—more often than he liked to think of—and lost more buddies to them than he liked to remember.

This was different. This was a dream come true. He could take his time, take careful aim—pick them off one by one, the way they had picked off so many of his buddies.

And still have time to enjoy their dying.

His slug rifle began to fire, almost of its own accord. Weasels dropped one after another.

Glassman's grin grew wider. This was great! A quick glance showed that Verzyl was doing just as well. Together they were wiping out the Khalian ambush patrol—in seconds!

Glassman shot another of the aliens and realized how enjoyable this kind of fight would be—if he could only get the sweat to stop dripping into his eyes.

"On this experiment, all initial encounters with the Khalia were concluded with a one hundred percent success rate for our troops. One hundred percent!" Rodman was projecting figures on the secondary monitor screens now; the main screen was still showing encounter footage from the battle-suit camera. "And not a single fatality on our side. Not one! As a matter of fact, in three different actions, Marines were able to render Khalian troops unconscious after disarming them in hand-to-hand combat! This has allowed us tremendous opportunities to psychiatrically analyze pirate mind-sets and begin plans aimed at bringing them under our operational control as well as the other Khalians!"

* * *

Glassman had finished five of the Weasels, shooting them down well before they could reach his position. Verzyl had been firing on full auto, spattering six more into wall decorations before he was able to gain control of his fear. The last Khalian was almost close enough for Glassman to touch now, and he decided to take this one prisoner. After all, that was part of the reason for this whole test, to find out why the pirates kept on fighting.

As the alien thrust his knife at Glassman's side, the Marine twisted to the right, bringing his rifle butt up and across and into the Khalian's abdomen.

Just the way they taught it back in BCT!

When the Weasel doubled over, Glassman finished the move, swinging the butt, with all its accumulated speed, down on the creature's head. The Marine was shocked when the Khalian's skull *shattered*, pouring blood and brains out on the floor.

Glassman looked down at the pile of bodies for a moment, jerking his head quickly to the side to dislodge the sweat from his eyes. Then, turning from the carnage, he motioned Verzyl forward.

They still had to take the control deck.

"You will note that both of the Marine squads treated with the Scalosian drug were fully involved in firefights within twenty minutes of their inoculation." New figures and charts appeared on the monitor screens. "In all cases, Marine activity and effectiveness increased from ninety to two hundred fifty percent of norm when the drug became fully assimilated into their systems. By way of comparison, our studies have shown that the Khalians are, by nature, some thirty percent faster than the normal Marine response time. In effect, we have *trebled* Marine effectiveness through the use of this drug!"

Glassman paused just inside the control deck. He was sweating constantly now, the salty water running down over his face and eyes, stinging, making his eyes blur. He could feel his heart pounding away, and he was starting to have real trouble getting enough air into his lungs. He began to suspect there was something terribly wrong with his battle suit.

Still, he was killing Khalians—faster and more easily than he ever had before. He knew it must be because of that stimulant the medics had hit him with. That was some stuff. He began to think about ways he might get some for recreational use—there was that little bosun's mate in medical stores . . .

Admiral Fursom spoke up for the first time. "Let me get this straight, Commander. You're telling us that you used a Marine boarding group as guinea pigs for some sort of superstimulant your science boys dreamed up?"

Rodman had been waiting for this, and smiled at the admiral. He knew the older man had never been within thirty light-years of *any* conflict, and had attained his rank through twenty-five years of errorless paper-pushing. Rodman's bosses had briefed him on what to expect from Fursom— and what he was to do about it: "That's right, sir. And I think you'll find all the paperwork was properly cleared through Fleet HQ."

"But why, Commander? The Khalia are beaten. Most of them are on our side now." That from Admiral Dunsal.

"The Khalia are not our sole problem, Admiral. As you well know, the Syndicate tamed the Weasels centuries ago. How do we know they don't have some other, even nastier, biological tricks up their sleeves? Our forces had *more* than enough problems handling the Khalia. Isn't it our duty to make sure they are prepared for their next challenge?"

The Khalian bridge was deserted. Most of the controls were smashed beyond repair. It was clear that the command crew had fled, probably back to the boat decks.

Glassman was glad of that. He was having even more trouble seeing now; his helmet had begun fogging over from the heat and humidity inside. He knew the atmosphere outside was unbreathable, and yet . . . he was mightily tempted to pull his helmet off and wipe his face off. He *had* to cool down!

He caught himself as his hand started to reach for the quick release—he knew he had to stay in control now, work his way back to the boarding tube and the frigate—cool off there. It was the only way.

He began to shuffle back down the corridor. He did not notice that Verzyl had slumped to the deck behind him and was not moving at all.

"By the end of the first half hour, Marine raiders had penetrated to all target points on the Khalian vessel— including the bridge and fire-control centers." Rodman's graphs were rapidly flashing now, showing very high readings in all Marine medical telemetry. Here and there, battle-suit cameras showed Marines on the deck, helmets off. Their faces were red and soaked with sweat. "However, the first problems with our drug also began to show up . . ."

Glassman could see the end of the boarding tube only a few meters away. He could barely breathe now, his panting growing faster and shallower by the moment. He had to get air—cool air. And soon.

He bumped into the side of the tube, barely managing to keep his feet—just a little farther . . .

The monitor screen showed Glassman as he reached the end of the boarding tube and collapsed into the arms of the waiting corpsman. All his suit monitors were in the red now. As the officers watched, brain activity flat-lined.

"It was here we realized that we had some problems with the drug we hadn't foreseen." Rodman indicated the medical telemetry. "Marines given the Scalosian serum began to collapse—heat prostration in most cases, although some did experience coronary problems."

Admiral Grissom didn't like the sound of that, he knew what Marine screening was like. "Marines don't have heart attacks!"

Rodman grinned wryly. "Absolutely right, sir. But Marine hearts, stout as they may be, are usually not asked to beat more than two hundred fifty times a minute—and never for this extended a period of time. We had never anticipated *that* as one of drug's effects, or that the human body would have so much difficulty dissipating the internal heat the increased activity and speed would engender.

"Autopsies on the raiders were performed immediately, of course, and showed that all deaths were the result of two causes: heart failure caused by stress to the overall cardiovascular system; and brain shutdown caused by the tremendous heat generated by the body's increased activity."

"How many casualties?" Admiral Fursom was deviating just a little from his script—couldn't be helped.

"Twenty-four Marines died in this action, sir."

"And how many were involved?" Grissom was looking a bit sharper now, Rodman thought. He'd caught the scent. The admiral had always had a bloodhound's determination, it was Rodman's job to make sure he sank his fangs into the proper arteries.

"There were thirty-six Marines in the boarding party, sir. Twenty-four of them were given the Scalosian drug. All twenty-four died as indicated."

"One hundred percent casualties?!" Even Fursom looked surprised at that—maybe his briefing hadn't been as complete as Rodman had believed.

"That's correct, sir. All the Marines testing the drug died from unforeseen complications." Rodman had new graphs and charts up on the monitor screens now. "However, I must point out that not a single casualty was the result of enemy action. No Marine was so much as scratched by a Khalian fighter. *All* the deaths were caused by the drug. We believe that this is a remarkable statistic."

Admiral Dunsal stood up, pacing behind the table. "So. You want us to convene a court on the scientists who dreamed up this stuff? Killed a couple of squads of Marines with their test?"

Rodman turned to his controls for a second, calling up a new menu of charts and battle tapes. The screens went blank for a moment, then started showing a new series of scenes. "Not exactly, sir—watch this for a moment."

* * *

Corporal Jane Martini rubbed her arm, even though her battle suit prevented her from feeling the motion. She had never figured out how the medics could do it—all those hypersonic injectors, high-speed syringes, all kinds of technology and they still couldn't give you a shot without it hurting.

She shook her head, no time to worry about it now. Worry about the Weasels—and about this drug they put into you. Supposed to make *us* as fast as the Weasels. Well, she'd see. Probably before she wanted to.

Martini shifted her slug thrower down into the ready position and gave her squad a quick hand signal. The boarding tube was about to open, and they'd better be frosty when it did.

"So what!" Admiral Grissom's deep bass cut through the lounge like a machete. "You going to show us more Marines dying of your damned drug? I've seen enough of that! Let's get on with . . ."

"Just a moment, sir. I think you misunderstand. This is the control group—they have *not* been given the Scalosian drug; the shot they got was glucose and water—just a placebo to make them *think* they'd gotten the same drug as the others."

"But they're moving like . . ." Grissom was sputtering now, completely confused.

"Just keep watching, sir."

Martini's squad had been assigned the escape-pod bay. They hurried down the mapped corridors, knowing that they needed to get into position before the fighting started around the control areas. Martini was already sweating heavily, the water starting to trickle into her eyes. Was the damned drug causing her to overheat?

She took a sip from her water tube and shook her head to clear her eyes; no time to worry about that either. She made a quick hand signal to her squad and they broke into double time. Behind them, the sound of slug throwers began to echo back along the ship's corridors.

* * *

"You will note that Admiral Grissom is quite correct. This Marine squad is moving no faster than an average group moves." Rodman indicated a register on one of the monitor screens surrounding the main array. "And keep in mind that they *know* that the Khalians will be rushing toward the position they're supposed to hold. I think we can assume that they are doing the best they can."

Grissom was near his rather low boiling point now. "What is all this driving at?"

"Be patient, sir. Just be patient." Rodman restarted the main data flow.

Martini stopped her people just before they reached the escape bay entry. There was always the chance the Weasels had beaten them there.

She motioned Karp forward. He had the heaviest weapon and was the best shot. They'd worked together for long enough that he knew what she wanted.

Karp planted himself at the edge of the bay accessway and set up, planting his bipod for greater stability. Finished, he looked to Martini, waiting for her to make the first move.

Martini took a deep breath, checked the safety on her weapon, and did it, bolting into the escape bay, eyes searching for any kind of cover even as the rest of her body cleared the edge of the entrance way.

"Indications are that the Khalian officers all moved to the escape bay as soon as they saw they couldn't outrun or outgun the *North*." Rodman was back at his desk now, running the show like some tri-d technician. "We think they had some sort of rendezvous planned and left their warriors to cover their escape. Whatever their reasons, they reached the escape bay well in advance of our Marine squad."

Martini found herself in the middle of a storm of firepower. Slugs, darts, even the occasional bolt of an energy weapon, washed around her. She hugged the scant cover she had found and waited for the rest of her squad to make their way in. Maybe this drug they'd gotten would make a difference. She hoped so. It didn't look like she had a chance otherwise.

"Note the medical telemetry on the Marine squad at this point." Rodman pointed at the appropriate screen, which he highlighted from his control panel. "You see that all the readings are at just the high side of normal. Keep an eye on them over the next few minutes."

Martini saw Karp come sailing into the room, slug thrower blazing on full auto as he dodged behind one of the escape pods. The Khalians started to move then, their weapons ready, zigzagging at incredible speed toward the two pinned Marines.

Martini knew they'd had it. There was no way she and Karp could handle that many Weasels moving that fast—just no way—unless . . .

Even as Martini began to fire, the Weasels began to slow down, almost as if a switch had been pulled. It's the drug! Martini thought. It must be the drug finally taking effect! The damned thing works!

Martini got to her feet then, calmly using her weapon the way she'd practiced for so long, placing her shots just where she wanted them, knocking down Weasel after Weasel. To her side, she could just see Karp doing the same thing, mirroring her own success.

From her rear, she caught hints of other flashing movements. The rest of the squad had come into the escape bay. Their weapons had no trouble finding targets.

"You see the biometry readings?" Rodman punched them up so they flashed golden on the screen. "Heart action, lungs, EEG, all are less than half what we saw on the Marines injected with the Scalosian drug—yet this squad is performing at about the same level of effectiveness as the others. In some cases, even faster!"

* * *

Just about all the Weasels were down now, piled on the deck where they'd fallen—almost at the feet of Martini and Karp.

No member of the squad had been hit.

"What a high!" That from Kanoche, as usual, the last man into the fight. "This drug is something else! I wonder who we see about getting more of it."

"Enough chatter." It was time for Martini to regain control, past time, really, but the reaction was just starting to wear off. "Let's check this place out and make sure no other Weasels are hiding out. Fast or not, we don't want to get hit from behind, now do we?"

The squad took her meaning. They spread out and started a search pattern through the pod bay deck. Karp and Zalewski had set up a little barrier facing the entrance door and to make sure no Weasel got in or out that way. Martini started a little prowl of her own, determined to make sure that nothing and nobody was missed.

"You will note that this Marine squad operated at nearly two hundred percent efficiency during this action—much higher than can be accounted for by adrenaline surge or any other stimulant we can think of." Rodman was highlighting all sorts of medical data now. "Further, they actually engaged more Khalians in this action than any other squad involved in the experiment! And their success rate was also one hundred percent! Now, watch this final sequence . . ."

Martini had just passed the farthest pod on the starboard side of the bay when she saw the Weasel. He was about twenty meters in front of her and doing his best to stay in shadow. He had a spacesuit on and was less than five meters from the manual bay controls. If he reached the evac button . . .

Martini raised her rifle. She had to ice this guy before he evacuated the bay—her people had battle suits on, but if they were vented out into space, the frigate's automatics would assume they were targets and fry them before they had time to yell!

Her sights centered on the Weasel's head, Martini

squeezed the trigger—and nothing happened! She cursed and dropped the useless hunk of metal. Only one chance, she pulled her battle knife and charged . . .

"Now, you will note that the Khalian is only some four meters from the control panel when the Marine makes her move. And she is more than twenty meters away." Rodman had the main screen in slow motion now, so everyone could see what was about to happen. "As some of you may know, the Alliance record for the forty-meter dash is in the area of four point four seconds . . ."

Martini knew she had to move fast—faster than she ever had before. Maybe the drug would give her the edge she desperately needed in this situation. . . .

She kept the K-bar up in front of her and as she got within five meters of the Weasel, she launched herself straight at his body, praying she could get her point in before he reached the controls . . .

"This Marine covered that distance in less than two seconds flat! Even the Khalia cannot maintain that sort of speed. Her momentum was such that . . ."

Martini's K-bar flashed through the edge of the Khalian's pressure closure and the neck beyond it. When she finally came to a stop against the bay wall, the Khalian toppled at her feet. Its head had been nearly severed from it's body.

Martini lay for a second, panting, then dragged herself trembling to her feet. "All right! Who was supposed to cover the starboard side!" Someone was going to get peeled for *this* screwup!

"I don't understand." Grissom was truly puzzled now. And his face told Rodman why so many officers enjoyed poker nights in the admiral's quarters. "If these Marines *didn't* have the drug . . ."

Rodman had finally gotten to his objective, if he could only hold these men for a few more minutes . . . "That's the whole point, sir. If these Marines could self-induce the sort of reaction they did *without* access to the Scalosian drug, the High Command has to ask: why can't they fight this way in normal combat?''

''Are you trying to say . . . '' Dunsal was trying to put it together.

''What the Judge Advocate General's office has instructed me to point out, sir, is that there must be a *reason* that Marines cannot achieve these results in ordinary combat.'' Rodman knew it was time to make his point now. ''This experiment has shown two things: first, that it is within our ability to create a drug that will increase the efficiency of the human fighter by two to three hundred percent—assuming that we can find a way to eliminate a few unsatisfactory side effects.''

''Like the Marines dying.'' Rodman had always known that Grissom was going to be the tough one.

''Yes, sir. But we've also seen that Marines who only *thought* they had been given the drug were able to operate at the same high level of efficiency—*without any side effects!* The question we must ask is . . . why can't they put out that sort of effort all the time?''

''Dammit, Commander . . . !''

''No, sir. Think about it. Is it not the duty of the Marine command staff to insure that their people operate at peak efficiency at *all* times? And if they have not accomplished that—is it not *our* duty to punish their lack of competence?''

''Are you trying to tell us . . .'' Grissom saw it now—he just didn't want to believe it.

''Yes, sir. The JAG office wants you gentlemen to deliver an indictment against the Commandant of the Fleet Marine Corps, and whichever of his subordinates you consider equally responsible, for dereliction of duty.''

Rodman lit up the screen again. The whole group watched as Martini and her squad moved back into the boarding tube, stepping aside as another Marine corpse, carelessly stuffed into a body bag, was carried through by the medical detachment.

"After all, gentlemen. It is *they* who are responsible for those deaths, is it not? And *they* who will be responsible for more if we must fight the Syndicate at our current state of readiness!"

"But surely it is merely human nature . . ." Grissom was grasping at straws now. Rodman could see he knew he was beaten.

"Human nature almost got us beaten by the Khalia, Admiral Grissom. We must insure it does not interfere with our actions against the Syndicate!"

In silence, the officers watched the last of the Marines limp out of the boarding tube. Marines who had no idea of exactly how well they had done—or how much they might yet have to pay for it.

INTERLUDE: Morale?

Back on Port the word "morale" was being written more often with a question mark than a period. The question being asked by this was almost invariably "how bad was it there?" The answer rarely was encouraging. This was hardly surprising. The Fleet, after hundreds of thousands of casualties and four years of major effort, had thought they had won a war. Its personnel, having joined in a burst of patriotic fervor, prepared to return home as conquering heroes. Instead, the men and women of the Fleet now found themselves faced with an even greater conflict. A battle against a human foe, who may have penetrated their ranks, and whose size and location were still unknowns. A war likely to last longer and be harder fought than the one they had just "won."

Internal security forces had found literally thousands of Syndicate agents had penetrated both the Fleet and related civilian enterprises. Nor did they question that they had missed thousands more. Hypnotesting and careful interrogations found men and women loyal to their "family" everywhere. It had been too easy, with all the Alliance's attention riveted on an alien species as the enemy, for humans planted by the Syndicate to infiltrate every vital office and department. Men who had served or worked together for years now watched one another suspiciously.

Slowly it became apparent that the new enemy, the Syndicate of Families, was a massive opponent. The interrogations of those spies captured alive painted a picture of a confederation of hundreds of worlds. No less than a total mobilization encompassing all the resources of the Alliance could be expected to prevail. A few prisoners belligerently predicted the Alliance would be smashed within months by massive Syndicate fleets. Others taunted their interrogators on how easily the Alliance had been deceived into thinking the barbaric, unsophisticated Khalia had been their real enemy. None of those captured expected to be prisoners long. A few even bragged that they had been promised appointments as planetary managers after the Alliance was conquered.

None of this did anyone's morale any good. Several attempts were made to improve this situation. Unfortunately bad morale is more stubborn than a drill instructor. Sports failed, tours by celebrities just reminded personnel, many of whom had been shipbound for over three years, just what they were missing back home. Perhaps the worst part was not knowing just how bad things were going to get. Discipline became lax in even the elite units, while drunkenness and addiction increased dramatically.

Then as weeks passed the Syndicate made a fatal error. No major battle occurred. Small conflicts brought home to the personnel of the Fleet that they were still a victorious and effective fighting force. Men can only wait so long for defeat. Then their frustration turns to defiance. Regardless, often despite the inept attempts by the Admiralty on Port to improve their morale, ships and infantry units regained their fighting trim. Each in their own way found how to cope and prepare for the total war they now faced.

PATRIOT'S SONG

by Judith R. Conly

When the Fleet first launched its squadrons
to police the worlds of men,
we discovered Khalians waiting
and engaged in war again.

Oh, we cursed and muttered, "Weasels"—
learned to hate a furry face—
for we found ferocious foemen
had encroached on human space.

Then we beat them back to Target,
where we thought their homes would fall,
but we found the vanquished Khalians
weren't the natives after all!

So we curse and mutter, "Weasels,"
When we spot a furry face
pouring out embittered anger
at the captors of their space.

When at last we won their home world,
what we conquered gave us pause:

the defenders—most civilians—
were reduced to clubs and claws.

So restrain your groans of "Weasels,"
and don't shoot that furry face,
for the enemy you're blasting
is too young to go to space!

Well, we couldn't fight forever,
so we made uneasy peace.
Now our struggles should have ended,
but instead they'll soon increase.

Now we smile when we say, "Weasels"—
learn to love a furry face—
for there's greater danger lurking
out beyond the Khalia's space!

MANDALAY

by Anne McCaffrey

HER INTERCOM SCREEN blinked. Amalfi Trotter looked up from the frustration of her life-support system reports, grateful for an interruption.

"Captain requests a meeting of all officers. Wardroom at 1630."

"Fardles, that's barely time enough to get there!" As a life-support systems officer, she was quartered on 9 deck, in the bowels of the troop carrier *Mandalay*.

With one hand, she toggled the acknowledgment switch as she began to strip off her coverall, stinking dirty from her latest wriggling tour of the air-conditioning systems. She'd been positive that she would find dead vermin to account for some of the pong that soured the *Mandalay*'s air. She was a conscientious officer and had done her best with filters, purifiers, and deodorizers to neutralize the pervasive reek.

She lay awake in her bunk night after night, trying to figure out what could be generating or perpetuating the odors. The odors that, she was certain, were one of the chief reasons why she—and most of the complement of the *Mandalay*—didn't sleep well. It was that kind of a nightmare combination of stench. Perversely enough, the heads on all decks were reasonably free of unpleasant odors.

In fact, Cookie had told her that it was getting to be a joke: go to the head for a cleaner breath of air. Cramming her fouled coverall into the reconditioner, she stepped into the jetter, turning swiftly in the thin mist allowed her for such ablutions. Thirty seconds for soaping and then the mist returned to rinse her body. It did her morale no good to realize that she had just added her sweat and ventilator dust to the pervading odor, but one didn't appear before the captain with visible dirt.

Could he have called an emergency meeting about the air quality? She had done her utmost to improve it. She knew how depressing it was to breathe bad air, and morale on the *Mandalay* was low enough. But she *had* tried.

After the Khalian surrender (the official one, although many enemy units refused to accept their defeat and the ignominy of yielding), while the *Mandalay* was on the surface undergoing minor repairs, Amalfi Trotter had scrupulously replanted the entire 'ponics garden, coaxing broad, shiny oxygen-supportive leaves from her vines with careful dollops of fas-gro. She had crawled through all the major ventilating shafts on an inspection tour and used remotes to sweep those that were too narrow for even her slight frame— was that why a pint-sized person was invariably made life-support officer?—and replaced every one of 743 vent filters.

Despite her best efforts, once they lifted from the planet, even the "new" air had quickly taken on the taint of hot metals, acrid plastics, body odors too intense to neutralize, and the faint but throat-souring smell of Khalian Weasel fur. Even after she had located and destroyed five badly preserved Khalian pelts, she hadn't quite eradicated that taint. The residue was probably due to having to flush out the systems while they were still on a Khalian-occupied world, and had given the air its final touch of pollution.

Her only success was in eradicating the sweet sickly smell of blood and singed flesh. Perhaps, she thought grimly, there was simply no way to eradicate the rank odor of fear on a troop vessel. And why now? The Khalian War was over. They'd all be heading back to the Alliance ports and demob. Surely the fear contaminant should be fading.

The fighting men and women of the 202nd Regiment, the Montana Irregulars, on board the *Mandalay* had survived nineteen major engagements. The MIs were crack troops, a great point of pride to the naval crew who transported them to the various theaters. With the war over, why were these veterans still churning out the sour pheromones of fear? She could understand it if they were moving on to yet another battle area. But they weren't. They were in a holding orbit, and as soon as essential repairs were finished, the entire squadron would very shortly be leaving it on a course for an Alliance world.

She fastened the closings on her clean shipsuit and grabbed up her clipboard of printouts on the air system. Complaints about the air, while justified right now, were analogous to complaints about weather on primitive planets. It was at least an impersonal, unemotive issue to bitch about. But she couldn't help feeling guilty when someone did. Clean air was her responsibility.

Maybe the captain had gotten the orders that would release them from orbit. Maybe that would reduce the stink. They'd been hanging about a long time now, going nowhere in never decreasing circles. Hope of that reprieve made her hurry down the narrow companionway to the g grav-well.

Once the troops knew they were going home, the air would clear up from the barracks' decks where it hung, an almost visible miasma of accumulated fear, stress, and pain. And when the old *Mandy* was back in a decent human port, she would scour the air system of this old bucket with good clean civilized air on a properly photosynthesizing planet.

Everything will improve, she assured herself, when we're on the way home. She scrambled off the null-grav lift onto the wardroom level. Her palms were sweating again. They always did when she anticipated criticism.

Her keen nostrils caught a new odor, a pleasant one, refreshing. She sniffed about her and realized that the smell was seeping from the wardroom. She identified the aroma with some astonishment. Lavender? In the wardroom? They were desperate.

She rapped the panel courteously and then entered, closing the door quickly behind her because she didn't want the outside air to dilute the fragrance inside. The odor came from a lighted candle on the wardroom table, around which ranged both naval and Marine officers. She slipped into the only remaining seat, between Marine Colonel Jay Gruen and Major Damia Pharr, head of the medical team. They gave her a nod but something about their tenseness communicated itself to her. The clipboard slipped out of her sweaty hands and clattered to the tabletop.

She muttered apologies that no one noticed. Then she, too, found herself trying not to stare at Captain August. His face was so expressionless that the flimsy that drooped from his fingers must contain bad news. The lavender was to soothe them all?

A sudden premonition shook Amalfi. They were *not* going home. She clutched the edge of the clipboard now as if she were squeezing the breath out of whoever issued such orders. Where in the Nine Pits of Hell could they be sent now? Not another pocket of Khalian resistance? Was that why there was such a stench of fear? Only how could the soldiers know the content of a message the captain could only have received within the past half hour? Scuttlebutt was quick but not that quick, and any important stuff came in code, which took longer to seep into general scuttlebutt.

Captain August stood. He had been a lean man when she first joined the *Mandalay* seven long years ago. He was gaunt now, the flesh stretched across the bone of his skull, the skin under his eyes dark with sleeplessness and stress. He'd been in command of the *Mandalay* since the outbreak of hostilities with the Khalia. He spread the flimsy, its message black ink bleeding tracks across the dirty cream of the recycled paper.

"In code, we have been given orders to proceed to a rendezvous in two weeks, GGMT, with the supply ship *Grampion*, which will have replacement personnel for you, Colonel Gruen, to bring the regiment up to full strength."

"Replacement personnel?" Gruen demanded, his light, oddly flecked eyes bulging slightly as he challenged the captain. "Full strength?"

"Yes, Colonel," August said. He scowled as he glanced around the table, at the stunned expressions that ranged from horror through disbelief to despair. "We are to reprovision to battle readiness."

"Battle ready?" The words exploded from Hamish Argyll, the gunnery officer.

On both sides of Amalfi came the mutter of mutinous curses.

"But, Captain, who's left to battle with?" No sooner were the words out of young Ensign Badeley's mouth than he tried to melt under the table from embarrassment.

"That information is omitted from this communiqué!" Captain August let the flimsy fall from his fingers. He scrubbed his fingertips on his thumb as if he'd touched something unclean. The sheet drifted slowly to the tabletop, all eyes following it.

"Then the scuttlebutt is true?" Colonel Gruen asked in a hoarse voice.

Captain August turned his head slowly toward him. "And you believe the scuttlebutt you hear, Colonel?"

"When it's affecting the morale of my soldiers, you bet your last tank of oxy, I do." Waggling a finger at the captain, Gruen went on. "I got to tell you, Captain, the morale of my troops is so low, I shall withhold this information from them as long as it is humanly possible."

"How can you keep it from 'em, Jay?" Major Loftus, the adjutant, demanded, raising his hands in resignation. "They know most things before we do. The air's full of fear stench." He darted a quick glance at Amalfi, who tried to scrunch even smaller between the two larger bodies.

"How could they possibly know orders which were only issued thirty-five minutes ago?"

"They don't," the colonel replied bluntly. "They won't. They're sunk so low in battle fatigue right now, such orders would result in a rash of suicides, brawls, and possibly even a mutiny attempt . . ."

"Not on my ship . . ." August began.

"You're exaggerating . . ." Brace, the naval science officer, protested.

"We can't cope with that," added Major Pharr.

Colonel Gruen eyed everyone dispassionately. "I've been the regimental commander now since we were mobilized to fight the Khalia and there's no fight left in my soldiers. I'll tell you this, I stay awake nights trying"—and his fist came down on the table—"trying to figure out some way to revive their morale. Right now, I doubt they'd even suit up. There've been wars before where there weren't any soldiers to fight it."

"How can you have a war if there're no fighters?" Ensign Badeley piped up.

"You have been apprised of my orders." Captain August rose to his feet. "We break orbit at 1200 tomorrow. If it's any consolation, the entire squadron is headed in the same direction, not just the *Mandalay*."

"It is no end of consolation, Captain," Gruen replied with bitter sarcasm, "to know that High Command isn't picking on us alone. I'd like permission to make a private call on the secure band, sir."

Captain August gave a curt nod and strode quickly out of the wardroom.

"Wait here for me," Gruen said, pointing a commanding finger at the others as he rose to follow.

"You bet!" Loftus replied, glancing about the table to see if anyone would be fool enough to leave.

Gruen's wife served on Stone's flagship *Morwood* and had often been able to discreetly reassure those aboard the *Mandalay* to their advantage.

"There is no way that I, as chief medic," Damia Pharr began in her gravelly voice, "would certify these troops as battle-ready. They can dress 'em up and kit 'em out and load 'em up but they won't fight!"

"Surely they'll follow orders?" Badeley asked, his round, youthful face screwed up in droll surprise.

He was alternately a headache, a laugh, and a raving bore. It was the universal opinion that he was likely to remain an ensign. Two years on a troop ship that had made four landings on hostile planets—and in which he had had to defend the *Mandalay* from vicious attacks by would-be boarders—had not shaken the down from his cheeks or given him any significant insights into Life and the Real World. He could be counted on to ask just such a stupid question as he had.

"No, laddie." Hamish's accent became thickly ethnic when emotional. "They wouldn't. And I, for one, would not lay a feather of blame on them."

"But . . . that would be tantamount to mutiny!" His eyes bulged.

"Wouldn't it!" Argyll agreed too amiably.

"It's inhuman to ask any soldier in his current depressed state to trundle off and fight another one." Loftus brought both fists down on the table, his expression deeply troubled.

"They've got to have some R&R on a decent planet, not one with the stench of Weasel and blood and death. They need sleep and unprocessed food and rest . . . Plague take it, Trotter, can't you do *something* about the air?"

Amalfi tried to hide behind Damia Pharr, who looked down at her with a slightly quizzical expression on her face.

"Yeah, Malf, isn't there something you can do? Who can sleep easy with tainted air in their lungs all night long?"

"I've done everything I can," Amalfi said, her voice just one note away from a whine. She brandished her clipboard. "I changed every plant in 'ponics when we were grounded. I've cleaned every duct, refitted every filter . . ."

"Had my gun crew jumping out of their skins when they heard her sweeping out the shafts above us," Hamish said, grinning encouragingly at her. "They thought the captain had found the still."

"Which reminds me," Damia said, "I'll need four liters tonight if I'm to get my patients to sleep."

"Has Farmeris come out of his coma yet?" Loftus asked.

"No, and I've done nothing to wake him up. He's better off asleep in that babbling bedlam I used to call my infirmary," Pharr replied, her wistful tone intimating envy of the man's condition. "He's okay apart from staying asleep. He's got the right idea. Sleeping it out till better days."

A tinny voice filtered through from Major Loftus's com

unit. "Major, fight broke out in D barracks: tranked nine combatants, but Infirmary says they've no room for 'em."

"That's right," Damia replied cheerfully. "Any injuries?" she added as an afterthought.

"No, sir. We had warning of the mood and arrived in time to restore order."

"List their IDs for Report, Sergeant Norly, then dump 'em in their bunks with wrist and ankle restraints. There's no more room in the brig anyhow." Loftus swore as the crackling of the intercom ceased.

"Do you think they feel safer fighting among themselves?" Pharr asked rhetorically, glancing about the room.

Amalfi saw Badeley open his mouth and she glared so fiercely at him that he subsided. A depressed silence fell on those waiting at the table. Two of the Marine captains who had listened intently to their commanders' remarks were now obviously trying to get a few winks of sleep in the lavender-scented air. Amalfi was only too relieved that no one started in on her again. The sound of boots clomping on the metal decking alerted them all. As one, they looked toward the door, anticipating Gruen's return and whatever hope he might have gleaned from his wife.

The blank expression on Jay Gruen's face as he entered was sufficient to depress all hope. He closed the door behind him with meticulous care and then leaned against it with the weariness of total dejection.

"The truth is so bad"—and he paused—"that not even High Command has the balls to put it in the orders."

"Well?" demanded Damia Pharr when Gruen let an atrocious span of time go by without enlightenment.

"I agree." He pushed himself off the door and toward the table. Loftus and Argyll made room for him as he folded, like a decrepit aged man, into the chair. "It would appear that the Khalia are not the primary enemies of the Alliance."

"Say what?" demanded Loftus.

Gruen clasped his hands before him, one thumb massaging the other. He didn't lift his eyes once as he continued to speak.

"The Khalia appear to have been the first line of defense of an oligarchy of Merchant Families—of human or human-oid stock—known as the Syndicate. The Khalians questioned named them the Givers."

"They Give war?" asked Damia softly.

"There are a lot of gaps about the Syndicate but one thing is sure: they subjugate any useful entities and massacre any that defy them." Gruen's voice mirrored the defeat in his expression. "The Khalian War, the one we just finished, is apparently only the prelude to the Big One. And the Alliance has got to win it or expect that every single planet and star system in the Alliance could, and would, be destroyed by the Syndicate."

"But surely in a large group, a Syndicate, there would be an outcry against wholesale destruction?" Brace asked. "It's just not economical to obliterate whole planets and star systems . . ."

"The Syndicate doesn't think the way we do. They may be technologically superior, but not sociologically," Gruen said, massaging his thumbs with such force the blood suffused the tips. "They're prime bigots—hate any alien race and enslave or exploit them. And we thought the Khalia were bad . . ."

"They were," Loftus muttered respectfully. "But surely if the Alliance sticks to our sphere of influence . . ."

"That would work with anyone but the Syndicate. And the Syndicate doesn't tolerate powerful neighbors."

"The Alliance isn't hostile," Badeley began. "We live in peace with lots of other species and civilizations."

"We blew the peaceful image by fighting the Khalia . . ."

"But, Colonel, they began the hostilities," Badeley replied belligerently, "we were only defending ourselves."

"Oh, plug it up, Badeley," Argyll said. "Jay, what about other regiments? Can they take another all-out offensive?"

"I don't have to worry about other regiments," Jay Gruen said, slapping both hands facedown on the table, his eyes averted. "I have to worry about mine. And mine are not ready to hear the score."

"We can't keep them in the dark for long," Loftus protested. "And if we don't level with them, whatever faith they have in us as commanders flushes right down the tubes!"

"You're right there. So"—and Jay Gruen glanced around at the others—"we've got approximately twenty hours to come up with a way to restore morale—which news of fighting a brand-new war is not going to do—before leaving orbit."

"But we won't be making the rendezvous for two weeks . . ." Badeley began.

"If someone," Loftus said, pinning Badeley with a hard glare, "isn't smart enough to figure out that we're *not* heading back to Alliance territory, there's nothing we could do to resurrect our once-proud regiment. And I'll just bite the bad tooth and get my discharge."

Badeley looked even more shocked but he shut his mouth.

"I'd sleep on that notion, were I you, Lofty," Damia Pharr said kindly. "Oh, Great Gods and Other Lesser Deities!" She slapped her forehead and expressions of amazement, anxiety, incredulity, and dawning hope flitted across her broad homely face. "Why didn't I think of that before!"

"Think of what?" Gruen asked with acid impatience.

"Sleep therapy! We could all use a really good sleep. I read about the therapy in the *Space Medicine Journal*. The surgeon general (someone named Haldeman) recommended dream sleep therapy for troops being transported from one theater of war to another. I don't see that much difference in this application. It could work. It should work. It sure won't hurt and it'll cut out all the brawling, that is . . . Arvid," she spoke sharply because the supply officer was quietly napping in his corner. "You still have all those barrels of hibernation gas, don't you?"

Startled, the jg had to have the query repeated. "Sure, yeah, hey, that stuff's probably the only thing we haven't used in this campaign."

"Deep sleep will not solve a morale problem," Gruen said. "It'll only defer it."

"Used as a hibernant, yes, but used to induce a deep and restful slumber, now that's another thing. We can't give the

men any R&R but we can give 'em S&D. Sleep and
dreams.'' Damia was so positive that some of her enthusi-
asm began to infect the others with hope. ''What your troops
need is restful REM sleep, to help relieve the backup of
willie-horrors . . .''

''And how in hell are you going to tend close to four
thousand sleeping troopers? They've got to be fed, evacuated, and . . .'' Gruen stopped and Damia, grinning broadly
now, waved her hands encouragingly to talk himself into
the next step. He stared at her with dawning comprehen-
sion.

''Yup, that's right. Battle-dress drill. I know you made
'em all service their suits on the surface. There's enough
nutrient fluid to keep every single one of them going for ten
days. And the suits do bodily functions as well as monitoring. Why must such expensive equipment be used only in
war?''

The others around the table, even those who had remained silent, began to talk.

''Malf,'' Damia turned to the life-support officer, ''can
you block off the barracks decks from Operations. You guys
still have to run the ship even if your passengers are all
asleep.''

''Ah, yes, I think so except I thought sleep gas is skin-
permeable. Wouldn't the suits . . .''

''Seal all the airlocks from the troop decks, and pene-
trating as that hibernation gas is, it won't affect the ship's
crew,'' Damia went on, sort of running roughshod over
objections.

''Now, just a minute, Dame,'' Gruen began.

''Shit, Jay, you need the rest more than your men. I
promise you, at the concentration we'll pour into the troop
quarters, everyone will go beddie-byes and dream sweet.
Dream themselves right back into rested, resilient minds
quite willing to take on this new challenge. Hell, if they're
deeply asleep, we can even do some sleep training, and
they'll be fit as fiddles when we rendezvous with *Grampion*.''

''You're sure it'll work?''

Amalfi had to look away from Colonel Gruen's face: the beseeching look of hope revived was almost more than she could bear.

Damia put her hand on Gruen's shoulder. "I don't know anything else to try. And sleep's not going to hurt anyone aboard this ol' tub . . ." She shot an apologetic grin at Brace and Argyll. "If the entire regiment is suited save the medical staff, and with a little help from the *Mandalay* personnel, we can check you all out."

"Is there enough protective garb, Arvid?" Loftus asked. "You gotta have the right gear or you'll end up asleep at the switch."

"Yeah, yeah, sure. Plenty," Arvid replied. Amalfi thought he hadn't taken in exactly what was being planned.

"Malf, can you handle your end of it? Blocking the vents?"

"I'd only need to block off at 3 deck. But I'll have to bunk in with someone else," Amalfi said. "I wouldn't mind sleeping through it all but I haven't got a battle suit," she added, responding to the lightening of mood.

"Good girl, Trotter," Gruen said, his eyes alive again in his face. "Now, Brace, how d'you think the captain will take this?"

The science officer, who was nominally the second in command to the captain, gave the colonel a slow smile. "I don't think he'll quibble, Jay, it's not exactly a naval decision. *Mandalay*'s proud to ferry the Montana Irregulars. We want to help. After all, if this Syndicate is half as bloodthirsty as rumor makes 'em, we've got to have at least one regiment fighting fit."

"Good. I'll just stop up to his quarters and give him the word. Let's get cracking. The faster we can suit 'em all up, the quicker we avoid problems." The colonel nearly bounced out of the wardroom, a cheerful Loftus and their captains, looking remarkably bright-eyed, following.

"Arvid," Damia Pharr said, "I'll just get the specs on that sleepy-time gas so I get the dose calibrated correctly. Can't have our beauties oblivious to wake-up time . . ."

She had the supply officer by the arm and was hauling him away.

"How many hands will you need, Mr. Trotter, to effect the seal off?" Brace asked her. Amalfi was running the figures in her head but Brace waved her to the wardroom console. "If this works, I might try a little compulsory shut-eye myself on the next leg of this voyage."

At 2302, following Captain August's devious advice, every alarm system on the *Mandalay* howled, hooted, and shrieked. Troopers on every deck, even those in the brig and infirmary, were ordered into their battle suits until the "break in the skin of the *Mandalay* could be mended."

As the seasoned troops, cursing vehemently, struggled into their protective battle armor, complaints were rife but there wasn't a breath of suspicion. Some may have thought it very odd that they hadn't been ordered to close and seal their helmets against loss of oxygen, but battle-weary troops don't do more than they're told to. The first insidious flow of the diluted hibernation gas spread across every deck simultaneously. Not one trooper noticed—and every one of them fell asleep, held upright in parade readiness by their stout battle suits.

The crew in their protective gear muttered about it being bloody unnatural to move through the rank and file, lowering each to the horizontal mode. To relieve the tedium of their caretaking duties, there was a spritely competition about who had the most outrageous snore, the longest, the most involved, the funniest. There was considerable controversy in the *Mandalay*'s wardroom about the competition: they didn't want the results to affect the Navy-Marine relationships when the troops were finally awakened. Captain August had been heard to chuckle as some of the snore tapes were replayed.

"You'll notice, Captain," Damia Pharr said shortly before they had reached the rendezvous, "that crew morale has also improved."

"Noted, Major. We can only hope that the improvement also includes our sleeping beauties."

"It will, sir, it will," Pharr replied so devoutly that the captain entertained no further doubts.

By the time the *Mandalay* eased into position in a docking bay at the gigantic supply ship, *Grampion*, even the air aboard had improved from barely breathable to quite pleasant.

The officers were the first aroused, for orders had come for them to attend a briefing on the flagship. If the sparkle in the eyes of Colonel Gruen and Major Loftus were any indication, Pharr's therapy had indeed worked its magic.

"We'll wait till our return, Pharr, to effect a full-scale revival," Gruen told his medical officer, ignoring her smug grin. "We just might have some good news to relay with the bad by then."

"Won't hurt. It's been so peaceful I almost hate to wake 'em up."

Damia Pharr responded with a huge, jaw-popping yawn. "I get a chance for some S&D first, Jay!"

"S&D?"

"No R&R, try S&D. Makes a difference. You will see."

Formally piped on board the flagship, the colonel found an anxious wife waiting at the airlock for sight of him. Her amazement at his rejuvenation was heartening.

"I can't believe my eyes, Jay," she said, giving him a quick but ardent kiss under the eyes of the grinning officer and ratings who were in the portal. "Two weeks ago, you looked ghastly . . ." She broke off without further detail of that clandestine contact and pulled him down the companionway out of sight. "And it's not just you. Hello, Pete, you looked rested and raring to go, too. However did you do it?"

"You can't keep a good regiment down, you know," Pete Loftus replied, grinning. Then a yawn escaped him, and chagrined, he belatedly covered his mouth.

"There was nothing wrong with any man in the Montana Irregulars, Pamela," Jay Gruen told his astonished wife, "that a good long sleep couldn't set right. A little S&D would do you no harm either. I'll tell you all about it on our way to beard the general in his lair."

INTERLUDE: Cat's Paws

Their sponsors, the Syndicate of Families, never expected the Khalia to win the war against the Alliance. They had expected the war to last at least a decade. The Merchant Families had begun arming and training the Khalia decades earlier with the intention to create a buffer zone between themselves and the expanding Alliance. To this purpose they created an entire branch of modular manufacturing. This was the only way things could be kept simple enough for the Khalian warrior to operate or repair. This led to riches for a few families (actually greater power) and opportunities for the scions of the lesser houses.

The Syndicate strategy was in some ways a flawed policy. By its defensive/aggressive nature the Alliance had to concentrate its expansion in the direction of the worst threats to its own security. In their misguided attempt to create a powerful buffer, the Syndicate actually managed to draw in their direction the bulk of the Fleet's forces. To counter this they redoubled their efforts to encourage the Khalia to fight back with ever-greater ferocity, turning a border conflict into a major war.

That all this was grossly unfair to the Khalia was never a concern. Within the Family Boards of the Syndicate the human chauvinism of the late Empire still prevailed. This gave rise to a philosophy of exploitation, or worse, for all non-humans contained within the Syndicate sphere. The typical Syndicate citizen was neither evil nor cruel. Not any more so than the typical British citizen during their empire's exploitive era during the nineteenth century. The system, though, assumed that the only value of an alien race was whatever it could contribute to the family that was appointed to "manage" it, no matter what it cost the native race. In the case of the Khalia, several families cooperated in arming a primitive society with modern weapons and spurring them into a hopeless war.

Even though the Fleet stunned most Syndicate combat managers with the speed of its victory, they were still confident of defeating the Alliance. After all, they had still nearly three decades of intense preparation and a decisive edge in intelligence. This gave them many more advantages than just infiltrating spies. Though smaller than the Alliance, their fleet was equal in number to their enemy's. Further, they had a massive edge in intelligence. Not only had they infiltrated the Fleet, but they had spent much of this time preparing surprises within the borders of the Khalian Empire. Surprises that would cost the Fleet dearly in both men and ships. A few of these were found early in the occupation. Some by luck, others by good intelligence work, a few by more unusual means.

TRIPLE-CROSS
by Janny Wurts

LIEUTENANT JENSEN PACED, spun in a tight circle, then hammered an angry fist on the chart table. Loose marker pins scattered from the blow, falling like micro-shot through furniture tight-knit as a battle formation. "Damn the man, what godforsaken plot could send him back to Guildstar?"

"Information, maybe," suggested Harris, who lounged with closed eyes on the wall bunk, his pilot's coverall in its usual neglected state of crumple. Quarters on *Sail* were far too cramped for displays of violent frustration; by now resigned to having sleep disrupted by his senior's obsession with the obscure motivations of a criminal, Harris chose not to fight the inevitable. "You can bet Mac James isn't making the run for any merchant's sake."

The model of a Fleet officer in a faultlessly fitted duty coverall, Jensen swore. Black-haired and classically handsome, he leaned on his knuckles and glared at his holo map of Alliance space, which hogged whatever paltry space their quarters had to offer. The display was crisscrossed with threads and speared with markers in three colors: blue for those sites the skip-runner Mackenzie James was rumored to have visited; yellow for a confirmed sighting, and red for any station or planet or interstellar vessel that had fallen prey to his penchant for piracy. Mac James being the most wanted criminal on Fleet record, the map was peppered red from end to end.

"Or else the source you bribed is selling you a line of crap," Harris added.

Jensen swore again. He smoothed back bangs razor-trimmed in the latest military fashion. "My informant isn't wrong. I pay another rebel to cross-check her."

Harris knuckled the orange stubble that roughened his jaw. He failed to open his eyes, or speak; but his silence on the subject spoke volumes.

"The two are *not* in cahoots," Jensen defended, hotly enough to see another pair of markers bouncing across the narrow aisle of decking. They fetched against the corrugated plastic of the shower stall, where the lieutenant irritably retrieved them. "My people don't even know each other, and since when does a Freer do business with a Caldlander without one sticking a knife in the other?"

Now Harris did sit up, incredulity etched across lines left by laughter and self-indulgence. "Damn, boy. You've been had. I know you're rich, and that you've dumped all of Daddy's allowance into tracking skip-runners, but didn't anyone tell you? Freerlanders never sell out on a comrade. Mac James has been named in their honor song since the day he jammed that surveillance station over Freermoon and knocked it out of orbit."

Jensen returned an arch look. "This Freerlander is the one whose ancestral burial grounds got slagged under nine tons of radioactive junk, direct result of that foray."

Harris flopped backward. "OK," he agreed in defeat. Jensen's backup informant wouldn't be lying for gain, but hell-bent on bloody revenge. Harris wasted no energy wondering who else besides rebels his aristocratic senior had courted for access to Mac James's secrets. He shrugged one shoulder and said, "So your damnable pirate has business on Guildstar? So what?"

Jensen's brown eyes narrowed. Because it made no sense, he thought, slipping into one of those sudden, uncommunicative silences that claimed him when he contemplated the skip-runner captain whose activities preoccupied him wholly since the Khalian wars wound down. Combat action was reduced to a minor few far-flung outposts, and the present best chance for glory and promotion remained the capture of Mackenzie James. And James, who was never careless, never forthright, and never in his life involved in honest trade, should have been anathema in a system as straitlaced as Guildstar. Half the merchants on the council there had suffered losses due to Mac's operations; his ship, the *Marity*, should in theory have been blown to bits the instant she applied for a docking bay.

Webbing creaked as Harris shoved to his feet. His pilot's reflexes spared him from stepping unshod on spilled tacks, but the near miss sent him muttering toward the galley cubicle for coffee, or beer, or the chocolate bars he ate after difficult flights that unjustly never fleshed out his middle; even his tailored dress uniform hung on him like a mechanic's coverall.

Jensen's lips thinned in distaste. Harris's sloppiness was tolerable only because he could fly the shorts off just about all of his peers. And if Harris resented his assignment on *Sail*, a three-man scoutship commanded by a lieutenant whose father had stonewalled all reasonable opportunity for advancement, the pilot was too lackadaisical to care. Jensen despised such lack of ambition, but kept his contempt to himself. Without Harris, *Sail* had no prayer of intercepting the *Marity*. Longingly, Jensen reached out and fingered the single green pin in the display. How would his pilot respond, he wondered, if he knew that Daddy's allowance had gone toward the spreading of false information? Would Harris file for transfer if he understood that the green pin marked a trap most painstakingly laid to entice the *Marity*'s master, precisely so that *Sail* could effect a capture?

But the *Marity*, damn her wayward, disingenuous traitor of a captain, appeared not to be buying; instead she was making a third run to Guildstar, decorously scheduled as the merchanter she assuredly wasn't.

Jensen loosened a clenched fist and retrieved a marker, a blue one; with determined steadiness he imbedded the pin by the existing pair over Guildstar, then muttered, "It makes no sense."

Though Harris could overhear from the galley, Jensen felt no embarrassment. While other officers jockeyed for leave to visit wives and families, the lieutenant curried favor with Intelligence. He was first among the lower ranks to hear that the Khalia had been armed and financed by the Syndicate; the shock just beginning to filter down from above was that war was far from over. The heated issue now was location of the Syndicate's worlds. Weasel sources held no clue, spies in the most sensitive positions drew blanks, and the brass was reduced to screening hearsay in a vain search for coordinates. Jensen viewed the dilemma with an eye for opportunity. His passion to trap Mackenzie James took on increased importance: a skip-runner who trafficked in state secrets and whose record held multiple charges of treason would be acquainted with the Alliance's enemies. The Syndicate should be numbered among his customers. If James did not know their home system, he would have a contact, or a base of operations that would open a direct lead. To capture him, to claim the hero's honor for uncovering the turf of the enemy, Jensen was prepared to stake his name and career.

Lieutenant Michael Christopher Jensen, Jr. tapped the blue pin into the holo map, then considered another red one with a speculative frown. Mac James had pilfered plans for prototype weapons the Fleet had in classified research; the designs had not turned up in Indy hands, as everyone first supposed; where had James sold his booty that time? *Where?*

The blue pin mocked, by Guildstar.

"None of this makes sense, damn you to Weasel castration!" Jensen exploded, as though the arch criminal he hunted could hear his curse across space.

In the galley cubicle, surrounded by crumpled cups and a fashion magazine left by the ensign, Harris lifted doubtful eyebrows under a crown of red-gold hair. "Obsessed," he muttered to himself, and the coffee just ordered from the dispenser sat cooling while he rummaged under the mission's accumulation of debris after his illicit cache of beer.

In a dusty rebel settlement far beyond *Sail*'s patrol, a bar had been erected from slabs of modular siding filched from derelict stations and an abandoned colonial settlement. The corners did not match, and the sand took advantage. The floors were terminally gritty. In a side room, walled off by a fringed curtain, a Freerlander raised her cowl to veil a vicious smile. Her narrowed, desert-weathered eyes caught topaz light from a candle flame as she shifted gaze to the man who sat in the shadows. "The young officer was told outright, Captain. Guildstar, the time, the date. Everything short of your com codes, but the word is he hangs back, still."

A dry chuckle answered from the darkness. Pale eyes flicked up and glinted, while on the wine-sticky tabletop, a pair of hands scarred by coil burns flexed and straightened and flexed with an ease that, by the nature of such injuries, never should have been possible. Over the noise of the spacers' bar beyond the doorway, a voice equally grainy and grim observed, "Then the boy is not quite the brash fool he once was. No point in renewing the lease to that merchanter when this run's finished. I'll recall *Marity* when she makes port at Guildstar. Let out word that my next move will be those private sector interests on Chalice."

A chair squeaked as the Freerlander sat straighter, and a sigh issued from the hawk-nosed man wearing Caldlander harness who lounged opposite. After a black glance at the Freer, the Caldlander said, "But I understood the take on Chalice was worthy of a raid? Is it not risky to be baiting an Alliance scoutship on site at a real operation?"

"Well, Godfrey," drawled the man with the scarred hands. "If that's what it takes to get me access to a documented Fleet vessel, there's the ticket to the party. My mate Gibsen'd find the heat more welcome than bus driving guild cargoes, there's certainty."

The Caldlander made a disparaging sound through his nose; the Freer readjusted her cowl.

Both were cultural signs of displeasure, ignored by the skip-runner captain who stretched and rose, still in shadow. He half turned, scooped up a rattling collection of weapons belts and hiked them over his shoulder. Then he exposed blunt teeth in an expression that Freer and Cald both knew better than to mistake for a smile.

"Gentleman," said Mackenzie James in his boyishly amiable fashion. "Lady. If one of you kills the other after I leave, take my point, I'll gut the survivor like a fish."

No sound answered but a whore's raucous laugh beyond the doorway.

"Good," Mac James concluded. Still slinging the weapons he had, after all, never promised to return, he spun and ducked out, a large-framed bear of a man with a tread that incongruously made no sound. The door curtain slapped shut after him and left two enemies face-to-face over a wildly guttering candle.

"Damn his arrogance," swore the Caldlander. His fist slapped irritably against the hip that now held neither knife, nor sheath, nor pistol.

The Freer expressed her frustration through silence and a twitch of steel-nailed fingers. She found she had something to say after all. "If it were only his arrogance, neither of us would have come here, nor agreed to run errands to benefit some snot-nosed boy lieutenant."

The Caldlander stiffened fractionally. His eyes showed wide rings of white. "You suspect the information on Chalice is a setup?"

The face under the cowl yielded nothing. "The question is, does Mackenzie James?"

The enemies parted then, each wrapped in their own breed of silence. Days later, when Freer and captain were both beyond contact, it occurred to the Caldlander that Mac James's formidible cleverness might have fallen short. This once he might have overlooked the significance of a past action that had slagged a Freer ancestral memorial.

Sail emerged from the queer, deep silence of FTL on a routine run to deliver dispatches to Carsey Sector base. The capsule was relayed, another received to replace it, and in the six-sided capsule that served as cockpit, Harris snoozed in his headset, bored. Behind him, in the command alcove reserved for Lieutenant Jensen, *Sail*'s third crew member slouched in the process of painting her nails. Sarah Ashley del Kaplin, called Kappie by her deckmates, was short, whip-thin, and full-lipped. She had inviting, dusky skin and a deep voice, and she had taken assignment on *Sail* knowing that the lieutenant was handsome, but an iceberg, and that Harris was a bum who pinched. The pinches she fielded with equanimity, until they got too personal to ignore. Harris received a bruise he swore happened in a shower that was gravity stabilized, and the iceberg lieutenant was left to his romance with the machinations of Mackenzie James.

"Why's his nibs not out here reading off new orders?" Kaplin mused, turning her wrist to admire her nails, which this round were metallic lavender.

"Huh," muttered Harris. One elbow on the astrogation unit, he scratched his chest through his unsealed collar, then added, "The lieutenant will return to duty when he's finished housekeeping his map tacks."

A shout emerged from crew quarters, followed by what sounded like a war whoop. Harris shoved out of his slouch, and Kaplin swiveled around, her almond eyes wide with astonishment. "Did I hear that? Could this mean we've been assigned leave for the next tour?"

Harris grunted again. "Small chance. Jensen spends leave doing volunteer scut work for the recon boys."

Kaplin's groan was interrupted by Jensen's explosive appearance at the companionway. His rangy frame filled up the narrow opening; lit by the overhead panel, his face was flushed and his eyes overbright with excitement.

"He's done it!" the lieutenant shouted, waving a recent message com. "He's finally taken the bait."

The "he" needed no definition; nothing short of obsession with Mackenzie James could cause Jensen to overlook the crew member who usurped his command chair, the nail polish a calculated affront to his dignity.

From the pilot's station, Harris drawled, "Let me guess.

We're going to go AWOL, maybe pay an unscheduled visit to Chalice? At least I presume all those messages coming and going between us and the private sector were not over an affair.''

Kaplin watched this exchange, her nail brush forgotten in her hand. "If our boy is even capable of an affair," she muttered sotto voce.

Jensen failed to take umbrage as he crossed the cockpit in a stride. Risking an undecorous crease in his trousers, he leaned on the instrument panel cowling. This drew a frown from Harris, disregarded as the lieutenant plunged on. "No. We go under regs, by the book. *Sail*'s a scout and recon owes me a favor. Once we've placed these dispatches, I can get us an assignment to do a discretionary patrol sweep. Since the mines on Chalice are the juiciest operation the military has going with private business, they'd naturally need to be checked.''

Harris raked his fingers through a rooster comb of red hair, then replaced his beret with its frayed Fleet insignia. "That'd work.''

Only Kaplin insisted on particulars. "What's at Chalice for us?''

Jensen let her sarcasm pass. "Everything. I've been months setting it up. We're going to capture Mackenzie James and through him trace the home worlds of the Syndicate.''

Kaplin raised pencil-thin eyebrows. "Oh? And what's in Chalice for Mackenzie?''

Smug now, Jensen smiled. "A trap. My trap. James thinks he's going to heist core crystals, ones engineered with the technology used to interface those fancy brainship modules with their hardware. But once in, he'll find out the booty was bait. *Sail* might not have all the latest tracking gadgets, but she's strong on gunnery. We're going to stand down the *Marity*.''

The nail brush by now was thoroughly dry. Tossing it aside in exasperation, Kaplin flipped back ash-brown hair. "You're crazy. You'll get us all court-martialed.''

"Or decorated," Harris interjected. "That's what happened last time."

That moment Jensen noticed the gaudy, nonregulation nail lacquer. "Ensign Kaplin," he rapped out. "One more breach of protocol on this bridge, and I'll have you confined to quarters." His voice did not change inflection as he resumed with orders for his pilot. "Harris, charge the coils and prepare for FTL. I want our dispatches delivered as if they were hot, and *Sail* on flight course for Chalice."

In fact the logistics took days to work out. On fire with impatience lest they miss their timing at Chalice, Jensen paced through *Sail*'s tiny corridors. He ran through his plan to trap *Marity* over and over again. Since the scoutship's living quarters consisted of two bunkrooms, a galley cubby, and the bridge, his crewmates grew sick of hearing it. Harris escaped by closeting himself in astrogation to watch his library of porn tapes. Kaplin got bugged enough to argue.

Her fingers tapped the mess counter as she voiced her list of objections. "First, you took a helluva risk assuming those recon boys you brown-nosed could wrangle us an assignment."

"Irrelevant point," Jensen snapped. "We've got our papers and the assignment, both on target."

Kaplin shot a glance at the soup he would not eat because of nerves, and her next nail snicked against the counter. "Second, the explosive you had that dock worker rig in case your plans went awry could misfire."

Jensen gestured his exasperation. "Not if you know, as the rest of Chalice personnel does, that the box with the self-destruct is a dummy. The crystals inside are fakes, a decoy for Mackenzie James."

"Oh?" Kaplin's eyebrows arched. "You told *everybody* about your plot? Even the janitors? Hell, man, if you left things that wide-open, your skip-runner's deaf not to know it. His intelligence network's better than Fleet's, if he's got connections with the Syndicate. So who's fooling who on this mission?"

"Mac's best style is recklessness," Jensen countered. "And he wants those interface crystals very badly."

Kaplin threw up her hands, almost banging the dish locker in her irritation "You're telling me nothing but insanity! Our success depends on Mackenzie James being quantum leaps dumber than you are."

Now Jensen grew heated in turn. "If you can devise a better plan, I'd sure be interested to hear it!"

The lilac-colored nails drummed an agitated solo on the countertop. "I can't," Kaplin said finally. "But God, we'll be lucky if our asses stay whole through this one."

The queer, intangible stagger that human time sense underwent through the shift from FTL came to an end, but confusion lingered. On reentry to analog space, *Sail* seemed to hesitate and bounce, as if she were a plane engaged in a turbulent landing. Then something moving and metallic impacted her high-density hull with an awful, ear-stinging clang.

"Jesus!" screamed Harris from the pilot's seat. "We've dumped slap into a war zone!" He spun the spacecraft, tossing Kaplin and Jensen hard into their couch stations.

The lieutenant strained against the pull of vertigo and managed to punch up an image on the screens. Instantly his eyes were seared by the glare of an expanding plasma explosion. *Sail* had not entered a war zone; instead, the station logged as her destination had been detonated to a cloud of gases and debris. Harris responded, reflexively kicked *Sail*'s grav drives into reverse with a scream of attitude thrusters. Small fragments rattled against the hull. The gravity drives accelerated into the red, and buzzers sounded warning.

Jensen stared at the blowing burst of destruction that Harris labored feverishly to evade. What could possibly have gone wrong? he wondered, and his shoulders tensed in anticipation of Kaplin's acerbic, "I told you so, you arrogant, stupid fool."

But Kaplin said nothing, only sat with her face in her hands, caution lights from the recon unit a glare of yellow against her knuckles.

"Je-sus," Harris repeated, the Eirish accent of his child-hood breaking through the more cultured tones he had ac-quired in air-tactics academy. A gifted sixth sense and instinct enabled him to quiet the drive engines; *Sail* de-scribed a smooth course just beyond the event horizon left by the explosion. "What now?"

Nobody spoke. None of the three in *Sail's* cockpit cared to contemplate what might have been had their scout probe broken through FTL just half an instant sooner. Jen-sen looked at his hands, found them clenched whitely on the arms of his crew chair. Since he could not change the fuckup, he forced his brain to work.

And the obvious stared him in the face.

"Kappie," he said sharply. "Engage sensors, sweep the vicinity for the presence of other warcraft."

"What?" Overdue, the ensign's reproach was cutting. "Have you gone nuts? You set a live charge on Chalice station, and now you're after the culprit who blew it?"

Lieutenant Jensen repeated his command, his voice back under control. "The charge I had rigged was a contained net explosive. If anybody set it off, even accidentally, it might have burned one sector. Not the whole station. We're seeing the afterimage of a plasma bolt. Now, *make your sweep*. Our lives depend on it, because the enemy who manned the weapon is still out there."

"Could be renegade Khalians," offered Harris.

Nobody had time to suggest otherwise. An alarm cut across the cramped cockpit, one that signaled an inbound distress call.

Kaplin locked in on the signal. "A survivor," she called crisply. "He's in freefall with no life support beyond a ser-vice suit." She listed distance and vector, then added fig-ures for Harris to calculate drift factor. The human bit of flotsam moved with the debris from the station, no less a victim of the blast. "He's got a maintenance coding," Kap-lin finished. "Probably a repair man who was caught out-side when the charge hit."

"Set course for intercept," Jensen ordered. "By regs,

we're bound to pick the fellow up, and maybe he can tell us what happened.''

A pilot other than Harris might have protested; laying course through a high-speed, tumbling mass of debris was hardly the safest of undertakings. But Harris leaned over his console, a half-crazed grin on his face. As he began the maneuver, he relished telling Kaplin that she'd better not unbelt to fetch a Dramamine. The vector changes were going to be fast, and violent, and if she was going to be sick from inertia, better that than wind up splattered against a bulkhead.

The interval that followed became a hellish parody of a carnival ride. Harris alone found the gyrations enjoyable. He leaned over *Sail*'s console with his nose thrust forward like a jockey, every sense trained on the attitude displays, and his hands almost wooing the controls. The spacecraft responded to his measure, rolling, twisting, and sometimes outright wrenching a clear path through pinwheeling debris. Harris pressed *Sail* to the edge of her specs and reveled in every moment. His voice as he announced that the survivor was now close enough to grapple aboard sounded near as he came to elation.

Lieutenant Jensen issued orders through his vertigo. As Kaplin set hands to her couch belt, he told her to stay on station. ''Keep the scanners manned. If we're not the only craft out here, I want to know it fast.'' Then, as if *Sail*'s cockpit were too small to contain his restlessness, he strode out to manage the loading lock and grapplers on his own.

In keeping with most scout craft, *Sail*'s utility levels were a warren of bare, corrugated corridors as poorly lighted as a mine shaft, and unequipped with simulated gravity. Experienced enough to disdain magnetic soles, Jensen made his way aft through the service hatch, hand over hand on the side rails. Although he had logged more space hours, Kaplin was more agile than he. She could zip through null grav like a monkey, never the least bit disoriented. Jensen's jaw muscles tightened. A lowly female ensign should not make him feel threatened; but thanks to the almighty wishes of his politician father, others as inexperienced had earned their promotions ahead of him. Kaplin might easily do the same, despite the fact she was apt to act flighty on duty, and her record held a collection of demerits.

The frustration of being continually passed over caught up with Jensen at odd moments. Intent on the injustices of his career, he drifted over the open-grate decking to the space bay, flipped open the grappler's controls, and slipped on the headset inside. He clicked the display visor down, powered up the unit, and initiated recovery procedure as if the drifting speck on the grid represented no castaway, but an enemy target in a weapon scope. Since Jensen held a citation for marksman elite, the mote of human flotsam was recovered in commendably short order. Jensen tossed the headset into its rack. Poised before the trapezoidal entry to the lock chamber, he engaged the space bay controls, then waited, his hand on the bulkhead to pick up the jarring vibration that signaled closure of the outer lock. His ears measured the hiss of changing air pressure as atmosphere flooded the chamber. Only greenhorns and fools trusted to idiot lights on the monitor panel. Electronics were never infallible, and there were prettier ways to die than voiding an unsuited body into vacuum.

The pressure stabilized within the bay. Jensen flipped off the manual safety and unsealed sliding doors through the innerlock. Inside the steel-walled chamber, the figure he had recovered drifted limply in null grav, clad in the bulky, ribbed fabric of a deep-space mechanic's suit. The elbows showed wear, the knees were grease-stained, and the tool satchels were scuffed with use. The hands in their fluorescently striped gloves did not rise to undo the helmet, and a second later, Jensen saw why. The face shield was drenched from the inside, with an opaque film of fresh blood.

Nausea kicked the pit of his stomach. He had not expected a survivor who was injured, or maybe dead. Hindsight made his assumption seem silly. The emergency tracer signal emitted by the suit did not necessarily trigger manually. The backpacks and tool satchel compartments were typical of a repairman's, and such gear often had a proximity fail-safe: if the worker wearing the rig accidentally came adrift from a workstation, the alarm would set off automatically. Jensen swallowed back sickness. He had seen death before, had once blown a man's brains out point-blank from behind. Now, duty demanded that he ascertain whether this suit contained a corpse, or a medical emergency.

Queasiness reduced to irritation, Jensen pushed off into the lock chamber. He bumped against the drifting figure, clumsily captured it in an embrace, and managed to hook onto the handrail before he caromed off the far wall. With one elbow crooked to maintain position, he wrestled the suited body upright, then flipped the clasps on the helmet.

As he lifted the face shield, the figure moved against him. A space-gloved hand gripped his waist from behind, and a hard object jabbed his side.

Probably just a tool appendage, Jensen rationalized, his pulse quickening. But the face behind the blood-streaked shield dispelled his last vestige of delusion. The lieutenant looked down into slate-colored eyes and an expression that held only ruthlessness.

"Godfrey, you boys are predictable," said the voice of Mackenzie James. The cheek in shadow beneath the face shield showed a smear of new blood, but the hold that gripped Jensen, and the arm that shoved what surely was a firearm against the lieutenant's side, were not those of a wounded man. Mackenzie James was bearishly strong, with reflexes not to be trifled with. Jensen had cause to remember.

Shocked by the skip-runner's presence and enraged to have lost the upper hand to a castaway, the lieutenant fought to stay calm. "I presume you deep-spaced the man who owned the suit you're wearing."

The query prompted an insouciant smile. "Cut the crap," said James, his voice multiplied by echoes off of the lock bay walls. "If you've got any scruples about killing, they're faked." He shook back mussed brown hair and nudged the gun barrel in the ribs of his victim. "Unfasten my suit clips."

Jensen saw no option but compliance; if James decided to shed the bulky suit, a way might arise to seize advantage while his enemy was encumbered by the sleeves. Convinced that the pirate had tripped the charge in the bogus crate of brain crystals, and that an accomplice on *Marity* had seen the explosion and opened retaliatory fire on Chalice, Jensen talked in an attempt to distract his enemy's thinking.

"You'll never get away with a hijacking. *Sail*'s courses are automatically logged, and she runs under check-in protocols. All transmissions are coded and routinely traced."

Mackenzie James said nothing.

"Give yourself up, man." Jensen set hands to the last shoulder clip. "If our schedule is disrupted a millesecond, we're presumed to be boarded by enemies. We're tagged and targeted for armed search, with orders to be slagged on sight."

The clip unlatched with a click. James raised insolent brows. "Let go," he instructed. As Jensen hesitated, James swung his body and wrenched the officer's fingers. Painfully freed, Jensen felt himself spun around, his right wrist looped neatly in a tool tether.

The lieutenant struggled, tried to jab an elbow in his enemy's face. The move was both anticipated and countered; after years spent in freefall standing ambush, Mac James had mastered null grav to a fine point. He did little but shift one hip. The result provoked a spin as he and his captive drifted in tandem from the rail. Jensen's fast movement added vector that hammered him sideways into the wall. James was protected by his suit; Jensen, caught on the inside, got the breath crushed from his lungs, and a bruise on the temple that nearly stunned him. Weakly he clawed for the lock. If he could reach the control, he might signal and warn the bridge.

The tool tie on his wrist jerked him short and rebound slammed him backward into James. Jensen tried to fight. A punch that ineffectively dented suit padding was all he could manage before a kick in the groin killed his resistance. Amid the chaos of motion provoked by his shoves and thrusts, the tool tie looped his other wrist. Mac James controlled his

random tumble. He shucked the suit, revealing blunt features and a pair of nondescript coveralls soaked like camouflage with bloodstains. Plainly the suit's original owner
had died from exposure to vacuum. Left queasy by pain,
and by the coppery sharpness of the droplets drifting in
freefall that unavoidably got inhaled with each breath, Jensen cursed.

The gun barrel was no longer pointed at his face. James's
hand on the grip was relaxed, even negligent as he loosened
the neck of his coverall; this action was an effrontery by
itself since Jensen was not fully helpless. His feet were left
free to kick; but to do so in null grav without use of his
arms was asking for a nasty crack on the head. Mac James
understood that Jensen was experienced enough to know
this. The skip-runner relied on that wholly, an arrogance
his captive found infuriating.

Jensen cursed again. He despised the notion that a criminal could so easily guess his mind. He decided any effort
was worth the inevitable concussion, but on the point of
action, James caught the tool tie and jerked it like a leash.

Snapped in line like a disobedient puppy, Jensen wrestled
with shoulders and forearms, half gagged by the taste-smell
of blood. His struggles skinned the flesh of his wrists, no
more; Mac James towed him expertly through the inner
lock. Crimsoned, coil-scarred fingers tapped across the
control panel. The skip-runner was no stranger to Fleet vessels, Jensen observed in bleak rage. The lock hissed shut,
fail-safe seals engaged.

"You lost your ship, at least," Jensen managed through
clenched teeth as he was dragged past the service access to
condenser and drive-engine compartments. "I hope she was
blown to a million bits as a result of your late misjudgment."

Mac James half turned. A glimpse of his snub-nosed profile showed a sardonically lifted brow. "Misjudgment?
Godfrey, boy. I'm exactly where I planned to be, which is
more than you can say for yourself."

Jensen returned an epithet, clipped short as he twisted to
stop a nose dive; Mac James towed him through the access

hatch into the upper level of the ship, and gravity slammed
his shoulders into the deck grid. The breath left his lungs
and his feet drifted stupidly in the gravityless well of the
service corridor.

"Up," said Mackenzie James. The pellet pistol was back
in his hand and fixed in nerveless steadiness on the vitals
of his captive. "Move, now!"

An impatience colored the skip-runner's tone that only a
fool would question. Jensen rolled, pulled his knees beneath
his body, then flinched as his captor clapped a hand to his
shoulder. He was ruthlessly hauled upright, spun, and
marched ahead. The tool tie tautened, stressed his arm
sockets without mercy, while the pistol nuzzled the base of
his skull.

"Now," said James in his ear from behind. "We're going
to the bridge. At the companionway, you will stop and in-
struct your pilot to set course for Van Mere's station in
Arinat."

Jensen automatically began to protest. A shake from Mac
James caught him short.

The captain qualified. "Your current orders permit you
to act on discretion. And discretion, if you wish to stay
alive, says *Sail* engages FTL for Arinat."

Aside from the weapon at his neck, curiosity urged Jensen ahead. That James knew the fine print on his orders was
a cold and disquieting puzzle. "Why Arinat? And what's at
Van Mere's except a trading colony for a remote agricultural
outpost?"

"Quite a bit," James said uninformatively. Then, as if
stating everyday business, he added, "The *Marity* didn't
blow to bits along with Chalice. She's spaceworthy, and
awaiting rendezvous, and will go under your escort through
the security zone checkpoint to Arinat."

At which point Jensen knew searing rage. He had played
blindly into an ambush. Months of intricate planning had
led him to this: not as the hunter, but the trapped prey,
forced to play puppet for the skip-runner Mackenzie James.

"Carry on, Lieutenant," the gruff voice instructed in his
ear.

Jensen did so purely out of hatred. He swore he would find a way to turn the tables, to bring this pirate to a justice long deserved.

Skip-runner and captive reached the galley nook; beyond lay the companionway to the bridge. The hand that poised the gun at Jensen's neck tightened ever so slightly. Since Mac James was never a man to act by half measures, Jensen squared his shoulders. He stepped up to the companionway, faced through toward the cockpit, and crisply called out orders.

"Ensign Kaplin, discontinue your search pattern. Harris, I want this ship on a new course for Arinat. Plot FTL co-ordinates for the security zone checkpoint, and from there to Van Mere's station."

Harris shot out of his habitual slouch. He turned his head, stared at his superior officer with an insolence peculiar to pilots, and said, "You want *what*?"

The pistol nosed harder against Jensen's neck. He swallowed stiffly. "Harris. You're insubordinate."

"When isn't he," Kaplin commented with her usual flat-toned sarcasm. She shut down systems for travel and spun her station chair, in time to see Harris narrow his eyes.

"No," the pilot said, quite softly. "We've done too many assignments together for me to buy on this one. I'll set course for Arinat on one condition, *sir*. Step in here and show me both of your hands."

Jensen had no chance to warn, no chance to act, just one instant of crystallized fear as Mac James shoved him aside. The pellet pistol went off, a compressed explosion of sound. Jensen staggered off balance, heard Kaplin's scream, and knew: Mac James had gunned down his pilot, even as he, on a past mission, had killed the *Marity*'s mate. In his own way, but for different reasons, Jensen shared such ruthlessness. He was not shocked, but only whitely angry, when he recovered his footing and saw the fallen figure sprawled in the helm chair. The pilot's beret had tumbled off, and the fiery thatch of hair dripped blood. The long, lean fingers that had performed feats of magic at the controls were not relaxed, but twitching in an agitation of death throes. Mac

James's pellet had taken Harris through the forehead. He'd probably died between thoughts.

A muffled sound across the cockpit reminded Jensen of his other, surviving crew member. Sarah del Kaplin looked sheet white; yet the makeup like garish paint over her pallor masked an unexpected death of character. Scared to the edge of panic, she hadn't lost it enough to stand up.

Which was well, for the murdering skip-runner shoved onto *Sail*'s bridge and snapped his next orders to the ensign. "Lady, your training included flight rating, and you'd better know the material, because you're going to push that body off the helm and fly this vessel to Arinat and Van Mere's."

Kaplin turned a shade paler. She lifted wide eyes to her senior officer; and prodded by the gun in twitchy hands at his back, Jensen said, "Kappie. Just do it."

She returned a jerky nod, rose, and struggled with Harris's cooling corpse, her hands with their extravagant nail polish shaking and shaking, but able enough nonetheless. She sat in Harris's spattered chair and engaged instruments to plot the skip-runner's course.

MacKenzie James followed the figures that flashed on her board. The criminal knew his astrogation, solidly; that he watched over Kaplin's shoulder told more clearly than words that there were stakes to this foray. A hum pervaded *Sail*'s hull, followed by deeper vibrations. The coil condensers began their charge cycle in preparation for FTL, and as if the change in the ship's drive galvanized Jensen's thinking, it dawned that *Marity* had blown Chalice station deliberately, her purpose to hide Mac James's tracks.

"You've stolen the brain crystal interfaces," Jensen accused, his voice muffled by his own epaulette as Mac James shoved his face down and to the side, and manhandled him sideways into the hanging locker reserved for officers' dress coats.

James responded with a grin that had no humor behind it. "You helped make it convenient." He pushed down, ramming his captive into the dusty closet. "Chalice security was busily watching your box of rigged bait. Really, boy,

I'm surprised. A man would expect you to learn not to *keep on* meddling beyond your depth.''

Jensen winced as his elbow caught on the door hinge. Jammed on a nerve, he gasped, sweated, and vainly thrashed for purchase in an area too constricted for bodily movement. ''Damn you,'' he grunted, before the fine silk of his officer's scarf was forcibly crammed in his mouth. James used a length of shock webbing to tie the gag in place, then shoved the door closed.

Jensen crouched in fetal position, his wrists lashed bloodlessly tight behind his back. Pressure against his cheek flattened his nose against his knees, and the toes of Harris's battle boots ground relentless dents in his buttocks. Unable to move, unable to speak, he still could hear. The dry tones of MacKenzie James instructed Kaplin to adjust her course; she'd missed a decimal point. The result, as James phrased it, would get *Sail* an unscheduled refit, since Van Mere's star had an asteroid belt that could skin the shields off a battle cruiser.

Jensen squirmed and managed to cramp his left thigh. He could not stretch to relieve the discomfort, but only sweat with the pain. The closet quickly became stifling, and somewhere between nausea and frustrated tears, he missed the shift to FTL. He knew the transition had happened when the cramp eased off, and he realized the vibrations from the condensers had subsided back to a whisper.

A light tread crossed the cockpit; not Kaplin's, Jensen determined. She tended to slap her heels down, result of a flirty, provocative hip-sway she habitually used to distract. Most men were not immune, but James would prove the exception. Jensen knew the skip-runner to be formidably focused in his actions. The steps paused, and the couch by the com station creaked.

''You'll tell me *Sail*'s security code schedule,'' James suggested in his gravelly bass.

Silence. Jensen squeezed his eyes shut and moaned. Kappie, he thought desperately, you'll go the way of Harris. He tensely awaited the shot.

''Godfrey, girl,'' said James. He sounded strangely tired.

"Don't shake so hard. I only shoot on sight when some-body's fixing to kill me. Your pilot kept a gun in the pocket next to his jock strap, or didn't you know that?" A pause. "No, I see not. His whores shared the secret, and for a pitiful bit of change, they talked."

In the closet, Jensen drew a shuddering, sweat-stinking breath. *He* had not known Harris packed a pistol, never mind under that ridiculously baggy coverall. Jensen's worst nightmare had never allowed that James might run a net-work that extended so deep, into the back streets of who knew how many worlds. The haunts of pilots on leave were notoriously varied, and scattered as stars to scope out. That this criminal's interest had focused so intently on *Sail*'s crew was a most unsettling discovery.

"The codes," reminded MacKenzie James, his voice gone strangely steely. Above the subliminal hum of FTL, the cockpit beyond the closet seemed gripped in waiting stillness.

Kaplin gasped as if hit. "I can't tell you," she lied. "I don't know them!" Her bravery held an edge of hysteria.

Jensen braced for a shot that never came. The chair by the comconsole creaked again as Mac James shifted his weight. "Dearie," he said in a tone of deceptive gentleness. "I'm running out of time. That means you talk, or I em-barrass the brass higher up."

In the closet, Jensen frowned; and Kaplin's tremulous silence became underscored by James's quick tread, then the tap of fingers over the keys on what had to be the com-mand alcove console.

"What are you doing?" Kaplin asked in a blend of fear and suspicion.

"Canceling our course coordinates," MacKenzie James replied. "We're going to stay in the Chalice system until a battle cruiser comes to investigate."

"You'll get us all blown to hell," said Kaplin with the acid bite she used to admonish her senior lieutenant.

"Very likely you're right." James left the command chair, and by the squeals of outrage that followed, Jensen judged that the skip-runner tied Del Kaplin to the pilot's station with his usual ruthless style.

There followed a wait, in which the skip-runner fixed himself coffee. In the protocols manual under the console, he found *Sail*'s security code schedule and ascertained the time for her next check-in. Then, with a style more flamboyant than Harris's, he spun the scout craft on a trajectory that blended with the expanding debris from the explosion.

Nauseated by vertigo, and jammed in the suffocating closet, Jensen felt a horrible, hollow lurch in his abdomen as the artificial gravity was switched off. More controls clicked in the cockpit as the skip-runner adjusted *Sail* for total shutdown, making her invisible to all but a tight-focus scan.

An hour passed, then two. *Sail*'s call-in was due in thirty minutes. Jensen sat, ears straining, to hear how MacKenzie James planned to handle the Fleet cruiser that was sure to arrive at any moment.

Kaplin must have been left facing the screens, because when the battle cruiser arrived, she spoke with tense satisfaction. "That's the *New Morning*. She's a flagship with an admiral aboard, and an escort fleet of six."

"Eight," James corrected. "Chalice got off a distress torp." He did not sound upset, but crossed to the comconsole and rapidly began punching keys.

"You're going to beg amnesty?" Kaplin said, just missing her usual sarcasm.

"No. Personal phone call," James qualified. "To your senior, Admiral Nortin." A burst of static hissed across the screen, followed by the chime that signaled a clear transmission. James spoke crisply, "Ah, Admiral, I seem to have disturbed you in the shower?"

Jensen tried to picture his crusty senior officer in a towel or a bathrobe. Imagination failed. Nortin was always, and ever would be, square-shouldered, tight-lipped, and well groomed, with a daunting row of medals on his chest.

In tones slightly rusty from surprise, the admiral answered, "Get to the point."

"Indeed." James paused for what had to be a nasty smile.

"I wish to know the security codes for the scout-class vessel *Sail*."

"She's on reconnaissance assignment." The admiral recovered fast; already his words had recovered their customary bite. "Why *Sail*?" Then the admiral's voice became softly menacing. "You on her?"

James made no verbal reply; instead, his fingers tripped lightly over the console. A moment later, Jensen heard the click of the drive in the log tape reader.

The admiral's voice came back jagged. "Where did you get that film clip?"

"From an extortionist who wanted something much too big for his resources. He got killed instead. His tape collection, unfortunately, survived him. Now, I want *Sail*'s codes, and quickly, or the fact you took pay to hang back from engagement at Elgettin will be broadcast to the satellite feeds."

"It was never so simple as that." The admiral sounded suddenly very aged.

"It never is, sir." A false note of sympathy colored Mac James's platitude. He was, after all, committing blackmail. Jensen raged at the indignity forced on the admiral, as, over com, he heard the old man calling information from security.

Sail's codes came through promptly after that, and Jensen despaired as he confirmed the accuracy of each sequence. MacKenzie James had done his legwork with the efficiency that trademarked his career. He humbled large men and small with the same evenhanded ruthlessness. For his pains, the skip-runner captain had gained himself a scout-class vessel with open search orders. He could travel the breadth of Alliance space, or any of a half-dozen security zones, and not be questioned; the *Marity* could accompany openly, masquerading under military escort.

The effrontery of the piracy cut Jensen like a razor. He did not mourn for Harris. He felt only passing sympathy for his admiral's private shame; but for his own whipped pride and the certain ruin of his career, his hatred burned murderously bitter. Fury did not allow for limits. Crushed and cramped into a hole not fit for a dog, Jensen twisted his shoulders sideways and strained against the tool ties. He forced numb and bloodless fingers to open and close and grope for the nearest object to hand, which happened to be Harris's scuffed, old battle boots.

Two places the Eirish pilot wore those shoes without fail: on deck during combat, and off on leave, where his hobbies had been whoring and brawling. The toes were reinforced with steel caps, and Jensen sawed his bonds feverishly against the metal in the futile hope of fraying through high tensile mesh.

Activity continued on the bridge. MacKenzie James reset the autopilot, then, in a masterful orchestration of instruments, cross-wired the grav-drive regulators and the life-support emergency generators to charge the coils in a split-second burst of power. *Sail*'s banks reached peak capacity and transferred into FTL in one screaming instant of vertigo. *New Morning*'s instrumentation would have seen the surge, but not in time to evaluate whatever had caused the burst. To keep ends neat, they'd chart the anomaly as an unstable bit of debris from Chalice's fusion reactor.

Assured that *Sail* was safely away, James confined Kaplin to the stores locker behind the galley. Jensen missed the light-footed tread that returned to the cockpit, but not the change back to analog space, and the voice that activated the com and summoned the *Marity* to take station to *Sail*'s rear.

Mac James relayed instructions to his mate. "I'll escort you through the checkpoint at the security zone, as planned. Once in Arinat system, we'll separate. *Sail* will execute patrol patterns while you transfer the goods and take payment. We'll rendezvous afterward off Arinat nine, darkside of the satellite called Kestra. That's the only blind spot in the Syndicate's sensor network, and it's a damned narrow one. Misplace a vector, and we're vapor, so be careful."

As the skip-runner closed contact and restored *Sail*'s altered circuitry to reprogram his original course, Jensen paused in his attempt to free his hands. Furiously he combined facts, those he knew with others he'd heard. His final conclusion was chilling. For MacKenzie James inferred that the agricultural colony beneath Van Mere's was a covert Syndicate outpost, undiscovered by the Alliance and, indeed, unlikely to be, since Arinat system lay within the Molpen security zone that ships could not enter without passing a military checkpoint. The added inconvenience should have discouraged spies; but in a backhandedly clever sort of way, the compromised location made sense.

Who knew, and who had ever thought to look for sophisticated technology underneath three continents of crops? The secret was viciously guarded, since James had risked acquisition of *Sail* to have her in system for his transaction. If the Syndicate faction behind Van Mere's valued their skip-runner contacts lightly enough to blow them out of space after goods transfer, the wisdom of *Sail*'s presence made sense. On patrol, her sensors would detect explosions or plasma charges. She would be duty bound to report such abnormalities and file for investigation. The spies on Van Mere's would wish to avoid such attention in the interest of preserving their anonymity. Stations that traded with agricultural outposts rarely acted with aggression, and that profile provided essential cover.

MacKenzie James had indestructible luck because he unerringly planned for contingencies. As Jensen resumed sawing at his restraints, he had to admire the man's genius. Mac's operations had the feel of a grand dance, precisely timed, and disarmingly masqueraded as coincidence.

That *Sail* should be commandeered for treason was no sane ending to contemplate. The lieutenant leaned back in the cubicle, flexed his wrists, and groped at his bonds with his fingertips. The webbing was not the least bit frayed, and a tug to test the knots showed his efforts had only chafed skin.

A man who hated less might have quit. Jensen rammed his shoulders against the wall and relentlessly sawed all the harder. He persisted though his muscles cramped into screaming knots of agony. He cut and cut and cut the tool tie across the toe cap of Harris's boot through the hours of passage to Arinat. His hands went numb, and then his wrists and elbows. He kept cutting. *Sail* completed her transit, kicked out of FTL, and the web of the tool tie he'd been tearing at showed the faintest trace of a nap. He rested, listening as James refined course and opened contact in an unfamiliar language with his Syndicate contact on Van Mere's.

Orders were relayed, and *Marity* assumed position for the sale of her stolen technology. Core interface crystals took years to manufacture, and there were many, many bodies left crippled from the war that waited, bathed in nutrients, in the hope of future service in a brainship. Since crystals were unique, and the idiosyncracies of each required a precise match with the consciousness of the individual they would be paired with, today's loss meant the death of hope for someone who valiantly clung to life in total helplessness. Jensen ran swollen, aching fingertips over the light fuzz on the tool tie. He acknowledged the sorry fact that he could never rip free in time to matter.

In the cockpit, MacKenzie James logged in *Sail*'s codes and established routine patrol at Arinat's. He set up a closed band connection with his mate on the *Marity*, and the core crystals came closer to changing hands.

Prisoned in the closet, Jensen shut his eyes. He reviewed every memory of Harris. There had to be a reason, besides steel toe caps, why the pilot insisted on a particular pair of boots whenever he flew into combat.

"Never catch me being lab rat for a Weasel," he had once confided over beer; Harris, whose whores had known he wore a pistol in a hip strap over his undershorts. Jensen reasoned furiously. The combat boots had metal-capped toes, but no ankle laces. It followed that Harris might have chosen the style to carry a knife in his boot cuffs.

Jensen strained to raise his arms, hampered as his elbows jammed against the back wall and the door panel. He lacked the space to flex and reach the boot tops only inches away from his wrists. He grunted, forced blood-starved muscles to contract. Using wall and door to wedge his shoulders, he raised himself inch by torturous inch and scrunched backward. He sat on the insteps of Harris's boots; while in the cockpit, MacKenzie James monitored the exchange of the crystals with a coolness that rankled the nerves.

Jensen groped, caught the left boot cuff between his knuckles. He pinched, kneaded, and crumpled the tired old leather, while his joints tingled horribly in complaint. He found nothing. Close to tears of frustration, he twisted at his bonds, forced his shoulders into an angle that all but flayed his back, and managed to hook the right boot. He found what he sought, not a knife, but a razor-thin strip of metal sewn between the seams above the ankle.

It took him a pain-ridden hour to work the implement free. By then utterly exhausted, he had to rest, his hands numbed lumps of meat, and his wrists scraped down to raw gristle. In the cabin, MacKenzie James wrapped up his transaction and gently set *Sail* on an outward spiral toward Kestra.

Jensen cut himself twice before he got the razor positioned against his bonds. He nicked the weave of the tool tie over and over, his hold precariously slippery with his own blood. The stubborn webbing gave way. Shivering, wretched with discomfort and relief, he wormed his arms into his lap and cradled his hands to his chest. He had to pause through an agonizing interval of time, until Mac James chose to leave the cockpit. Jensen dragged off his gag. He used the spoiled silk to wrap his gashed fingers, then, uncontrollably shivering in a cold sweat, he stole his moment to act.

The lieutenant tripped the catch to the closet and spilled unceremoniously onto the deck. His legs refused to obey him, and his manual dexterity was shot. Aware that he had only moments, he half dragged, half rolled his body across the cockpit to the weapons locker. More seconds were lost as he blotted blood from his hand so the security sensor could read his palm print. The lock clicked open. Not trusting his aim with a kill weapon, Jensen chose a riot pistol armed with stun charges. Then, scuttling crabwise, he positioned himself against the companionway bulkhead just as Mac James stepped in through the access corridor.

The skip-runner saw the opened closet and instantaneously jerked out his pistol. Formidably fast, he spun sideways, almost into cover as he punched the switch to shut the access hatch.

Jensen's charge nipped through the fast-closing panel and hammered the skip-runner in the shoulder. Nerves and muscles went dead and the pellet gun clanged to the deck. The barrel wedged in the hatch track. The door jammed, leaving a sliver of a gap; enough for Jensen to squeeze off another round.

Luck favored him. The charge caught Mac James as he leaned to kick free the jammed pistol. He grunted what might have been a word, then crumpled and sagged to the deck.

Jensen could not resist a crow of triumph. He might not have the *Marity*, might have lost the precious interface crystals to the enemy, but he had MacKenzie James. And along with the most wanted skip-runner in Alliance space, he could deliver the first definitive proof of a spy connection with the Syndicate. The wreckage of his plans at Chalice had not ended in failure.

The sweetness of victory and the sure promise of promotion made his recent humiliation worthwhile. Gripping the stun pistol in his swollen, lacerated hands, Jensen pushed to his feet. He had details to arrange, a criminal to secure, and no choice but presume that the spies on Van Mere's monitored military com channels. He'd need to withdraw from Arinat system as if nothing untoward had happened, and initiate FTL before he dared call for an escort. *Marity* was still at large. The mate left on board would know James had encountered problems when rendezvous failed behind Kestra. Yet unless MacKenzie's man wished to broadcast Fleet connections and face reprisal from Van Mere's, he'd be powerless to pursue until too late.

Jubilant, drunk on his own triumph, Jensen cleared the companionway door. He gave the stunned body of his captive a vengeful, self-satisfied kick, then squeezed past to free Kaplin from the supply cubby. She could damn well reset their course log, since her infernally manicured fingers were probably not mangled to incapacity. As he stumbled on nerve-deadened feet, Jensen acknowledged that he desperately needed to use the head. He considered his ruined uniform, and wondered, between planning, whether his efforts to escape the hanging locker might have bloodstained his best battle jacket.

Well after the code check at 1700, Ensign Kaplin drifted cross-legged in the dimly lit corridor by the space lock. Unimpressed by Jensen's bubbling elation, and unconcerned that her hair needed fixing, she sullenly chipped enamel off a broken thumbnail. Her thoughts centered darkly around the admiral whose record was impeccable, but whose past was anything but. Her future in the Fleet would become deadlocked as a result of the tape she had witnessed. The lieutenant was a fool if he thought the captive held trussed in the lock bay was going to sweeten an admiral whose private shame had been leaked to the crew of a minor class scout. As Kaplin saw things, MacKenzie James might never see trial; more likely he'd die of an accident, or someone would pull strings to set him free. He hadn't gotten where he was without connections in high places. His record of success was too brilliant.

Kaplin jabbed at her fingernail, plowing up a flake of purple lacquer. Jensen was an idealistic idiot, and Admiral Nortin a desperately cornered man; no need to guess who'd survive when the dirt inevitably hit the fan.

A discreet tap at the lock door disrupted the ensign's brooding. She started and looked up, saw the haggard face of MacKenzie James drifting by the small oval window. His hands were bound; he'd managed the knock by catching the pen from the bulletin alcove between his teeth and rapping the end against the glass.

"Damn," Kaplin muttered under her breath as her grip slipped and mangled a cuticle. She sucked at the scratch, pushed off from the floor grate, and, still cross-legged, peered through the glass. "What do you want?"

Other than a leak, she mused inwardly. If the stun drugs had just worn off, that's what most people wanted.

Mac James ejected the pen from his teeth. "Talk," he

said, his succinctness blurred by echoes. He bunched his shoulders against the webbing Jensen had contrived to confine him. The result would have tethered a bull elephant, Kaplin felt, but hell, she was only the ensign. She unfolded elegant legs, set her shoulder against the lock, and lightly braced on the door frame. "Should I listen?"

James managed a grin. His forehead had somehow gotten cut during transfer from the bridge to the lock bay, and a bruise darkened the stubble on his jaw. "You might want to." He tossed back tangled hair and added, "I'd hate like hell to be left at the mercy of an admiral whose secrets were compromised."

Kaplin pursed her lips. "You're quick."

James's grin vanished. "Always."

The ensign considered her torn thumbnail, then elegantly unfolded her body and tapped the controls to her left. The lock unsealed, and a rush of cold air from the barren metal bay raised chills under her coverall. She shivered. "Speak fast. I'm not sure I should be listening."

"Be sure," said James. "I can get you reassigned. To another division, under another admiral, with a few less demerits on your record."

Kaplin regarded him carefully. Trussed hand and foot, his massive shoulders twisted back, James did not seem discomforted. His expression was much too confident. He watched, his eyes steely and level; as she noticed the scar over his right carotid artery, and as she lingeringly weighed the rusty stains that remained of a Chalice mechanic that patched his threadbare flightsuit. He was a man who had seen death from many angles. The possibility the next might be his own failed to move him.

"You'd have to free me, get me back to rendezvous at Kestra," he finished in a voice that was dry with disinterest.

A pirate should have owned more passion, Kaplin felt. The list of criminal charges did not seem to fit with the man. She thought deeper, while those gray eyes followed; her hand tapped involuntary tattoos on the railing. MacKenzie James, skip-runner, should have gunned the other crew down with Harris. His hold over the admiral was all he truly needed to commandeer *Sail* without questions.

As her oval chin rose obstinately, Mac James seemed to follow her reasoning. "I didn't kill Jensen because I need him. His obsession is a tool, invaluable because it's genuine. A man's hatred is always more reliable than the best of laid plans."

Kaplin narrowed her eyes. "Who are you," she demanded. "You'll tell the truth, or we don't talk."

Now Mac James studied her. He no longer seemed boyish, or hardened, but only unnervingly perceptive. "I take orders from Special Services," he said, his face like weather-stripped granite. "And my criminal record is genuine. I could be tried and convicted on all counts, and no pardon would come through to save me. I am legitimately skip-runner, traitor, and extortionist, and because of that, I have served as the Alliance's contact to disclose the motives of the Khalia and, now, the Syndicate behind them." A strange thread of weariness crept into the prisoner's voice. He tried, but did not entirely hide a ghost of underlying emotion. "Sometimes it takes a bad apple to know one. And through *Sail*'s surviving officers, the Fleet is free to deal with what Van Mere's is actively covering. *Marity* is not involved, my cover is kept intact, and the Syndicate's best outpost is exposed to counterespionage before anyone inside knows they're compromised."

He was not pleading, Kaplin decided. He was appealing to her loyalty on a higher level; loyalty to humanity above her oath to serve the Fleet. She considered what he had not said, the threats he had not outlined: that *Marity* was yet at large, that *Sail* was still a long and lonely distance from the nearest battle cruiser or station, and that the Special Services branch of Intelligence often stooped to ugly tactics to free its operations from interference.

Fractionally, James shook his head. "Gibsen won't pursue. He's under my orders, and he won't break. Not to spare me from arraignment. The Syndicate outpost was always our target, whether I am sacrificed or not."

Kaplin chewed her lip. "Damn you," she whispered into

the echoing chill of the lock. "What about the interface cores? And the outright murder of Chalice station?"

Now James lowered his lashes. His inscrutable expression cracked into a grimace of wounding compassion. "The cores we traded were genuine. The thirty pieces of silver, as it were, to confirm the presence of the enemy. And Chalice personnel, curse their bravery, defended their post with their lives."

Kaplin drew a shuddering breath. She bunched her hand and slammed the closure button; and the lock hissed shut, leaving the skip-runner and his haunted bit of conscience to the solitary chill of the space bay.

"Oh, damn you," Kaplin muttered. "Damn you to deepest hell." She needed a coffee, she decided; and every other habit that was ordinary to quiet a vicious inner turmoil. For the favor that MacKenzie James requested for the higher good of the Alliance was nothing short of mutiny. As she left her post and propelled herself through null grav toward the galley, she reflected that Jensen was going to dismember her.

Lieutenant Jensen snapped awake to the realization that *Sail*'s vibrations had changed. She was no longer traveling FTL, but powered by her more obtrusive grav drives. The lieutenant glanced at his chronometer, his worst fear confirmed. *Sail* had deviated from his chosen course and orders. He leaped from his bunk, jammed his legs into the nearest set of coveralls—Harris's by the smell of beer and sweat—and raced full tilt for the bridge.

He found the pilot's chair deserted. The course readout on the autopilot confirmed trouble well enough: *Sail* was currently under gentle acceleration out of the Arinat system. Directly astern, like a thing cursed, lay the cratered lump of rock some forgotten mapper had named Kestra.

Jensen was too enraged to swear.

He spun, plunged through the companionway hatch, and hurried with all speed through the service corridors.

He reached the lock to the space bay. A furious survey showed Kaplin drifting cross-legged in the chamber, twist-

ing and twisting the shock webbing that once had confined
MacKenzie James. She had been weeping. The mechanic's
deep-space suit was gone, of course, along with the skip-
running criminal who had killed its owner for hijack.

"My God, Kappie, why did you let him go?" Jensen's
voice was a scream of unmitigated anger.

The ensign looked up, startled to fear. "Sir! He's Special
Services, and on our side."

Jensen heard, and a greater rage crashed through him.
His handsome face twisted. "Damn you, girl. He's the biggest con artist in the universe. You were *had*, and he was
lying. You're nothing but his pawn, and a traitor." There
would be an inquiry over Harris's death, Jensen's frantic
mind understood. A trial would follow, and under investigation and cross-examination, the flimsy plot arranged at
Chalice would surface and ruin his reputation.

The lieutenant ceased thinking. He reacted on the reflex of a cornered animal, and hammered the green, then
the yellow, then the orange button on the console. The
lock door hissed shut, cutting off Kaplin's panicked
scream. Warning lights flashed, but the hooter that signaled a deep-space jettison never sounded. Kaplin had
disconnected the alarm to release MacKenzie James for
his rendezvous.

For that reason, her pleas could be heard very clearly.
"Jensen! Listen to me! You're MacKenzie's best pawn, and
he knows it!" She launched away from the wall, hammered
her model's hands against the innerlock. "We could stop
James, both of us could stop him! Blow his cover with Special Services, and he's lost his righteous reason to keep
skip-running. You didn't see his face, but I *know*. The re-
morse would put him over the edge."

Jensen's lips stayed fixed in an icy half smile. Deaf to
pity, mindful of nothing beyond the ambition that was his
life, he ground his palm hard on the red jettison button.
The outerlock doors cycled open. Atmosphere vented outward, along with the corpse of the ensign who had dared to
turn triumph into failure.

* * *

Admiral Nortin's office on *New Morning* was sumptuously large, but bare to the point of sterility. On the hard metal bench by the doorway, Jensen sat in his dress uniform. He kept his eyes straight ahead, resisted the urge to search the impeccable white of his jacket for bloodstains the cleaners had soaked out. He waited, rigidly correct, while the admiral's pearl-white fingers paged front to back, through his report.

The words matched the circumstances closely enough: *Sail* had happened across a raid on Chalice station and picked up the trail of a skip-runner who had stolen core intelligence crystals. The lieutenant in command had given chase, followed the space pirate MacKenzie James to Arinat, Van Mere's station. The log spool on the admiral's desk held proof positive of a Syndicate spy post, in the form of a recorded transaction between James and a covert network on Van Mere's. *Sail* had maintained a standard patrol pattern, then pursued as the *Marity* made her getaway. Battle had resulted. *Sail*'s bridge had sustained severe damage, her pilot and her ensign dead in the course of duty. Jensen, sole survivor, had nursed his command back to base.

The admiral finished reading. He raised bleak eyes to the impeccably dressed lieutenant before his desk. He did not point out the unmentionable, that the log spool might hold proof of a Syndicate spy post, but events differed drastically from the report. Neither Jensen nor the admiral wished the particulars of that tape examined for documentation. Jensen staked his future on the surity that Nortin held the power to misplace, or alter, or erase, the flight logs and checkpoint records of *Sail*'s passage between Chalice and Arinat. Jensen balanced everything on an extortionist's secret embedded within proof of his own crimes. Only the admiral's guilt could spare him from certain court-martial and a firing squad.

A minute passed like eternity.

The admiral's cragged face showed no expression when at last he drew breath for conclusion. "Young man," he said sourly. ''For outstanding service, and for your discovery of a Syndicate spy base, you'll report for commendation, decoration, and promotion. Then you'll be transferred into Admiral Duane's division, and I trust we'll never need to set eyes on each other again.''

INTERLUDE: Cavalry

The Syndicate policy of exploiting aliens was often more ruthless in theory than fact. It is good business to have a healthy and productive population. Nor did the managers of the families overlook the value of greed as an incentive. Still, occasionally there was a race too valuable to not exploit. When your family's need is for protection, you seek out a race that could protect your leaders. When the need is for production, you deal with production, you deal with races that are suited to factory work. When you are building toward a military conflict, a race whose culture has bred them for unswerving, if unthinking, loyalty and almost mindless courage is invaluable.

Among the several hundred stars that comprise the Syndicate cluster, almost a hundred alien races have developed. In most cases these were deemed not worth exploitation and their planet was merely watched to insure it was no threat to the Syndicate worlds. You never know when each race might be useful later. Those races that develop into a threat were quickly "adjusted." Sometimes a plague was judged to be most effective, occasionally bombardment from space.

The planetwide culture of the Kosantz was at a level comparable to the Earth's bronze age. Being descended from the unusual combination of herd animals and omnivores, the

113

centaur-shaped Kosantz were endowed with fanatical loyalty to their group and equally fanatical ferocity. Once considered a likely candidate for adjustment, their value in the upcoming war with the Alliance was recognized by the Fleish family.

The Fleish were not one of the fifteen families whose Fathers shared unquestioned power over the Syndicate. They were one of the two dozen lesser families whose holdings rarely were greater than a single world. Two centuries ago there had been over four dozen of these lesser families and ten great ones. Of the two dozen that had made a bid for major family status, five had succeeded and the others had been totally destroyed. Among those expected to attempt to better themselves in the near future, the Fleish family was considered by many the most likely to succeed. With the Kosantz, the ruling Fathers of the Fleish family thought they had found the way. They would ride to prominence on the backs, figuratively, of the Kosantz. The family that controlled the elite infantry of the Syndicate could be no less than a great house.

The Fleish worked with careful patience. They had already been trading with the centauroid aliens for decades. Over a period of five years the Kosantz clans were wooed and traded with. Able to offer wealth and items far beyond their primitive technology's ability to produce, it was not long before the Fleish family representatives became a dominant part of the Kosantz culture. Rather than moderate the Kosantz love of battle, the Fleish then began two years of conquest. It's not hard to be a brilliant general with satellite observations and the careful application of high-tech weaponry. Soon the humans were recognized as the unquestioned leaders of all the Kosantz clans. Those who had questioned this authority were dead or in hiding. In great numbers the Kosantz warriors swore their fidelity to the Fleish family combat managers. An oath they felt was binding for life. Upon taking their oath each Kosantz warrior was given a tempered steel knife and badge sporting the Fleish family crest, signs of their fidelity. Most would die before allowing either to be taken from them. All would attack suicidally, without hesitation, when so ordered.

CHANGE PARTNERS
AND DANCE

by Jody Lynn Nye

THE PARTY OF armed Khalian warriors backed up against the bulkhead of the Fleet destroyer *Colin Powell*. Crouching in a defensive position, they growled fiercely at the surrounding company of Marines. A few of them flicked nervous claws at the safety catches on the Fleet laser rifles they clutched.

The leader hissed out a warning, which was translated by a tall, brightly feathered Nedge who stood well out of the way of the action. "Do not attempt to follow us," the Nedge repeated in heavily accented Alliance Standard to the human Marines surrounding them. "We do not need you softskins to help us kill Khalian traitors. We are more than capable of dealing with them ourselves." Fiercely, the Khalians feinted toward the open hatch of the lift leading to the shuttle bay. The Marines, with long-suffering glances toward their sergeant, moved to stop them.

The *Colin Powell* was hurtling toward the last-known destination of the Khalian pirate Captain Goodheart. After running hard for thirty hours, it had passed the last-known location of the ship that had been carrying the late and now-legendary Commander Lohengrin Sales in pursuit of the pirate vessel. Traces of debris and matter swirling through the space around the *Colin Powell* had been analyzed by the

sensors as belonging to a Fleet vessel and another ship. By
the telltale impurities, the second one was judged to have
been constructed of materials manufactured in both Alliance and Syndicate shipyards. Evidently, the Fleet ship and
the pirate had destroyed each other.

When it reached the general area, the *Colin Powell* began
scanning the local system for signs of the pirate's safe port.
Life existed on three of the ten planets and two of the many
moons circling them, revolving around the yellow star, according to long-range telemetry. It would take time to pick
out the best prospect. The troops within had nothing to do
but hone their skills and wait, and try to reason with their
new allies, a squad of Khalian warriors.

"Look, Blitvan, it's bad enough we have to work with
you musty-smelling, rat-faced furballs," "Tarzan" Shillitoe complained, "but you're making the exercises unnecessarily difficult by arguing every order with me." The
Nedge translator chirped out the sergeant's words in Khalian, and the warriors scowled. The big sergeant was beginning to regret issuing laser rifles to the Weasels for weapons
exercise. He figured they'd try mutiny or something equally
stupid sooner or later. It had only been a matter of time
after the deck officer taught the Weasels to use the power
lifts, giving them access to every part of the ship except
Engineering, Arsenal, and the bridge, to keep them from
feeling trapped on the cabin level. They learned quickly,
and now here they were, making a break for it. The shrinks
were likely right when they said the Khalia were scared
shitless, and too proud to show it. The Alliance ships were
out of their control, and they were surrounded by large enemies with unlimited firepower. Even a Khalian warrior had
to sleep sometime. These lads were beginning to show the
symptoms of fatigue.

Blitvan snarled out a few syllables, and the Nedge hastily
repeated his words in clipped Standard. "Flattery will not
serve here," was the chieftain's reply. "It is our honor to
dispose of the dishonorable thieves of our race, and we do
not wish to share it with you."

"Your supreme chief ordered you to serve me," Shillitoe

spoke slowly and clearly. He pushed up to Blitvan and glared down into the Khalian leader's eyes, which were glowing with fury. Blitvan wasn't very big for a Khalian, but he was feisty. "I am in charge of this mission, and you will be deployed as I see fit. Otherwise, you're not getting to the shuttle bay or on that landing craft, and I won't give you any oxygen equipment if you do manage to get aboard." The Nedge hesitated, ducking its beak protectively toward its breast feathers. "Translate, dammit!" Tarzan roared. His voice echoed in the metal-domed chamber.

"He understands you," the unit's medical officer, Dr. Mack Dalle, interposed quickly, watching the Khalian's face. "So do a few of the others. They must speak some Standard."

"Then why do we need him?" Tarzan pointed at the quivering Nedge.

"Point of honor," Blitvan said suddenly in Standard. "I am deprived of the rest of my entourage, but I demand at leasht a few of my perquithites. I will communicate with you in your language since my chief demandsh it. But I object to the indignity of the thituation."

Tarzan controlled his face with difficulty. Blitvan had a ridiculous lisp to go with his oversize front teeth. Some of the other Apes were grinning openly.

When the general order had come down that the Khalia had surrendered and were now part of the Alliance, there was disbelief and fury among the Fleet personnel. How could the Khalia, who had been the Alliance's fiercest enemy, suddenly change sides? It wasn't believable. Medical Service's headshrinkers were kept busy analyzing the nightmares of combat veterans who couldn't take the change in status. Protesters filled the x-waves communicating their displeasure with their representatives in the Alliance Council.

But orders were orders. Fleet personnel were expected to welcome their new brothers-in-arms with, if not friendship, at least well-veiled hostility. In the Apes' quarters, the disposer was kept busy, disintegrating kilos' worth of war trophies: Khalian-tail coats, skin rugs and chair covers, and

other, more unusual constructions. Jordan was persuaded
with difficulty to conceal his ear collection, since he couldn't
be bullied into burning it.

The Apes had a slightly easier time adjusting to Weasels
as allies than did most of their fellow Marines. After their
experiences on Target, and what followed after, it was a
reasonable progression, if not a simple one. The shrinks
listened to them one at a time for a few days, and pronounced them ready for joint missions as soon as Command
required. His fellow sergeants harassed Shillitoe about being a Weasel-lover, and predicted that the faithless Khalia
would probably let him down when he needed them most.
Tarzan ignored them and tried to go on with business as if
it was usual. Privately, he was proud of his men for handling the situation better than the other units.

Specialist Pirelli and Medical Officer Mack Dalle spent
hours in the rec chamber instructing the others in a few
phrases of Khalian, mostly military orders and queries about
health. Pirelli was a Khalian convert, after Weasel volunteers had risked their lives to help him when he had been
wounded on Target. Some of the Apes were more responsive than others to the lessons. Sokada had more or less
adopted the Khalian cub he'd orphaned during their mission.

"What about insults?" Dockerty had asked, shouting
above the voices of the others, who were repeating aloud
the squeals and hisses for "set lasers to pinpoint" and "can
you move your forelimb?" "We want to know when they're
calling us names. You've met Blitvan."

"Yeah, that's true," Pirelli had said. " 'Why are you
called Apes?' he wanted to know. 'Are you humans not all
Apes?' Miserable Weasel. I wonder why we don't mind
calling ourselves names, but we don't like to hear it from
other types."

Dockerty pressed Dalle. "You know it won't be all nice-
nice. I want to be able to respond appropriately. Come on.
It could help dispel the tension."

The two instructors looked at each other. It was a reasonable request. The Khalia certainly weren't all taking the

change from enemy to ally that well, either. Mack shrugged his narrow shoulders and, with Shillitoe's permission, turned to the translation program in the comp system for Khalian equivalents to "your mother wears army boots."

As a result of the instruction, the Marines could understand some of the muttering going on in the ranks of Khalian warriors. It increased in volume and ferocity when Blitvan accepted grudgingly Sergeant Shillitoe's orders and commanded them to back away from the lift car.

"But I will not acthept the rank of common soldier," Blitvan sneered, as the Apes made way for them.

"Dockerty is my second in command," Shillitoe stated. "You will be equal with him, with insignia to match." Keeping his expression bland, Dockerty made a half salute to the glaring Weasel. "All right? No more backchat. I'm going back to the rec room now. You can join me there if you want. Or go take a nap. At ease. Dismissed!"

Within a few hours, telemetry announced that there was a likely prospect in the star system dead ahead of the *Colin Powell*. The fourth planet had a nitrox atmosphere, and .90 g gravity. It was inhabited; sensors picked up a hundred-odd life readings.

"Some of them are human," Dalle announced, reading off the data as it scrolled up the screen embedded in the recreation-room table.

"We already knew there were humans helping them," Shillitoe replied, his feet crossed on the table next to a half-finished beer. "Take that ugly spud helping them, the rat-face, what was his name? There must be others. How many Khalians? Command figured there couldn't be too many, not more than a hundred or two. Still, that's too many for our unit to take, even combined with the Khalians. I registered a protest with Captain Slyne, but he's still got the idea that it's smart to land the units thirty minutes apart. So he won't lose any more than he has to, he says. They must give them stupid pills in Officers' Training. An interval like that could kill us."

"I can't make sense of the other readings." Mack continued to study the screen. "The blood pressure and body temperature are right for Khalia, but the body-mass indicator is all wrong. Too high."

"Probably a screwup in the program," Shillitoe said, peering over the screen. "Missing a decimal point or something. Ask for a clarification. I bet you it says the humans weigh five hundred kilos each."

As Mack reached for the keypad, the screen cleared, and a red-bordered graphic appeared in its place. "Attention. Attention, please," came the pleasant voice of the communications officer. "We are approaching orbit. Landing parties to the shuttle bay."

Tarzan tossed back the last ounces of beer and rose to his feet. "Okay, boys and ferrets," he roared, his booming voice carrying to the rear of the recreation chamber over the clamor of voices and the clatter of game pieces and crockery. "Just like in the drill. Move it!"

The mission was slated for three units, under the command of Captain Slyne. The Apes were A Unit, put down ahead of two other units completely comprised of human Fleet Marines. Their job was to secure the command post and destroy communications gear as quickly as possible, holding off the other unfriendlies until the second and third units arrived. With the help of the Khalians, Shillitoe was to identify and capture leaders.

Within the landing capsule, the Khalians watched suspiciously as the Apes locked down their suit helmets, activating instrument lights and comlinks. There were two Apes for every Khalian, a force of numbers that made them very uneasy. Blitvan had flatly refused retooled armor for his party, insisting that they would interfere with his warriors' mobility. Instead, they were issued medical wristlets and back-mounted oxypacks, and fitted with communication earplugs, an obsoleted version of the helmet comlink. Furry ears twitched around the capsule as the connection tone sounded, hooking them into the Command frequency.

"How do they know where we are going?" asked Thalet,

Blitvan's lieutenant, in Khalian. "Their priests use no incantations that I recognize."

"Silent prayer," Blitvan hissed swiftly. "Keep your eyes and ears open, as a brave warrior must, and we may yet return to our home world."

The audio pickups carried every word to Shillitoe and his corporals, who exchanged wary glances.

The capsule thudded down and burned along the ground through deciduous undergrowth, burying itself partly into the soft soil of the fourth planet from the yellow star. The air beyond the hatch was warm and fragrant, peppered by the sharp taste of industrial pollution somewhere in the distance.

"These pirates must have repair or manufacturing facilities out there," Shillitoe growled. "We'd better find out what it is they're making. I don't want to destroy unnecessarily. By the numbers, now. Move out! One! Two! Three!"

Following the sergeant's barked orders, Marines and Khalians sprang out of the hatch, weapons at the ready.

"Douse that fire before the pirates see our smoke!" Tarzan shouted, pointing at the undergrowth that had burst into flame from the capsule's frictive landing. Two of the Apes ran to obey, carrying handheld extinguisher units from the capsule's storage.

They had landed at the concealed top of a ridge with the sun behind them, to make it difficult for anyone in the forested valley below to see them. It was late afternoon, local time. Lights were beginning to come on in the habitations in the valley.

"The locals can't be expecting us," Ellis said, peering through the brush with infrared binoptics. "They must not have much in the way of advance tracking systems."

"Traitors do not deserve to have the highest grade of equipment," Blitvan observed.

"Methinks the Weas—Khalian doth protest too much," grumbled Viedre.

The soil underfoot was soft and lightly packed. Each footfall kicked up little clouds of dust. The G force was noticeably lighter here than was standard on Fleet vessels. Effortlessly, Jordan threw his heavy plasma cannon up in the air and caught it, smiling at the reduction in its weight. Marks hoisted another cannon onto his back and paced beside Jordan into the valley. Dockerty beckoned to his sharpshooters, fanning them out through the undergrowth. Shillitoe nodded approval. "If we have to go hand-to-hand, activate grav boots. I don't want something tossing you around because you mass less down here."

Unbuckling the holster guard of his laser pistol, Mack Dalle sniffed the air and looked around. The Fleet doctor wasn't much of a soldier, the sergeant thought, but he was resilient and observant. Shillitoe relied almost as heavily on him as he did on his Apes.

The Khalians hunched in a knot behind the stern of the capsule, peering over the valley below and growling to one another, paying no heed to the sergeant's order to form up.

"What's the matter with you?" asked Shillitoe, stalking up to Blitvan. The Nedge translator stepped forward. "I don't want to hear it from you," the sergeant forestalled him, waving a finger at the chieftain. "I want to hear it from him."

"This does not smell Khalian," Blitvan said in a suspicious tone. "There is something else here."

"Tell me. Keep your voice down; the audio pickup will transmit everything you say."

"The lights are too high, and there are too many of them for this much starlight."

"Perhaps the pirates took over a human colony," Ellis offered.

"Negative," Shillitoe said. "There are no Alliance colonies in this system." He worried again that the captain had weakened them unnecessarily by dividing the forces too far. Investigating an unknown situation, the units should have come down boom, boom, boom. He strode to the head of the file next to Utun, who was point officer. Training the telemetry units forward, she stepped out.

Silently, the unit moved down the slopes of the hill under the shadow cast by the ridge. A tiny thread of warm cooking smells passed by on the wind, and the distant lowing of herd animals mixed with the susurrus of swaying grasses.

"Nice place," said Dalle suddenly, from the back of the line.

"But not Khalian," Blitvan insisted, the lisp crackling on open audio frequency. "See."

As they broke out of the woods a third of the way from the bottom of the valley, they came upon corrals of farm animals and huge, hangarlike structures inside which the Marines could just make out the shapes of steel-based machinery and square bales of dried grasses.

"Too high for Khalia to use," Shillitoe agreed. "So this is a human complex. But whose? A renegade human colony on the edge of Khalian space?" He changed frequency on his commset and listened. "B Unit? C Unit?" He clicked back. "Neither of the others have made the drop yet. No one's in our range. Dammit, this is an anomaly!"

Within a few hundred yards, they reached a cluster of low wooden houses in a clearing. Along one side of the close-set buildings lay a communal vegetable garden, in which wooden poles lashed together in pairs and festooned with leafy vines stood among lower plants hung with ripening cucurbits and capsicums. Rising up from the center of the small community was a tall, white building constructed of the local stone. It had no windows below the second story, and an array of spiral antennas above a barred window at the top of the square central tower.

"Krims, if that doesn't say 'Look in here,' nothing does," Viedre stated. "We'll find our pirate leaders in there, if anywhere."

Softly, they made their way along a muddy path through the garden and into the midst of the village. The pathways among the houses were well worn. Sodden patches had been filled in here and there with gravel. The wooden walls of the houses showed signs of age. Water rot had swollen patches and caused corners of boards to flake and crumble into shards. The doors of the houses all faced inward, toward the white building.

"Bad planning. There's only one exit from that structure."

"This has been here a long time," Mack said. "Did the pirates take refuge with humans? Or has this rebellion been building longer than we ever guessed?"

"Why would we, or you, need these big doors?" Blitvan hissed, annoyed at having to respond to yet another of Shillitoe's subordinates. "See, they are double, swinging out in two vertical sections."

From the wide gate of the stone structure, the Marines heard the sounds of marching feet on stones.

"The night watch. Conceal yourselves."

The Marines were just barely hidden within the shadows when six guards emerged from the gate and passed under the lantern at the corner of the barbican. Shillitoe studied them, and let out his breath.

"Humans, all right," he said into his comlink. "How many are there?"

"Don't know," Utun complained, holding out her unidirectional scan. "Could be one, could be dozens behind those. Something in this white stone screws up transmission."

"Syndicate!" Ellis added excitedly on the private channel to Shillitoe, studying the approaching men. "I remember those uniforms from briefings. But whose are those badges? Red rectangle with blue 'X' corner to corner. I don't remember that family."

"Sarge, they're coming right at us. They must know we're here," Utun announced urgently.

"So much for a concealed approach. Utun, are they carrying any instrumentation?"

"No, Sarge."

"Then they're relying on eyeball contact. Prepare to withdraw. We've got to learn what this place is before we go diving in. Blitvan, keep your men, er . . . well, men behind us."

"I hear," muttered the Khalian into his pickup. "What is before us?"

"Humans."

Blitvan crept up behind Shillitoe, followed by his entire force of ten Weasels. He watched the guards come within feet of them, and then turn away, following the path to the left. "But those are Syndicate humans." His small eyes shone with a red light. He turned to his warriors and let out a warbling cry. The warriors answered, and they rushed forward into the midst of the approaching humans, the Nedge following, flapping its feathered upper limbs and shrieking.

"Where's he going? Blitvan, come back here!"

"I told you they'd defect," spat Dockerty. "The Syndicate owned them first. We never had their loyalty. We're going to have to kill all the damned Khalians before we can get through to the Syndicate men." Dockerty flung himself onto his belly and aimed his laser rifle, giving orders to his concealed sharpshooters to do the same.

Shillitoe, too, was afraid the Weasels had turned back to their former masters. If the Khalians turned against them, there would be only a scant handful of defenders until B and C Units arrived. By the time Blitvan's warriors reached the Syndicate men, he realized he needn't have worried. The Khalians threw themselves on the stunned guards, tearing at their faces and throats with razor-tipped claws.

"Evil humans, we defy you!" crowed the Nedge, translating Blitvan's triumphant cry. "We serve our new masters, the Alliance. Death to you!"

"Yeah! Come on, men!" Shillitoe whooped, arcing an arm over his head and running after the Khalians. "We can't let our furry brethren have all the fun."

Screaming and battering at their small attackers, the guards backed up into the courtyard, calling out for help. Surprise had prevented any of them from reaching for weapons. They seemed bewildered by the speed of the Khalians' reactions. Any time one of them put a hand on a holster, sharp teeth closed on his fingers, and the same creature raked talons through the fabric of his uniform or the flesh of his throat. Almost before the Fleet Marines had entered the courtyard, two of the Syndicate men were dead. Dockerty's sharpshooters had taken out two more before having to rise and run after the rest of the Alliance unit.

"Pause all skyward!" cried a deep voice, as floodlights on in the stonewalled enclosure flared sunbright down onto the battle. From a doorway in the tower appeared a tall, impressive man clad in the same uniform, but decorated at the shoulders and throat with silver.

"He says break it up," the Nedge translated for the Apes.

"An elder cousin or first brother," said Ellis. "This is probably his proprietory."

"Take him!" Shillitoe ordered. "He's one of the ones we have to get for Command."

The Marines made for the tall man. He smiled at them, his gray eyes glittering, and stepped backward through the double doorway. From behind him strode two lines of huge, centauroid monsters, clad in armor and carrying spears as well as oversize laser pistols. The Fleet sergeant stared, trying to see faces in the folds of thick, hairless skin at the front of the heads. The eyes were evident, glowing slits under heavy semicircular ridging; and surprising saw-edged teeth lined the lipless mouth at the bottom of the expressionless faces. The ridges also guarded parallel sets of arcing frills, which bracketed the eyes and mouth. Ears? Noses?

The two monsters in the lead pulled spears out of the quivers slung on their backs, aimed, and threw. The Apes barely recovered enough to duck out of the way in time. The Khalians, tearing up the human guard, paid no attention.

As soon as the last of the gray-green monsters was out of the door, it slammed shut, sealing the Syndicate man safely inside.

"Get past them if you can! Take him alive!" Shillitoe ordered. "What in hell are those?" he demanded, rolling. He slid on the cobbles and came up with his own laser pistol out. The gray-green creatures advanced on four huge, round, flat-soled feet, sturdy as tree trunks and every bit as stable.

"Bodyguard," Ellis panted. "But what kind of creature I have no idea. God, are they ugly."

"They are Kosantzu," chittered the Nedge, pressing itself into a corner away from the fighting. "The ones who stand. Even when they die."

The Kosantzu, moving with a sleepy, slow-motion grace, each reached behind it and pulled another spear from its quiver. The spear shaft rested like a feather in the angle between three massive manipulative digits, which looked like the business ends of horseshoe magnets. As one, the Kosantzu raised their spears.

"Down!" shouted Shillitoe, though there was no cover in the courtyard behind which they could hide. They would have to keep moving. "Fire at will!" The Kosantzu seemed to be obeying the order, showering the Marines with the spears they seemed to prefer to their oversize rifles.

Dockerty's men were good, scoring on Kosantz flesh no fewer than one out of two shots. The wounds bled redly but laser fire seemed to do little to stop them. Even a direct hit on the face was nearly impossible. The Kosantz would slit its eyes closed and draw in the flaps of flesh, leaving a featureless expanse of gray. Fortunately, the four-legged giants moved slowly, deliberately, giving the humans time to maneuver. There was no way a human could survive *corps à corps* fighting with one of these. They were doing a very effective job of keeping the Fleet unit away from the entrance to the tower.

"We need more firepower than this! Jordan!"

"Cover me," the Marine said, dropping to one knee with his plasma cannon on his shoulder. His fellows kept up a steady barrage of laser bolts and slugs while he aimed at the Kosantz closest to him.

There was a deafening burst as the plasma bolt struck the Kosantz full in the chest. The explosion tore one of the centauroid bodyguards apart and rocked the creature behind it up on its back feet. Stunned, it dropped its spear and rifle. Shillitoe and three others rushed in and bore the Kosantz over. It thudded heavily to the ground and snaked out its flexible arms, grabbing for them. It caught hold of Sokada's leg and started to squeeze. The Marine's face drained of blood, and he fell over.

"Sarge!"

Shillitoe jumped in with his sword drawn and hacked at the arm. Sokada kicked at the Kosantz's face, but it merely shut up its features behind the protective skin ridges. The creature maintained an impressive level of strength for one whose thorax had a hole blown right through it by a plasma charge. In less than a minute, shock caused it to lose its grip. It flailed its arms blindly until it stopped moving. Shillitoe pulled Sokada clear and helped the man limp over to the corner where Dalle waited with the Nedge.

Dockerty and Marks singled out another Kosantz. They discovered that not only were the giants slow-moving, but they had almost no neck, and the "waist" wasn't very flexible, so it was possible to keep one spinning on its huge feet while they peppered it with lasers, searching for vital organs or vulnerable spots. The tough, loose skin seemed to absorb slugs, so those served only to annoy more than injure. Something was getting through to its slow brain, because the slitted green eyes were becoming wilder. It had run out of spears, and was returning laser fire, but its aim was poor because its targets kept moving out of the way. The Kosantz roared, furiously trying to hit the Marines with laser blasts. The courtyard was full of etched and half-melted cobbles.

"How in hell do you make one of these stop?" Viedre panted, dodging.

"It's got to run out of blood eventually," Dockerty said. "It's getting tired. Marks, ready when it's got its back to you. The spine is your best bet."

Marks steadied the plasma cannon on his shoulder, waited, and fired. The burst glanced off the Kosantz directly in the middle of the horizontal portion of its back. The bulk of the shell burst far beyond the battle. Shrieking, it dropped its laser pistol and reached for the smoking wound with both hands. Unbelievably, the arms were jointed to allow movement as good behind as before its body.

Dockerty stared in disbelief as the Kosantz pulled its arms forward again, swiveled on two feet, and charged straight for Marks. No more lumbering giant—this beast was mad.

He and Viedre tried to head it off, firing steady beams into its chest, but it paid no attention to the burning wounds. It bore down on Marks, hoisting its limp rear legs forward behind it. As Marks gaped up into its face, the Kosantz seized his chest between its hands and squeezed.

It was over almost before Dockerty could turn around. The plasma cannon fell off the man's shoulder with a clatter. Marks let out no more than a breathless squeak before the life was crushed out of him. With visible effort, the Kosantz flung the Marine's limp body against a wall. It watched, swaying, as Marks struck and slid down into a heap. Then the upper body collapsed, slowly folding forward until its hands brushed the ground. But it never fell over.

Shillitoe left Sokada with the doctor strapping his leg, and surveyed the courtyard. Blitvan and his brood were in trouble. Khalia weren't as strong as humans. The low gravity of this planet gave them an advantage, but the human guard had superior weaponry and armor, which protected them from a lot of the Khalia's favorite attacks. Three of the Khalians still standing had bad burns and wounds. In a little while, there would be no Khalians left alive or no Syndicate soldiers, and Shillitoe needed prisoners.

"Blitvan!" he called over the comlink. "I've got a better place you can use your speed. Come and help us clean up the Kosantzu. They move slowly, but watch it! They're strong!"

The Khalian's head swiveled toward him. "Do I have autonomy to order my warriors? And your cannon weapons?"

"Yes, dammit, just move before they know what we're doing! Jordan, you shoot where Blitvan tells you."

"Aye, sir."

Blitvan shrilled out a cry, and the Weasels poured away from the amazed human guards, who watched them disengage from their individual battles and run away. The captain of the guard recovered and, wiping blood from his face, ordered pursuit of the furred menace. They were met halfway by the Fleet Marines.

The Khalians swarmed all over the slow-moving Kosantzu. Blitvan was a clever general. On his orders, his warriors struck swiftly, tearing at the protective flaps covering the Kosantzu's features, digging talons into the sensitive eyes and nostril slits, and tearing open their torso armor, and then jumping away before the slow giants could grab them. One of the Khalians was knocked down and stomped to death by a Kosantz before it could move out of the way, but it looked like an accident to Shillitoe. Once a Kosantz was blinded, the Khalians concentrated laser fire on the back of the massive neck and the curve of its spine until the creature went limp.

One of the blind Kosantzu went berserk, throwing the small Khalians in all directions. On Blitvan's shrieked orders, three of them picked up one of the Kosantz's discarded spears and held it angled upward between the courtyard wall and the cobblestoned floor. They screamed taunts at the giant, goading it into charging them. Unable to see the pike, it blundered forward, hands out to grab its noisy little opponents. Its body rammed itself almost eight feet along the spear's shaft before it died.

Shillitoe and the others moved in on the human guards. Ellis knocked one down and ripped the helmet off the man's head when his mouth began to move. A big male with a curved sword charged toward the sergeant. Shillitoe backed away and parried with his own sword.

"Sarge, this one was radioing for help!" Ellis announced over the comlink.

"Knock him out and give him to the doc. We'll keep him for Captain Slyne. Let me see if I can raise our fearless leader yet." Shillitoe nudged the frequency selector with his chin and listened for voices, watching his opponent closely. The man had a silver insignia on his chest instead of the simple blue ones worn by the other guards. This could be a prize, if the Marines could take him alive, but the man was good with his sword. The guard parried under Shillitoe's sword and scored on the flexible armor over the sergeant's midsection.

"Doesn't this radio machine work, human sergeant?" Blitvan's voice inquired over the headset.

"Do gerbils chew cardboard?" grunted Alvin as he side-stepped a blow from the guard's sword, and riposted with one of his own. Ah, near miss to the other man's temple. He was getting closer.

"I do not know if we will survive this fight, so I must ask, at risk of giving offense. Why are you and your followers called Apes? Are you humans not all apes?"

The question would have bothered Tarzan before, but now he just smiled grimly. "Yeah, but we're special. We're more ape than any of the other apes."

"I think I am honored to know you, Sergeant of the Apes."

"That's Tarzan."

"A Unit, do you copy?" It was Captain Slyne, on inter-rupt frequency.

"Thank Krim, where are you? Sir," Shillitoe exclaimed, jumping back to avoid a slice.

"About a hundred yards behind you, on line-of-sight contact, with B Unit. C Unit is just landing. They were monitoring and insisted that the time interval was too great, and I agreed."

"Our medical officer is holding a couple of the Syndicate men alive and unconscious for your questioning. But we've got other problems," Shillitoe said, looking for an opening. He didn't want to kill the guard, but the man was making it difficult for him to get in a knockout blow with the flat of his sword. His own body armor was nicked in several spots.

"I see 'em. Holy earth mother, what are those?" asked Unit B commander over Shillitoe's headset.

"The Syndicate's new flunkeys. Care to try a turn with one of them?"

"God, no. They'd probably step on my feet."

"Well, they're tough, but they don't move too quickly. Would you mind getting in here and helping? If it isn't too goddamned much trouble? One of our prisoners was just transmitting a cry for help!"

"Well, Sergeant," demanded Captain Slyne sternly, "if the Khalian pirates aren't based here, where are they?"

Did all brass have ball bearings for brains? Shillitoe tried to keep his voice level. "Captain, with all respect, I'd say the pirates—or any Khalians—are the least of your worries this time around. This is a Syndicate base. Would you mind doing something about our big friends here? We haven't got the complement to deal with these things." He took a quick step back and risked a quick glance around. Almost half the Khalians were down or visibly wounded. His own men had formed along the perimeter and were firing at the massive aliens whenever they could get a clear shot. "The Khalians can't hold them off forever."

There was a short pause while Alvin could hear metal rattling over the open command link.

"Time to dance, Sergeant. Tell your men to flatten out when I give you the word."

Alvin managed to slap his sword into the unprotected head of his opponent. Flipping over to general broadcast he barked the order. "Blitvan, everyone, hit the deck!"

The barrage of heavy laser fire started one second after the captain gave the order. Only later did Shillitoe realize he had thought of both the humans and the Khalians as "his men." Even the massive Kosantzu couldn't absorb the energy from a direct hit and survive. The air thrummed from the power contained by the five-centimeter-thick laser beams passing inches over the squatting noncom's head. To Shillitoe, it was the prettiest dance music he had ever heard.

INTERLUDE: Loyalty

The level and mechanizations of those who revel in the mind games called intelligence and espionage are at best convoluted. The infiltration of the Fleet was accomplished on many levels. A generation ago the far-ranging traders of the Syndicate watched as the Alliance absorbed or conquered each culture it encountered. By its very nature the Alliance had to overwhelm or destroy every threat to its existence. The lessons of the long dark age after the fall of the Empire were still too fresh to allow for any other policy.

To the fiercely competitive managers of the Syndicate, it was apparent that being included in the Alliance would mean the eventual destruction of their own way of life. Too many of their policies directly opposed the more liberal tenets of Alliance politics. Nor would their populations accept the structured way of life that characterized their worlds if the vista of unlimited opportunity was an alternative. While to the Alliance the Syndicate was responsible for the millions of deaths caused by Khalian raids, those raised on Syndicate worlds saw themselves as patriots using whatever they had to stop inevitable Alliance aggression. They were fighting to maintain a society established over hundreds of years. If more repressive and suppressed, their citizens were also more secure, supported by the paternal family. If those in the Alliance would find abhorrent the low level of freedom of a typical Syndicate citizen, a Syndicate resident would be no less repulsed by the poverty and even hunger allowed by the laissez-faire policies of the opponent. Each side saw the other as evil. Each viewed their actions as being necessitated by defense. The result was that most Syndicate spies remained loyal to their family, even after capture. Even more importantly, surprisingly few of their deeply planted sleeper agents had "gone native" and changed their allegiance to the Alliance.

Caught in a situation that could only end in defeat, the Fleet began to react with desperate measures. With the war increasing in intensity and ship-to-ship actions growing from duels to full squadron actions, the need to find their enemy's base of operations became imperative. The best and the newest technology was soon allocated exclusively to finding the Syndicate systems and ascertaining their strength.

SMASH AND GRAB
by David Drake

THE RECEPTIONIST FACING Captain Kowacs wasn't armed,
but there was enough weaponry built into her desk to stop
a destroyer. Her face was neutral, composed. If she was
supposed to do anything besides watch the Marine captain,
she was fucking off.

This was like going through a series of airlocks; but what
was on the far end of *these* doors was a lot more dangerous
than vacuum.

The inner door opened to admit a guide/escort—
Kowacs's third guide since hand-delivered orders jerked
him out of the barracks assigned to the 121st Marine Reaction Company.

His company, his Headhunters. And would to God he
was back with them now.

"If you'll come this way, please, Captain Kowacs," said
the guide.

This one was a young human male, built like a weight-
lifter and probably trained as well as a man could be trained.
Kowacs figured he could take the kid if it came to that . . .
but only because training by itself wasn't enough against
the instant ruthlessness you acquired if you survived your
first month in a reaction company.

Captain Miklos Kowacs had survived seven years. If that wasn't a record, it was damn close to one.

Kowacs was stocky and powerful, with cold eyes and black hair that curled on the backs of his wrists and hands. The Fleet's reconstructive surgeons were artists, and they had a great deal of practice. Kowacs was without scars.

On his body.

"Turn left at the corridor, please, sir," said the escort. He was walking a pace behind and a pace to Kowacs's side. Like a well-trained dog . . . which was about half true: if the kid had been *only* muscle, he wouldn't have been here.

Here was Building 93 of the Administration Annex, Fleet Headquarters, Port Tau Ceti. That was the only thing Kowacs knew for sure about the place.

Except that he was sure he'd rather be anywhere else.

Building 93 didn't house clerical overflow. The doors were like bank vaults; the electronic security system was up to the standards of the code section aboard a command-and-control vessel; the personnel were cool, competent, and as tight as Nick Kowacs's asshole during an insertion.

"Here, please, sir," said the escort, stopping beside a blank door. He gestured. "This is as far as I go."

Kowacs looked at him. He wouldn't mind seeing how the kid shaped up in the Headhunters. Good material, better than most of the replacements they got . . . and Marine Reaction Companies always needed replacements.

He shivered. They'd needed replacements while there were Weasels to fight. Not anymore.

"Have a good life, kid," Kowacs said as blue highlights in the door panel suddenly spelled SPECIAL PROJECTS/TEITELBAUM with the three-stars-in-a-circle of a vice admiral.

The door opened.

Nick Kowacs was painfully aware that he was wearing the pair of worn fatigues he hadn't had time to change when the messenger rousted him; also that the best uniform he owned wasn't up to meeting a vice admiral. He grimaced, braced himself, and strode through the doorway.

The door closed behind him. The man at the desk of the

lushly appointed office wore civilian clothes. He was in his mid-forties, bigger than Kowacs and in good physical shape.

Kowacs recognized him. The man wasn't a vice admiral. His name was Grant, and he was much worse.

I thought he was dead!

The man behind the desk looked up from the hologram projector his blunt, powerful fingers toyed with.

He grinned. "What's the matter, Kowacs?" he said. "You look like you've seen a ghost."

Grant gestured. "Pull a chair closer and sit down," he said. He grinned again. There was no more humor in the expression the second time. "Hoped I was dead, huh?"

Kowacs shrugged.

The chairs along the back wall had firm, user-accommodating cushions that would shape to his body without collapsing when he sat in them. The one Kowacs picked slid easily as his touch reversed magnets to repel a similar set in the floor.

Keep cool, learn what hole you're in, and get the hell out.

Nobody likes to talk to the Gestapo.

Though if it came to that, Reaction Company Marines didn't have a lot of friends either.

Assuming the office's owner was the vice admiral in the holographic portrait filling the back wall, Teitelbaum was a woman. In the present display, she wore a dress uniform and was posed against a galactic panorama, but there were probably other views loaded into the system: Teitelbaum and her family; Teitelbaum with political dignitaries; Teitelbaum as a young ensign performing heroically in combat.

Special Projects.

"You work for Admiral Teitelbaum, then?" Kowacs said as he seated himself carefully.

"I'm borrowing her office," Grant said without apparent interest. He spun the desk projector so that the keyboard faced Kowacs, then tossed the Marine a holographic chip. "Go on," he ordered. "Play it."

Kowacs inserted the chip into the reader. His face was

blank, and his mind was almost empty. He hadn't really felt anything since the Weasels surrendered.

The message was date-slugged three days before, while the 121st was still on the way to Port Tau Ceti. An official head-and-shoulders view of Kowacs popped into the air beneath the date, then vanished into another burst of glowing letters:

FROM: BUPERS/M32/110173/Sec21(Hum)/SPL
TO: KOWACS, Miklos Alexeievitch
SUBJECT: Promotion to MAJOR

Effective from this date . . .

Kowacs looked across the desk at the civilian. The air between them continued to spell out bureaucratese in green letters.

Grant's face was too controlled to give any sign that he had expected the Marine to react visibly. "Here," he said. "These are on me."

He tossed Kowacs a pair of major's collar tabs: hollow black triangles that would be filled for a lieutenant colonel. "Battle-dress style," Grant continued. "Since it doesn't seem that you have much use for dress uniforms."

"I don't have much use for any uniforms," said Nick Kowacs as his tongue made the decision his mind had wavered over since the day he and his Headhunters had taken the surrender of the Khalian Grand Council. "I'm getting out."

Grant laughed. "The hell you are, mister," he said. "You're too valuable to the war effort."

The data chip was reporting Kowacs's service record to the present. Part of the Marine's mind was amazed at the length of the listing of his awards and citations. He supposed he'd known about the decorations when he received them, but they really didn't matter.

His family had mattered before the Khalians massacred them.

And it mattered that the 121st Marine Reaction Company

had cut the tails off more dead Weasels than any other unit of comparable size.

"Fuck you," said Nick Kowacs distinctly. "The war's over."

"Don't you believe it, mister," Grant replied. There was only the slightest narrowing of his cold blue eyes to indicate that he'd heard *everything* the Marine had said. "We've got a real enemy, now—the Syndicate. The humans who've been using the Weasels for their cannon fodder. The people *behind* the whole war."

Kowacs shut off the projector. The list was reminding him of too much that he usually managed to forget while he was awake: hot landings . . . civilians that neither God nor the Headhunters had been able to save from the Khalia . . . Marines who hadn't survived—or worse, who mostly hadn't survived.

"I don't . . ." Kowacs muttered.

"We'll be raising mixed units of our best and the Khalia's best to go after the Syndicate," Grant said. "You'll want to be in on the real kill, won't you?"

From his grin, Grant knew *exactly* how Kowacs would feel about the suggestion of working with Weasels. It was the civilian's response to being told to fuck himself.

"Besides," Grant went on, "what would *you* do as a civilian, Kowacs?"

"I'll find something," said the Marine as he stood up. "Look, I'm leaving now."

"Siddown, mister!" Grant said in a tone that Kowacs recognized because he'd used it often enough himself; the tone that meant the order would be obeyed or the next sound would be a shot.

Kowacs met Grant's eyes; and smiled; and sat in the chair again.

"Let's say that you're here because of your special knowledge," the civilian said. Grant could control his voice and his breathing, but Kowacs saw the quick flutter of the arteries in the big man's throat. "If you know who I am, then you know too much to think you can just hang up your uniform anytime you please."

But I wouldn't have to work much harder to be buried in that uniform.

Aloud, Kowacs said, "You didn't call me in here to promote me."

"You got *that* right," Grant said, his voice dripping with the disdain of a man who doesn't wear a uniform for a man who does. "We've got a job for you and your Headhunters."

Kowacs laughed. "What's the matter? Run out of your own brand of sewage workers?"

"Don't push," said the civilian quietly.

After a moment, Grant resumed, "This is right up your alley, Kowacs. The Syndicate used cut-out bases in all their dealings with the Khalia, so the Weasels don't have the locations of any of the Syndicate home worlds. But we think we've got the coordinates of a Syndicate base—so you're going to grab prisoners and navigational data there before the Syndicate realizes they're at risk."

Kowacs frowned as he considered what he'd just been told. *There had to be a catch. . . .*

"All right," he said. "What's the catch?"

Grant shrugged. "No catch," he said.

"If there wasn't more to this job than you're telling me," Kowacs said, unsure whether he was angry, frustrated, or simply confused, "we wouldn't be briefed by the fucking Eight Ball Command, *mister*. Is this some kinda suicide mission, is that what you're telling me?"

But that couldn't be right either. Normal mission-control channels hadn't shown any hesitation about sending the Headhunters on suicide missions before.

And the Headhunters hadn't hesitated to go.

"Nothing like that," said Grant. "It's safer than R&R—you won't even risk catching clap."

Kowacs waited.

"You see," Grant continued, "you're going to use APOT equipment for the insertion. All points are the same point to the device you'll ride in. The Syndicate won't have any warning."

That was the fucking catch, all right.

The 92nd MRC had tested APOT equipment on Bull's-Eye. Sometimes it worked, sometimes it got them dead. *Dead* wasn't the scary part of the stories Toby English and his Marines had brought back from that operation, though. . . .

"I . . ." Kowacs said, ". . . don't know how the guys are going to react to this. Seems to me that maybe a unit that's already got experience with—"

"Wrong, Major Kowacs," Grant said. He didn't shout because he didn't have to shout. "You know exactly how you and your company are going to react. Because it's orders, and everybody knows what happens to cowards who disobey orders in wartime."

For a moment, Kowacs couldn't see anything for the red film in front of his eyes. When his vision cleared, he noticed that one of the civilian's hands had dropped out of sight behind the desk.

There was no need for that. The room's automatic defensive system would trip faster than a human could if somebody tried to attack the man in Admiral Teitelbaum's chair; and anyway, Nick Kowacs wasn't out of control, was *never* out of control. . . .

"As a matter of fact," Grant said in what was almost a conciliatory tone, "the Ninety-Second was the original choice for the mission, but they're still in transit. They've been switched with the backup company. Yours."

Kowacs swallowed. "You got the coordinates from a captured Syndicate ship?" he said, sure that he'd be told that sources and methods were none of his business. He had to change the subject, or—or else.

Grant smiled again. "From the mind of a prisoner. Before he died. The prisoner you captured on Bull's-Eye, as a matter of fact."

"From his *mind*?" the Marine repeated. "How did you do that?"

"Pray you never learn, mister," Grant said.

"Right," said Kowacs as he got to his feet. He wondered whether his escort was still waiting outside the door. Probably. "I'll alert the company. I assume formal briefing materials are—"

Grant nodded. "Already downloaded to the One-Twenty-First databank," he said. "I'll take the lock off them immediately."

"Right," Kowacs repeated. He reached for the latchplate of the door, then changed his mind and turned.

"Just one thing, *Mister* Grant," he said. "My Headhunters aren't cowards. If you think they are, then you come on a drop with us someday."

"Oh, I will," the civilian said with the same mocking terrible smile as before. "As a matter of fact, Major Kowacs—I'm coming with you on this one."

"Our job," said Nick Kowacs in the personnel hold of the intrusion module, "is to—"

The high-pitched keening of a powerful laser cutter rose, drowning out his voice and thought itself.

Sergeant Bradley glanced around flay-eyed, looking for the source of the noise. It came from somewhere between the module's double hulls. He started for a hatch, wiping his palms on his fatigues to dry the sudden rush of sweat.

Kowacs grabbed the sergeant with one hand as he put his helmet on with the other.

"Right," Kowacs said over the general frequency. "Lids on." He looked to see which of the new replacements needed to be nudged by their neighbors before they figured out that the rest of the briefing would be conducted by radio even though the Headhunters were all in one room together.

"Our job," Kowacs went on, "is to capture personnel, databanks, and anything that looks like it might be navigational equipment. We *aren't* going in to blow the—"

The laser shut off. A woman with commander's collar pips on the uniform she wore under her lab coat walked into the bay with two male technical representatives, speaking among themselves in low voices. Heads turned to watch them.

Sergeant Bradley grimaced.

"—place up, we're going in to gather information before

the *enemy* blows it up. We've only got seventeen minutes. That's one-seven minutes, period. Anybody who—''

The trio in lab coats gestured Marines away from a portion of deck and knelt down. One of the tech reps took an instrument from his pocket and placed it cup-end down on the decking. He frowned at the result; the commander growled at him.

''—loses sight of the mission will have me to answer to,'' Kowacs continued.

''And they'll wish they'd never been born!'' added Sergeant Bradley. The field first sergeant got enough venom into the justified threat to take out some of his frustration about the way the briefing had to be held.

And the way the mission was shaping up.

Kowacs was holding the briefing here because the module's hangar was the only space in the huge headquarters complex both big enough to hold a hundred Marines—*and* cleared for this particular dollop of Sensitive Compartmentalized Information. Unfortunately, the module was still under test, and the technical crews dialing in the hardware had precedence over the briefing.

The Marines who were about to ride the hardware into the middle of enemies worse than the Khalia couldn't argue with the priority, but it didn't make life simpler.

Kowacs touched a stud on the control wand a Grade P7 Fleet technician had given him. For a wonder, the system worked perfectly. The hold's circular bulkhead was replaced by a holographic display, the simulated interior of the Syndicate base the Headhunters would be attacking.

''We'll be landing inside the docking bay,'' Kowacs said as a slow hammering sound began to work its way across the ceiling above him. ''In all likelihood it'll be under atmosphere, but we'll be wearing ten-minute airpacks for an emergency.''

The two tech reps got up and walked toward the hatch, a rectangle with rounded corners in the midst of a holographic gantry. The commander followed them, shaking her head. She turned in the hatchway to frown at the deck she'd been examining.

"Suits?" asked Laurel, a squad leader in 3d Platoon.

"Weapons Platoon will be in suits," said Kowacs. "They'll provide security for the module. The remainder of us'll be traveling light. We'll fan out in three-man teams. You'll all have prebriefed objectives, but don't hesitate to divert to grab anything that looks like it might be valuable."

Something *pop*ped within the hulls. The encircling holograms vanished. All the lights in the bay went out. First the display, then the lights came back on moments later.

Somebody swore bitterly.

Corporal Sienkiewicz—the tallest, possibly the strongest, and certainly the toughest member of the 121st—looked bored as she lounged against a bulkhead covered by the image of an open corridor. She knew what the Headhunters' job was this time out—and she knew her own job on every operation, to cover Kowacs's back and keep him alive till the next time. The whys and hows of the operation didn't matter to her beyond that.

"Sir," said a newbie named Bynum—five years a Marine but on his first operation with the Headhunters. "I looked this boat over and she don't have engines. No shit."

"The ship," said Kowacs harshly, "is none of our business. Do you hear? The ship just gets us there and brings us back."

"S'posed to bring us back," somebody muttered in what should have been general silence.

"Listen!" Kowacs snarled. He had to take a tough line, because they all knew this could be a rat-fuck, and the only way his Headhunters were going to go through with it was by rigid obedience. "If there's any of you who don't think you want to chance life in a reaction company anymore, I'll approve your transfer *now*. Want to be a cook? A recruiter? Just say the word!"

Nobody spoke. A number of the Marines looked down, at the deck, at their hands.

They were a good bunch, the very best. They'd charge hell if he ordered it . . . only in part because they knew if it came to that, Nick Kowacs would be leading from the front.

The laser cutter shrieked as it bit into an interior bulkhead again.

"Is this an Eight Ball Command job?" asked Lieutenant Timmes of Weapons Platoon.

"Yes, it is," Kowacs said flatly.

He looked around the crowd of hard faces and the blank visages of Marines who had opaqued their helmet visors. "If anybody's got a problem with that, the transfer offer still stands."

"No problem," said Timmes. "Just wanted to know."

"*Them* bastards," said a sharp-featured trooper named Fleur. "You never know what they're playing at."

Kowacs suspected Fleur had been a disciplinary enlistment—volunteer for a reaction company or face a court-martial—but Kowacs had no complaint to make of the Marine. He didn't guess any of the Headhunters, himself included, were good civilian material.

"You don't know what anybody who's got any real authority is playing at," Kowacs said. He was restating the argument by which he'd more-or-less convinced himself. "It's just that people like you and me at the sharp end, we don't see the regular sort, the admirals and sector commandants. The boys in Interservice Support Activity, they may be bastards but they're willing to put themselves on the line."

"Gotta give 'em credit for that," chuckled Bradley.

The laser cutter had stopped. The sergeant removed his helmet to knuckle the bare scar tissue of his scalp.

"I don't gotta give 'em a fuckin' thing but a quick round if I get one in my sights," muttered Fleur.

Kowacs opened his mouth to react, because you weren't supposed to shoot putative friendlies and you *never* talked about it, neither before nor after.

Before he could speak, Sergeant Bradley changed the subject loudly by asking, "D'ye mean we don't gotta wear those fucking APOT hardsuits that the Redhorse had all the trouble with on Bull's-Eye?"

Kowacs looked at his field first. Bradley gave Kowacs a half wink; Bradley and Corporal Sienkiewicz would straighten out Fleur, but it didn't have to be now and in public.

A man in a white lab coat entered the hold and began making his way through the listening Marines. For a moment he was anonymous, like the noses in the hull and the other intruders who'd been focused on their technical agenda.

"I don't know," the newly promoted major said. "I'll have to—"

The big technician in the corner of Kowacs's eyes suddenly sharpened into an identified personality: the man in the lab coat was Grant.

"Fuckin' A," Sienkiewicz muttered as she drew herself alert.

"I'll take over now, Kowacs," the spook said with as much assurance as if the Headhunters had been his unit, not Nick Kowacs's.

Grant wore a throat mike and a wireless receiver in his right ear, though he had no helmet to damp out the ambient noise if the laser started cutting again.

He stared around the assembled Marines for a moment, then looked directly at Kowacs's bodyguard and said, "No, Corporal, for this one you'll be using the same stone-axe simple equipment you're used to. If you tried to open an APOT field inside an existing field—the intrusion module . . ."

He smiled at the big woman. "You wouldn't like what happened. And I wouldn't like that it screwed up the operation."

Grant met the glares and blank globes of the waiting Headhunters again. "For those of you who don't know," he said, "my name's Grant and you all work for me. You'll take orders through your regular CO here"—he jerked his left thumb in Kowacs's direction without bothering to look around—"but those orders come from me. Is that clear?"

Beside the civilian, Kowacs nodded his head. His eyes held no expression.

"And since you work for me . . ." Grant resumed as he

reached beneath his lab coat, "I've got a little job for one of you. Private Fleur—"

Grant's hand came out with a pistol.

"Catch."

Grant tossed the weapon to Fleur. It was a full-sized, dual-feed service pistol, Fleet issue and deadly as the jaws of a shark.

The Marines nearest to Fleur ducked away as if Grant had thrown a grenade. Kowacs, Bradley, and Sienkiewicz were up on the balls of their feet, ready to react because they'd *have* to react; they were responsible for the unit and for one another.

"Private Fleur," Grant said, "I'm afraid for my life. There's somebody planning to kill me. So I want you to clean my gun here and make sure it's in perfect working order for when I'm attacked."

Nobody spoke. Other Marines eased as far away from Fleur as they could. Even without combat gear, the Headhunters packed the hold. English's 92nd MRC was a demi-company half the size of the 121st. . . .

Fleur stared at the civilian, but his hands slid over the pistol in familiar fashion. He unlatched one magazine, then the other, and slammed them home again.

"Careful," added Grant as he grinned. "There's one up the spout."

"I . . ." said Fleur.

If Fleur's trigger finger tightened, Kowacs would get between the private and Grant . . . but he'd have to be quick, since Sie would be going for *him* and Bradley was a toss-up, Kowacs or Grant or Fleur, the only thing sure being that the sergeant would do something besides try to save his own hide.

"My cleaning kit's back at the billet," Fleur said. He swallowed. "Sir."

"Then you'd better return the gun, boy," said Grant. "Hadn't you?"

Fleur grimaced. For a moment he looked as though he were going to toss the weapon; then he stepped forward and presented the pistol butt-first to its owner. Fleur's hand was dwarfed by that of the civilian.

The laser started cutting again. Grant aimed his pistol at the open hatch. Marines ducked, though nobody was in the direct line of fire.

Grant pulled the trigger. The flash*crack* and the answering *crack* of the explosive bullet detonating somewhere out in the hangar removed any possibility that the weapon had been doctored to make it harmless.

The cutter shut down. Technicians shouted in surprise, but nobody stuck his head in through the hatch.

Grant put the pistol away under his lab coat. "All right, Fleur," he said. "You're relieved. Go back to your quarters and pack your kit. Your orders are waiting for you there."

Kowacs felt exhausted, drained. Sienkiewicz gripped his shoulder for the contact they both needed.

"Your new assignment's on an intra-system tug," Grant added. Then, as harshly as the pistol shot of a moment before, "*Get* moving, mister!"

Fleur stumbled out of the hold—and the Headhunters. A few of the Marines flicked a glance at his back; but only a glance.

Grant exhaled heavily.

"Right," he said. "This is going to be a piece of cake, troops. The bastards won't know what hit them. There's just one thing I want to emphasize before your major here gets on with his briefing."

He grinned around the bay. Sphincter muscles tightened.

"The module will be on-site for seventeen minutes," Grant went on. "That's not eighteen minutes, it's not seventeen minutes, one second. Anybody who isn't aboard on time spends the rest of his life in Syndicate hands.

"You see," the smiling civilian concluded, "I couldn't change the extraction parameters. Even if I wanted to."

An electronic chime warned that the Headhunters were three minutes from insertion.

The hatches were still open. The intrusion module's bulkheads were hidden by images, but the hologram was not a

simulation this time. The present view was of the hangar in
which the vehicle had been constructed and the twelve sealed
black towers surrounding the module at the points of a com-
pass rose. The towers would presumably launch the module
. . . somehow.

"Everybody's aboard," prompted Sergeant Bradley, stating what the green bar in Kowacs's visor display already
told him.

"Grant isn't aboard," Kowacs said, finger-checking the
grenades that hung from his equipment belt.

"I don't get this," complained a Marine to no one in
particular. "We can't ride all the way from Port Tau Ceti
packed in like canned meat. Can we?"

"Fuck Grant," said Sienkiewicz.

The eighteen members of Weapons Platoon carried the
tubes, tripods, and ammunition of their belt-loaded plasma
weapons. Their rigid hardsuits of black ceramic stood out
from the remaining lightly equipped Marines like raisins in
a pound cake.

Kowacs saw Grant's image coming across the hangar floor
with long strides. The civilian wore fatigues, but he carried
what looked like a briefcase. His com helmet was nonstan-
dard.

Grant's pistol hung muzzle-up in a harness beneath his
left armpit.

"Right," said Kowacs. "Six to all team leaders"—his
helmet's AI switched him automatically from the private
channel he shared with Bradley and Sie to the general command frequency—"administer the gas antidote to your
teams, then dose yourselves."

Grant entered the module. The hatches closed.

There was barely enough room for equipment and the
ninety-three personnel aboard the spherical vessel; if the
Headhunters' line establishment had been at full Table of
Organization strength, Kowacs would have had to cut some
people from the operation.

What the Marine who'd complained didn't understand—
what *Kowacs* didn't understand, though he accepted it—was
that the Headhunters weren't traveling through space, not

even sponge space, on this operation. They were using the Dirac Sea underlying the universe, *all* universes and all times, to create congruity between a top-secret hangar in Port Tau Ceti and the Syndicate base they were about to attack.

At least that's what they were doing if the notion worked. The closer Kowacs came to the event, the less likely it seemed that the notion *could* work.

"Hold still, sir," said Bradley, the administrative head of the team to which Kowacs belonged operationally. He jerked the tab on the front of the major's blouse.

The integral injector pricked Kowacs as it filled his bloodstream with chemicals. The drug would provide a temporary antidote to the contact anesthetic sprayed from bottles that every third Headhunter carried for this operation.

The chime announced *two minutes.*

Grant turned his briefcase sideways and extended its legs. When he opened the lid to expose the keyboard and display, the case became a diaphragm-high workstation. Despite the crowding in the bay, the Marines gave the civilian plenty of room.

A Third Platoon team leader pulled his own tab. He collapsed jerking as reaction to the drug sent him into anaphylactic shock.

Lieutenant al-Habib, the platoon commander, pushed toward the casualty, swearing in a combination of concern and fear. Everybody was supposed to have been reaction-tested before now; and testing was a platoon responsibility.

Kowacs's eyes narrowed, but he said nothing. If he and al-Habib both survived the operation, al-Habib was out of the Headhunters.

If.

The warning chimed *one minute*. The holographic displays vanished, leaving the bulkheads bare for the moment before the hold's lighting flickered and went off. Grant's face was lit from below by his workstation, making him look the demon Kowacs was sure he really was.

The lights came on again, but they were red.

Kowacs opaqued his visor. He figured he could keep his expression neutral, but he didn't want to bother any of his people if by chance they correctly read the terror behind their major's eyes.

The module drifted. It was more than weightlessness. Kowacs had the horrible feeling that he was rushing *somewhere* but had neither control nor even sensory input, as though his vehicle were skidding on ice in pitch-darkness. He heard some of his troops screaming, and he didn't blame them.

The world switched back with the abruptness of a crystal forming in a supersaturated solution. The lights became normal; holograms covered the bulkheads again.

The holograms didn't show the hangar. They didn't show anything at all, just a gray blur without even a spark to pick it out.

Grant was talking angrily, but his helmet contained his words. His big, capable fingers rapped a code into the keyboard. The gray blur shifted slowly through violet to a green like that of translucent pond scum. Though the color changed, it remained featureless.

"What's hap'nin to us?" somebody demanded sharply. "What's—"

Sergeant Bradley's knife poised point-first in front of the panicked Marine's right eyeball. The blade wouldn't penetrate her visor, but its shock value was sufficient to chop her voice off . . . and if she'd take time to reflect, she would have known that the edge could be through her windpipe before she got out the next syllable.

"Hey, Grant," Kowacs called.

Grant continued talking to someone on the other side of his communications link. His anger was obvious even though his words were inaudible.

Kowacs raised his visor and leaned across the workstation from the opposite side, putting his face where the civilian couldn't ignore him.

Grant's fist clenched. Kowacs grabbed his wrist and squeezed.

For a moment the two powerful men struggled, as motionless as neighboring mountains. Sienkiewicz moved just out of the range of Kowacs's direct vision, but Kowacs didn't need help.

The civilian relaxed. His mouth formed a command, and the shield of silence dropped away from his helmet. "What the fuck do *you* want?" he snarled.

"Where are we?" Kowacs whispered. Everyone in the module was watching them, but only the nearest Marines could hear the leaders over the hiss of nervous breathing. Grant shook his hand, trying to get feeling back into it.

"There's nothing wrong," Grant said. "We're not where we're programmed to be—or *when* we're programmed to be—but there's nothing wrong. If they can't straighten it out, we'll just return when the seventeen minutes are up."

We hope, Kowacs's mind added, but that wasn't something even for a whisper.

"Right," he said aloud. "I'm going to calm everybody down; but Eight Ball Command pays, understand?"

Grant probably didn't understand . . . yet.

Kowacs didn't key the helmet intercom, opting for the more personal touch of his direct voice.

"All right, Marines," he bellowed. "We're on R&R for the next fifteen minutes or so, courtesy of the Special Projects Bureau. But you all know the Fleet—what we get's one room and no sandy beaches."

Siekiewicz laughed loudly.

"Hey," called al-Habib, "you can keep your sand if you find me a cathouse!"

Kowacs grinned broadly at the lieutenant whose quick understanding had just reinstated him in the Headhunters. "Naw, Jamal," he said. "When you join the Marines, you get fucked over—but you don't get laid."

This time the laughter was general. The holographic light bathing the walls shifted slowly back to gray.

Kowacs lifted his helmet to scratch his close-cropped scalp.

"Okay, now listen up," he resumed in a tone of command. "This is a good time for you all to go over your missions again by teams. The delay doesn't mean that we're off the hook. Even Special Projects—''

Kowacs waved toward Grant, bent over his workstation. ''—and Eight Ball Command are going to get things right eventually. I want us *sharp* when the time comes. Understood?''

''Yes *sir*!'' from a dozen throats, and no more eyes filled with incipient panic.

''Then get to it!'' ordered Sergeant Bradley.

Helmet-projected maps began to bloom in the midst of three-Marine clusters, teams going over the routes they expected to take through the hostile base.

Kowacs leaned toward Grant again. He expected the civilian to be visibly angry at being made a laughingstock to defuse tension, but there was no expression on the big man's face.

Which proved that Grant was a smart bastard as well as a bastard; and that wasn't news to Kowacs.

''I'm in contact with echelon,'' Grant said. ''Everything is proceeding normally.''

''Except we're not where we're supposed to be,'' Kowacs said. Bradley and Sienkiewicz were close behind him— everything was close in the module's hold—but they were facing outward, watching the company for their major.

''They've refined the parameters,'' Grant said. ''We should be able to turn it around at the end of seventeen minutes and go in immediately, without docking.''

''Fine,'' said Kowacs without expression. ''That's almost as good as having the shit work right the first time.''

''Just have your troops ready to go, mister!'' the civilian snapped. ''Got that?''

''You bet,'' said Kowacs as he straightened. ''You just get us to the target; we'll take it from there.''

And they did.

The alarm chimed, the interior lights went red, and the intrusion module was within a cylindrical bay large enough to hold a liner—or a battleship. The trio of courier vessels docked there at present were dwarfed by the volume surrounding them.

"Artificial gravity and standard atmosphere!" Kowacs shouted, relaying the information that other Headhunters might not think to check on their visors, as the hatches—*only two fucking hatches, as though this were a bus and not an assault craft!*—opened and the dozen Syndicate maintenance people visible in the bulkhead displays gaped at the module that had appeared in their midst.

Bradley was through the hatch first because he had the shotgun and it was the close targets who were dangerous—though none of the Syndicate personnel, all of them human, seemed to be armed. The woman a hundred meters away, running for a courier vessel, was probably the biggest problem because she'd been smart enough to react.

Kowacs shot her. He was second through the hatch because the 121st was *his* company, not Sie's, however much the corporal might want to put her body out there first when the action was going to start.

The target flopped on the walkway with her limbs flailing. There were dots of blood on the back of her tunic, and a great splash of scarlet and lung tissue blown by the keyholing bullets onto the walkway where she thrashed.

Taking prisoners had to wait until there were enough Headhunters out of the module to secure the area.

Bradley ran for the corridor marked D on the maps from Eight Ball Command and 6 in yellow on the girdered lintel. Kowacs followed his field first toward what was the transient wing of the base according to data sucked from the prisoner's brain. The major fired a short burst into a glazed office, shattering the clear panels and sending the staff to cover behind banks of short-circuiting equipment.

As usual, Corporal Sienkiewicz carried the considerable weight of a shoulder-fired plasma weapon in addition to her regular gear. She lighted the bay with a round of plasma into the nose turret of both courier vessels on her side of the intrusion module.

The dazzle and *crack*! of the miniature fusion explosions forced their reality onto the huge room. One of the turrets simply slagged down, but ammunition detonated in the other. Balls of ionized gas bubbled through the vessel's open hatches.

The navigational computer of *that* boat wasn't going to be much help to the spooks back at Port Tau Ceti, but the raiders couldn't risk somebody arming the turrets before teams detailed for vessels in dock got aboard the couriers.

Coming back without the desired information was better than not coming back. Even Grant, monitoring all the teams from the belly of the module, would agree with that.

Bradley carried a bottle of stun gas. It was a volatile liquid intended for contact application, though the fumes would do the job if they had to. The sergeant directed the bottle's nozzle into the office Kowacs had shot up, angling the fine jet so that it sprayed the terrified personnel hiding behind their bullet-riddled equipment.

Pickup teams would secure the prisoners later, though they'd be stacked like cordwood beneath Headhunter boots during extraction. *Provided casualties didn't clear too much of the module's hold.*

The corridor formed a Y. Bradley followed the left branch, as planned.

There were rooms on both sides. The third door down quivered as though in indecision. Kowacs riddled it. He was switching to a fresh magazine when the fat man in garish silks and ribbons tumbled out into the corridor, still clutching his pistol.

He'd have been a good one to capture—if that had been an option compatible with Kowacs staying alive.

Belt-fed plasma weapons fired short bursts from the docking bay. Timmes's platoon was taking an active definition of perimeter security. Light reflecting down the corridor angles threw momentary harsh shadows.

The docking bay was out of Kowacs's direct sight. He could have viewed the module by switching his visor to remote images, just as he could follow the progress of any of his Marines either visually or by a digital readout.

He didn't bother. The Headhunters were too experienced to need their major looking over their shoulders—

And anyway, their major had enough on his own plate.

An emergency barrier began to slide across the corridor twenty meters ahead.

"Down!" Kowacs shouted as his left hand snatched a grenade from his equipment belt. He flung the bomb side-arm as he flattened.

A pair of security men in helmets and uniforms ran from a cross-corridor just beyond the sliding barrier. They leveled sub-machine guns. Bradley sent an arc of stun gas in their direction, but the bottle didn't have quite enough range and Kowacs, sliding on his right shoulder, couldn't twist his assault rifle on target fast enough to—

The antitank grenade struck the barrier, clung for an instant, and went off with a deafening crash. The barrier bulged inward, jamming in its track. The shaped-charge warhead blew a two-centimeter hole through the metal and cleared the corridor beyond with a spray of fragments and molten steel.

The shock wave skidded Kowacs back a meter from the blast area. The frangible casing powdered harmlessly, as it was intended to do, and com helmets saved the Headhunters' hearing.

"Go!" Kowacs cried.

Sienkiewicz was already on her feet and past the barrier, the near limit of the station's transient accommodations. The corporal paused beside the first door to make sure Bradley was ready with his stun gas, then smashed the panel open with her boot.

Bradley sprayed the interior with his nozzle set on mist. The gas glowed like a fluorescent rainbow in the flicker of distant plasma discharges.

Another team sprinted past Kowacs and broke left at the cross-corridor. Automatic fire blasted.

The team leader spun and fell. His number two dropped her bottle of gas and dragged the leader beyond the corner of the main corridor, across from Kowacs.

The number three, under cover also, started to lean out to return fire with his automatic rifle. Kowacs waved him back, then whipped a cluster of fragmentation grenades around the corner with a motion that exposed none of his body.

The cluster rebounded as a unit from the far wall of the cross-corridor, separated into its component sections with a triple pop, and detonated in a white sleet of flame and glass shrapnel.

Kowacs dived into the corridor in the shadow of the blast. Bradley was beside him and Sie covered their backs, facing the opposite direction in case company tried to intervene down the other leg of the cross-corridor.

There were three uniformed Syndicate personnel in the corridor, two sprawled on their faces and a third staggering toward safety as a barrier ten meters away slid to seal the hall. Kowacs and Bradley both fired.

The security man flung his arms out and lurched forward. His back was splotched with slits from the airfoil charge of Bradley's shotgun; there were three neat holes between his shoulders—Kowacs's aiming point.

The barrier ground to a halt. The security man's body might not have been enough to stall out the motor, but his helmet was. There was just about enough room for a man to squeeze through the opening between the barrier and its jamb.

Somebody on the far side of the barrier fired. The bullets ricocheted through the gap, howling like banshees and all the more dangerous for the way they buzzsawed after deforming on the corridor wall.

"Cover me!" screamed the other team's number two. She bolted past Kowacs and Bradley, snatching up her bottle of gas as she ran.

Kowacs poured the remainder of his rifle's magazine through the opening. Bradley unhooked a grenade cluster. His shotgun's pattern was too wide to get much of the charge through the opening at that range, and the airfoils wouldn't ricochet effectively anyway.

A bullet zinged past the running Headhunter, close enough to pluck a pouch of ammo from her belt and half spin her, but she reached the dead zone behind the barrier without injury. She fumbled with her bottle of gas. Bradley's arm went back with a grenade cluster.

"D—" Kowacs shouted, but he didn't finish the "Don't" because there wasn't much chance the sergeant would miss the risky throw—and anyway, Bradley was going to do what he pleased in a firefight, whether Nick Kowacs thought it was a good idea or not.

The grenade cluster arced through the narrow slot and burst with a triple flash waist-high above the corridor floor. At the blast, the number two poked her gas bottle into the opening and began to spray a mist of anesthetic into the other side of the barrier.

The firing slackened. A woman in the bright, loose clothing favored by Syndicate bigwigs slumped across the opening and lay still. A pistol slipped from her hand.

Unexpectedly, the Headhunter dropped her gas bottle and collapsed also.

The fucking seventeen-minute delay. The gas antidote was wearing off!

"Headhunter Six to all personnel," Kowacs said as he lurched to his feet and another Syndicate bullet whanged through the slot. "Stop using gas! The antidote's—"

Sienkiewicz fired the last round from her plasma weapon through the opening. The wall thirty meters down the corridor bloomed in a sun-hot fireball as the jet of directed plasma sublimed the metal-and-ceramic structure into vapor in a microsecond.

"—wearing off!" Kowacs completed as he hit the slot a step ahead of Bradley, who'd been that much slower getting to his feet, and two steps before Sie, who rocked back with the violence of the bolt she'd unleashed.

The major went through sideways. His equipment belt hooked on the edge of the barrier anyway, twisted but didn't hold him.

The corridor dead-ended. The four rooms on the left side were glowing slag from the plasma charge. A security man knelt in an open doorway across from where the bolt had hit. He'd dropped his rifle and was pawing at his eyes, possibly blinded already and certainly dead when Kowacs walked a one-handed burst across his chest.

The shooters didn't know anything worth carrying back to Tau Ceti.

The end door on the right side was open a centimeter when Kowacs saw it, slamming shut an instant thereafter. He hit its latch bootheel-first, springing fasteners that were intended for privacy rather than security.

The interior lights were on. There were two people inside, and a coffin-sized outline taped to the back wall of the room. The people were a man and a woman, both young, and they were starting to lock down the helmets of their atmosphere suits.

The man's gauntleted hand reached for the sub-machine gun across the bed beside him. Kowacs fired, but Bradley fired also and at point-blank range the rifle bullets were lost in the plate-sized crater the shotgun blew in the target's chest.

The back wall exploded outward. The outline had been drawn with adhesive-backed explosive strips, and the vaguely familiar woman detonated it as she finished fastening her helmet.

The other side of the wall was hard vacuum.

The rush of atmosphere sucked the woman with it, clear of the Headhunter's guns. Loose papers, bedding, and the helmet from the corpse sailed after her.

The mask of Kowacs's emergency air supply slapped over his nose and mouth, enough to save his life but not adequate for him to go chasing somebody in a proper suit. The suit's maneuvering jets would carry the woman to a regular airlock, when the raiders left and it was safe to come back.

The room lights dimmed as the atmosphere that scattered them into a useful ambience roared through the huge hole. Kowacs reached for the male corpse, lost his balance, and staggered toward death until Sie's huge hand clamped the slack of his equipment belt.

"Let's go!" she shouted, her voice attenuated to a comfortable level by the AI controlling Kowacs's headphones. "We're timing out!"

"Help me with the body!" Kowacs ordered as the three of them fought their way back into the corridor. The wind was less overmastering but still intense.

"We don't need dead guys!" Bradley shouted, but he'd grabbed the other leg of the body, clumsy in its bulky suit.

"I got it," said Sienkiewicz, lifting the corpse away from both men. She slammed it through the gap at the barrier in what was half a shove, half a throw.

"We need this one," Kowacs wheezed.

The corridor was empty except for Syndicate corpses. Headhunter pickup teams had gathered the casualties as well as the loot and headed back to the module. It'd be close, but Kowacs's team would make it with ten seconds to spare, a lifetime. . . .

"We need this deader . . . " he continued as they pounded down the hallway against the lessening wind-rush. Sie had the body. "Because he's wearing . . . ensign's insignia . . . on his collar."

The module was in sight. A man stood in the open hatch, Grant, and goddamn if he didn't have his arm outstretched to help jerk the latecomers aboard.

"*Fleet* ensign's insignia!" Kowacs gasped.

The receptionist looked concerned, and not just by the fact that Major Kowacs carried a full load of weapons and equipment into her sanctum.

Or as much of his weapons and equipment as he hadn't fired off during the raid.

The escort, rising and falling on the balls of his feet at the open door of these third-tier offices, was evidently worried. "Come this way, please, sir," the youngster said. Then, "He's been waiting for you."

"I been waiting for a hot shower," Kowacs rasped. Powder smoke, ozone, and stun gas had worked over his throat like so many skinning knives. "I'm still fucking waiting."

The escort hopped ahead of Kowacs like a tall, perfectly groomed leprechaun. Kowacs could barely walk.

The adrenaline had worn off. He'd seen the preliminary casualty report—*with three bodies not recovered*. There was a ten-centimeter burn on the inside of his left wrist where he must have laid the glowing barrel of his assault rifle, though goddamn if he could remember doing that.

There were bruises and prickles of glass shrapnel all over Nick Kowacs's body, but a spook named Grant insisted on debriefing him at once, with your full equipment, mister.

The door flashed SPECIAL PROJECTS/TEITELBAUM an instant before it opened.

"Where the hell have you been?" snarled Grant.

His briefcase lay open on the desk. A gossamer filament connected the workstation to the office's hologram projector. Fuzzy images of battle and confusion danced in the air while the portrait of Admiral Teitelbaum glared down sternly.

"I had to check out my people," Kowacs said as he leaned his blackened rifle against one of the leather-covered chairs. He lifted one, then the other of the crossed bandoliers of ammunition over his head and laid them on the seat cushion.

"I said *at once*," the civilian snapped. "You've got platoon leaders to baby-sit, don't you?"

"I guess," said Kowacs. He unlatched his equipment belt. It swung in his hands, shockingly heavy with its weight of pistol and grenades. He tossed it onto the bandoliers.

God, he felt weak....

Grant grimaced. "All right, give me your helmet."

Kowacs had forgotten he was wearing a com helmet. He slid it off carefully. The room's filtered air chilled the sweat on the Marine's scalp.

The civilian reversed the helmet, then touched the brow panel with an electronic key. Kowacs knew about the keys but he'd never seen one used before.

Line Marines weren't authorized to remove the recording chips from their helmets. That was the job of the Second-Guess Brigade, the rear-echelon mothers who decided how well or badly the people at the sharp end had behaved....

Grant muttered to his workstation. The ghost images shut down. He put the chip from Kowacs's helmet directly into the hologram reader. His own weapon and shoulder harness hung over the back of his chair.

"Didn't your equipment echo everything from our helmets?" Kowacs asked.

He remained standing. He wasn't sure he wanted to sit down. He wasn't sure of much of anything.

"Did a piss-poor job of it, yeah," the civilian grunted. "Just enough to give me a hint of what I need."

He scrolled forward, reeling across the seventeen-minute operation at times-ten speed. Images projected from Kowacs's viewpoint jerked and capered and died. "Too much hash from the—"

There was a bright flash in the air above the desk.

"—fucking plasma discharges. You know"—Grant met the Marine's eyes in a fierce glare—"it was bughouse crazy to use a plasma weapon in a finger corridor. What if the whole outer bulkhead blew out?"

"It didn't," said Kowacs. "You got complaints about the way the job got done, then you send somebody else the next time."

Grant paused the projection. The image was red with muzzle flashes and bright orange with pulmonary blood spraying through the mouth of the man in the tattered spacesuit.

"Smart to bring back the body," Grant said in a neutral voice. "Too bad you didn't capture him alive."

"Too bad your system didn't work the first time so we could've kept using the stun gas," Kowacs replied flatly. The parade of images was a nightmare come twice.

Grant expanded the view of the dying man's face. "We've got a hard make on him," he said. "There was enough residual brain-wave activity to nail him down, besides all the regular ID he was carrying. Name's Haley G. Stocker, Ensign . . . and he disappeared on a scouting mission."

"A Syndicate spy?" Kowacs said.

"That's what the smart money's betting," the civilian agreed.

He backed up the image minusculely. The blood vanished like a fountain failing, the aristocratic lips shrank from an

O of disbelieving horror into the sneer the ensign bore an instant before the bullets struck.

"Only thing is," Grant continued, "Ensign Stocker disappeared thirty-five years ago."

He looked at Kowacs and raised an eyebrow, as if he were expecting the Marine to come up with an explanation.

"Bullshit," said Kowacs. "He's only about twenty. He was."

"Close," the civilian agreed. "Twenty and a half standard years when you shot him, the lab says."

He let the projector run forward. The spy, the *boy*, hemorrhaged and died again before his mind could accept what was happening.

"I don't get it," said Nick Kowacs. He heard a persistent buzzing, but it came from his mind rather than the equipment.

Grant looked . . . tired wasn't the right word, lonely wasn't the right word, but . . . Grant had paid a price during the operation too—

Or he'd never have been talking to a line Marine this way.

"It looks like we still don't have all the bugs out of the APOT intrusion system," Grant said. "The best we can figure now, the second pass was early. Thirty-five years early."

He spoke to the voice control of the holographic reader. The image paused, then expanded.

The face of the woman who'd escaped was slightly distorted by the faceshield of her helmet, and she was considerably younger—

But the features were beyond doubt the same as those lowering down from the portrait of Vice Admiral Teitelbaum on the wall behind.

INTERLUDE: Deep Cover

Space is big. That is a gross understatement. No better description has been given. This is such because there are no words for a concept incapable of being grasped by the human mind. Picture three items, red balls perhaps. Now five. Okay seven. Now try for a million. Not the number, but the image of a million individual balls. There are millions of stars in the spiral arm of our galaxy that housed the Alliance, and the Syndicate. At top speed these average about a week apart. Nor are they evenly spaced. Some clusters contain hundreds of stars. In the emptier areas a ship could cruise for weeks and not pass within sensing range of a planetary system. Even if they had the luxury of time, there was no way the Fleet could simply find the Syndicate home worlds. With small fleets of Syndicate ships already ranging into Khalian space, there was no time at all.

Somewhere among the hundreds of thousands of stars bordering Alliance and Khalian space, maybe, could be found the worlds of the Syndicate. The secret of their location in an otherwise nondescript cluster of fifty thousand stars was the most vital piece of information needed for the Fleet to act. No effort was too desperate. Until then the Fleet was no better than a blind man flailing wildly to defend himself against an unknown number of club-carrying assailants.

The hidden military facilities prepared by the Syndicate were often interspersed among the Khalian worlds. Many of these were bases prepared for future action, now only lightly manned by a few family members and their guards. Since the Syndicate technicians completely controlled the Khalia's ability to travel between worlds, it was a simple matter to lock out any areas they did not wish to have visited. Even after they had sworn allegiance to the Alliance, no Khalian was capable of alerting the Fleet to this threat in their very midst.

When such a world was discovered, it was necessary to act swiftly. Only on them were men who knew the vital information of the whereabouts of the cluster containing the Syndicate home worlds. No information could be gained from slag and rubble. Even the most poorly defended had to be taken by assault. Such attacks tended to high casualty rates, but when the alternative was certain defeat in a defensive war, the Syndicate's location, or even just clues, were worth any price.

BIRTHDAY PRESENT

by Janet Morris

THE MESSAGE THAT English left with the MAC/ASD receptionist said, "Gone to Electro Research Station for therapy—Capt. Tolliver English, 92nd RMC, SERPA/J36/ TACOPS."

Being on ice for forty-five days behind the lines didn't mean you were cooled out; Toby English was living proof of that. Ever since his outfit, the 92nd Marine Reaction Company (Redhorse), had carried X-class weapons into battle for Eight Ball Command, they'd been getting more and more "special." And English had been getting into more and more trouble.

"Special," out here at Military Assistance Command/ ASD, *meant* trouble. Special Electromagnetic Research Projects Agency (SERPA) had its own huge, privileged station at the MAC/ASD facility, orbiting a gas giant that the command-and-control facility was using as a power plant.

The first time that English had seen the space base, he'd known he'd be lucky if he ever got Redhorse out of there alive. The 92nd was coming off a sterilization mission for ISA, the Interservice Support Activity. You couldn't blame the brass for wanting to segregate them: nobody in the regular Fleet was liking Redhorse real well these days; everybody they'd killed or arrested as enemy spies during the ISA mission had friends. But you could blame Eight Ball Command for handing you over to SERPA to spend your downtime as guinea pigs. Or maybe the rest of your lifetime.

There hadn't been any choice that English could see. There still wasn't. They were here until the *Haig* came to get them when the destroyer was finished with its purported retrofit. Or until they got killed in SERPA experiments.

After a month and a half of psychovers and various therapies, English still wasn't sure which fate he preferred. His outfit wasn't just a Marine Reaction Company any longer; SERPA had turned them into something euphemistically called "Electro Research." And English didn't like being the tactical operations arm of SERPA one bit.

He didn't like the equipment. He didn't like the implications of the kind of retraining they were being given. But nobody gave a damn what he liked except the sex therapists, who couldn't understand why he wouldn't take advantage of their services.

All the therapy Toby English needed was down here in the Virtual Prototyping bay of the Electromagnetic Research Station.

He pushed his hand against the palm-ID imprinter and peered into the retinal scanner. A sharp puff of air stung his eyeballs.

The door ending the short, featureless corridor said, "Please identify yourself by voice."

"English, looking for a couple hours in the funhouse." It didn't matter what you said. The AI guardian just wanted to be sure that he wasn't too spiked to go beyond this point.

It compared his voice with the template on file, and then considered his palmprint and galvanic skin response, the dilation and mapping of his pupils, the pressure in his eyeballs.

The door swung back, which meant that the Station AI had decided he wasn't about to go berserk. Which, considering the weapons behind the heavy door of the ERS, was a real consideration when you were deciding whether to let somebody through.

It was sleep cycle for the command-and-control facility.

English didn't expect to run into any humans in here. So it was strange that the lights were lit in the halls.

Last time he'd come down to the funhouse this late, they hadn't been. Still, he'd come to get some time in on his customized hardsuit and the Associate AI and APOT weaponry that went with it.

He didn't need to disturb some clerk working here late. He knew where everything was. He'd been spending all of his waking hours "consulting" with the SERPA techs, tweaking this twitchy gear up to something like combat readiness, while he was waiting for his replacement personnel.

The tour refit specs were easier to meet than the personnel specs. They'd gotten three new guys. They'd fitted them to hardsuits and neurotyped them for the second-generation Associate electronics that powered the battle-management systems in the suit helmets. And then, two days ago, Greco, one of the new guys, had had a heart attack during a Difficulty Seven simulation.

Now SERPA wanted to tear everything down again and find out why. English turned a corner and a light above a doorway blinked on, scanned him, and opened the door to the locker room for him.

The door shut behind him. The lights all flicked red for a minute before they came back sunlight-spectrum. He hand-printed his locker and it opened. Greco, the dead guy, was simply ready to have a heart attack, English had tried to explain. He'd seen it before, during drop phase. Something always went wrong with special operations. When you got operations this special, things were going to go wrong during training.

That suited English fine. A corpse is lots less trouble when he's in a nice clean research facility than when he's in your com circuit and battle plan minutes before you jump into a hot landing.

Stripping down to his antistatic skivvies, English tried not to look at himself reflected in the mirror. He was looking at a coward: somebody who didn't have the guts to make the fuss necessary to keep Redhorse out of this particular billet.

Funny, it didn't show on any of his workups, not even his psychover. The psych therapists didn't care about his dreams of dead guys, any more than the physical therapists cared about the weird little tics he'd developed in the wake of using the A-potential (APOT) electromagnetic beam weaponry, or the tan he'd gotten from spending so much time in the simulators' mixed fields.

He was "well within the curve," and looked healthier than he could ever remember. His muscle tone was great, optimized by the artificial gravity of the station and the cushy living conditions at MAC/ASD. His long-limbed frame had filled out; he was carrying about twelve percent fat; his rest pulse rate averaged sixty-five and his stressed pulse rate averaged eighty-five.

Only he felt like death warmed over, but you couldn't put that in any report. He'd tried. He had a formless dread that everybody told him was just normal, considering that when the Khalian enemy had surrendered, the Alliance had found out there was a bigger, badder, higher-tech power behind the Khalia—enemies that humans might not be able to defeat.

The scuttlebutt had it that those Syndicate enemies were human. Toby English had grown up killing Weasels, furry Khalian enemies whose tails he collected until he had a coat and bedspread's worth.

He wasn't exactly unwilling to kill humans. But he was unwilling to get himself killed so that SERPA could report to OPSCOM through Eight Ball Command that, yes, indeed, there really was a humanoid threat out there.

He felt old and tired and he really did have a pathological hatred for APOT rifles. Never mind that SERPA was sure that the weird shit he saw when he fired one was just a backwash of excited electrons spinning through his skull from another universe—nothing to sweat.

As he got out his hardsuit and clamped the metal-composite body armor over him, the sticker revealed in the back of his locker reminded him: STATIC IS THE ENEMY.

"Bullshit," he told it. Human error was the enemy. He still wasn't satisfied that he or any of his men really were neurotyped sufficiently for this customized equipment. Or, if they were, that field retrofits were possible, if you lost a soldier and had to cannibalize his equipment the way you could with regular gear.

He slung his ELVIS (Electromagnetic Vectored Integrated Scalar) pack onto his back, got the APOT rifle from its hook, and then fitted his helmet and gloves into the system.

Snapping his visor down, he brought up his displays and went through his self-test. Then he said, "Bay One, Conflict Scenario," and started down the hall, waiting for his Associate AI to tell him what was playing in the funhouse tonight.

His Associate said, "Scenario in progress."

Shit, he hadn't meant that he wanted to walk in on a running game . . . "Reprogram. Display options."

The heads-up showed him a complex, quadranted grid that was no different from a real battle plan, with blips of various colors and digital call signs beneath.

English's sphincter muscles tightened. Things had been screwy with the simulator ever since Greco had had his heart attack. SERPA kept saying that it hadn't impacted the AI sysop to monitor a human death, but SERPA said what served SERPA . . .

When he got to the holo bay, he realized that somebody was already in there. He relaxed. There was nothing wrong with the sysop for the funhouse. Even better, there was nothing really wrong with his Associate. He'd had trouble with the previous model in combat, when his Delta-One Associate had usurped his command prerogatives.

Now he had an override switch, in case that happened again, that allowed him to cold-voice-code the entire electro/transducer/battle-management system.

If he ever needed it, he was going to enjoy the hell out of the moment he got to pull the Associate's plug. . . .

The simulator was running hot and heavy. English's breathing and pulse rate were beginning to respond to the visual cues of conflict on his heads-up display, even though he'd been in the simulator countless times and knew that a Virtual Prototyping module was a big, empty bay with holographic and electro-imaging capabilities, and that was all.

English said to his Associate, "What's the scenario?"

It came up on his screen: *Syndicate Base Raid; Difficulty Level, Ten.*

They'd had a guy die of fright at Difficulty Level Seven. Who the fuck was in there, anyway?

He asked the Associate for a patch to whoever was playing through. There were other teams training here, English knew—small, seven- to twelve-man assault units, nothing as big as his fifty-man demi-company. Maybe it was Sawyer. Sawyer, English's line lieutenant, was crazy enough to test the limits of these systems just to make sure they were safe for his men to use. . . .

"Hey, Sawyer? That you?" The dual-com English voice-actuated would only come up in Sawyer's helmet.

No answer.

English was punching his code into the combination lock, because he was damned if he was going to wait in line for what he rightly considered the 92nd's funhouse, when he heard a voice:

(*Static.*) ". . . fratricide between these systems, Incoming User. Sending 3.5 GHz; repeat, freq stabilizer F coming your way."

Well, well. English punched the last combination number into the lock and the door opened. He'd see what this guy from some other unit had for stones, once their suits locked up.

A Ten Simulation didn't scare English. He'd done the first field test of this equipment, in combat, without a familiarization run-through beforehand. And lived to be told not to talk about it.

As the door slid back and he stepped down into a chaos that came in through all his sensoring packages, making his head swim, he braced himself: you felt everything in this funhouse you'd feel if you were really discharging your weapons.

For all he knew, he really was punching a virtual hole in space-time every time he laid on his trigger in this test bay. His trigger finger always felt shocky, like it did with the real thing. The friendly fire problems of this equipment were pretty serious, though, and nobody was admitting to these practice rifles being the same as the real ones.

Still, you shot what you got on your display, you felt what you felt when you were shooting for your life.

Somebody else shot—either the other player, or the sysop. English hit the deck, his visor whiting out because he was taking fire point-blank.

Game in progress.

On his belly, he wriggled forward, talking his systems through a damage assessment, waiting for his visor to clear itself. When it didn't, immediately, he was suddenly afraid that the simulator was going to tell him he was dead. So he asked for enemy targeting and positions of his "men."

He got a quick visual of something like a football field with five black towers that he could see. Then his Associate showed him a putative field-of-fire grid, with twelve three-teams, a command-and-control vehicle, and three two-teams designated in various grid squares.

And he got the other player, live: a yellow bead lit on the left upper quadrant of his visor and a voice said, "You reading me, Eye-Cubed-Ell?"

"Delta Two," habit took over, "to Yellow Shooter. What the hell's Eye-Cubed-Ell?"

"Oh. Sorry. Thought you were someone else. I³L: Ingenuity, Innovation, Intelligence, and Luck. You almost bought it back there, Delta Two. Want to integrate me? You've added lots of synth shooters."

"Yeah. Take Omega Leader, it's close to where you are." He toggled out, told his Associate that Omega was now a three-team with a live leader who had dual-com requirements, and then back in: "We're running. What's the target? You've been playing this longer than I have."

"Target's black tower, twelve o'clock, my plot point."

"Right," said English. It wasn't a game any longer. At least, it didn't feel like a game. There was enemy fire pin-

ning down three of his synth teams, and his Associate
wanted him to retreat to the C&C vehicle.

"Omega Leader, I'll want point."

"Come get it, hotshot—Delta Two."

"On my way. We get there, touchdown, you buy the
drinks."

"Be the first time in synth history, but sure—you're alive,
you got it."

English got off the dual-com and onto all-com. Sweat was
pouring down into his eyes. His suit turned its climate control up and he began to shiver.

It was a long way to Black Tower N and there were four
enemy blip configurations headed straight toward him.

You could get killed doing this. Greco had. There was
no such thing as not for real, especially with this equipment. He fired a burst at something that popped up on his
far right, just as his Associate targeted it for him. They were
synced better than ever. But that didn't stop the weird-ass
effects: his soul turned inside out. A hot wind blew through
there. He saw strange clouds and funny flora and fauna.

Bullshit he wasn't shooting real zero-point energy through
his rifle. He felt the world rock under him.

It was now a matter of pride that he would run this simulation through without losing a single synth team, from the
point, so that he could collect his drinks from the cocky
son of a bitch who was with Omega. Never mind that Omega
was a synth team.

Toby English was a bad loser.

He talked his synth teams into position. He brought up
his C&C car and ported data to it so that it would clear a
broadband swath to the target.

Then he ran like hell, dodging synth fire, talking his teams
through in a shorthand that his Associate and he had developed, until he was up by Omega's grid square and right
below Black Tower N.

He asked for a head count. Not one casualty. Then the
virtual reality program that had been showing him terrain
in his heads-up whenever he asked for it showed him an
actual person as opposed to a simulated person.

He could tell because the helmet turned toward him, black visor down, had "Cleary" stenciled on it, and the asshole wearing the helmet was pointing an APOT rifle at him.

In that moment he thought: ISA. Grant's sent somebody to waste me, unattributably. And I walked right into it.

Then he thought, as sweat made his eyes sting and his suit hummed and aspirated, trying to cool him, Get the fucker, as his body lunged forward and he caught the barrel of the other rifle over his, and jerked up before he swatted sideways.

If it were some plan of Grant's, he couldn't shoot the other guy. Not if there'd be an Eight Ball Command inquiry. And not if one, or both, of these rifles were as live as his felt.

Profanity came through his dual-com, then: "Asshole! What do you think, I'm an enemy simulation?"

"Don't point your gun at a superior officer, sonny, ever—not under any circumstances. Now, Omega Leader: You wanted me. Here I am. Let's take the tower."

Right then, the tower opened, and a nightmare's worth of counterforce poured out of it.

English hit the deck and called on his C&C car for air support: "Smart, fast, all the missiles you've got. Level the thing."

And the simulation ended abruptly.

Toby English was lying facedown, his chest heaving, the rifle butted against his shoulder, in an empty bay that showed clearly through his grid-hashed faceplate.

The Omega Leader was lying beside him. English thought: He's a little guy, this Cleary. He said: "What the fuck was that?"

His dual-com bead lit and Cleary said, "The end of the Ten Simulation, I guess. Never got this far before. Just let me stow my gear and shower, and I'll buy you all the drinks you want, Delta Two." Rolling sideways with a grunt, Cleary offered a gloved hand.

After only a slight hesitation, English took it. The youngster just hadn't been in combat enough to know you don't point a gun at somebody like that.

"You bet," said English. "Shower and drinks."

Trotting through the white, pristine, empty bay with his rifle over his shoulder, English could see the holo projectors. And a couple places where the walls looked like something had impacted them pretty hard. But it wasn't his job to worry about bay damage. His gear was getting heavier by the moment, the way it always did after action.

He kept ahead of the little Omega leader. No need for Cleary to realize how hard English's suit was working to keep him cool inside it.

Once he'd checked his gear and stowed it in his locker, he picked up his clothes and headed for the shower. Cleary's locker must be in another part of the station. This was the first time that English had seen anybody from the other teams rumored to be training.

He was stiff, his antistatic jockstrap and undershirt—even his socks—were soaked. He hung them on a blow-drier and slapped it onto full before he got into the shower, where steam was already rising.

"Hey, Cleary," he said as he opened the door—and stopped talking.

Water from the shower head sprayed him in the mouth and reminded him to shut it.

Nothing for it but to get the rest of the way in, close the door, and tough it out.

You bet Cleary was little. Cleary was a woman.

Bent down, washing her legs, so that only her white ass was truly visible, she said, "Yeah, what, Delta Two?"

He couldn't think of a damned thing to say. He didn't usually come out of a shooting situation, pumped up beyond measure, and find himself unexpectedly confronted with a white, wet ass in primo physical shape.

He'd been going to piss in the shower. Which meant he wasn't exactly in the right state to greet a colleague, either, unless that colleague was as pumped as he was.

He said, "Nice simulation," lamely, and reached for some soap on the ledge, trying not to look at her slick butt.

He couldn't see anything else.

"Thanks, Delta Two," she said. Her voice was throaty,

deep; over the com it had sounded like a guy's. But then, he'd been expecting a guy.

She wasn't short, for a woman; she was finely made, narrow but round where it counted, and her skin looked altogether too soft.

He stepped in under the shower head next to hers and turned it on full bore, not caring much how hot or cold it was. *Just keep busy.*

There weren't any women in the 92nd. There wasn't any reason for that, not really. They were half the strength of most companies. . . . He pissed when the tepid spray hit him and started soaping his blond hair. Even with his eyes closed, he could still see that first sight of her bottom. He could probably cup both her buttocks in his one spread hand and put his fingers inside her at the same time; she was tiny.

He couldn't seem to think the things that would get his body under control. His breathing was still too deep when she said, "Damn," and her soap dropped on his foot.

She reached for it.

He reached for her. His left hand just slid under her butt of its own accord, and the logistics were exactly what he'd thought they'd be.

She gasped in surprise and straightened up. In that instant, he was in nearly combat-heightened awareness. There was no way to back out now, even if he could convince himself. . . .

His right arm went around her from behind and she didn't twist out of his grasp.

But she didn't say anything when his fingers found her breast. Instead, she leaned back and against him.

All along his length, wherever they touched, his body tingled. He said into her wet hair, "Please . . . don't tell me to stop."

His fingers, exploring her, were telling him he had a chance.

Then she did twist and he let go, quick, to make it clear he wasn't going to push this. This wasn't any kind of assault. But he knew it was too late for that. . . .

Then he saw her face, covered with spray, water dripping

from her lips. "You better not stop, soldier, until I find out if you fuck as good as you fight." And she took a step toward him and raised a leg high, almost over his buttocks.

The rest was something his serial memory wasn't capable of storing. She climbed him like a tree, he was sure of that.

And he was sure that her heart was beating just as fast as his. And that she was everything a sex therapist wasn't. He did remember saying, when his legs were threatening not to hold them, "Easy there, Omega. I haven't used this thing for a long time."

But she just laughed and reached behind her to turn the shower off. She had black hair, blue eyes, and the softest, whitest skin he'd ever touched over muscles like a swimmer's. "I suppose you still want me to buy your drinks," she said, finally, and he didn't have the heart to make her do anything she didn't want to do.

He said that.

She said, "See you around the simulator," and went off toward her locker to dress.

So he never did ask where she was billeted.

When he had his clothes on and went down there to find her, she was gone. And the *Haig*, he learned when he stumbled back to his quarters, was scheduled to dock in the morning, just long enough to pick up English's 92nd.

So he'd have no time to look for her if he wanted to: he had to shape up his outfit for imminent departure, new weaponry and all, and he had only seven hours left to do it.

It wasn't thrilling English that the *Haig* was refitted with APOT guns too. And newly equipped with zero-point drivers as well, if the rumor mill was right.

Jay Padova, the *Haig*'s captain, must not have been listening when the 92nd came off the Bull's-Eye insertion, short a Beta three-team and bitching like hell about X-class weapons that got Marines killed down there.

But it was still good to be back on Padova's little destroyer, close quarters or not, Fleet protocols or not. Once they were under way and English and Sawyer had shoehorned their forty-seven men back into the familiar belly of the ship, English went to pay his customary courtesy call on the captain, leaving Sawyer to check the manifest and settle-in the two new guys.

If Sawyer, his blue-jawed line lieutenant, chose to have some private reunion with the *Haig*'s ranking Intel officer, one Johanna Manning, while English was gone, then that was their business.

English didn't have to formally disapprove their relationship unless it was negatively impacting Sawyer's performance. Until it did, it wasn't any of English's goddamn concern, he told himself. Anyway, Manning was their lifeline to ISA, an Eight Ball Command as well as Fleet Intel staffer.

Now that the 92nd was a Special Electro Research outfit, she was indelibly inked into English's command chain. They might be needing Manning's goodwill like never before.

So he had lots of reason to make himself scarce, given that he'd gone out of his way plenty of times to let Sawyer know that he didn't like his first officer messing around with a dual-hatted spook like Manning. If it hadn't been so crystal clear that Sawyer couldn't wait to be rid of him, it wouldn't have rankled so.

The 92nd was still English's responsibility, wasn't it?

Jay Padova's office hadn't changed a bit, right down to the pall of blue cigar smoke.

"Take a load off, Captain," said Padova, once English had been admitted. "How was refit?"

"About like yours, sir," said English, taking a seat opposite the paunchy captain's desk. Something wasn't right here. He could see it in Jay's face: the balding, jowly man's features were too carefully arranged.

Then English thought maybe he knew what it was: the SERPA dogtags his Marines were wearing these days. He reached into his blouse pocket and handed over his orders as if nothing had changed.

Padova took them as if nothing had changed. Then the destroyer's skipper tapped the folder on his desk, making no move to open the packet, scan the hard copy through his decrypter, or view the accompanying chip. "I think you have a right to know that we're up way beyond milspec for the foreseeable, Toby."

Real stiff. And yet trying to be chatty. English said, "I heard something about that. Sir, if I may say so, I'm not sure you're going to like this particular batch of black boxes. . . ."

"We'll have a chance to find out, together, unless I miss my guess." Padova puffed on the cigar, pulled it out of his mouth, and looked at it critically. "You know I pride myself on keeping the *Haig* on the techno-edge."

Enough that she was usually pushing the bounds of what was strictly legal. Everybody who shipped with Padova was proud of his technical expertise and nearly arrogant about what their destroyer and her captain could do.

"This tech's real . . . unpredictable, sir. I hope they told you that the . . . human . . . effects of it are—" Shit, he didn't know whether he had any right to be saying what he was saying. So he stopped. Stood up.

Padova waved him back down. "We're just keeping up with you boys, Toby. Did I tell you how proud I am that your ER company's come out of the *Haig*, and that you've come back home with what you've learned?"

"No, sir, you didn't," English said weakly. Oh, great. Now the 92nd was some kind of sexy, elite technocombat team, so far as the Fleet was concerned. Even if he didn't experience severe equipment failure during his next mission, that kind of reputation by itself could get the whole outfit killed.

"Sir, this just sort of . . . happened."

"We know, Toby. And every sailor on the *Haig* is proud to be a part of it." Some of the masking dropped from Padova's demeanor. The barrel-chested Navy captain leaned forward: "Once Manning and I have looked everything over and we have you back up here for your briefing, we can really talk about this. But I want you to know how important CINCFLEET thinks this next mission of yours is—to the whole war effort."

This wasn't the Jay Padova that Toby English had known.

This was some guy with more on his plate than he could handle, no longer the fatherly authority to whom English could turn when the 92nd tail was caught in a door somewhere.

"Look, sir, we've got two new guys who need orientation and I ought to get back to it. When you and Manning are ready to brief me . . ." A courtesy call was just that. This wasn't the moment to be trying to warn Padova that his thirst for leading-edge hardware might choke him, this time. Anyway, if the destroyer blew up the first time it used its new gear, English and his boys either wouldn't be on board, or wouldn't know what hit them.

So he ought to get out of here, back to where he knew what was expected of him.

"I understand you're busy, Toby. But if you want to talk, or just compare notes, feel free to drop in on me. Anytime."

Surreal. Impossible. English ran a hand through his hair and got to his feet, this time less tentatively, eyeing the unopened packet on Padova's desk. He'd never expected to come up here and *not* have Padova open his orders . . . .

"Thanks, sir. I'll do that." He just stood there, waiting for Jay to dismiss him.

The thick, blunt fingers of the destroyer's captain drummed on the packet that English had brought from MAC/ASD. "Don't worry, Toby. We're ready for this. We've been thoroughly briefed. It's my considered opinion that the *Haig* can handle ten times her weight in Syndicate vessels. We'll get you where you're going. And back. You have my word on it."

So Padova knew what was in English's orders. Or thought he did. English stared at the ship's captain and said, "Then you know more than I do. Sir."

Padova didn't blink. English's eyes began to sting. The visual game of chicken continued until Captain Padova said, "Let's just say I know which way the wind's blowing, like a good sailor should."

Padova looked away, finally, down to the chronometer on his desk. "Your new technical advisor's being billeted up here. Manning was very persuasive. What say we crack these eggs at 0100, when everybody's nice and relaxed. Until then—''

''Technical advisor?'' This was getting weirder and weirder. Yeah, Greco's death had left the 92nd with one empty slot, but . . . ''Nobody said anything to me about—''

''You know command decisions, Toby. The way I heard it, your Ninety-Second was going to get this advisor or a Weasel advisor, and I was very relieved that Manning politicked for a human.''

English just wanted to get out of there, now that Padova was through with him, and hole up somewhere so he could assess his damages. ''Yes, sir. Well, I guess Manning will introduce me to my new TA soldier when she's damned good and ready. Sir.''

Padova chuckled. ''I guess she will, Marine. All right, you're dismissed.''

Thank the Lord.

He wandered down through the decks, trying not to think about what Jay was implying. Of course, the *Haig* had had to undergo a refit to bring it up to Syndicate-fighting specs, if his 92nd was going to ship inside it with all their new ER gear.

And of course Jay was pleased as punch, and privy to a lot more data than English was. A Navy captain and a Marine captain weren't anywhere near parity in rank.

You did the best you could. English decided that, since there was no funhouse on the *Haig*, the best thing he could do was to go to the officers' mess and see if he could get a little buzz on—one that he could work off before his briefing.

There wasn't anyplace else he could think of going that he wouldn't run into Johanna Manning. Damn meddling Eight Ball bitch.

The officers' mess had a dark corner and English was half asleep there, having made it secure and defensible. His kinetic kill pistol was on the table beside a half-empty glass of beer and he was meditating on it.

There'd been a time when he would have said that whatever he got himself into, that pistol could get him out of, one way or the other—on his feet or in a rubber bag.

But that wasn't true anymore. His most trusted ally, his .10mm sidearm, had failed him. You couldn't shoot Manning and you couldn't shoot Grant, the ISA honcho who had it in for Toby English, personally, and everybody in the 92nd because of Manning and Sawyer.

English and Sawyer had *tried* to shoot Grant, and failed.

If Sawyer hadn't saved English's ass repeatedly, English would have torn into Sawyer right now about getting so goddamn familiar with somebody who was handing down orders cut at Eight Ball Command level. But Sawyer had, and English couldn't, so he settled for wishing.

Settled for it, that is, until Manning came in with a crowd of laughing sailors and some of his troops.

"Hey, Manning," English called across the room. "Get over here a minute."

He was surprised at how angry he was. The sight of her was making his hands shake. Or maybe he was drunker than he thought.

He checked his watch as she approached. Still had three hours until his briefing. Okay, then.

"Hey there, Captain English. Good to see you." Manning was a mean, little woman with a sharp face and hair habitually cut shorter than English's own. She had people with her but English was too pumped to look at anything but her cold, brown eyes.

"Well, it's not good to see you, Manning. What's this about you havin' some tech advisor of mine stashed up on the Intel deck instead of down with my company? You think you've got some kind of carte blanche to change Marine rules and regulations?"

Manning had been messing around much too much with English's men and his command chain. It had to stop. He couldn't let Sawyer's situation impact his judgment.

"English, shut it down," Manning said, taking a step

toward him. The tops of her thighs hit the table. She picked up the pistol there and pretended to examine it. "I've got your tech advisor with me, ready to report. I had to do a prebrief on the situation, tech parameters only. It's all by the book."

"Whose goddamn book?" he muttered. Then, "You keep my people—my TA—out of my reporting chain, and you call yourself an Intel officer? Who're you working for?" Almost a whisper.

He shouldn't be starting this argument. He knew it.

Manning knew it too. "Look at me, English."

He did.

"You're drunk, and you've got a briefing in three hours. Maybe the most important briefing of your life. So we'll forget this. You took care of me when I came a little loose. I haven't forgotten. We're on your side. You've got to realize that."

"We?"

She wouldn't answer that, not say "ISA" or "Eight Ball Command" right out here in public. And the crowd she came in with was trying to look busy.

But you could bet they were listening. Nobody'd even sat down, although a couple had gone to the bar.

"We," she said softly, and put the gun down, just the way she'd found it. "I'll get your tech advisor."

"I don't want a technical advisor."

"Command doesn't care what you want, English. You're getting what you need to keep you—and your unit—alive. The best we've got. And you're lucky you pulled a human technical, rather than a Weasel tactical, advisor. So you smile, and you be nice. And don't you make anybody's life more of a hell than it's got to be. You hear, buddy?"

Or else he'd have her to deal with. Of all the tight-assed Intel officers English had known, Manning took the prize. "I give, Manning. Truce." He squinted at her and tried to smile.

"Fine," she snapped. "Let me get your outfit back to full strength." Manning turned, whistled, and motioned.

Somebody came through the crowd to join them at the

table. English was looking at his hands. He'd better find a way to make peace permanently with Manning. He couldn't imagine how he'd let things go so far, over some Intel protocol.

He looked up, ready to say something placatory and greet the 92nd's new tech advisor, his hand out to take the file the advisor was holding.

And blinked. Swore under his breath. Manning was watching him steadily. So was the technical advisor that Eight Ball Command had decided that the 92nd needed.

The person holding out the folder was Cleary.

He took the packet as smoothly as he could and said, "Thank you, Officer Manning. If you'll excuse us, I've got to huddle with my new TA . . . ."

He started to get up. Manning said, "You'll have to stay here for a half hour or so, English. You can show her the ship's belly later."

He didn't even ask why. He was having enough trouble just covering his misery and shock. "Sit down, please," he said to Cleary.

Her pale blue eyes were wide as she sat across from him and Manning sauntered back to her group.

"Give me one good reason why I shouldn't dump you for good and sufficient cause, right now, Ms. Technical Advisor," he said in as close as he could manage to a whisper. His damned voice was shaking.

Cleary leaned forward, her starched uniform sleeves smearing the wet-rings on the table. "You've got to believe me, Delta Two, I didn't know. Not my assignment; not who you were, beyond that you had a C&C profile in the simulator." She reached out as if to touch his hand.

"Damn it, don't do that." He sat back as if her touch was lethal. "Look," he said in a rush. "We've never had a female *any*thing in this company. And we don't need a technical advisor—"

"Yes, you do, sir." Her brand-new uniform had all the appropriate mission patches, including the Redhorse patch. But it also had the crossed lightning bolts over a universe spiral: ISA.

"Look, Major, I've got spooks up my ass on this. I've got Manning, who's not my favorite person. Because of Manning, I've got her boss, Grant, breathing down my neck. Shit, if it weren't for Manning and Grant—"

"I don't want to hear it. Sir. I think when you've read my orders you'll realize that, given the circumstances, although it's your company, you're not in any position to 'dump' me. So let's just forget what's happened up until now—all of it—and start over." Her delicate jaw squared.

"Okay, cowgirl. Let's do that. You tell me, in fifty words or less, why I need you—any TA. Here. Now."

She didn't even look over her shoulder before she spoke. She reached into her breast pocket and tweaked a field generator; he could feel it come on: all the hairs on his forearms rose and fell.

She said, "In a nutshell: SERPA's been dual-tracking a Syndicate reconnaissance effort. Grant and—some people— took a Track A shot at coming home with targeting data and intel. They blew it off pretty bad: some folks say they never even left the launch bay. So we're the Track B effort. And if we don't come back, the data's *got* to. That's what your briefing's going to say."

"So, why do I need you? I been coming back just fine for . . . a hundred and twelve combat drops so far."

"Because the *Haig*'s going to take us into Syndicate space, and cover us while we do something very similar to what we were trying to do in that Ten Simulation, you and I."

"I still don't copy the 'you and I.' "

"Mister . . . Captain English, not only do you need me, but you yourself can't get any farther into action than the hold of an APC unless I certify you fit and ready. So be nice to me. Or you'll sit this out and your second in command will have all the fun. And I know you wouldn't want that." She smiled as if she'd been telling him a joke.

So he laughed like she had. Seeing them sit back from their close huddle, Manning started toward them again. With her, now, was Sawyer.

Then English looked closer and saw most of his 92nd in

the room (where they shouldn't be because this was officers only), as well as Jay Padova and most of the officers from the destroyer—everybody who wasn't working, it seemed.

The lights went out.

English grabbed for his pistol just as the hologram behind the bar came back on.

It said, in big, glowing letters, HAPPY BIRTHDAY, CAPTAIN ENGLISH.

And Manning, rushing over, reached down to hug him: "All's forgiven, Toby. Everybody gets bitchy around their birthday, once they're over thirty."

Sawyer had, of all things, a birthday cake with what looked like a million candles on it.

He couldn't even remember how old he was, in elapsed time: relativity aged you. And then he did, sort of. Whether you were chronologically some age or other ought not to matter.

But maybe Manning was right: turning thirty wasn't something you wanted to dwell on, not when you were just going into a new phase of an escalating interstellar war.

Maybe that was all that was wrong with him: turning thirty. But, Cleary. Damn. What the hell was he going to do now?

He couldn't believe, during the sponge transit into Syndicate space, that Cleary actually expected to jump into combat with the 92nd.

Drop, maybe. But not jump. He had enough to do without knowing that one of the blips on his screen was somebody he'd fucked once and now was fucking him over, every way she knew how.

It was just unacceptable.

But, command being what it was, nobody gave a shit what he thought, and he couldn't very well be event-specific, so there they all were, in the APC, suited up, with a woman technical advisor who probably thought that when the going got rough, the simulation stopped and you went to the showers and got laid.

The Syndicate bases' coordinates weren't his problem,

but Cleary was sure Padova had the right ones. So sure that she'd packed life support beyond normal need into the little APC.

That spooked everybody. Even Sawyer. And when Sawyer was spooked, there was no way to pull the Marines out of it.

So English was talking himself hoarse in the jump bay. They weren't doing anything but sitting there. He handed out protein bars and cigarettes and told every joke he knew.

Nobody had their helmets on; they weren't free of the *Haig* yet, just sitting in her belly in another layer of arguably survivable hull.

Cleary had insisted they spend the last hour of sponge jump ready to rock and roll. She was Omega leader on his com, because he wasn't about to let her forget what had happened.

When they dropped, and he had his helmet on, he was going to talk to her the way he hadn't been able to during the briefing or in the interim.

If she wanted to do this job, he was going to give her the on-the-job training she needed. Or die trying.

He gave up trying to make the men feel any better than he did and sat down in a corner, with the bulkhead behind his back. There was bench space, but he didn't want it.

It was like a morgue in the APC. Their Nocturnal Operations Clandestine Module (NOCM) had been refitted for Syndicate encounters, like everything else on the destroyer.

It carried APOT guns as well as underbelly cannon. The pilot and copilot couches had enough command-and-fire electronics to run the insertion from the bird. If they needed to.

Sawyer was up there on the NOCM's flight deck, with Manning, getting last-minute orders of some kind. Or getting head, for all English knew. The bulkhead door was closed.

He looked at his watch again, and then at Trask, his top sergeant: "Trask, knock on the door. See if we can get privy to any of what Manning's got to say."

"Right, boss," said Trask, ducking his dark head as he

slid off the bench, unwinding from his crash webbing too
jerkily for English's liking.

This was going to kill his guys, if anything did, all this
extra high-torque waiting.

"Cleary," he said in exasperation as Trask knocked on
the forward bulkhead, "get over here and talk to me about
these fratricide problems from the *Haig*'s APOTs you say
you think you've fixed." Fratricide meant, in general terms,
one system screwing up another's ability to function. You
normally worried about it in terms of coms.

But Cleary was worried about it in terms of—

The bulkhead opened to Trask's knock. Manning stuck
her head out, saying, "Clear of sponge. Jump phase count-
down in—"

Cleary was moving toward him, and the space-time
burped a little as the destroyer settled into real-time. So did
Cleary. Staggering, she grabbed for webbing.

English checked his watch. They were ten minutes early.
So much for perfect planning. "Ninety-Second: ready up.
Com checks. Lock and load."

The hell with Cleary. This was something he didn't need
a tech advisor for, a major or any other kind.

Inside his helmet, the world of the APC began to look
manageable.

She was Omega leader; her yellow head lit and turned
green, blinking for privacy: his Associate gave him
dual-com before he could ask.

"Something's wrong," she said without preface.

"He's early. So what?"

"Something's wrong. I've got stuff you aren't monitoring."

"So, what do you advise, Omega?"

"You might as well drop. The destroyer's already engaging whatever popped it out of sponge early."

Shit. The Syndicate had something that could pull you
out of a spongehole? English shivered. "Okay, Omega
Leader. Stand by for all-com." He didn't want the men
hearing any of this.

"Drop in one minute," he told them. He could hear Sawyer swear when he got the separation order without warning.

Sawyer's com bead lit, purple privacy and blinking: "Treat me like I'm still somebody you'd drink with, Toby, for chrissakes."

"Sorry. Got busy. TA's got scary stories about there being some unfriendly fire out there when we separate. I was about to get to you with it."

The purple bead went off. English punched it back: "Keep Manning in the copilot's seat. We got one woman, we might as well have two. Maybe we're the only ones'll go home from this."

"Crap. Too long an APC ride," Sawyer said. And: "Thanks."

English toggled into the tune-up that Trask was giving their Marines, and prayed like hell that there wasn't a space battle going on around them when the APC dropped out of the *Haig*'s belly.

But there was. If the APC hadn't been Clandestine, with all the stealth that implied, they might have gotten hit before they made their first orbit.

As it was, they had too long a ride to atmosphere.

"Play dead," Sawyer advised from the flight deck, and everybody shut down everything, including movement, coughs, or unnecessary communications, until the red drop light started to strobe.

The APC skipped in and out, then into the Syndicate world's atmosphere like a stone on a pond. Somebody lost hold of a rifle, which went banging around the bay until Trask caught it.

English didn't have to look to know it was Cleary. He decided he was going to shoot her himself if she screwed up once more. So far, she was running zero-sum: he'd given her one point for calling the hostile fire warning, which evened her up for the point she'd just lost, letting her weapon get loose and bang around like that.

Noise could get you killed in this mode. Purported dead pieces of crashing equipment didn't make human noises.

He was holding his breath.

Then the burn of attitude stabilizers told him he didn't have to, and he got ready to drop his teams.

Sawyer said, "Got one full ground track," in his privacy com. "Here it comes."

English's visor display showed him the APC's collection of imaging and signature intelligence from the planet.

And damned if Cleary didn't break right in with, "If we've got that much, maybe we should send it back. Or go back with it to the *Haig*."

"Maybe?" English said icily. She shouldn't even have been able to penetrate purple mode. "Sawyer, port that data to the *Haig* and wherever else Manning wants, however else she wants. Tell me when it's done. Don't drop anybody until we know it's safe."

Damn, this was his worst nightmare.

Trask was cued up to talk to him, his green light blinking. "Yeah, Trask?"

By then his field first was waving at him urgently. "Sir. We can't assume we can hold parameters during another pass. Integrity of insertion voided. Repeat: jump now or pull out and try another day."

Otherwise, Trask was saying, they'd be tracked all the way down.

And from the cockpit, Sawyer said, "If we can. We've just been acquired on somebody's scope."

When you were acquired, you were a target.

They were, at this point, sitting ducks. He wasn't feeling like suicide today.

"Cleary," English said, and his Associate made a command decision to bring her up in privacy mode. "What do you say? You want to die here? We're a target as of now."

Something Sawyer did on the flight deck threw everybody to the right before she could answer.

"Cleary? How bad you want that insertion? As our TA, we'll jump if you insist."

Time to see what she was made of.

"Delta Two," came her voice, "you're the captain. If you say the situation's too dangerous—"

They took a hit that English hoped was glancing. The NOCM shivered and began to spin.

The question of command was now academic, but he gave Sawyer a direct order anyhow: "Delta Three, get us back to *Haig* if you can. Intel's more important." Fucking SERPA *had* a goddamn scenario-able picture of their drop coordinates, anyhow. Cleary had verified for him that it was the same location. Difficulty Level Ten.

No fooling.

He had to grab webbing himself as Sawyer wrestled the NOCM out of the atmosphere. Then the ride steadied as they came out into cleaner space.

But English wasn't getting lucky today. Sawyer told him: "I'm porting you a view of the engagement at the *Haig*. You'll want to call this one yourself, Delta Two."

When he saw the space battle, he blinked twice because it couldn't be this bad: telerobotics were all over the *Haig*'s skin, like ants trying to get into an overripe pear. He could see the little puffs and bright flares of the destroyer's reactive armor as it met the telerobotic attack. Then he said, "Omega Leader, to the flight deck."

He met her there, and there was just room for the two of them, plus Manning and Sawyer.

"So? Now what?" Sawyer's voice through the Associate-assisted four-way was attenuated with protective scrambling.

"Damned if I know," English said, leaning one hand on his rifle. "I just came up to watch the show from a better seat. TA, what do you think?"

Cleary leaned over Sawyer and touched something on the imaging screen. The view got better.

"Must be fratricide: the *Haig*'s APOTs are interfering with her jamming and other defensive systems." English thought he heard a sigh. "Maybe I could fix it, if I got on board."

"Can't you tell 'em what to do?" Manning wanted to know, her one-eyed visor turned toward Cleary and polarized flat black. "It'll take us a while to get back inside."

Manning didn't say, "We might not be able to get back inside."

English started estimating what he and Sawyer could do to clear the hull.

"Manning, Cleary, you guys send them some stabilizing data." He remembered Cleary giving him that sort of thing when he entered the simulation.

"Sawyer, you and me are going to drop the 92nd onto those telerobots and pick 'em off by hand."

"Whatever I can't get with a quick orbital pass," Sawyer amended.

When English got himself pulled off the skin of the *Haig*, he asked for a head count, lying on his back in the NOCM, breathing hard and staring at the nice, low ceiling as if he could see the wonderful, precious atmosphere floating there.

His APOT rifle was still in his hands; its barrel was up against his helmet.

Until everybody called in, he was still reserving the option of shooting Cleary, who was hanging, tangled, in the webbing across from him, looking as if he'd have to cut her free.

When the last Marine checked in, the last grid square checked out as empty of telerobots, he knew he wasn't in for any more surprises: none dead or MIA. Three wounded bad enough to need special retrieval. Not great, but nothing they couldn't handle. The telerobotic enemies weren't programmed for men.

They just looked like the upper halves of big, nasty guys with shiny steel arms and integral night-vision goggles on their heads. The first time one had looked up at English on that hull, he was acutely aware that, somewhere down on the planet's surface, somebody human was taking his measure.

So he'd given whoever-that-was the bird, before he trashed the robot.

English relaxed a little and toggled to Sawyer, "You know, this Associate retrofit ain't half bad."

"Good thing," came his lieutenant's voice. "We're continuing pickup. Want to get with Manning about the *Haig*'s damages and how she'd like to handle the docking procedures?''

''Sure thing. Patch her through.''

Manning's imported com said, ''Delta Two, the *Haig*'s not so crippled that we can't augment her and fly her out of here, if I give your TA what she needs to know.''

''Us? Fly her—'' He realized that he was sticking his nose into an intelligence protocol problem, and stopped before he went on the record. ''You bet we'll fly her, push her, or pull her. Whatever TA and you think, Intel.''

''Thanks for the vote of confidence, Delta Two. FI out.''

FI: Fleet Intelligence. Such as it was, it was going to save the *Haig*, or blow her. Manning hadn't said it, but English understood: couldn't give the Syndicate a Fleet vessel with experimental hardware to study. He wouldn't want Manning's problem.

English was monitoring his pickups and helping guys in the door when his Associate shunted him Cleary without a single convention.

''Got the late news, Cleary?'' he asked. He wasn't angry anymore. He was helping Trask pull the last of his wounded in the door, and you couldn't be angry at live people when you were so glad to see hurt people.

''I just thought you'd like to know: Padova's going to be okay; so's the bridge personnel in general. We've got a tight time window, though, before the Syndicate recovers enough to send up something else from groundside.''

Something that could kill them.

''Yeah, well, you're the technical advisor. All you have to do now is teach a bunch of Marines what they need to know to salvage a partly crippled destroyer enough to kick her butt out of here. Can do?''

''Can do, English. No sweat.''

''Great, Omega. Delta Two, out.''

INTERLUDE: Family

When society began to break down during the rapid fall of the last Empire, societies and peoples sought ways to survive the chaos that followed. The Alliance found their solution in mutual support. On the worlds that evolved into the Syndicate of Families, a type of high-technology feudalism developed. Not densely settled at the beginning of the era, the depredations of pirates and similar raiders soon decreased the population even further. The industrial base that did survive tended to be concentrated in the hands of those few who had retained the skills and knowledge necessary to maintain them.

On many worlds the collapse of the highly technical infrastructure of their society created a backlash against those few capable of maintaining what was left. When you live in an animal power society and have been bombed by spaceships, those who could build spaceships become your enemy. Too often entire planets fell into feudal barbarism, each little valley controlled by a warlord. Very often the technical expertise that was retained did so by being passed down within a family. Precious technical manuals and tapes became family treasures. These families soon began to think of themselves as something separate from the illiterate society around them. When the worlds recovered enough that the merchant class were again more important than the soldiers, then these highly skilled families rose to dominance.

Even then the military barbarism was often replaced by competition between a few robber barons who controlled virtually all means of production. The situation was soon complicated by the reappearance of space-traveling traders as the area outside their cluster began to recover. Much like Japan, after a period of open trade, the families that dominated continents and now often entire worlds felt threatened by the change. Unlike feudal Japan, these same families valued technology and so began to seek out and adapt the developments and rediscoveries of the worlds outside their cluster for their own use. The threat of outside influences destroying their firm hold on their world's populations also caused the most powerful families to unite. Together these fifty families were able to both isolate their worlds and gain domination of those few planets within their boundaries that were not already under one of their number's sway.

It's a funny thing about loyalty. When you were raised under the expectation of unquestioned obedience to a group, it's a hard habit to break. This was particularly so when you were one of the privileged few. With something as strong as the concept of family, where you felt you were part of the group because of the very blood in your veins, then the loyalty was even greater than could be aroused by an abstract concept like an Alliance, or even a Fleet.

DOVE

by S.N. Lewitt

BEFORE HE GAINED consciousness of pain, the last thing Tony Lucca remembered was dying.

Weasels to port, two o'clock. The scout didn't have enough shielding to do this, and the scout didn't have a plasma cannon, not even with one charge. One single second of white brilliance, one amazing revelation. Tony knew he wasn't going to make it. Time spun and vaguely he thought about how mad his folks were going to be, and Theresa wasn't ever going to forgive him.

And he had promised them all, too, that he wasn't in any danger. Not like the war, anyway. Although as an occupation and native populations specialist he could get sick to his stomach on some of the things considered honors in primitive societies. He had laughed and made faces when he told Theresa the worst he was going to encounter was being presented with a meal that resembled one of Lovecraft's Older Gods.

And now he was going to die. Vision telescoped, his peripheral completely in darkness. Like entering a long tunnel, he thought, surprised to find that he wasn't aware of pain. Pleased about that too. From some ancient and innocent memory he dredged up the words he had learned by rote

*before memory even began. "Now I lay me down to
sleep . . ."*

*They weren't the right words, he knew, but he wasn't
worried. The brightness understood that he was muddled
and new at this. He hadn't died before and so it was all
very confusing. But he thought that somebody would understand that he really was very sorry for having cheated on
the seventh-grade math final.*

The scout needed more room for electronics, surveillance
devices along with the consumer perks that should win some
native hearts. Plenty of omni screens and relays. The Bain-
bridgians might only be culturally subnormal due to years
of Weasel occupation, not to some intrinsic inferiority. According to the report the natives still practiced stick agri-
culture and lived in hand-built huts without running water.
But every one that had been exposed to omni had immediately loved it.

Or so the reports had said. "The natives are friendly,"
Tony had muttered to himself during the briefing. Not that
he minded, not at all. Preparing the area for occupation was
not going to be easy even with native cooperation, and it
was Tony's job to insure the locals were with the Fleet all
the way.

Tony wasn't worried about the locals. There had been
some reports of Weasel diehards on suicide runs in the region, and he didn't like that one bit. No way. He wasn't
some Hawk Talon wannabe like his cousin Jimmy Apache.
He wanted the whole occupation of Bainbridge to go just
like the cases he had read in the textbooks back in training
on Port.

But the Intel boys had assured him that the last bit of
Weasel insurgency had been "cleaned up." Which, given
what he knew about the Khalia, meant that they had been
eliminated in a permanent manner. Much as he had had his
doubts about how thorough they could be, given the terrain
and large uninhabited sectors on Bainbridge, he had agreed
that it was better to carry more omni equipment than weapons.

Besides which, he wasn't really qualified to shoot any-

way. One of the reasons he had become an occupation specialist in the first place—he couldn't shoot. At anything at
all, including a target. The doc had said it was a sight-line
disability, not will. They'd called it a "Wild Eye."

That hadn't made the other guys in basic like him any
better. Behind his back he knew they called him a coward
and a pacifist and a bleeding-heart girl. When he'd opened
his locker to pack to move out of the barracks and begin
training in alien culture, he'd been showered with a flurry
of white feathers. Tiny little things that probably had been
taken out of some old-style pillow someone had brought
from home.

He knew what that meant and it hurt. And he had vowed
to prove them wrong. No matter what it took, no matter
how long, he was going to show the whole Fleet.

And maybe he had. He knew the scout had to have evap-
orated. There wasn't any hope at all. Which was why he
couldn't understand why he hurt so badly. Being dead was
being beyond the pain—at least that's what the priests had
said. And while he didn't have a whole lot of faith in the
priests, they knew more about death than anyone else Tony
had known.

And then a soft voice cut through the sharp wall as relief
very slowly enveloped him. "That should keep you for
now," the voice said. "Do you want some water?"

Water sounded wonderful. He tried to say yes and only
managed to grunt. A straw touched his lips and he began
to sip.

"Slowly," the voice said. "Just a little."

The water was tepid, and after a few sips Tony could feel
it lying in his stomach, sloshing and heavy. The straw was
removed and he was grateful. Moistened somewhat and
drifting a little apart from the pain he was able to rest again.

"That was a bum shot you took," someone said, bringing Tony to full consciousness. He'd been wavering on the
edge for a while, not wanting to surface and unable to stay
in the safety of sleep. This voice was a man's, with a slight
rasp as if the speaker had hurt his throat.

"Yeah," he agreed. "I didn't even get down."

"Too bad," the man sympathized.

It was only then that Tony realized that he couldn't see anything. The painkillers had kept him in a warm haze that had relieved any anxiety. He was afraid like he had never been afraid before. Slowly he tried to open his eyes and found they were bound shut. He started to lift a hand to his head, but his arm was much too heavy and resisted.

"No, no, wait," the first voice said, alarmed. "You have an IV in that arm. Now what's the trouble?" she asked soothingly.

"I can't see," Tony said, his mouth sticky from medication and his throat dry.

"That's because you have bandages on," the woman said. "Your eyes were hurt in the blast. We did surgery as soon as you were brought on board, and all indications are that you will regain your sight. But you have to rest and you can't be tearing off the dressings."

"Yes," he assented, recognizing the authority behind that soft voice. He couldn't tell if she was a doctor or simply a corpsman and it didn't matter. Just so long as she was right. The panic retreated to a distant place in his mind, but it wasn't completely gone.

Then he giggled. Maybe the surgery had corrected the flaw that had made him a Wild Eye in the first place. Then he could show those Marines. He'd learn to shoot with the best of the them. Comforted, he let his curiosity free. At least answers would occupy his mind and keep it off the dull throb that threatened to encompass his entire body.

"This has gotta be the *Salah Al-Din*, right?" he asked just for openers. "Has Ivan Yagudin or Samiah Zin been down to check up on me?"

Yagudin had been his best friend and roommate aboard the *Salah Al-Din*, an engineer who was all geared up to go down to Bainbridge and start constructing accommodations for the Fleet personnel who would take charge of the area. Ever since the discovery of the Syndicate there was plenty of burrowing into newly acquired territory, securing and holding every position. But Tony figured that if he had been brought aboard the *Salah Al-Din* wounded, Ivan at least would have asked after him.

Samiah, on the other hand, was a long shot. He'd admired her for a long time and she knew it. Still, it didn't hurt to ask.

"The which?" the raspy male voice answered. "*Salah Al-Din?* No, you're on the *Cardiff*. We were closer to the position you got blasted to, like way over the other side of Bainbridge."

"Oh." Tony couldn't keep the disappointment from his voice. He'd wanted to be back on his own ship with his friends and the familiar rivals, where he knew the order of the day and the mission objective. Still, he knew he shouldn't be too disconcerted. Probably the *Cardiff* had been closer and would pass him back once he was recovered enough to move.

No question about it, really. The *Salah Al-Din* was in synchronous orbit over Bainbridge's largest continent, the one where they had been planning to set up shop. And he knew perfectly well that for this kind of assignment no more than one cruiser could be spared. No doubt *Cardiff* had business elsewhere to attend.

"By the way," the man said, "I'm Alex Schurr. Your roommate here in sickbay for the duration. Weapons officer."

"What're you doing in sickbay?" Tony asked, only half interested in the answer.

"Would you believe I tore out a ligament in my knee playing inversion deadduck? And bones they can knit like nothing, but ligaments are completely beyond control. Not important enough to bother with an entire branch of medicine and technology, unless you happen to be the person on the receiving end. Then it hurts like a son of a bitch."

Tony had to smile at that. At least his injury had been acquired in the line of duty. With that much confidence, he introduced himself, braced for the usual nasty cracks from a line officer to an occupation specialist. The expected barb didn't come. Instead, Schurr seemed almost interested. "I've never met an occupation specialist before," he said perfectly amicably. "You guys are sort of the advance team, aren't you? So what's going on on Bainbridge? The natives aren't exactly human. You think you can get them to accept a Fleet presence? This would be a great staging area for this sector, I guess, if you can win over the locals, right?"

"Well," Tony started slowly, "I don't want to bore you. Weapons officer and all."

Alex only laughed. "Whatever you say has got to be less boring than lying here watching the bulkhead rust. They don't give *me* any juicy drugs to dull the pain. Just endless reruns of last month's least favorite omnidisk. Believe me, in two days you will know more than you ever wanted to know about the life cycle of Lyrian avian predators."

Tony warmed to Alex a little more. After all, he'd never met a weapons officer this friendly. And it was his one chance to prove his theory.

Lucca had always been convinced that if he could only get hold of one of those arrogant line types, get them to stay listening, he could convince them that his speciality was not some catch-all for misfits. He knew that a little education went a long way with local populations, and from the data the same would work perfectly well on his shipmates. Only before now he'd never gotten a chance. Besides, Schurr had all the good qualities of the line types, that immediate assumption of camaraderie and a trusting, open nature.

"How much do you know about Bainbridge?" Tony asked conversationally. "About the natives?"

"Not much," Alex admitted. "I only shoot at them, I don't study them."

Tony began to nod but that made his head spin. He leaned back into the crisp pillows and collected his thoughts. "Bainbridge was prime Weasel territory," he began. "The native population was peaceable and easy to control, the attack routes into Alliance space immediate. Besides which, it was an excellent place to hide and cut out supply lines. Not that you weapons officers ever think of that, but without supplies the repair bases of Mainstay and Ace of Clubs wouldn't function for more than a week. And as much as anyone else, they're responsible for keeping ships on the line against the Khalia after the Weasels lost Bethesda.

"Anyway, even though most of the resistance was wiped out early on in the settlement campaign, there were a few diehards out there. They're the ones who must have got me. Even you guys aren't infallible, you know. Anyway, with full native cooperation Bainbridge is the perfect place to direct sector activities. Both to finish up any pockets of Khalian resistance and to penetrate farther into the Syndicate. We might not know where their home worlds are, but those shadow-types in Intel think they're somewhere in this general direction. Which means that we're going to have to have Port Junior in some corner. And Bainbridge is perfect. Great climate, nice air, lots of veggies, not too much gravity, everything everyone ever wanted in real estate.

"The only catch is the locals. Who just happen to love omni. Haven't found a sentient species that doesn't, including the Weasels. At least when you've got programming they're interested in. Anyway, I was going to set up omni on Bainbridge. We've got disks already translated into the native dialect with a good variety of programming. All subtly playing up the Fleet and the Alliance, naturally.

"I have a complete research plan to advance the programming and use it to influence the culture, to bring it to Alliance level and invite a Fleet base on planet. That's really the crux of my job."

"Well, if you need it, I know where you can get a great disk on deviant wildlife," Alex volunteered. Tony almost laughed but it hurt too much.

He felt good, safe, pleasantly warm from the conversation, but he was tired, too. Talking was wearing. There was so much more he wanted to tell Alex, about how programming was chosen and how his research plan fit into the long-term plans of the Fleet. But now he was only exhausted.

He drifted into the twilight stage of sleep and became vaguely unsettled. Although everything had been positive so far, he felt some nagging vague anxiety at the edge of consciousness.

Crazy, he told himself. It was just the drugs and his injuries, the constant worry about his eyes. That had to be it. All the reassurances in the known universe weren't going to mean squat until they took the bandages off and he knew for a fact that he could see.

But the disconcerting fear did not evaporate on identification. Exhaustion and drugs were dragging him deeper into sleep, but the fear remained like a wall through the night. He slept restlessly, woke, slept again. It wasn't until waking for the second time that the word was clear in his head and he understood.

Cardiff. Who the hell was Cardiff? Tony Lucca had been a history buff all the way through school. He knew the stories of most of the cruisers' namesakes. Salah Al-Din, Alexander Haig, Hamilton, Morwood, Bolivar. He'd known them all, their exploits and places in the history of humanity. But Cardiff? He'd never heard the name, he was certain.

Come off it, he told himself. You don't know the name of every hero of humanity of every planet for all time. What do you think you are, some kind of professor or something?

But the name kept running in his mind and he couldn't sleep. The whole thing was somehow—skewed. A name he didn't know. A friendly weapons officer. And a strange ship near Bainbridge. To his knowledge there wasn't anyone else in the vicinity. *Salah Al-Din* should take care of business just fine.

So he must have wandered onto one of the "dark" missions that were so popular as plot devices on at least sixty-seven of the omni series that he was familiar with. His mind was crystal clear and his curiosity was sharp, but suddenly he found the anxiety of the earlier evening gone. This time he really knew what was wrong, and it was exciting enough to induce fantasies of revenge on all those in training who had laughed at him. Maybe the surgery had corrected his eyes, and by the time he was healed they would be out of range of the *Salah Al-Din*, and he would become an undercover operative who was legally dead in the Alliance. And at the very end he would come back and testify in front of the men who'd called him a coward and a weak sister.

All a plot from a bad late-night series if he'd ever heard

one. But then, life sometimes imitated trash. Tony Lucca fell asleep and this time he had pleasant dreams.

"Hey, Alex, who was Cardiff?" Tony asked the next day when breakfast was brought. "I never heard of him, and I sort of collect stories from different ships I've been on."

Alex hesitated. Tony could hear the coffee mug being set back on the tray. "I'm not sure I really know," Schurr answered slowly. "I mean, I haven't been aboard very long and haven't quite gotten all the details yet. If you want to know, I'll bet Kassa knows. You know, the medic who bosses us around. I have this funny feeling that she does that mostly because we rank her and she likes having us in her power. You think?"

Tony agreed and continued the conversation but his mind was elsewhere. He'd never in his life met anyone in the Fleet, officer or enlisted, who couldn't tell the story of his ship's namesake with pride. It was the sort of thing everyone learned as soon as they got an assignment, practically. And not only didn't Schurr know, but he had tried to distract Tony from the question as well.

Slowly the clarity of the night came back. Only this time he didn't embellish it with his own fantasies, lifted wholesale from omni entertainment channels. This time he decided to help reality along. After all, he had watched the same scene on *Early Earth* ten million times. The perfect sting when the victim didn't even know he'd been taken. Somehow that seemed a more appropriate image this morning.

So he followed Alex's chatter, noticing that the other was eliciting information that could actually be useful to the Fleet's enemies. Objectives on Bainbridge, for example, along with operating methods in this sector and which ships were where in the occupation process.

By the time Kassa served lunch Tony knew he'd been pumped by an expert. No, the right word was interrogated. Even though he usually associated that with pain and resistance, with drugs and pointed questions, he knew that somehow Alex had gotten him to talk freely. Maybe the drugs they fed him had something to do with that, but Lucca felt sure that the whole thing was a setup. Alex was too friendly for a weapons officer, too interested in things that most people in his position would find actively boring.

"Yeah," Alex was saying, "I loved omni as a kid. Couldn't get enough of it. I think I just about lived for *Hawk Talon*. I used to make up Hawk stories on the way to school in the morning."

"Yeah, me too," Tony agreed. "And when I had to study or take a test I always played I was Hawk at the Academy." A plan was starting to form in his mind, nebulous and uncertain. A test of something, that's what he needed. So far Alex had flunked on everything a Fleet officer in his position should know. But Tony needed something more, something final, something that couldn't be explained away, either by personality or cultural differences.

Alex laughed. "I'll bet that's why they had those flashback scenes, to make sure the kids buckled down to the books."

"What was your favorite episode?" Tony asked innocently.

"Wow, I'd really have to think about that," Alex answered reasonably enough. "I loved the whole third season and most of the fourth. Not that I didn't like the others, but those years they were the absolute best. Or maybe I was just the right age."

"Mmm," Tony agreed. "I liked that one where Hawk tells his brainship to shoot, and the brainship asks who. And Hawk says, 'The bad guys.' I always thought that was a great line. And the brainship was pretty good. What was its name? *Dove*?"

"Yeah, *Dove*," Alex agreed. "I hadn't thought about that one for a long time. I always liked it especially when Lisa Nakumba was playing the senator's daughter. She was something, though. You know what she's doing now?"

Tony answered, somehow managed to keep talking casually while his mind raced. Because he knew. Maybe he had set Alex up, maybe the other really didn't remember. But Tony Lucca couldn't buy that. No one who had been that much of a Hawk Talon fan could forget the brainship's name. The brainship had been a more popular character than Hawk himself. *Derv*, not *Dove*, he thought. Lisa Nakumba. They had prepared Schurr extremely well. He knew the details, the things that should throw someone like Tony way off the track.

Only he couldn't know all the details. No one who hadn't been born and raised Alliance could know all the tiny nuances that cut across the various planets and cultures that comprised human space. Alex Schurr was an imposter.

But Tony kept talking, pretending that he hadn't noticed the slips. Like yesterday, he thought. Only the drugs weren't affecting him so much, or maybe he was simply healing enough to need less of them. He had to play along, somehow keep Schurr from guessing that he knew. Tony went through Lisa Nakumba and then through almost every other actress of the period, and almost every one of their features. He hadn't been an omni buff for nothing.

Finally it was time for dinner and sleep. Lucca was docile, didn't resist the drugs Kassa poured into his hand. She didn't see that he held the pills firmly anchored under his tongue while he sipped the water and then lay back to feign sleep.

Waiting was hard. He made his body relax and concentrated on his breathing. Just like Sri Hananda on the education yoga program on channel eighty-nine had instructed his students. Count to four while breathing in, hold for four and then count four while exhaling. At least the counting and breathing gave him something to do.

He waited until he thought it was safe and then he waited more. There wasn't going to be a second chance, he told himself. Better to do it right the first time. So he went through the breathing exercise and reran old *Hawk Talon* episodes in his head. And waited.

At some point he thought he heard a rustling in the chamber, but he couldn't be sure. The sound was so soft, as if whoever was making it was being very careful. If anyone was making any sound at all.

Finally he couldn't wait any longer. He lifted his good arm and pulled the gauze from his face. For a moment he was still in darkness, until he realized that this darkness had a different quality to it. There was shadow and shape around him and he could see into the depths of the dark and perceive the subtle play of ambient light through the gloom. So he could see. The bandages had been to keep him from searching his surroundings or his companion.

He glanced over at the other bed, where according to Alex's voice the other bed should be. It was there, all right, made up in stiff military style, the white sickbay sheets gleaming dull gray against the pitch-black. No one was in the bed. It looked deserted, abandoned, as if Alex had never existed.

And for a moment Tony wasn't sure he had. After all, without seeing the other, it was always possible that a computer-simulated voice had questioned him. Not that it mattered. What mattered was that they had the information. And more. He had taught them a few more angles to this sting, this very complicated con game. And if they could dupe other Fleet officers, pilots, and weapons types and tacticians, then they were more dangerous and more treacherous than he had realized. After a lifetime of the Khalia, it was hard to think of any humans as the enemy. But there was no doubt in Tony's mind that these were, and were a hundred times more dangerous because of it.

Carefully he removed the two tubes in his arm. The drip had to contain drugs to dull his critical thinking and make him more receptive to the interrogation—to giving the Syndicate all the details it needed. Once free of the drug IV, he slipped out of bed. At least they had seen fit to keep him dressed in sickbay-issue pajamas. He hoped to find some more suitable garb somewhere in the vicinity. He began to rummage through the doors and lock component for something to wear.

Finally he found what appeared to be a medical uniform. No more question of the Fleet here, the symbols and cut were nothing Tony had ever seen before. No wonder they had bandaged his eyes. He dressed quickly, and then stuffed the old pajamas under the covers to make an acceptable lump on the bed. Not quite enough, really, but in the dark it would cover for an hour or so.

And then, as he made his way to what he hoped was the door out of the sickbay, he froze. He didn't know what he was going to do. Escape, his mind jabbered, send a message and tell the Fleet about this Syndicate plot to trick Fleet captives.

And who would believe him? Tony thought, anger lancing through the hurt. Those Marines who left feathers in his locker? The officers who couldn't wait to get rid of him? None of them would even listen, let alone believe. As for Intelligence, they barely recognized that anyone else in the Fleet could talk and walk on two legs, let alone come across data that Intel did not have prior knowledge of. No, Tony realized the more he thought about it, there wasn't anyone he could tell. Anyone who would listen and do something.

And meanwhile the *Cardiff* would go on, collecting strays and getting better and better at its game. The *Cardiff* had to be destroyed. Lucca came up hard against that single fact. The Syndicate had to learn that they couldn't get away with this scam, that any Fleet member could find them out. Then maybe they wouldn't try it again.

Nor could he let the *Cardiff* go with the data he had given them about Fleet plans for Bainbridge and this region. The Alliance hold was still too fragile here to risk. The presence of the *Cardiff* proved that this area was sensitive for the Syndicate, as well. No one, not even the shadowy human enemy that Tony Lucca still could scarce believe existed, would commit a ship of the *Cardiff*'s size and special capabilities just to prove a point in some unimportant sector of space.

What the hell would Hawk Talon do?

Tony found himself smiling. Hawk would blow the *Cardiff* to smithereens while escaping in a fast scout. Which, come to think of it, was not a bad idea. Only two things were wrong. First off, Tony didn't know where the scouts were on this ship or even if he could fly one. Second, he wasn't sure they could blow the cruiser. That was all easy enough on the Omni, but real life made things difficult.

One thing was certain. He needed a plan before he left sickbay, and he had to leave before the night crew was replaced by the fuller day-cycle staffing. He didn't even know the layout of the *Cardiff*, where he could hide or where the weak points were.

Well, small details like that never bothered Hawk Talon. There had to be some immediate, direct action. Of course, if he could melt down the plasma cannon so that when they fired they would explode in the ship itself, that would be ideal. But Tony didn't know if the Syndicate even had plasma cannon, and if they did, he didn't know where they were or how to go about sabotaging them. No, there had to be another weakness to exploit. Something that not even the alienness of the Syndicate ship could completely eliminate.

And then a smile spread slowly across his face. He found what he needed easily enough in the coffee cabinet in the sickbay. One large box that he tasted and verified. And one large size old-fashioned lighter. Someone had left it lying out next to a heater ring that indicated the whole rig was set for experimentation. A beaker rested above filled with black liquid, and a single sniff assured Tony that the whole setup was some ancient, complicated coffee-brewing mechanism.

Good enough. The lighter disappeared into a pocket hidden in the cuff, and the box he held casually in his hand. No one would think twice about an off-duty med carrying around an extra-large ration of powdered sugar.

Thank the fates that the ship was large enough that new faces didn't attract undue attention. Nor would newness to the ship's complement. He found an equally new-seeming youngster without any rank markings on either her sleeves or collar and asked how to get to the observation deck. The young woman didn't seem to find the question untoward. Two decks above and at the end of the main corridor. He hurried, before he lost the stamina or the nerve.

On arrival of the observation deck he was pleased. There were certain things that humans took for granted, needed in great quantities, and did not deviate from some prehistoric norm. The need for open space and to see the sky and smell growing things was the same, Alliance, Fleet, or Syndicate. The observation deck here was not much different from any of those he had seen before. Oh, some of the plantings were unique. These seemed to tend toward aromatic fruit trees and overhanging arbors, but the basic idea was the same.

The large, open space felt like a park. Smelled like one, too. It had to be used for oxygen production as well as foodstuffs, not to mention the necessary psychological balance. All around were observation-transparent walls. Outside he could see the stars glittering cold against the eternal night. He spared one last, loving glance at those distant points, and then turned his attention to the task at hand.

There had to be a feeder duct around here somewhere. Sitting very still, just like Sri Hananda taught, he listened for the half-hidden sound of an intake valve. A tiny hiss caught his attention and he prayed quickly. Theresa would hate him forever. He just hoped that she understood that he really had no choice at all. That it didn't have anything to do with the Marines or Hawk Talon or any fantasy. That just at that moment he would give a very great deal to wake up home.

He sniffed at the valve. Pure oxygen intake filter, just as he had hoped. There were a few ideas so good they had to be universal. Tony peeled back the bladder of the box and fit it into the intake. Only seconds went by until the whole vent resembled some fabled Christmas snowfall. He watched as the white powder drifted deeper into the ventilation system. With pure oxygen and a little something to burn—

Tony muttered a quick prayer and silently asked Theresa and his parents to forgive him. Then he flicked the mechanism on the lighter and watched as a long torch flame was sucked into the oxygen hole.

By the time the *Salah Al-Din* responded to the emergency hot-spot in the vicinity there was nothing even their most advanced fire-fighting equipment could do. The blaze had raged down to the munitions locker and blew enough ordnance to supply the Weasels with another six months of resistance. There was nothing left to mop up except random chunks of debris.

"At least the crew suffocated fast," one of the Marines on cleanup muttered.

The others didn't respond. Burned bodies stuck to melted metal made them want to retch in their suits. Not a good idea. It didn't pay to look too closely.

It wasn't until the wreckage was analyzed days later that they found Tony Lucca, perfectly identifiable in the debris. He had barely been singed. The fire had been sucked down into the oxygen mix, depriving the observation deck of breathable air.

"What the hell was he doing on a Syndicate ship?" the officer in charge of the investigation asked no one in particular.

"Exactly what any Fleet officer would have done," the Marine captain responded. "Blowing it up. He finally found a target so big even he couldn't miss."

INTERLUDE: Timescale

In a few seconds a ship using FTL drive could travel several million miles. The beam from a power laser traveling at the speed of light, in effect, took only a small fraction of a second to reach an opponent during ground combat. Too often the duel between two small ships was resolved in a matter of seconds. Hand-to-hand combat between a Marine and a Khalian pirate typically lasted under thirty seconds, no matter who won.

In contrast, the time required for a Fleet warship to travel between stars could seem very long; it took a newly completed heavy cruiser almost two months to make the journey from a Vegan shipyard to Duane's fleet where it was massing off Khalia. Even a fast courier boat couldn't make the journey from the high-command Port to Khalia in less than a month. A typical scouting mission would last six months and include less than two dozen systems. Some of the specialists were trained for almost a decade before being adjudged sufficiently skilled to dismantle and assemble such delicate items as the Cooper FTL drive.

From another perspective, it was almost as long a journey from most Syndicate family navy yards to Khalia as it was from Port. A scout leaving the cluster and sneaking into

Khalian space inevitably returned with data no less than a month old.

As a result, the first battles in what was to prove one of the most costly wars the Alliance was to ever face were mostly minor skirmishes. Intelligence was deemed by both sides to be more important than real estate. Even after the general location of the Syndicate's worlds was known, it was several more months before Duane could assemble a force that could enter the hostile cluster with any expectation of surviving.

Actually both sides needed to know some important facts before acting. The Syndicate combat managers had to be sure that Duane's forces would not make a drive into the cluster at a time when their aggressive actions left it comparatively defenseless. They also had to learn what use the Fleet was making of the Khalian worlds, what infrastructure of bases were being constructed, and judge how committed the Alliance was to preserving the worlds of their newfound allies. Meanwhile the changing allegiance of the Khalia was proving to be a much greater problem than had been expected when the decision was made that it was no longer cost effective to support them. Finally, the Khalian War had ended much more abruptly and sooner than expected. Final plans had to be made and ships completed before the campaign against the Alliance invaders could begin.

On the Fleet side six months were spent just piecing together the clues and confirming the location of the major Syndicate worlds. Hundreds of ships had to be repaired and tens of thousands of replacements trained before Admiral Isaac Meier was confident Duane's battle fleet was capable of offensive action. Finally the Alliance too had to be sure that their own much more greatly dispersed worlds would not suffer from the absence of Duane's fleet when it did take the war into the Syndicate cluster.

The result of all this was that after the violent intensity of the final days of the Khalian War there was a period of boredom and frustration for most of the spacemen on both sides. This delay may have served the Fleet better than their foes. It certainly provided them with a necessary period of preparation. Morale was restored and new ships replaced those lost. Still, as the months dragged by, it became harder to maintain constant vigilance. To those back home, no battles meant peace. So much so that the politicians in the Senate actually began to question the huge, new expenditures the Admiralty demanded.

During this period the war was characterized more by personal duels than big battles. Ships and spies fought for scraps of information or to protect vital industries. These were duels whose winners were determined by many factors other than firepower. Though having the biggest gun certainly helped.

MANSTOPPER

by Katherine Kurtz and
Scott MacMillan

IT HAD BEEN extremely easy for the Syndicate to recruit
"adjustors" from ambitious junior executives who found
the complex business structure of the Alliance too restrictive
for their own freewheeling egos. Rewarded with staggering
wealth for manipulating information, misdirecting supplies
and raw materials, and occasionally taking a hands-on role
in some of the more unpleasant business transactions of the
Syndicate, these "adjustors" were run by blind control,
never seen by their Syndicate masters, and only retired to
a sanctuary planet in the cluster if their exposure jeopard-
ized a continuing Syndicate operation within the Alliance.

To combat the adjustors, the Council authorized Fleet to
recruit "regulators" whose job it was to balance the books,
and if possible penetrate to the core of Syndicate intelligence. Totally trusted by Fleet and the Council, regulators
were given the broadest possible powers to complete their
tasks; they were expected to perform miracles, with no
questions asked.

Rykker was one of the first, and certainly one of the best,
regulators given an active commission by Fleet. For two
years, he had moved through the industrial wasteland of the
Alliance picking up the threads of intelligence that, woven
together, produced a tapestry of Syndicate activity with one

man in its center. Working in deep cover, Rykker set out to
bring in Planetary Resources Exploitation Executive James
Coleman Melton.

The fight had lasted the better part of the day, and it
wasn't until his partner was dead and his own life suit damaged that Rykker had decided to give up and take his chances
as their prisoner. He scraped what was left of Connors off
the blast shield of his helmet and, crawling back to the
smoldering heap of his ex-partner, stuck his own identity
disc into the still-steaming mess of congealed flesh and
melted life suit. The thermal grenade had opened the side
of their ground rover, and in the process only partly vapor-
ized Connors. Rykker reasoned that they'd rush the hulk in
a matter of minutes. If his luck held, he'd have just enough
time to lose his ID somewhere deep inside Connors. If it
didn't, then he wouldn't last five minutes, once they were
inside the ground rover. His luck held.

The first to reach him was a Thalmud; short, long-necked,
and with the shoulder-length, greasy-looking hair that made
them stand out from the other semhoms—semi-hominids—
in this sector. The smell of the Thalmud's hair was thickly
sweet. They perspired through their hair, with the result that
even under the best of conditions they had a faintly musty
smell, like gym clothes forgotten over the weekend in a
locker. The Thalmud roughly dragged Rykker across the
twisted deck and wrenched off his helmet before giving him
a stunning blow to the side of his head. Thalmuds were
rough, but they didn't eat you. Gerns did.

A pair of humans had entered the ground rover through
the hole created in its hull by the thermal grenade. As they
began to paw through the wreckage for anything of value,
a Gern carefully clicked in through the breached hull and
with spiderlike delicacy moved over to Connors's slowly
cooling remains.

Carefully, the arachnidlike alien lowered its thick body
down into a pool of Connors's body fluids and, with one of
its small upper arms, pulled all that was left of the human
torso closer to its small head. Using both of its stronger

lower arms, it brought the charred torso up to its body and, with the aid of its vestigial legs, gracefully maneuvered the lump of flesh and melted life suit under its own dull bottle-green body.

Slowly, as though it was making love to Connors's body, the Gern began to gently slide back and forth on the congealing blob that had been Rykker's partner. On the Gern's belly, short, coarse hairs bristled as they were dragged across the charred flesh, tasting Connors's, telling the Gern that this was human meat. With deliberation the Gern raised itself above Connors and, extending its siphon, pressed down, plunging the hard, yellow-green tube into the body. The Gern shook and jerked obscenely as it moved its siphon deeper into Connors until at last it was through the charred outer layer and into the soft, raw innards.

Rhythmically the Gern rocked back and forth on Connors as its siphon felt out the organs deep within the abdominal cavity, its small, razor-sharp tongues pulping the meat and muscle that then was sucked up the siphon and into one of the Gern's stomachs. As its siphon sucked out Connors's guts the Gern used the small, crescent-shaped claws on its stunted top arms to open an incision along the side of what had been Connors's neck. Once the cut had been made, the Gern inserted its long, curved mandibles into the wound and began chewing.

On the other side of the ground rover's deck, the two humans were sifting through the space lockers of Rykker and Connors when the Gern's siphon found Rykker's identity disc. Along with bits of heart and liver, the sharp tongues had passed the plastellic disc back to the throbbing tube that had eagerly sucked it in along with other, more savory morsels.

The disc entered the siphon sideways, slicing and tearing the delicate membrane that lined the walls of the Gern's feeding tube. As it moved along the inside of the siphon, drawn along by the powerful sucking action that scavenged the food, it became momentarily stuck and like the damper in the flue of a stove pipe, rotating on its axis, closing off the passage of food and fluid to the Gern's stomach.

The effect was both immediate and profound. The Gern's siphon collapsed, sending the Gern into a screaming frenzy of explosive pain, excruciating beyond endurance. Screaming, bits of Connors dripping from its mandibles, the Gern tried to retract from the body cavity but couldn't. The identity disc, slightly larger than the channel that had admitted the siphon to Connors's body, now served to anchor the siphon firmly in the flesh. Unable to withdraw its siphon, the Gern reared up on its lower back legs and began to tear at Connors's corpse, as the sheer weight of Connors's remains began to rip the no-longer-rigid siphon out by its roots. Insane with pain, and with its own body fluids beginning to mix with Connors's, the shrieking Gern turned and lunged toward the two humans, who stood transfixed in terror as the spiderlike Gern came bearing down on them.

The Thalmud fired two quick blasts from his slug gun, both driving home into the gaping wound created by the loss of the siphon. For a brief moment the Gern paused; and then, as the two slugs detonated, it exploded, spattering the interior with its cream-colored viscera. One of the humans vomited.

The sound of the detonations brought Melton in from the Fleet tractor that Rykker and Connors had been following for the past three days. Unlike the others, Melton didn't look like a Fleet deserter or renegade scum. He was expensively dressed in the top-of-the-line civilian life suit, one of the 9SB models that cost more than a troop of Fleet Marines would earn in a year. Like a few of the privileged executives, he wore a sword that looked like it had been in his family for generations—although to judge by the scars on the guard, Melton knew how to handle a sword. It took a good deal of skill, and confidence, to parry an opponent's blade on the guard.

It was the briefcase, however, that said it all. Leather. Real leather—not the chemical composite stuff that most of the elite used, but the outside covering of a cow. A cow that had lived in a field, eaten grass, given milk—Rykker had tasted bio-organic milk and beef once—and finally, after feeding the top directors of the company, had had its skin processed into leather. A leather briefcase was worth more than some minor planetary despots could extort in their lifetime. And Melton had one. He was scum, but had a great sense of style.

Melton looked at the mess in the ground rover, but didn't bother to comment. Instead he walked over to where Rykker was propped up in the corner, reached into one of his pockets, and produced a "come along," a mildly hypnotic drug used by police to assist them in controlling anyone they thought might be unruly. The Thalmud held Rykker's head while Melton placed the cup of the aerosol syringe over Rykker's left eye. For a brief instant Rykker thought of slamming his boot into Melton's crotch, but the stinging sensation of the drug hitting Rykker's eye prevented him from carrying out the action. Instead, he found himself wondering how much Melton's self-cleaning boots had cost.

Inside Melton's tractor, Rykker was given a more primitive form of sedative; one of the humans slammed him hard behind the ear with a blackjack, and Rykker slipped into a painfully starry oblivion.

Rykker came to, facedown in the sand with someone's boot planted firmly on his neck. He twisted his head enough to see that it wasn't Melton; the boot wasn't clean enough. That left the Thalmud or one of the humans—not that it mattered. He knew that any physical resistance—now—would just get him killed.

That bothered him. Not getting killed; that was always a risk you took, if you were going to be what the Alliance called a regulator. No, it was the being kept alive that Rykker couldn't figure out. For some reason Melton wanted him alive, or he would have finished him off at the ground rover. The boot on his neck moved. It kicked him in the ribs.

Rykker felt the wind rush out of his lungs as two pairs of hands jerked him to his feet and dragged him over to an onger, one of the six-legged pack animals used by remote Alliance prospectors. Biogenetically engineered a few hundred years earlier, they were shipped in freeze-dried and provided to any prospector on any planet that had class-A vegetation. They ate little, drank less, and carried prodigious weights. They were uncomfortable to ride, but in a pinch could be eaten, although they tasted horrible. Rykker was thrown on the back of the onger and his ankles were tied together under the animal's belly. Melton reached into another of his wonderful pockets and produced the titanium handcuffs that he ratcheted tightly down on Rykker's wrist.

From his vantage point on the onger's back, Rykker was able to survey his surroundings—not that it told him much. Like most of the planet, it was desert, gritty gray sand with the odd outcropping of rock sheltering sparse class-A vegetation. Basically unproductive soil with low-grade mineral deposits, it had been a backwater where the Alliance sent miners with no future: low priority, low technology, low yield. And low lifes, like Melton.

Melton's sand scooter glided silently toward the cluster of men standing next to Rykker, the deep purple of its ground effects beam momentarily turning the gritty gray sand a shimmering silver as it gracefully bobbed and floated over the undulating terrain. When he was next to them, Melton paused for a moment, balancing on the sand scooter like an acrobat on a teeter board, and then signaled his men to follow. The Thalmud grabbed the lead line of the onger, one of the humans slapped it in on the rump, and Rykker and his three companions moved off single-file behind Melton and the scooter.

They had traveled for about two hours when Melton called a halt. Rykker's "come along" had worn off, but every muscle and sinew of his body ached from the effort of staying on the swaying back of the onger. His life suit, designed for work afoot, had rubbed the inside of his legs raw from the pressure exerted to keep from rolling off the animal's back and under its belly; he knew that if he survived the ordeal, it would be a long time before he was comfortable sitting at the controls of a spacecraft, let alone sitting down for dinner.

One of Melton's men untied Rykker's ankles and pulled him from the back of the onger, half dragging him to where Melton was sitting in the meager shade of a derelict mining shed. Melton took off his sunglasses, an expensive pair of

civilian lenses with a silver laser-coat that obviated the need
for the human eye to dilate in response to changes in light
levels, and turning his face away from Rykker gazed out to
the horizon.

"You have been very inconvenient," he said, slowly returning his gaze to Rykker. "Not to mention expensive."

Rykker tried to remain impassive, but failed as his legs
gave way and he crashed to his knees. Melton stood up,
brushing a few particles of sand from his life suit, and
walked over to where Rykker was kneeling. Bending briefly
to remove the handcuffs, he peered closely at Rykker.

"Mr. Campbell," Melton began, reading the name tag
on Rykker's life suit, "you are a prospector, right?"

Rykker nodded in agreement.

"Well then, you are undoubtedly aware of the dangers
posed by deserted mines?"

Rykker said nothing, allowing Melton to continue.

"Not only is there the danger of being trapped in a shaft
by a sudden cave-in, there is the peril of falling into a sand
pit; an all-too-real peril in your case, I'm afraid." Melton
stared intently into Rykker's eyes, as though hoping Rykker
would beg for some sort of mercy. He was disappointed
when Rykker spoke.

"Look, mister, I don't know who you are, or why you
attacked my ground rover, but I can tell you this: the Fleet
is scheduled to cruise by this godforsaken hunk of rock
within the next two days to pick up me and my partner, and
you aren't about to get away with murder. You and your
pals would be a lot better off just packing up and leaving
now, before the suns up there delay things for you for at
least eighteen hours." Rykker knew as well as Melton that
the sunspot activity caused by the system's twin stars would
prevent any attempt at taking off from the planet for a good
while when the two stars were in eclipse.

Melton regarded him impassively for a few seconds and
then turned and headed for his scooter, sliding on his glasses
as he made his way across the brittle gray sand.

The Thalmud was perspiring heavily, the thin, hairlike
tubes that covered his head emitting a viscous golden fluid

that rolled down his head and shoulders and spread across his glistening body, protecting it from the heat generated by the twin stars that high overhead moved closer and closer into conjunction. They walked only a few hundred meters to the abandoned mine, where Melton had parked his scooter in the shade of one of the sand-scarred derricks, but in the mounting light and heat it could have been miles. Rykker was dying for a drink—even electrolytes would have been welcome—but for some reason he doubted that they were going to offer him one.

Leaving the sand scooter in the shade, Melton motioned them to follow him to the other side of the mine. Sticking to the shade of the abandoned buildings, the five of them moved single file past the once-productive ore-processing plant and then out into the blazing light and heat and across the sand toward the pit.

The pit was nearly fifty meters across, with steep sides that dropped sharply to a bowllike bottom. At one side, a thin sliver of shadow provided a dark crescent that pointed to a gaping hole five meters across in the center of the pit. Like a vortex in the sea, it was ready to swallow anything— or anyone—that fell into it.

Melton produced a canteen and poured some of its refrigerated contents into his hand, letting the silvery stream trickle through his fingers and onto the parched sands, which darkened for only an instant before the ovenlike air sucked the moisture from the dessicated gray grit. Without looking at Rykker, Melton tossed the canteen into the pit, watching it slide down from the rim toward the bottom.

The canteen had barely come to rest halfway down the side of the pit when Rykker found himself first floating, then falling over the edge of the pit and down toward the vortex in its center. He had tried to grab one of them as he went, but as luck would have it the Thalmud was the closest, and no amount of strength would provide a grip on its oily body. Despite the lower gravity, Rykker still hit hard when he finally crashed into the side of the pit.

Even as he began to tumble, Rykker knew he only had one chance to avoid falling all the way into the vortex. With

sand abrading his hands and face, he spread-eagled and tried
to dig in with fingers and toes. Facedown, his forehead
bleeding and his mouth and nostrils filling with sand, he
continued skidding toward the very bottom of the pit, but
finally slowed and came to a precarious halt in the soft sand
just before the mouth of the vortex. Coughing and spitting,
Rykker raised his head cautiously and looked up at the top
of the pit, but Melton and his men were gone.

As the twin suns rose higher, one thing was certain in
Rykker's mind. Melton wasn't really concerned if a body
was found or not. And if Melton wasn't concerned about
leaving a trail, then it meant he had to be pretty well protected by someone high up in either Fleet Command or the
Alliance. Either way it didn't matter. If Rykker didn't pull
himself out of the sand pit before the suns met in conjunction, he would be baked to a crisp.

Looking at the shortening shadows, Rykker estimated that
he had about twenty minutes left. Not much time, but all
he needed, if he was lucky. The first priority had to be
water—the canteen that Melton had casually tossed into the
vortex before giving Rykker the big push. Slowly, carefully,
Rykker raised himself up onto one elbow and scanned the
sides of the pit for any trace of the canteen.

Nothing. Very gently he shifted to scan the other side,
only to feel the coarse sand begin to give way and start him
sliding again toward the bottom and oblivion.

Rykker spread-eagled and checked his descent. At least
he had spotted the canteen. Moving like an amphibian, he
half swam and half crawled his way around until at last he
was facing downhill, toward the black void that was the
very center of the vortex. The canteen was ahead of him
and slightly to his left. Rykker dug his hands deep into the
sand, burying his arms up past the elbows, and slowly,
painfully slowly, started pulling himself closer to the edge,
never knowing when the next movement might cause a violent shift in the sands and send him cascading into the
bottomless vortex.

The minutes seemed like hours as the twin suns rose
higher, and Rykker's damaged life suit found it harder to

keep up with the demands of his exertions in the steeply sloping sands. Finally, and with intense effort, Rykker was within reach of the canteen. He screwed his right arm deep into the sand, all the way to the shoulder, and then with deliberate effort managed to spread the fingers of his right hand in an attempt to more securely anchor himself.

Shifting his weight slightly, Rykker reached for the canteen. It moved. Only the faint rustle of sand coursing over sand broke the stillness of the pit as the canteen slid several feet closer to the edge of the vortex.

Rykker stopped short of cursing. His whole life had been spent in avoiding the futile, and right now cursing was futile. When he had the canteen, he could curse: a long, joyous string of profanities ending in the delightful taste of the silvery wetness contained in the canteen.

But not now. Not until he had the canteen. He reached again, slower this time, and again the sand began to shift. It was his anchor, his right arm plunged deep in the sand, that caused the subtle disturbance responsible for the canteen sliding away from his grasp.

It was an interesting problem. If he pulled his arm out of the sand he might just reach the canteen. Then again he might not. He might go sliding ever faster down the side of the sand vortex and pitch headfirst into the bottomless nothing at its center. Two chances to die, and maybe only one to live. Rykker closed his right fist tight, and slowly began to pull his arm out of the coarse gray sand. Beneath him the sand gave way.

Suddenly Rykker was sliding toward the center of the vortex and reaching for the canteen, flailing his arms and legs in an attempt to check his downward descent. Even though his mind raced, trying to find some way of saving himself, events seemed to move in slow motion. Instinctively he grabbed the canteen as he continued to slide, and instinctively, too, he shot his arms out in front of him and dug the edge of the canteen into the sand. It acted like a sea anchor, and slowed him immediately. Spreading his legs and digging in his toes as well, Rykker finally came to a halt.

The suns were high and nearly in conjunction as Rykker squirmed his way around into an uphill position again. He was not out of trouble yet. He could feel the heat burning into his back, even through his suit, and he knew that he had only minutes left to shield himself from the full effect of the conjoined stars, and only one option for survival. Quickly, using the edge of the canteen as a shovel, Rykker began to dig into the sand, hoping that by burying himself he'd survive in his tattered life suit. He reasoned that if he could get under the sand, he had enough liquid to sustain himself for perhaps as long as two hours; long enough for the suns to move out of their deadly conjunction and to give him a second chance at getting out of the pit.

Rykker had burrowed down almost two feet when the canteen struck metal—soon revealed as a section of smooth, cylindrical tube nearly four feet wide, and of indeterminate depth and length. Sitting on the shaft and kicking furiously with both feet Rykker was able to shift enough sand to realize that he was sitting on some sort of a pipe that seemed to run from the abandoned mine above the pit down toward its center.

Rykker nearly laughed as he realized that he was sitting on an illegal garbage chute. The miners had been using the vortex as a dump, clearly in violation of Fleet and Alliance directives concerning the natural ecology of exploited planets. If only there were some way into the chute.

Rykker's eyes ached from the intensity of the searing light overhead, and his hands were blistering from the touch of the hot metal pipe he was straddling. He began to hallucinate from the heat, and for the first time since his ground rover was blown off its tracks, Rykker thought he might die. He fumbled with the canteen, nearly dropped it, and slipped off the side of the pipe, sliding slowly toward the end—the end of the pipe where garbage from the processing plant had gone down into the vortex.

Oddly, he had plenty of time to think about what he was doing, this time. Very calmly he was able to reach out and grab the edge of the pipe end as he came abreast of it. Miraculously, his grip held. Almost before he realized what he was doing, he crawled up into the shade of the open garbage chute. The floor of the chute was smooth, as were the walls. But overhead was a series of handholds like a ladder riveted to the top of a giant aluminum cigar tube. Using one of the handholds to steady himself, Rykker allowed himself the luxury of a small drink from the canteen before starting up the incline of the tube. But he had gone on only a few meters before he cursed softly. A ten-foot vertical shaft led down from the mine to the garbage chute, its smooth walls impossible to climb without a ladder.

At that point, Rykker didn't care. After taking another swig from the canteen, he looped its strap through one of the handholds, hooked his arm through its loop to keep from sliding back out of the tube, and laid down to sleep.

It was dark when he awoke, at least as dark as it ever became on any planet in a binary system. It took Rykker a few minutes to size up his situation and settle on a course of action. He couldn't climb up the vertical shaft. The walls were too smooth to provide any sort of grip, and they were too high to jump to the top and pull himself over. His only chance was to try and throw a line of some sort over the edge, hope it would catch on something, and then pull himself out. Rykker took another swallow from the canteen and then peeled off his life suit.

Naked in the shaft, Rykker realized how hot it really was on the planet. Sweat poured from him as he tied one leg of the suit to the strap of the canteen. The small vertical shaft was oppressively hot, and even the slightest effort made his head swim. Blinking the sweat from his eyes, Rykker held tight to one arm of the life suit as he twirled the canteen over his head like a lasso before launching it over the edge of the shaft. He heard it hit with a dull thud and then pulled it toward him. It caught momentarily on something, pulled free, and then caught again. This time it held.

Pulling hand over hand along the life suit, Rykker walked up the wall of the shaft, his feet burning from the latent heat of the metallic walls. When he reached the top he used both hands to heave himself up and over the top. Exhausted, his chest nearly bursting from the exertion, Rykker reached for the canteen, pulled it free from a tangle of scrap metal, and savored the silver liquid as it washed down his throat. After a few minutes his strength began to return, and he hauled up his life suit and struggled to pull it on.

Inside the ore-processing plant, things were much as they had been left several years before when the mine had been shut down as no longer profitable. Any equipment that was judged to be either too heavy or too old-fashioned to justify the expense of shipping back to the home planets had simply been left behind. When the Alliance ceased operations in any sector, they left behind them a legacy of discarded technology, neatly mothballed and ready for service should the Alliance ever return.

Rykker explored the processing plant and soon found the abandoned crew quarters. The lockers were empty, for the most part. Rykker found a stash of girlie magazines, some discarded socks, and a baseball cap. One locker yielded up a towel, and in another he found a pair of sweats almost his size.

Off the crew quarters was a shower room, and Rykker tentatively tried the taps, laughing to himself as the pale blue sterile cleansing solution sprayed out of the chrome nozzle and bounced off the tile floor. He found a hardened sliver of soap next to one of the sinks, and for the next fifteen minutes reveled in the simple pleasure of washing.

It was, he decided, his first shower in weeks, possibly months. The life suit kept you clean and odorless, but for some reason Rykker had never been able to clearly understand, he only felt clean after a real shower. He shoved his head under the nozzle and let the spray wash the lather from his hair, the suds running down his back and legs as he switched the temperature control from hot to cold before finally turning off the shower, grabbing the towel, and roughly drying himself off.

Back in the locker room he pulled on the sweats he had found in one of the lockers and, barefoot, padded into the galley. He knew that there would be no fresh food, but hoped that the emergency rations would have been left behind as not worth the bother of shipping back. Neatly stacked in one of the stainless steel cupboards Rykker found the small emergency ration packets, each containing a small block of more or less tasteless matter compressed into a sandwich-sized morsel that provided all the nutrients required to sustain life. Rykker shut his eyes as he bit into the gray-green lump, and thought of a real beefsteak, in the fond hopes of deceiving his palate. It wasn't fooled.

Dinner over in a few bites, Rykker headed down to the computer room to see what memories he might retrieve from the central computer banks.

One thing that the Alliance didn't leave behind was anything useful in the computer's memory. A quick scan through the menu showed Rykker that most files had been cleared; what remained were the basic plant maintenance programs, a map of the mining complex—and a complete copy of Handiman's Complete Encyclopedia of Technology.

Rykker smiled gently to himself. Everything he needed was right here in the "useless" information files.

Rykker's fingers typed out the first command, and a cobalt laser screen flashed up a map of the mining complex. The mining operation had been a small one, covering only a few dozen square miles, with the ore-processing plant located well away from the central administration complex. Rykker pressed a key and the ore-processing plant glowed a dull pink on the screen. A few more keystrokes and Rykker knew that the nearest buildings were nearly two miles away. The big question, though, was where were Melton and his pals?

Rykker typed out another command. "Request status all life-support systems."

One by one each of the stations on the map began to glow, first a dull pink, then turning to a hazy yellow—all that is except two. The ore-processing plant and the executive wing of the central administration complex both throbbed a dull pink on the cobalt screen. Rykker's smile broadened. He knew where they were, and best of all, they thought they knew where he was.

Rykker pushed himself back from the computer terminal and stared up at the ceiling. Several long minutes passed before he decided on his next move. He stretched once and, knitting his brow, leaned back over the keyboard. The index to the Complete Encyclopedia of Technology scrolled lazily onto the screen. Rykker stopped it several times until he found exactly the entry he was looking for.

Reading and rereading the entry, Rykker decided that although crude, it was undoubtedly effective. Now, the question was whether or not he could make a slug thrower from the material at hand. The computer quickly provided an inventory of material in the ore-processing station, and then cross-referenced that inventory with the requirements set out in the Encyclopedia. Another scan through the computer indicated that the machine shop in the ore-processing station could handle all of the milling and machining. The question Rykker now faced was a choice of propellant.

Most slug throwers used a capacitive energy discharge to launch the projectile. Rykker's design was based on the use of gunpowder ignited by a fulminate charge placed under sudden and severe percussion. Rykker tapped in the formula for black powder and asked the computer to locate a material that would have similar characteristics that could be used for a substitute. The computer immediately supplied a list of over six hundred materials, and cross-indexing these with the inventory of the ore-processing station Rykker was able to find his propellant.

Taking a hand modem with him, Rykker headed down to the machine shop. Here he fed in his material requirements to an ancient laser lathe, plugged the hand modem into its control panel, and headed out to collect his propellant.

The mine had used several different methods of ore displacement, and according to the computer, all of the reagents were stored in a bunker a few hundred feet from the exit of the ore-processing station. Rykker trotted down the corridor to the airlock and once inside pressed the automatic release. Nothing happened. Rykker hit the green button again and still nothing. Realizing that full power wasn't on, Rykker spun the manual control that retracted the bolts sealing the airlock doors and slowly pushed the door open.

The outside temperature was like an oven, and Rykker

flinched as the wall of heat came crashing down on him. Shading his eyes from the binary stars overhead, he could just make out the opening of the bunker shimmering in the convection currents that rose from the sand. Barefoot, the sharp gray grit of the planet's surface scorching the soles of his feet, Rykker trotted to the cool shade of the bunker's doorway. Using the manual access control he entered the bunker and descended the cool metal stairs to the main storeroom. The glowing bacteria lights threw a soft green glow into the corners of the room, and it took Rykker's eyes a few minutes to adjust to the contrast with the harsh sunlight outside. Then he searched for several minutes until he found the Codex-3 fissure separators. Grabbing a small box, he turned and retraced his steps.

In the machine shop the laser lathe had finished turning out the component pieces of Rykker's slug thrower and had deposited them in a basket ready for Rykker to assemble. Taking the basket with him, Rykker headed back to the computer center to make sure that he assembled everything in the correct order.

Back in front of the display terminal Rykker built his weapon. Handiman's Encyclopedia of Technology had given a detailed history of the slug thrower, and Rykker was at great pains to see that it was carefully assembled. Of course, there had been some modifications to the original design—Rykker's ammunition was electronically detonated, percussion caps being a bit thin on the ground, and the grips on his slug thrower were a polymer-based resin, not walnut. Still, it was faithful to the original design, right down to the loading lever that would be used to pack the Codex-3 into the chamber and then seat the slug on top.

Rykker hefted the assembled weapon. It felt right, as though it were a natural extention of his arm. Well balanced, it reminded him of his favorite sword—form following function. He knew that he had chosen the right weapon from the thousands catalogued in the Encyclopedia; even the name was right, recalling as it did other battles fought long ago on nameless seas by other fleets—the Colt Navy revolver.

Instinctively Rykker twirled the pistol around the index finger of his right hand, his thumb catching the hammer and snapping it back into its fully cocked position. He laughed to himself as he set the gun down and turned his attention once again to the computer.

Slugs were the main problem. According to Handiman, the 1851 Colt Navy revolver was designed to fire a 9mm conical or spherical bullet made of lead, a substance that had virtually disappeared from use by the end of the 21st century. He had checked and cross-checked the computer inventory, but there were no substitutes available from the stores here in the ore-processing station. After feeding in the performance parameters required of the substance used to make the slugs, the computer provided Rykker with a short list of commonly encountered elements and alloys that could be substituted for the required lead. It even went so far as to tell Rykker where these elements were most likely to be encountered, and if there were any of these items in the station.

Rykker scanned the list, noting that none of the items were in the station. None, that is, except item twenty-two: life suit, model G-14 Alliance issue, priority 87. Rykker's life suit. Worn like a second skin, life suits were designed to be powered by the electrical charge inherent in the human body. In order to most effectively capture this current and use it to power the life-support systems, the entire suit was lined with a fine mesh made of gold wires no thicker than a human hair, separated by a space of one tenth of a millimeter. It might be possible to make four, five, or even six slugs from the gold-wire grid in a life suit. The problem was, without the grid the life suit wouldn't work. And without a life suit, Rykker knew he wouldn't last two hours on the surface of the planet.

Rykker trotted back to the crew quarters where his damaged life suit lay in a heap outside the shower where he'd left it. Picking it up, he headed back to the machine shop. Here he stuffed the life suit in a crucible and then placed it in a low-power solar oven. Five minutes later only the molten gold remained in the bottom of the crucible.

Rykker used a tiny ladle to scoop out a small quantity of the molten gold. Standing on a table, he poured the gold into a bucket of ice-cold water placed on the floor. The falling gold congealed into a ball as it hit the water. It took several tries before he had the right amount in the ladle, but two hours later he had managed to drop-cast five golden slugs, and still had enough gold left over to almost form a sixth. Using a hammer, he pounded the last bit of gold into a thin sheet, which he wrapped around a ball of the Codex-3.

Following the instructions of the computer, Rykker rolled more of the Codex-3 into a thin rope, thick enough to just fit into the shallow chambers of his Navy Colt. He placed a gold slug on top of each chamber and, rotating the chamber under the loading lever, rammed each ball home. As the golden slugs were forced deep into the chambers a small golden ring was swaged off of each ball and fell onto the table where Rykker was working. The last projectile—a bit of Codex-3 wrapped in gold like some sort of lethal confection—Rykker seated by hand, using his thumb to push the slug down on its charge.

In the locker room Rykker pulled on two pairs of the discarded socks and then stepped into the shower. Standing under the cool spray, he reevaluated his chances of surviving the three kilometers that separated him from Melton and his crew. His sweats, now saturated with the sterilizing fluid from the shower, would probably dry out during the first twenty minutes; sipping from the canteen, he could probably last another fifteen minutes before the heat and glare would get to him. Pushing, he might last another ten minutes. So that was it. He had to cover three kilometers in forty-five minutes and still arrive in good enough shape to tackle Melton. It just couldn't be done. So, on to plan B.

On the map of the mining complex there was a shed halfway between the ore-processing plant and the administration complex. Rykker decided to head for that carrying a bucket of water. He'd leave the water, come back, pick up another bucket, and return to the shed. Two buckets of water ought to be enough to soak his clothes a second time and continue on to Melton's retreat.

Dripping water as he made his way through the crew quarters, Rykker paused only long enough to put on the yellow baseball cap as he headed toward the door.

Outside, the searing dry heat sucked at Rykker's lungs, making his legs buckle slightly under the added weight of twenty liters of slowly evaporating liquid. Forty minutes later, Rykker had reached the corrugated shed, his clothes dry and caked with perspiration. Despite the heavy charge of electrolytes in his canteen, he was beginning to feel the first waves of nausea as he stepped through the door and came face-to-face with one of Melton's goons—fortunately, one of the humans.

The man moved fast, but not fast enough. Rykker swung the water can hard at the man's head and caught him a glancing blow off the side of the jaw. The human fell heavily on his side, and as he hit the deck Rykker could hear the man's arm snap under his own weight. Before the human could fully regain his feet, Rykker was on top of him, bending the broken arm backward until it snapped again and the man shrieked in pain, going limp in Rykker's grasp.

Rykker relaxed his grip slightly, but the man suddenly twisted to the side, pulling a knife from his boot top and slashing furiously as Rykker jumped back. The tip of the knife caught Rykker on the front of the thigh, tracking a hairline cut down toward the knee. Rykker grabbed the man's wrist and twisted the knife away form his body as he slammed his knee into his opponent's face. Still holding the man's wrist, Rykker drove the knife deep into his assailant's chest as the man tumbled forward.

The exertion had nearly been more than Rykker could stand, and for twenty minutes he lay flat on the floor gasping for air and hoping he wouldn't retch again. Finally he was able to sit upright and take stock of the situation. The large puddle of dried blood around the human told Rykker that the man was definitely down for the count. As he leaned over and pulled the knife out of the man's chest, he managed to somehow short out the dead man's life suit. The corpse gave several galvanic jerks as the system short-circuited, and Rykker caught an unpleasant whiff of singed body hair.

Looking around as he wiped the blood from the blade of the knife, Rykker realized that there was no going back to the ore-processing station. In the scuffle with Melton's thug he had spilled his water, and there was no way he could make it back in dry clothes. The creep's life suit was damaged beyond repair, even if it could be peeled off its lightly fried former owner. Rykker eyed the dead man's boots, but even at a glance could tell that they were too small. He slowly stood up and walked to the back of the shack, the Navy Colt making a large bulge in the waistband of his sweatpants.

Halfway across the room Rykker froze in his tracks. Outside the small corrugated building, he heard the sound of someone walking in the sand, pacing along the other side of the wall, moving in the direction of the door. Dropping to all fours, Rykker scurried across the floor and took up a position where he would be able to kill the first two people through the door. He decided to use the knife on the first two, saving his six shots for whichever of Melton's men remained outside.

Slowly the door inched inward as Rykker crouched to spring, knife at the guard position. As the door swung fully open, Rykker launched himself from his hiding place and was immediately knocked flat on his back by the onger. The six-legged beast bowled past Rykker and headed straight to the corner of the shack, where it buried its nose deep in an automatic watering trough and drank for several minutes. Its thirst satisfied, it turned to go, but Rykker closed the door.

Rykker stared at the beast for several minutes before deciding that it would be futile to try to ride it; he didn't know how to start, stop, or turn the animal, and past experience had taught him that the ride was far from comfortable. He opened the door and let it out. Walking back to the corner of the shack, he pulled off his sweatshirt and stuck it in the watering trough, soaking it thoroughly before putting it back

on. He had just pulled off his sweatpants when the other
human pulled up on a sand scooter and came in through the
door.

Half-naked, Rykker didn't have time for the subtleties of
hand-to-hand combat. Before the human's eyes had adjusted
to the dimness of the shack Rykker, crouching close to the
ground, picked up the Navy Colt, cocked it, and fired. The
110-grain gold ball spun down the rifled barrel of the pistol
and, traveling faster than the speed of sound, smashed into
the forehead of the man at the door, tore through his frontal
brain, and exited from the top of his head, tearing out a
piece of skull the size of a small orange.

For a moment neither Rykker nor the two dead men
moved. Then, very slowly, with a look of utter amazement
frozen on his face, the man standing at the door slowly
crumpled to the ground. Rykker stood up, looking first at
the dead man and then at the gun in his hand. There was
something about the Navy Colt that made killing with it far
more personal than using a modern weapon.

To begin with it was loud. It thundered out its message
of death where other weapons barely whispered of their le-
thality. It slammed back in your hand—recoil shoving your
whole arm back into your shoulder—giving you a taste of
what it must feel like to be on the receiving end of one of
its deadly projectiles. Finally, it left a thin residue of burnt
propellant hanging wraithlike in the air, a specter of battles
long forgotten, now summoned forth to remind the victor
that one day he too may be the vanquished. Rykker liked
his Navy Colt.

It wasn't until he was halfway to the sand scooter outside,
with the twin suns scorching the backs of his legs, that
Rykker realized he was still naked from the waist down.
Back in the shack he pulled on the waterlogged sweatpants,
not bothering even for a second to consider taking the dead
man's life suit. With the sand scooter, Rykker could be at
Melton's bolt hole in the administration complex in less than
ten minutes.

On the scooter, Rykker pulled his yellow baseball cap
down low over his eyes and cracked the throttle wide open.

The deep purple of the land effects beam threw a rooster tail of sand high behind the scooter that changed from a glittering silver to dark pewter as it fell to the ground. The hot air stung Rykker's eyes as he raced over the dunes, and by the time he reached the administrative complex his sweat suit was bone dry.

Rykker let the scooter glide to a stop in the shade of the building and dismounted, moving quickly along the side of the structure to the entrance. Inside, the building was cool, the solar-powered life-support system providing the maximum comfort for Melton. Unlike other areas of the mining complex, the floors in this building were highly polished stone, glass smooth and slippery under Rykker's feet. Rykker tugged off his socks and savored the smooth, cool stone floor soothing the blistered soles of his feet as he made his way toward the executive wing of the complex.

Room by room Rykker checked out the executive complex until he came at last to the recreation lounge and, beyond it, the galley. Peering carefully through the acrylic double doors that led from the main corridor to the lounge, Rykker could just see Melton sitting in an egg, one of those specially designed chairs that provided the maximum in auditory stimuli but were totally silent except to those seated in them—like Melton's nearby briefcase and self-cleaning boots, another outward symbol of Alliance success.

Rykker pulled away from the doors and headed back down the corridor, deciding that the best way to get at Melton was through the galley. Turning to his right, he followed an intersecting corridor until he came to the service passage leading to the back entrance of the galley. The door was designed to open outward, smooth on Rykker's side, without handles, so he used the tip of his knife to pry the door open enough to grip it with his fingers and then slowly pull it open. Inside, the silver metallic sinks and cupboards reflected the soft green glow of the bacteria lighting, filling the room with an eerie luminescence.

Dropping to all fours, Rykker began crawling toward the far exit. But as he moved cautiously across the galley floor, he became vaguely conscious that there was something about the room that was different, something that was trying to reach through to his subconscious, to warn him . . . the smell. He wasn't sure when he first detected it, but the odor was there, and its strong, cloying sweetness was getting thicker. You only had to smell that aroma once to remember it forever. It was the Thalmud.

Rykker dropped flat on the floor just as the Thalmud fired, the flechette from its needle-gun splatting into the cabinet inches above Rykker's head. Rykker rolled hard to his left, coming to his feet in a crouched position between two serving carts. The Thalmud fired again, and the cart nearest Rykker pinged and rolled a few inches under the impact of the slug.

Flat on his belly, Rykker crawled along under a long row of serving tables, hoping to catch even a glimpse of the Thalmud's legs as he went. At the end of the tables, Rykker flattened himself out and broke to the left, coming up against the door of the walk-in freezer. Slowly, with his back against the door, he pushed himself up into a standing position. The Thalmud stood with its back to Rykker, not ten feet away, a small, low-yield needler in its hand. From where Rykker stood, he could see the tiny red glow on the back of the weapon, indicating that it was fully charged and armed. Rykker's hand reached for the Navy Colt at his waist. It was gone.

Still unaware that Rykker was behind it, the Thalmud cautiously turned around, bringing its weapon to the ready position. Instinctively Rykker rushed to the attack, throwing himself over the serving tables and smashing into the alien. The impact of his body sent them both crashing to the floor, a fine golden mist of the Thalmud's secretions hanging in the air before heavily raining down on the two combatants. Rykker grabbed for the needler, but covered in the Thalmud's oily secretions it shot from his grasp and slid across the floor.

The Thalmud reacted quickly to the attack, smashing its fist repeatedly into Rykker's ribs. Rykker thought he felt one of those ribs crack, but he ignored the pain and twisted enough to bring his fist down hard on the side of the Thalmud's face. Its central nervous system working overtime, every fiber on the Thalmud's head was secreting thick golden slime that poured over its body and covered it with a slippery protective coating. Rykker's fist slid off its mark without doing significant damage.

Rykker tried to bring both hands up in an effort to gouge out the Thalmud's eyes, but found one of his arms pinned by a viselike grip. Rykker head-butted the Thalmud between the eyes and felt its grip momentarily weaken. Using all of his strength, he brought one leg up against the side of one of the galley cabinets and shoved for all he was worth—and managed to break free.

Almost as quickly as Rykker was up, the Thalmud got to its feet, only to be stopped halfway by a well-placed kick to the chin that sent it back down again. Seizing his chance, Rykker wrenched open the door to the freezer and dashed in, the Thalmud right behind. The freezer was large, some twenty by thirty feet, and held several randomly placed cases containing ongers held in deep storage against the day Alliance miners might return to the planet. Rykker's bare feet wanted to stick to the frozen metal floor, and his breath hung frozen in front of him. Around the top of the freezer walls, twin blue neon tubes cast an eerie luminescence. Rykker's sweat-matted hair began to harden with frost.

It took the Thalmud several seconds longer than Rykker to adjust to the low-level illumination, but that did nothing to lessen its aggressiveness. Shivering, its heavy breath hanging on the still air of the freezer, the alien moved cautiously from box to box looking for the human.

Rykker moved, and had to stifle a cry of pain as frozen skin was ripped from the sole of his foot. Limping slightly, Rykker moved from box to box, positioning himself between the Thalmud and the freezer door. In the intense cold of the freezer, he stripped off his sweatshirt and, holding it out by the arms, spun it around a few times until it formed a sort of rope. Then he crossed the cuffs one over the other forming a simple knot with a large loop, a noose ready to toss over the Thalmud's head.

In the few seconds that he had stopped moving to fashion

his noose, his feet had frozen to the floor again. Rocking
back and forth, using every ounce of willpower to avoid
crying out in pain, Rykker ripped his feet loose, the blood
and skin freezing in two dark blotches on the floor as his
tears froze on his cheeks.

But the cold was also having its effect on the Thalmud.
A kind of hoarfrost glistened on its body as the Thalmud's
bodily secretions reacted with the extreme cold of the
freezer, causing them to first thicken like syrup and then to
freeze over on the surface. The Thalmud crackled as it
moved, as its frozen body coating shattered and as quickly
refroze. The Thalmud stopped not far away with its back to
Rykker, turning its head first to one side then the other,
perhaps catching the sound of Rykker rocking back and forth
on his feet to prevent them freezing to the floor again. The
long neck swayed left and right, small bits of its frozen
bodily fluids drifting silently to the floor of the freezer like
amber snowflakes.

Rykker slammed a fist into the small of the Thalmud's
back with all the force he could muster. The Thalmud's
knees buckled, and Rykker had his noose over the alien's
head in a flash, pulling the sleeves of the sweatshirt tight as
he did so. The Thalmud reached back with both hands and
grabbed Rykker's sweatpants, its scaly palm and fingers
locking onto the fabric and pulling Rykker forward, top-
pling him off balance.

Holding on to the arms of the sweatshirt for dear life,
Rykker twisted as they fell, managing to remain on top of
the Thalmud, now facedown on the freezer floor. Pulling
for all he was worth, Rykker dragged the semiconscious
alien toward a pile of boxes near the freezer door and
climbed up, dragging the alien after him. With effort, he
tossed one of the arms of the sweatshirt over one of the
small cooling pipes in the low ceiling and tied it fast.

Twice the alien started to struggle, its hands tearing at
the cloth biting into its throat, choking it, strangling it, and
both times Rykker kicked and punched it into limp compliance. Finally, with the sleeve knotted tightly around the

pipe, Rykker kicked over the pile of boxes, leaving the Thalmud hanging like a side of beef in the freezer.

Outside, with the freezer door shut behind him, Rykker's feet throbbed with pain, their soles almost stripped of skin from having stuck to the floor of the freezer. Sitting down with his back against the freezer door, Rykker ripped off the legs of his sweatpants and wrapped them around his feet like makeshift moccasins. He found his Navy Colt lying on the floor near the door to the executive lounge. Each step was agony, but with the slug thrower in his hand Rykker suddenly felt a whole lot better.

Melton's egg was facing away from the galley door, so he didn't see Rykker come in. He was listening to the flower duet from Delibe's "Lakme" at full volume, the egg sending its alpha-wave transmission of the music so deep into his sensory centers that he didn't realize Rykker was standing in front of him until he felt the very cold presence of Rykker's gun barrel pressed hard against his forehead. As his eyes focused on the intruder, Rykker reached in and turned off the music.

A slow smile spread across Melton's face, but behind the lenses of his glasses the eyes remained impassively cool. Rykker took two steps back.

"Get outta the egg, Melton. Slow, real slow."

Melton shrugged slightly, and then slowly rose from his seat.

"Now, over to the table and open your briefcase."

Melton started toward the table and then turned to face Rykker.

"How would you like to be really wealthy? I mean richer than even level-five executives?" Melton stood, arms casually folded, looking at Rykker, waiting for a reply.

"Forget it, geek. Just give me the briefcase." Rykker motioned toward the table with his Navy Colt.

"I take it, then, that your answer is no." Melton sounded faintly bemused. "Too bad, you'll have to die."

Rykker was about to tell Melton to shut up when the unmistakable aroma found his nostrils. The Thalmud was halfway across the room when Rykker fired, his first shot taking the alien high in the right shoulder. The impact of the slug caused the Thalmud to stagger as he was hit, and Rykker's second shot missed by inches, smashing into the far wall. Rykker thumbed back the hammer and squeezed off his third shot, which slammed into the alien's stomach and stopped it just long enough for Rykker to put one more round into its chest. The Thalmud ran another few feet and then collapsed at Rykker's bleeding feet.

Melton had made it to the table and gotten as far as pulling his needler from his briefcase by the time Rykker turned and, bringing up the Navy Colt, took deliberate aim and snapped off his last shot.

As the hammer of Rykker's pistol hit the back of the cylinder it completed the electrical circuit that detonated the remaining charge in the Navy Colt. The electronic discharge also energized the gold foil wrapped around a ball of Codex-3 explosive. At 650 feet per second, the explosive round crossed the twenty feet separating the two men in milliseconds. The sound of Melton's face exploding was inseparable from the report of Rykker's weapon.

Later, after he had put Melton and the Thalmud in the disposer unit in the galley, Rykker enjoyed a long shower. He toweled off and, in a pair of Melton's lightweights, sat down to inspect the contents of the briefcase. Glancing over the documents inside, two things became clear: first, Melton had been waiting for a Syndicate ship to take him to the cluster, and second, no one in the Syndicate had ever seen Melton.

He finished Melton's drink and then climbed into Melton's life suit, tugging on the self-cleaning boots over his tender feet. Finally, before heading out to the waiting Syndicate shuttlecraft, he tossed the Navy Colt into the briefcase.

INTERLUDE: The Family Business

The basic forms of the Alliance culture were derived from a wide range of traditional institutions. This was because the lesser level of destruction suffered by the early Alliance meant that there was still a measure of continuity from the Empire and before. In the Syndicate cluster the much higher level of cultural collapse meant that most of this prior culture was lost. Further, the families' struggle to overcome the warlords permanently disaffected them regarding the only other remaining body of tradition that had survived intact, those of the military. As a result the titles and structure of Syndicate culture were derived from the only two institutions they retained knowledge of, business and the family. Most titles in the Syndicate refer to one of these. Further complicating the nomenclature was the fact that all business was controlled by members of an extended family. The head of a family was the Father. His immediate family were referred to as the heirs or sons (even when female). The leadership of any organization was the management. A military officer was a combat manager. Space-force ranks included vice presidents for weapons, transport, and the like, assistant managers, associate V.P.s, and even field managers. Foremen were the equivalent of sergeants. There were no diplomats or ambassadors, but instead liaison managers.

Superimposed over everything were the complicated designations of family relationship. These reflected not only relationships based upon birth, but often changed as a family member grew in importance. A second cousin, a level barely recognized as a family member at all, could rise through ability until he or she himself became a son and potential heir to the Fathership. The reverse could also occur. In all cases there was no way that any nonfamily member could ever hope to gain status equal to even a mere cousin.

A subtler implication of the Syndicate's cultural heritage was that all aspects of life were treated as being part of a business. Every citizen on a family world was judged almost entirely on their ability to contribute to the family's welfare. The military was viewed not only as a cost center, but also as a profit generator. Every mission was analyzed not only for its military necessity, but also if the risk could be justified by the potential gain. A gain that was often not only measured in military advantage, but in increased family assets as well.

WITHOUT PAINT

by Bill Fawcett

LOCATED ONLY FOUR light-years from Target, the small, verdant world was code-named Brown. No one was sure if this designation was the name of its discoverer or the color of its shallow, muddy seas. The planet was best described as pleasant, having a generally mild climate and friendly natives. Except for two recent developments the world would have held no interest for anyone, let alone a full admiral. The first of these was Happy Town. This was a Fleet Class II R&R station that had already grown by the addition of several hundred unapproved "recreational facilities." These were built mostly by enterprising businessmen, primarily employing business girls and boys of an amazing variety. Occasionally this monotony was broken by the still-unlit neon lights of an only mildly dishonest gambling club. Once Duane's fleet completed its current training maneuver and began sending transports full of spacemen and Marines to Brown on leave, fortunes would be made literally overnight.

Abe Meier stood staring in awe at his first view of the planet's other claim to distinction. If somewhere in Africa was an elephants' graveyard, like that made famous by the revered writings of Kipling, this was truly its technological equivalent. Spread for miles across the valley they had just entered were the hulks of hundreds of Khalian spaceships. Some were visibly gutted, others had portions of their hulls missing; all were severely damaged in some way. The entire scene was a mute testimony to the effectiveness of Fleet weaponry.

Auro LeBaric watched his superior's reaction as the O. D., a Lieutenant Bromley, explained the sight. He couldn't help but notice that even in the ornate uniform that went with his new rank, Meier still managed to look rumpled.

"Admiral," the lieutenant began, clearly enjoying having the complete attention of the only admiral in a four light-year radius, "for longer than we had guessed, the Syndicate used this planet as a dumping ground, a graveyard for all the wrecks that they felt were beyond the ability of the Khalia to salvage."

He paused as Meier turned to look once more at the valley spread out below them. The lieutenant had taken a devious route to this point so as to preserve the dramatic effect of the view. This graveyard of ships was filled with examples of every type of vessel the Khalia had used and a few that had to be captured Alliance hulls. Incongruously growing around and occasionally through the ships was a carpet of the waist-high yellow-green "grass" that covered most of this continent. A few saplings had even pushed up through those hulls left here the longest, their branches emerging from portholes and ruptures in the still-glistening sides of the fallen warships. Standing slightly off to one side, Auro also noticed dozens of small shapes moving purposely among the wreckage. Their guide resumed talking, quickly as if he had memorized the speech and was afraid of having his concentration broken. It probably wasn't very often that an admiral and war hero visited this outpost on official business, and he wanted to make the best impression possible.

"Intelligence says they were afraid to leave these cripples on Target or Khalia for fear some bright Weas . . . er, Khalian would take something apart and figure out how it worked. They appear to have been recently training a few thousand Brownians on how to dismantle or even repair some of the equipment, but hardly made a dent before they had to evacuate."

"I thought the Brownians were not a technological cul-

ture?'' Auro interjected, unable to resist checking if the
O. D. would fluster easily. He did it also because the newly
promoted captain was just beginning to realize he outranked
the other man, even though he was almost a decade younger.
Besides, the lieutenant had been ignoring him.

Bromley was plainly annoyed at having his carefully
thought-out spiel for the visiting admiral interrupted. Auro
wasn't yet twenty and looked as young as he was, but now he
sported the insignia of a captain. This promotion was a belated
reward for being Meier's second in command during their in-
tervention in the battle above Target almost a year earlier.

Eyeing the two clusters of valor metals and battle honors
on the youth's chest, the lieutenant chose discretion and
directed his reply to both of the visiting officers.

''Those are just some elves. We call the Brownians
'elves.' The locals are actually quite competent technically.
They already had some knowledge of electricity and even
atomic theory before the Khalia conquered them,'' he explained. ''And they seem to learn our procedures quickly,
if they are a little slow on theory.''

''I didn't notice any cities from orbit?'' Also newly promoted, Admiral Abraham Meier ended the statement with
the rising in tone that indicated an explanation was expected. He had noticed their guide was ignoring his young
aide and was enjoying his discomfort. Abe had come to like
this boy who had come to him as a spoiled cadet almost
eighteen months ago, and felt such slights personally. As
an admiral he had pulled rank to gain the privilege of watching the main screen as they approached Brown. Their entry
had been somewhat rushed as the planet's moons were the
planet's only drawback as a resort world. These moons had
so far failed to coalesce into any body larger than twenty
miles on a side. But what they lacked in size was made up
in number. Several thousand moonlets followed irregular
orbits around the world, virtually encompassing the planet
in a thin, but dangerous sheath of stellar debris. Most were
now marked with beacons and easily avoided, but dodging
through them in a gig had entailed a bumpy ride.

''There aren't any,'' Bromley answered, glad he didn't

have to correct an admiral. "Not aboveground anyhow. The elves live underground. Some of their warrens extend for miles. No one knows how many or where. The Brownians themselves aren't much for organization. No government or anything, just leaders who seem to appoint themselves when something needs to get done. Sociologists are having a ball trying to figure them out. Most elves love gadgets and are glad to work or be interviewed in exchange for vouchers that we honor at the PX."

At this point a party of Brownians was passing nearby. They were carrying a section of hull plate. Meier suspected it was on its way to becoming the roof of some brothel. But that wasn't really a problem yet. There was enough scrap metal out there to build a city full of brothels. He had been sent to assess what value the Fleet could gain from all these wrecks. His briefing had told him that many were known to contain salvageable modules, even working drives and power units. It was already apparent the graveyard was going to be of immense value to the war effort. Abe's subconscious was already churning away at a plan to salvage the working parts from those hundreds of ships in the valley below. He had to admit to himself that obtaining working Cooper FTL drive or shield units that only cost a few vouchers for paying the local laborers appealed to him. It certainly would make the budget bashers back on Port happy.

"You over there," their lieutenant bellowed at the natives, who halted instantly. Carefully, they set down the hull plate and walked purposely toward the Fleet officers.

"Can I be of service?" one asked as they approached. His Standard was almost without accent. Auro had to agree that he did seem eager to please.

"They learn quickly, mostly by rote," Bromley explained, noting the surprised expression on the faces of his two charges. "Great way to learn a language. Just don't ask them to conjugate a verb. Like I said, lousy at theory and great at following orders. The sociology types say they can adopt minor behaviors easily, but are much more driven by instinct than most races. Can't change the basics or look

beyond the surface. It took them thousands of years of observation to get their science to where it was at.''

It was readily apparent why the Brownians were nick-
named elves. Slightly smaller than Auro, they had large
pointed ears, green skin, and tufts of flesh that resembled
nothing so much as a beard and mustache. The illusion was
completed by immense golden eyes, slitted like a cat's, but
horizontally. Most wore clothing made from cloth imported
by the humans—much of it suspiciously like that issued for
the repair of uniforms.

Before either visitor had a chance to say anything the com
unit in their grav car bleeped urgently three times. Auro
and Abe recognized the code: urgent transmission waiting.
Lieutenant Bromley looked surprised and hurried over to
the vehicle. After a short exchange that neither Abe nor
Auro could hear, he turned to them and spoke even more
rapidly than before.

''I have to take you back to the command center, now.''
The words were clipped and Bromley started climbing into
the driver's seat before he had even finished them.

As they climbed in beside him Auro noticed that the man's
face had lost all of its color. Only awareness of his newfound rank kept the captain from quizzing Bromley on the
short flight back to the metal dome that housed the command center. It constituted the Fleet's only nonrecreational
facility on the planet.

Their route back took them directly over the valley. To
Auro's surprise Meier seemed too fascinated by the wrecks
they flew over to show any other emotion. The new captain
tried to relax then, emulating his superior, almost assured that
if Abe wasn't worried, he shouldn't be. What could be wrong
on a world whose only purpose was rest and relaxation?

On the far side of the graveyard was another valley containing a shallow lake on whose shore was located the official R&R center. Pastel buildings had been skillfully
designed to fit in to their pastoral surroundings. The complex had been completed only a few days before; one of
Meier's scheduled activities was to officially open it. Skill
games blinked and bonged appealingly, ice was made and

melted in sinks behind half a dozen bars, all awaiting only the staff and customers to appear. Dozens of construction engineers, reluctant to finish a job so preferable to their normal, hazardous spaceborne duties, still lingered among its buildings, adding final touches and enjoying the facility's best.

To one side of the complex was located the utilitarian shape of the command dome. At first glance, the spaceport beyond this appeared busy. Its ferro-concrete surface was dotted with dozens of small shapes. One or two were always lifting or landing. This had surprised Auro when they had first landed, but exiting the gig he had realized these were yachts belonging to the local entrepreneurs. All were unarmed and incapable of FTL flight. Many could barely make it into a stable orbit. A few were visibly overengined and likely destined to participate in races once there were spacemen here to bet on them. All of these ships had been ferried here in the holds of larger transports alongside supplies of such necessities as liquor and gambling equipment. Several of the more gaudily painted, he suspected, were outfitted for recreational use by those who preferred their entertainment in zero g.

Auro's fantasies of orbital love were immediately grounded by the look on the face of the captain commanding the construction unit as he ran toward their landing grav car. The man had been all smiles an hour earlier; now tension pinched his features. The man dashed across the parking area and was nearly crushed by the descending grav car.

Without even bothering to salute, the engineer poured out the details of their predicament: a message torp had just arrived. It was from Target. A Syndicate force of almost thirty ships had appeared off that planet. With most of the Fleet ships off on maneuvers, those remaining had been barely able to fight them off. When the Syndicate ships had turned and run they had continued in pursuit. During that pursuit an unknown number of the enemy vessels had split off from the main body. Projections of their turning arc indicated that they were headed for Brown.

Everyone quickly realized that the Syndicate was about

to rectify their oversight in leaving so many hulls to be
salvaged. The Fleet commander, an Admiral Nortin, had
not felt his force was strong enough to send any ships after
those that had split off. His first concern, the message had
justified the action by saying, had to be to protect the vital
port facilities on Target. He had sent a message torp to
Duane, but they could expect reinforcements no sooner than
a week after receiving this message.

The eight to ten Syndicate ships should arrive at Brown
in approximately two more days. After appointing Abe
Meier, as ranking officer present, to command the defense
of the entire planet, Nortin ended by wishing them all luck.

An hour later Admiral Abraham Meier followed a long
and hallowed naval tradition and held a staff meeting. Its
intended purpose was to organize the defense of Brown.
Abe wasn't about to give up such a rich prize as this graveyard without a fight. After the first few minutes of discussion, the quartermaster was beginning to share the
construction officer's panic.

Their situation wasn't just hopeless. It was light-years,
parsecs beyond hopeless. The total armament of all Fleet
personnel on Brown consisted of seven laser rifles and four
slug-throwing pistols carried by a unit of shore police. If
every engineer on the work force worked without sleeping,
there was a chance they could cobble together as many as
half a dozen laser cannon from the wrecks. Of course this
was less than were mounted on the smallest ship coming at
them, and his cannon would be unable to move after firing.
Once they opened fire, the location of each of these weapons would be known, and seconds later they would be destroyed by an overwhelming number of Syndicate missiles
and laser beams.

Nor could they even expect to do any damage. The Syndicate ships needed only to establish themselves in a sta-
tionary orbit and then casually beam or bomb every wreck
in the graveyard to useless slag. In orbit their screens could
operate and would deflect anything the defenders could jury-
rig. Being planetbound, Meier's forces couldn't even acti-

vate any screens they might salvage from the wrecks. The screen was a beneficial side effect of a ship's Cooper drive, but the result of engaging any FTL drive or screen within a few kilometers of even a small asteroid was a most spectacular explosion. Starting such a drive in the command dome would turn the entire seven-mile-long valley around it into a neatly scooped hole several hundred meters deep.

Meier (quite naturally not having been concerned with them when on a fact-finding mission for the quartermaster's corp) now asked what armaments the Brownians had. He was confused, at first, by the laughter and groans that greeted his question. Finally, Dr. Skiep Neiberger, the head of the sociology mission, explained their amusement.

"The Brownians are highly intelligent in their own way." His voice quickly adopted lecturing tones. "They obey instructions, even innovate and adjust when forced to. Sometime in their past some spur must have driven their species to develop intelligence. But so far we cannot find any trace of a single living predator. The problem is that the elves simply have no concept of armed conflict. They are wholly noncompetitive by nature. There not only aren't any words for 'war' or 'murder' in the Brownian language, there aren't even any for 'disagree' or 'argue.' The closest to 'fight' that any Brownian phrase translates to actually means 'to flee to safety.' "

"A planet full of bloody pacifists," one of the more grizzled combat engineers added, "and thousands of them are gonna get fried when the Syndicate slags that valley."

Finding himself in command of a planet populated by the pacifists, one with no obvious means of defending itself, facing an overwhelming enemy force, and no hope of timely reinforcements, Abe Meier had an uncomfortable sense of déjà vu.

"How is the planet's stock of paint?" he asked the ranking engineer, more in an attempt to remind himself that no situation is truly hopeless, than in expectation of useful information.

"Used the last yesterday on the resort's orbital fliers"

was the discouraging reply. "Got a requisition in for a few hundred gallons more, mostly gray and regulation blue."

No paint. For some reason this information seemed to make his aide, LeBaric, even more depressed. Meier wondered if their situation could really be completely hopeless. There seemed to be no alternative but hide while his ships were devastated. Surrender wasn't even an alternative. The Syndicate ships wouldn't risk themselves close to the planet for a few prisoners. Nor was anyone who stayed in this valley likely to survive the numerous target shots that were inevitable in any orbital bombardment. There were hundreds of civilian flyers out there. Maybe his only choice would be to order an evacuation of the civilians to a distant continent and to pray the Syndicate's scanners didn't pick up all the new construction in this valley. It promised to be a very long two days, followed by a very short, and completely one-sided, battle.

The meeting adjourned with empty promises by all to keep on the problem. Abe suspected most were going to go back and pack, hoping he ordered the evacuation in time.

Two hours later, sweat blinded the admiral as he pulled himself up through the charred gash in the hull of what had once been a Khalian light destroyer. The front third of this ship must have been hit by a laser mounted on a dreadnought. Everything forward of engineering simply wasn't there. A missile would have been less selective and all that remained would have been dust.

It was the fifth ship Abe had crawled through. The nervous energy of frustration powered his actions. With each hulk he visited Abe's determination to prevent the loss of his graveyard grew. The problem was he still had found no way to defend it, no matter how badly he wished to.

Outside, Auro waited beside the grav car, confused but patient. He had seen his commander pull off one miracle. He didn't know how or what it could be, but was hoping for another. As Meier dictated his findings between labored breaths, Auro wondered once more why they were there. Like three of the other wrecks, the drive or shield genera-

tors of this fifth ship were intact. Evidently the Syndicate
had planned to salvage or repair these hulks at a later time.
None of the hulls were anywhere near intact and there wasn't
even enough time for the engineers to cobble together even
one complete ship—if they knew how. And even if they
succeeded, there were no trained crewmen to fire the weapons when it faced an entire Syndicate squadron.

One of the civilian ships buzzed overhead. Meier suspected word had leaked out and soon the sky would be filled
with fleeing ships. Another orbital flyer sped straight up
under emergency lift, her drive whining audibly under the
strain. The quartermaster in Abe was annoyed. The maneuver was a waste of fuel since the enemy wasn't expected for
thirty-six hours. Watching it diminish to a dot and disappear
in the green sky, Meier realized that the pilot of the latter
ship intended to hide among Brown's moonlets. A good
plan *if* he stayed undetected until the relief force arrived.
None of the Syndicate ships would get too close to any of
the moons. Ramming even one of the smaller rocks would
prevent the use of shield or strain one that was engaged.

A few moments later Auro was amazed to see the smile that
had blossomed on Meier's face. He had seen it once before.

As expected, the civilians had screamed when Meier
commandeered their yachts. Few accepted his assurance that
most would be returned intact. Some had to be threatened
with the gig's single laser cannon before they volunteered
their ships. If he lived, unless his plan worked, there would
be the piper to pay. Then again, if his plan failed, there was
only a very slight probability that he would survive the
bombardment that would follow.

Like most of his ideas, the entire idea was so far out that
the quartermaster was reluctant to discuss it even with
LeBaric. The separate parts of Abe's plan eased into gear.
Once they had been shown how, the Brownians began to
flood the spaceport with Khalian drive and shield modules.
A surprising number of these were still functional. As
quickly as they arrived, these were loaded into a commandeered yacht and flown into space by an engineer. By the

time these ships reached their destinations, the necessary wiring and modifications Meier had ordered were completed. Abe didn't point out, and hoped no one else noticed, that even if they lost, he would have at least succeeded in preserving thousands of manhours' worth of drive units. The last few engineers had just disembarked from the last pickup boat when Auro radioed that the gig's instruments had registered nine ships dropping back from FTL several million klicks from Brown.

After hours of waiting alone in the gig, Auro was almost glad to see the enemy arrive. He waited another few minutes for the ships to approach and then opened the awkward ship's throttle wide and drove straight at them. Auro almost wished he could see the faces of the officers commanding the Syndicate force when they realized he was diving on them. They would have to assume he was insane. Slaving the gig's small laser cannon to the combat computer, he forced it to open fire while still out of range. It didn't really matter if he hit anything.

For a few moments the young officer hoped that the entire squadron would take the bait, even considering he was it. But their commander was either cautious or very smart. Two of the lighter ships peeled off and turned to meet the smaller ship. Auro spun away from the oncoming destroyers and dived among Brown's shell of moonlets. The Fleet beacons that were hidden on all of the larger rocks allowed him to maneuver through the clutter much more quickly than his pursuers. So Auro slowed down and waited for them to catch up.

The three ships had orbited a quarter of the way around the planet when the first destroyer passed close enough to a fifty-yard-thick chunk of rock. The destroyer's shield instantly interacted with the shield module hidden on the moonlet as it was activated by a yacht's proximity alarm. Part of the irony of the situation was that because both units were Syndicate made, they were attuned much more closely to each other than any Fleet and Syndicate shield unit pair would have been. The result was even more impressive than

Auro expected. Destroyer and moon both disappeared in a burst of raw energy that darkened his screens for several seconds.

The second ship, possibly damaged by the explosion, fired a few half-aimed laser bolts through the spreading debris in Auro's general direction and broke off pursuit. The young captain didn't bother to fire back. He did allow himself the luxury of a victory roll, but only after he had cleared the belt of moons and was entering Brown's atmosphere.

Auro was in the command dome two hours later when the Syndicate commander risked a second ship. This made a lone attempt to penetrate what had suddenly become a threatening cloud of moons that kept him away from his target. This ship made it halfway through the belt before its shield interacted with one hidden on an asteroid barely larger than itself. There were just too many pieces of rock, and until the yachts powered up on a signal from Meier, no way to determine which were traps. The result was another spectacular, if brief, burst of violet light in the Brownian night sky.

After nearly a day passed with no action by the orbiting Syndicate squadron, Auro almost allowed himself to believe they had won. Meier, he noticed, seemed more worried than ever. Abe had snatched only a few hours sleep, and that in a chair that sat in front of the main command console. The youngest captain in the Fleet felt his hopes that it was over die when the Syndicate ships began blasting away at Brown's moons.

Auro realized that the Syndicate commander had not been discouraged. He had done what Auro might have in his place. If the moons were a problem, get rid of the problem. It had taken time to plot the courses of all of those moons that would pass at a set time through a corridor leading to the sky over the valley containing the graveyard. The number of missiles needed to destroy them all would be extravagant, but not prohibitive. Lasers from a low orbit would be enough to destroy everything in the graveyard in less than an hour.

As the first shielded ship crept through the artificial void the Syndicate fire had taken three hours to create, Meier

launched four of the closest speedsters that had survived the
Syndicate missiles. Their autopilots and anticollision systems had been reversed and all four streaked toward the lead
Syndicate ship. Even assuming it would take a human response to reprogram the combat computers to accept civilian ships as threats, the Syndicate response was unforgivably
slow. Only two of the overpowered civilian ships were destroyed by antimissile fire and the third failed to energize
its shield unit and passed harmlessly a few meters behind
the dodging destroyer. The distraction this provided allowed
the fourth ship to get close enough that when its FTL drive
unit kicked in, another burst of light was visible low in
Brown's dawn sky.

An hour passed, then a day. The seven remaining Syndicate ships hung unmoving a dozen planetary diameters
overhead. It was only three days until help would arrive.
Maybe they would make it. Auro found that warm breezes
and soft Brownian sunlight encouraged his optimism. He
was beginning to believe that Meier had pulled it off again.
The warning scream of the engineer who had volunteered
to watch the scanners brought both Auro and Abe Meier
into the command center at a run.

The entire Syndicate force was descending, slowly, almost insolently, in a tight mass. Only after a careful review
of the sensor readings did Auro realize why. Though many
new moons had orbited into the gap they had blown, the
commander of the Syndicate ships had realized the key to
their vulnerability was not the moons, but their own shields.
The planet's only defense had been to cause their own
shields and drives to interact destructively. So they simply
shut them off.

All seven remaining Syndicate ships were carefully picking their way through the crowded belt of moons with their
shields down. They were much more vulnerable to collision
damage, but their corridor was still comparatively open.
Any more civilian ships would be easily destroyed by the
antimissile defenses, as could be the limited number of
moonlets that stood in their path.

They had no way to stop this attack. Auro turned away

rom the monitors. He wondered if it might be more spec-
acular to watch their destruction from outside the dome.
'hen reminding himself that he was a captain of the Fleet,
e forced himself to concentrate on the readouts scrolling
cross the bottom of the command console. Auro calculated
heir rate of approach with clinical detachment. In eleven
ninutes the first Syndicate ship would be below the moons.
'he bombardment should begin in less than twenty min-
tes. Determined to go down fighting, and unwilling to sim-
·ly wait to be blown apart by plasma torpedoes or fried
vith laser fire, Auro prepared to ask for permission to take
he admiral's gig for one final, futile attack.

Six minutes later Meier had refused Auro's request. Keyed
p as he was, the youth would have been uncontrollably
nnoyed except that his boss was wearing that same relaxed,
opsided smile again. Then he noticed that Meier was hum-
ning contendedly under his breath, glancing occasionally
t the chronometer behind them.

When the Syndicate ships were exactly halfway through
he moonlets, a pair of ships on each of the four of the
argest nearby moons received the signal to activate the FTL
·rives crammed into their living compartments. Each had
·nly enough power to create a Cooper field for only a few
·econds. Each pair also sat only centimeters apart. The
·rives of all the pairs interacted as expected.

Even though the blasts were close in stellar terms they
vere far too distant to harm any of the Syndicate vessels
·irectly. By the time the wave front of the explosions
·eached the descending ship's sensors, they had weakened
·o much they produced only slight blips on the radiation
·etectors. But the Syndicate ships' collision alarms sounded
·n time for most of the Syndicate fleet to reverse directions,
·ut not soon enough to escape. The tens of thousands of
·ragments that followed close behind them had a much more
·ramatic, and destructive, effect.

It was a tribute to the solid construction of the Syndicate
·hips that four still managed to climb away and drop up to
·TL space only a few hours later. An intelligence report
·onths later told Meier that all had been riddled by the debris

and had lost credible percentages of their crews. Of the forty Kosantzu accompanying the mission, none survived the unexpected, rapid decompression. Nor did the commanding officer, which, considering he had lost most of his command to an unarmed foe, was probably just as well.

Back in the command dome Meier looked both exultant and relieved. He had switched into an even more than usually grubby fatigue, but was striding around taking congratulations like a king. Abe gleefully commented that "this time I did it without paint." The comment confused everyone else, but Auro was almost prostrated by uncontrollable laughter that was also part sheer relief.

When the Fleet squadron arrived it discovered that Abe Meier had bettered his record of destroying thirty-seven enemy ships using only twenty-four lightly armed freighters by this time destroying three destroyers and three light cruisers using only a lightly armed admiral's gig and unarmed civilian yachts. It was possible that Abe was the highest rated Ace in the Fleet. They predicted galactic clusters and seats on the Senate for both the admiral and Auro. The civilians who had complained the most vehemently a few days earlier could not have been more profuse in their thanks. Auro quickly found himself the recipient of passes for free services at two dozen brothels and casinos, all of which were now delighted to have to open two weeks early. Thanks to the Syndicate attack there now was a full squadron of spacemen due there in less than a day.

It was just after the incredulous commander of the relief force had left clutching a detailed report of the entire defense that Abraham Meier made what Auro realized was his first direct order to his aide since they had landed on Brown.

"Let's go paint the town red," the admiral said with a grin.

Auro figured anything involving paint would make for a very interesting evening.

He was right.

INTERLUDE: Incentive

Cousin Arkham of the Rogger family was dangerously close to losing his renowned control. For weeks he had badgered Jou Ronica, combat manager of the combined families' fleet, to act. To Arkham, at least, it was apparent that Duane was not yet ready to take the offensive, even if his spies had confirmed the Fleet's gaining knowledge of location of their worlds. That wasn't a reason to hesitate. It necessitated immediate action. They had to bring the war to the Alliance before it came to them instead.

"We are nearly ready to begin," the gray-haired manager assured the Rogger family fleet liaison. His expression was one of feigned confidence, or maybe it was just boredom, Arkham realized. He had been saying this same thing for weeks. "I am just waiting for a few more ships to arrive and confirmation that Duane is not ready to move." The combat manager repeated the same explanation for inaction he had given each time he was urged to risk the largest fleet ever assembled in the cluster.

Arkham took a sip of chilled water, as an alternative to smashing his fist down on the table and screaming in frustration. Half the warships in the cluster were already gathered here. Piracy was on the rise along the fringes. They would not win this war by doing nothing. Didn't the manager see that?

The older man had been a compromise. No family had wanted to turn command of their ships over to the combat managers of another. Ronica had a reputation for independence, too much so for the comfort of his own family. His choice had engendered enough discomfort among his relatives to justify the decision at the time. Now Arkham Rogger was regretting it.

"We could begin sending preliminary probes into the Khalian system," a Fleish manager suggested from several seats farther down the table. The Fleish were always ready to interject their opinion. By the end of the war they would either be a great house or extinct. Arkham wasn't sure which he preferred.

Ronica looked unhappy. He was used to unquestioned obedience. Even more so from a combat manager placed almost seven seats from the head of the table. Perhaps though he should agree. It would place the burden of error on the Fleish family and he could still garner the credit for any success on himself.

"The plan calls for near complete surprise," corrected another combat manager before their leader could reply.

Damn, Ronica muttered to himself. It was the representative of his own family . . . trying to be helpful of course. Now he had to disagree with the Fleish suggestion or appear to be correcting his own cousin. Standing to increase the impact of his refusal, the fleet's manager was interrupted by the entry of the flagship's tech and comm manager. Everyone watched silently as the technician placed a single sheet of printout in front of Ronica. Not being even a cousin he was forbidden to speak in the council chamber and withdrew nervously.

The families' fleet had been cruising at sub-light speeds just outside the cluster that contained their home worlds. While moving in the general direction of Khalia, their speed, when compared to FTL travel, was negligible. Lost in the vastness of space, they had felt safe from discovery. Now one of the Khalian raiders that had remained loyal to them had dropped out of FTL and was imploring their aid. It was being pursued by a Fleet ship with seemingly magical abilities. Ignorant savages.

Turning from the table Ronica muttered an order that would send a dozen smaller ships to intercept the Fleet vessel when it dropped out. They had to destroy the intruder before it escaped with the knowledge of their fleet that even a quick scan would bring it.

Then the gray-haired combat manager reached under the table and activated the command holo. If by some miracle the Fleet ship did escape, the decision would have been made for him. They would have no choice but to begin the offensive.

Arkham studied the screen as the input of a hundred sensors labeled the suddenly appearing Fleet ship as being an overpowered cargo vessel. Sitting to the combat manager's left, the Rogger liaison watched as the green blip appeared among the hundreds of points of white light that represented their fleet and wondered if he was hoping for the impudent freighter to escape or be destroyed. . . .

TESTFLIGHT

by Diane Duane and Peter Morwood

INCOMING FIRE BRACKETED the target, and for a brief instant it became a star whose light seemed to rival the other ancient fires of heaven; then it choked on its own destruction and all became darkness again.

"Impressive," said Roj softly, and meant it. "This thing may be a barge that even the Weasels wouldn't want, but the specs on its weapon installations don't really do them justice." Senior Captain Roj Malin of the Fleet and the brainship Minerva had between them seen most of the forms of destruction modern technology could presently hand out, and this was right up there with the best of them.

"I thought the Olympus-class was just fine, thank you very much." Minerva managed to convey boredom, irritation, and a sense of being imposed on, all in the one short sentence. Granted, she'd had almost three weeks since launch to perfect that tone of voice, but Roj felt pretty sure she wasn't quite done with refining it further.

It was unusual for brainships to be any bigger than a Juno-class corvette, tops—Minerva had been an Olympus long-range scout in her last incarnation—but somebody at Fleet Ops had decided to experiment a little with the control capabilities of a brainship command core. The refit had been fast: Minerva and her brawn had come back to Orbital Facility Two-Twelve for nothing more than debriefing and a standard overhaul. Instead of which they had removed her brain-core like someone seeding an avocado, and with as little ceremony, to plug it into a brand-new Valhalla-class hull shell that after the responsive Olympus scout, apparently felt as cumbersome as lead waders.

"Without so much as asking," she grumbled for the wearisome thousandth time.

"It looks to me as if you're getting used to the feel of it," said Roj soothingly, and as if to prove his point punched up all the data for the past six test firings. Minerva scanned them and uttered a grunt like the metallic crunch of a bad gear-change. She wasn't impressed. Roj couldn't really blame her, even though with his new rank-tabs still glittering at the collar of his uniform, he seemed to feel it his responsibility to get something besides records out of this particular shakedown—though so far there was little enough apart from paperwork in the whole damned voyage.

Even the weapon tests were boring. Somebody somewhere had decided that until the new shell's flight characteristics had been collated, the Valhalla-class vessels shouldn't be put through a full-scale combat routine. Apparently that same somebody was afraid that the combined stresses of weapons and battle maneuvers would prove too much for the new hull shell, even though at three-hundred-meters-plus the *Valhalla* hull was bigger than an Iowa-class battleship of Old Earth, and was armored in the new Alfa proof, a self-replicating ablative that had maybe six long-chain molecules in the entire cladding. To be informed that people presumably in the know were unsure about the structural integrity of such a juggernaut did not fill Roj or Minerva with confidence.

"Besides which the bugger has a sensor cross section like a small moon."

Minerva had said so within a few seconds of her sensory inputs being reconnected, and would probably say it again before this particular duty tasking was out. They had both considered running the test routines in such a way that the notion of oversize brainships would be scrapped, but that

would make this the first mission that either of them had
undertaken that had proven less than successful. It would
just have to be an argument between whatever the flight
recorders said, set against the voices of experienced opinion.

It was just that joint experience that had earned them this
relatively cushy mission in the first place: they were apparently the most successful and best integrated brain/brawn
team in the Fleet. Also, between the pair of them, they
represented probably the biggest single investment of active
duty time, combat experience, and plain old money in any
one vessel short of a first-line light cruiser.

That was why they were out here, in one of the deep-
space fire-and-maneuvering ranges located just about as far
from any action as it was possible to be in this sector of the
galactic spiral arm. Nobody wanted to run the risk of being
the officer whose orders wasted such an accumulation of
knowledge. They were deodorant specks in one of the arm-
pits of space, but an armpit that didn't even sweat. . . .

"You want to hear something *really* cheerful?" said Roj.

"Kristos, boyo, surprise me if you can."

"I know they'll be working up a new class of brainship
from what we bring back to them; but I don't think either
you or I are going to have any part in it." Minerva made a
wordless interrogative noise and Roj shrugged. "I just don't
think we'll be going back in the line when this is over—
because I think they've got us slated for one of the teaching
academies."

"What . . . ? Roj, you have *got* to be joking." He could
feel all her lenses staring at him, iris shutters wide as they
ran everything from visual light through IR and thermo-
graphic over him in the hope that he was indeed making a
funny. Minerva was out of luck; it wasn't the sort of thing
that even he made jokes about.

"How many times during that last refit did they try to
transfer combat-experience data from your main banks?"

"Three, maybe four. I was shut down for part of it, so I
don't really . . ." Minerva's perfectly modulated voice
trailed off in a crackle of static as she realized the impli-

cations behind what Roj had just said. "And they couldn't make it work?"

"Nothing but dates and times and facts. Same with me. No matter how long they debriefed, I couldn't explain why we'd used this maneuver or that weapon rather than something else. Like I told them a dozen times, you had to be there, in a combat situation, under combat stresses, before all those combat instincts start to gel and produce some sort of sense. It's not something that can be dumped down to a data chip. So"—he shrugged grimly—"I guess we get to teach it."

"Roj, they are *not* putting me into some shitty ground-based simulator."

"Or me behind its console, lady." Roj smiled the slow, lazy smile that was becoming his trademark in the Fleet. It was a smile that said, "mess with me and pull back a bloody stump," and it was one of those expressions once seen, never forgotten. He was getting almost as well known among the tightly knit community of brainship brawns and their commanders as Captain Hawk Talon, Hero of the Spaceways, had become among the Omni-watchers. Except that there was nothing fictional or special-effectsy about the violence Roj could visit on people who annoyed him. . . .

"You're not suggesting something illegal, Captain?" said Minerva, speaking very carefully so that there was no chance of her being misunderstood. Roj listened to the absolute lack of inflection in her voice and recognized it as a tone he had heard several times before their service association. It meant that whatever he decided, she would support him to the hilt, and that he would be expected—no, he would be required—to back her up to the same degree.

"Oh, no, XR-14376," said Roj with equal formality. "Nothing of the kind. We're both far too busy right now." To continue with "but maybe later . . ." was both tacky and superfluous—even though both of them had heard the words just as plainly as if they had been spoken aloud.

Tweep!

Roj twitched slightly, and maybe Minerva did as well, deep down behind the armor of her core. Even though the sound was no more than her com circuitry acknowledging an incoming signal, after what they had been carefully not-saying during the past few seconds, any contact with the outside world was less than immediately welcome.

"Nothing on the screens," said Minerva an instant later. "We're clear, out to extreme range."

The com system ran a high-speed analysis, then flipped its findings up onto the main viewer. Roj glanced at it, then looked again and swore under his breath. The war with the Khalia might have come to an official end, but it was still recent enough for distress code prefixes to send that familiar ugly little shiver down his spine. "Somebody's in trouble," he said softly. "And I don't think it's just a cat caught up a tree."

"Enhancement and decryption systems coming on line, signal source tracking engaged," Minerva began briskly. Then she hesitated, and when she spoke again there was suddenly suspicion in her voice. "Do you know if Rear Admiral Agato has any connection with this shakedown exercise?"

Roj stared quizzically at her main lens array, as close as he could get to looking her right in the eye. "Not that I'm aware of," he said at last, but even so, there was a lot less concern than at first in the way he studied the newly de-coded signal. "According to this, a Fleet tender has come under attack by"—he cleared his throat significantly, but failed to shift the disbelief that hung heavy in his voice—"by a Khalian raider. Now that's strange. I thought the Weasels were on our side now. You think maybe this is just another drill?"

"I'm not sure what to think where Agato's concerned."

For as long as they had known him, Rear Admiral Julius Agato had maintained a connection with Fleet Intelligence and at the same time with R&D (Weapons). It made for an interesting combination, with "interesting" having the same value as in the old Chinese curse. Agato was eminently suited to his post—whatever its official title might be—because the man's brain, undoubtedly powerful and imagi-native, was also sufficiently convoluted to pull corks all by

itself. It was not beyond him to have arranged a sector-wide
alert just as some sort of test for the brainship-brawn team
that were his favorite guinea pigs.

The only drawback was that they didn't know yet what
the right response was supposed to be. Was it a test of
readiness, so that they should drop everything and go
scorching off to answer the distress call? Or was it meant
to check how determined—or otherwise—they were to complete the butt-and-brain-numbing shakedown duties without
letting every little thing distract them? Not that a sector-
band alert could ever be regarded as *little*. And there was
always the possibility that it wasn't a drill at all. . . .

"Any enhancement on that, Minerva?"

"On the screen. It checks out: coordinates, ID codings,
the lot. Either it's a bloody good simulation, or it's the real
thing. Treat it as real?"

"Close enough for jazz."

"Und jetzt fur Schrage Musik auch, Junge." Roj looked
blank, and Minerva chuckled. "Military historian's pun.
Check the new dorsal weapon installations sometime." The
monitors flipped from comms to navigation and a little
promissory vibration went through the *Valhalla*'s structure
as Minerva brought the main drives back on line. "They've
given us a last-spotted escape vector," she said, all business
now that they were doing something more than just another
drill. "I'm laying in an intercept course. Get a message
squirt off to Command, let them know what's going on."

"What *is* going on?"

"Call it, uh—call it a live-firing exercise. Under combat
conditions. They can work the rest out for themselves. Now
let's see what this thing can *really* do. . . ."

One of the things that the *Valhalla* could do was to ac-
celerate to maximum pursuit velocity far faster than the old
Olympus could ever have done. So that they didn't have to
discuss it—the revelation looked likely to put Minerva out
of sorts if she dwelt on it too long—she and Roj sifted all
the other information out of the damaged tender's data
squirt. There was a lot more information coded into it than

just a yell for help. During the war with the Khalia it had become standard Fleet procedure that a distress transmission should include as much detail as possible on the cause of that distress. In this case it was data on the attacking ship: speed, projected weapon capabilities, and last-known estimated escape course.

Minerva was now locked onto an intercept vector. If the raiding ship was to have any chance of avoiding her long-range scanner sweep, it would need at the very least a ninety-by-ninety degree change in its recorded course, and if its sub-light speed as recorded by the tender was accurate, there wasn't any Weasel ship yet built that could take such a strain without shredding itself. Even though the pursuit might take thirty hours or more, once they locked onto its energy-residual track they stood a better than even chance of catching the ship they were looking or. And if necessary, blowing it to scrap.

The interception came close to being a one-pass, one-shot knockdown. Close, but no cigar. The raider was there all right, one small ship that was a bright blip on the outer rim of the scan globe—but not where it should have been, right under their guns.

"Whose fault was that?" Roj muttered, not pleased.

"Don't look at me, honeybunch," snapped Minerva. "I just followed the coordinates. It's a pity the Weasels weren't so obliging as to leave the Scene of the Crime at their top speed after all."

They were Weasels, that much was certain: the track comparator had picked up enough of its energy residue to run an analysis and venture an opinion of the probable source. The Delta-class corvette was a vessel they had met before—distinctly short on creature comforts, even so far as the Khalia reckoned such things, but very well suited to its basic function of blowing things up and running away afterward. It had been one of the fastest ships in the Khalian fleet, and that it was now being operated on a freelance basis didn't make it any slower. The problem had two solutions: either they could give up right now, or settle back for the long sub-light pursuit that would eventually, very eventually, enable them to bring the Khalians to bay, because while they weren't close enough to open fire even with the *Valhalla*'s enhanced weaponry, they were still too close to warp up and catch the raiders that way. At least, not unless they wanted to overshoot by a factor of several billion. . . .

"They're heading out of Khalian space, Roj," said Minerva, speaking much more calmly than she had done at first. "It confirms a suspicion."

"Which is . . . ?"

"That they're nothing to do with the Khalian government, such as it is. Honorable defeat in honorable battle permits an honorable alliance with the honorable victors . . . ." Minerva rattled the litany off like a slug thrower, then made a sound of harsh amusement that was more like a cat with a hairball.

"Most likely this lad's one of those ship captains who saw profit in a bit of freelance looting before this sector of space becomes too quiet and orderly. He'll probably roll in and surrender with a claim that he was out on the frontier or something, and there'll be no questions asked, and God knows how many people he'll have killed before he decides the pirate life is getting too hot for him. . . ."

"I think not," said Roj. He settled into his acceleration chair and fastened the eight-point harness comfortably. "If we're the sole representatives of the Fleet in this sector of space, then we also represent, uh"—he hunted through his memory for a particular old-fashioned phrase that had been eluding him—"the powers of high, middle, and low justice."

"The powers of judge, jury, and executioner." Minerva's voice was soft, betraying nothing.

"If they surrender, well and good—if not, they get smoked. Seems fair to me."

"Maybe I should have a new paint job on this hull shell when we get back to Facility Two-Twelve. Something sharp in, say, black and white, with maybe a few red and blue strobes above the flight deck. If we're going to play at being the Galactic Patrol I might as well look the part. Pity a siren isn't any use in vacuum.''

Roj took note of the fact that Minerva wasn't laughing much at her own joke, and shut up about justice and anything connected with it, turning his attention instead to a good firing solution on the fleeing Khalian. Just in case. There was always the possibility that the Weasels would surrender; and then again, there was always the possibility that they'd do nothing of the sort. Let Minerva say what she pleased: he didn't have a brainship's ability to compartmentalize things logically, and he'd regarded the Khalia as The Enemy for a lot longer than he considered them as semiformal allies. Roj was glad enough the war was over, but with the memories inside his skull that could still keep him from his sleep, he wasn't able to join in the round of ''kiss and make up and forget it ever happened'' that seemed to his jaundiced eye to have overtaken the politicos. It wasn't as easy to turn off years of propaganda—never mind the painful experiences of reality—as they seemed to think.

The Weasels surely knew by now that they were being followed, because the pursuit was entering its fifteenth hour and not even renegade Khalians would let so long go by without at least glancing at the rear-quadrant monitors. Or maybe they would. Roj checked the scanner readouts for what had to be the thousandth time, and still there was no change in the *Delta*'s energy state. Maybe it was some sort of elaborate bluff. And maybe the tender they had tried to shoot up had given them more than they'd bargained for, and ruptured the weapons-system power-packs. . . .

''Fish in a barrel,'' Roj said aloud.

''Khalians are mammalian,'' Minerva corrected. ''But I get your meaning. Damaged power-cells?''

''Something like.''

''I've had them. No fun. No fun at all. But it should help persuade them to surrender and come back for trial. A military tribunal of their own people seems fair enough to me.''

''Considering the likely verdict, it's a long way to be bothered dragging them.'' Roj looked hard at Minerva's main lens, as if he were trying to read a reaction from its crystalline structure in the same way as he might gain information from a human eye. There was only his own distorted reflection in this one.

"High, middle, and low justice—but not summary."

"Anyway, you're assuming they'll offer to surrender."

"And I'm assuming you'll give them the chance. Don't disappoint me, Roj. We've been through too much together for you to—" Minerva broke off, distracted by something. Then the main viewscreen flickered from tracking mode to a tactical schematic, and in the same instant all of the DEW proximity klaxons started to blare at once. There was a ship on the long-range scanner, right on the edge of sensor pickup, as far beyond them now as the Khalian raider had been during the first moments of the failed interception. A moment later there were two more. Then another ten. . . .

When fifty more scan returns formed on the screen in squadron blocks that were segments of a gigantic globular holding pattern, a sphere composed of more warships than either Roj or Minerva had ever seen gathered together in one place, there was no more doubt. There was an entire bloody battle fleet out there, and they were running at full sublight velocity right into the middle of it. It couldn't be anything other than a battle fleet, not with the battle computer classifying each of the huge scope returns at the core of the formation as a dreadnought. Like the Fleet's Emperor-class—except that these dreadnoughts were half as big again.

"Starting deceleration sequence," said Minerva crisply, and there was an edge in her voice that seemed to anticipate her brawn's response of "What? But we've almost got them. . . ." She silenced the rest of his complaints by simply switching the com board's output over to the main speaker array and letting him draw his own conclusions. The Language-One unit started emitting the chittering sound of Khalian speech, and Minerva let him listen to it for a couple of seconds before patching in the translator circuitry.

". . . pursued, warning, we are pursued, alarm, alarm, alarm! Aid us, Givers! Aid us! Warning, we are pursued, warning. . . ."

"You hear? Givers! Dammit, Roj, those are *Merchant* ships."

"Heaviest-armed merchantmen *I* ever saw," said Roj with a tight little grin.

"Funny man. I was listening to that Intel briefing, even if you weren't. These are the arms dealers who've been supplying the Weasels—that entire fleet belongs to the Mercantile Syndicate. Forget the *Delta*, Roj, their friends outgun us. Time to leave!"

"First things first," said Roj. He activated the main fire-control system, tabbed in a weapon-selector prefix, and watched it track briefly on the Khalian corvette. "We'll be locked on in just a few more seconds. . . ."

"I said, time to leave." Minerva spoke sharply, irritated at his persistence; and under that irritation, partly hidden by it, was a very real worry about the scale of the opposition facing them. It looked as if the Khalia had only been round one of this war, and she was watching the seconds leave the ring before the bell rang for round two. Watching from the wrong side of the ropes. "If we can see that fleet, its point-defense pickets can certainly see us. And there's the little matter of reporting what we've found out here—if we can get away."

A slight rhythmic shudder ran through the *Valhalla*'s hull, and Roj glanced in satisfaction at the dozen arrowhead symbols that had just appeared on the tactical display. A full salvo of Mk-22 torps accelerated toward the Khalian corvette at fifty-plus g. "Oh, we'll get away all right," he said, and whether he was feigning the sound of confidence or really meant it, he sounded pleased enough. "It's more than the Weasels will. Now we can leave."

Minerva's sound system uttered an angry exhalation of static. "I hope so," she said, "I really hope so. . . ."

For all his jauntiness, Roj was uncomfortably aware that his hands were sweating, and more aware still that Minerva had noticed that they were clenched in an attempt to conceal it. The *Valhalla*'s primary weapons controller was neither faster nor slower than the *Olympus* on-boards, but it had still seemed like an enternity before all the predictors re-

turned a ninety-nine percent firing solution and were cleared
to open fire. It was one of those eternities when only he
seemed slow, for in that same achingly protracted two seconds, the readouts beside every ship in the battle fleet had
flipped from standby to combat active. That was the reason
why he had emptied an entire rotary at the only ship in
range: with luck, the flare of multiple thermonuclear detonations would blind their scanners long enough for he and
Minerva to get out of the way.

With luck.

That luck was nowhere in sight. Even as the Khalian corvette opened up with its rear batteries in a desperate attempt
to destroy the incoming torpedoes and the first warhead
went up in a sensor-scrambling pulse of heat and light and
radiation that blocked out the screen, Minerva began reporting a shift in the fleet's formation. It was no longer a
holding pattern, but a pursuit—with everything up to and
including the dreadnoughts coming after them.

And then the threat receptors screeched, reporting that
230 search-and-track sensors had begun to sweep the area,
hunting for something their weapons could lock onto . . .
shoot at . . . destroy.

The gunners and the fire-control computers on the Delta-
class corvette fumbled their catch, just once. When the catch
was for a 200-kiloton warhead homing in at sixty-five kilometers per second, once was enough. The Khalian ship
became superheated plasma in an eyeblink, its sole remaining useful function to remain between Minerva and the
Mercantile Syndicate's targeting screens for just a few seconds longer. . . .

"Dear Mr. and Mrs. Malin, Fleet High Command regret
to inform you that your son was killed because he didn't
have the brains to run away," said Minerva, all sweetly
vicious as her navcomps tried to pick out some safe direction for flight. There was no such direction: there was only
dangerous, and very dangerous.

"Thanks a whole heap for that vote of confidence," Roj
said, glaring. "I—"

"—agree, I hope. There's not much else you can do."

"If it's not too much trouble, I could take over the gunnery controls and let you concentrate on getting us out of here."

"Hoity-toity." Minerva was silent for several seconds, then popped the firing yoke out of its protective recess and switched the monitor to the targeting configuration for manual free fire. "All right, do it. There you go, space cadet. Keep them off my back for, oh, fifteen seconds."

"Done." The new gunnery override of the Valhalla-class vessels was meant to give a brawn almost as much fire-control capability as a brain-core; at least so far as using a tool could ever match the reflex ease of using just one extension of a body that was technological state of the art. It was obvious that no human could ever use the facility to its fullest extent, piloting and navigating while at the same time maintaining a full systems monitor and firing on as many targets as the ship had weapons systems to aim at them. Performing the tasks sequentially was understood to be possible, of course—but simultaneously, as the brainship's core could and did, was impossible.

That fifteen seconds were among the most hectic in Roj Malin's life, and somewhere around the ninth or tenth he had decided that a teaching post at the Academy wouldn't be a bad thing at all. Assuming he survived the next five seconds or so intact enough to take up any offer they might think of making.

Had Minerva not been busy about her own affairs, she would have called off the incoming fire in a voice of dreadful calm that Roj had come to know and hate. It was a tone that invariably meant she and her brawn had ended up with their necks on the chopping block again, whether through the machinations of Rear Admiral Agato, Fleet IntelSec, or simply by crash-landing on the Khalian hearthworld only a few hours ahead of an invasion. Whatever the reason, Minerva always sounded the same: dry, dispassionate, and apparently barely concerned at all over what was going on. Roj knew her better than that, but knowing that she was probably as scared as he was did nothing much to help.

Right now she was handling not only the navigation programming, but the ECM and evasive-maneuver randoms as well. It kept the torps from about their ears, but did nothing at all for the accuracy of Roj's fire as he tried to nail anything that hadn't been decoyed or dodged. At least the Merchants were still firing wild, without preprogrammed guidance in their warheads so that the torps had to rely on what they could find for themselves. He could tell as much from the peculiar curves and spirals of each missile blip as the seeker head searched in three dimensions for a potential target. Some of their circuitry had probably been fried by the detonation that had taken out the Khalian corvette—but with the size of the battle fleet and the number of ships in it, they could probably fill this sector of space with live warheads and still not run short of ammunition.

And the second wave of torps wouldn't be suffering the guidance problems of the first. *That* was likely to be interesting. . . .

"Course plotted and locked in, Roj." Minerva sounded pleased with herself. "Two jumps initially, and a third if we need to."

Roj swatted two torps with a sidewise slash of fire from X turret, and realized there were no more. Not for the next twenty-odd seconds, anyway. He sagged in the acceleration chair, breathless as if he had just run a race, and blinked at Minerva's main lens pickup. "Why, for pity's sake?"

"In case they can track me FTL. *Shearborn* could, I can, and the equipment's no longer what you might call fresh off the drawing board. So, two, maybe three jumps: one to get away from here, one to lose them, one to get some damned hot news to Intel—before they find out by tangling with those battlewagons out there."

Another wave of torpedoes were closing fast, and this time they were coming in a cloud thick as midges in May. Roj looked, swallowed, and said, "So don't talk about it. *Do* it!"

"Uh, okay," said Minerva, and did.

Seven minutes later she said a great many more things, connected mostly to the parentage and sexual preferences of whoever had checked the Khalian astrography charts and pronounced them fit for human consumption. "Problems?" said Roj grimly, knowing perfectly well that Minerva didn't swear without good cause.

"Plenty. I picked up a tracer lock just as we jumped, so expect company. And the data charts on this sector are nothing more than guesswork. They might as well have little puffy-cheeked Cupids in the corners and bloody sea serpents in the middle for all the use they are to me."

"Here be dragons?"

"Dragons I could tolerate. Here does *not* be the asteroid field I was aiming for. . . ."

"Again, please? I could have sworn you said 'asteroid field.' "

"I did."

"Minerva," said Roj carefully, "I saw that old vid, and I didn't like what I saw. Explain what you're thinking about, please, so that I can get out and walk from here if I have to."

"You," said Minerva, "obviously haven't given any thought to this. I'm not planning any slalom run. But try this: there would be multiple returns on a scanner, most of which would be rocks. And maybe a few of the remainder would be loose torps with proximity fuses. By the time anybody found out we weren't here, we, uh, wouldn't be." Minerva grunted with disgust. "Except, no asteroids. Just a grungy little star and half a dozen grungy little planets."

"And imminent pursuit."

"Quite. Pursuit we daren't lead back to Fleet headquarters. The Merchants'll get there soon enough, you'll see." She thought in silence for a few seconds, and Roj was able to watch how she considered and then rejected various possibilities by the way the bridge telltales for various onboard systems lit up, then dimmed again.

But when the main viewscreen came to life with an enhanced image of local-space astrography overlaid with a targeting grid, Roj was on his feet and shouting "Oh no, you don't!" before Minerva had a chance to speak. "They'll decommission you, court-martial me, and we'll both be back out here trying to put right whatever damage you're planning to the astrography records.''

"There are none, Roj," she told him soothingly. "No maps, no charts—at least, only the Khalian ones, and they're of small use as I think I've proved already. So what are we doing wrong . . . ?"

"It's not even as if this ship has the weaponry to do it," he said, as if that was the final argument.

"Are you sure?" Minerva's voice was a cajoling purr—and behind it was a steely edge that suggested *no* was not an answer she was willing to accept. There was a devil of destructiveness in that voice, and a final loss of patience with being chased from pillar to post by enemies and orders in equal proportion. "Wouldn't you like to see what the *Valhalla* shell can really do?" she tempted, and then threw in a clinching argument. "Before the Merchants get here and try doing the same thing to us . . . ?"

Minerva had been right in her estimate of how much time they had to spare: not much at all. They used up most of it in making sure that the system was as lifeless as initial scanning had suggested, and the little that remained in finding an appropriately small moon in orbit around one of the outer planets. It had a high concentration of nickel-iron and some very interesting rare metals in its structure, and it occurred to Roj that the less-known parts of Khalian space could well provide a good return on the investment of a certain decorated Fleet vet. It also meant that this particular moon, properly broken up by the judicious application of megatonnage against its plate faults, would provide just the sort of echoes and false returns that they needed to cover a quiet retreat.

Even so, they cut it almost too fine, because a proximity alert started to bleat just as all of Minerva's carefully targeted bombardment warheads curved down from orbit to hit the moon's weak points with a simultaneous hammer blow of 350-plus bevatons yield. It came to pieces. Big pieces, little pieces, and an expanding cloud of irradiated metal-heavy fragments that made perhaps the best and most impenetrable chaff that Roj and Minerva had ever had the privilege of hiding behind.

It also made the best bang that Roj had never heard.

What the Merchant cruiser made of it all, he never knew, since neither he nor Minerva waited to ask. They had a report to deliver: on the efficiency of the *Valhalla* hull-shell; on the destruction of a Khalian raider; on the approach of a potential new enemy of the Fleet—and a confession that for various reasons, the maps of Sector Two-Twelve really *did* need to be redrawn after all. . . .